READ WHAT FANS AC
ARE SAYING ABOUT . . .

The Great and Terrible, vol. 1: Prologue: The Brothers:

"An amazing book. . . . The whole story was great, but the ending gave me goose-bumps and the best feeling inside. Can't wait for the next volume."

—Hila Hopkins

"One of the greatest books I have read in a long time. . . . I actually cried while reading it. . . . Everyone should read this book—if not for the unique spiritual insights, then for the great story. I am buying volume two first day out."

—Joshua Dance

"Thought-provoking and compelling. . . . I love the way it has caused me to think differently about my mission on earth and to look at my husband and children in a different light."

—Hillary Johnson

"An excellent read. It was both thought-provoking and spiritually uplifting. Even my teenage son thought it was 'an awesome book.'"

—Dale Lyman

"It feels so real. . . . It is so intriguing, readers will keep turning the pages until the very end."

—Brenda Ramsbacher, President, Reviewers International, Scribblers

PRAISE FOR CHRIS STEWART

Shattered Bone

"Stewart writes with . . . Clancy's knack for spinning a thrilling global techno yarn."

—CNN Sunday Morning, Off The Shelf

"A top-notch techno-thriller. . . . An impressive debut, complete with suspenseful action, plausible geopolitical scenarios, and authoritative detail."

—*Kirkus Reviews*

"*Shattered Bone* is a splendid thriller."

—W.E.B. Griffin, author of the best-selling series *Brotherhood of War, The Corps,* and *Honor Bound*

"Knuckle-whitening flying scenes. A terrific novel."

—Douglas Preston, best-selling co-author of *The Relic*

"A new technothriller star has been launched. If you enjoy books where the action starts with a bang on the first page and ends with a bang on the last, you'll devour *Shattered Bone*."

—*Tulsa World*

The Kill Box

"A commando-lean plot with nick-of-time saves and edge-of-your-seat theatrics."

—*Publishers Weekly*

"A thriller writer who knows how to deliver."

—*Flint Michigan Journal*

"The plot builds to a page-flipping climax."

—*Booklist*

The Third Consequence

"His mix of fact and fiction explodes off the page with the immediacy of a live CNN war-zone video feed.

—*Publishers Weekly*

"Pins the reader to the seat of his pants."

—Eric L. Harry, author of *Arc Light*

"Fast and furious. The author writes in a crisp style and tells the story with a certain authentic touch."

—*Stars and Stripes*

WHERE ANGELS FALL

THE GREAT AND TERRIBLE SERIES

by
Chris Stewart

VOLUME 1
Prologue: The Brothers

VOLUME 2
Where Angels Fall

VOLUME 3
The Second Sun

VOLUME 4
Fury and Light

VOLUME 5
From the End of Heaven

VOLUME 6
Clear as the Moon

THE GREAT AND TERRIBLE

VOLUME 2

WHERE ANGELS FALL

CHRIS STEWART

SALT LAKE CITY, UTAH

First printing in hardbound 2004.
First printing in paperbound 2010.

Visit us at DeseretBook.com

All characters in this book are fictitious, and any resemblance to actual persons, living or dead, is purely coincidental.

Library of Congress Cataloging-in-Publication Data

Stewart, Chris, 1960-
Where angels fall / Chris Stewart.
p. cm. — (The great and terrible ; v. 2)
ISBN-10: 1-59038-289-7 (hardbound : alk. paper)
ISBN-13: 978-1-60641-683-9 (paperbound)
1. Middle East—Fiction. 2. Terrorism—Fiction. I. Title.
PS3569.T4593W48 2004
813'.54—dc22 2004014722

Printed in the United States of America 72076
R. R. Donnelley, Harrisonburg, VA

15 14 13 12 11

To Neil and Clara Jensen,
two of the most giving people I know.

prologue

It was calm. Peaceful and sweet. Like that brief moment in the morning before waking thoughts settle in, before the dim light filters through and the morning winds blow. It was the intense calm of nature, a peace that man cannot produce, like the silent roll of dark clouds before the coming storm or the calm of glassy water before the first raindrops fall. The peace seemed to emit from both above and below, from the sky and the ground and rock underneath, as if the earth herself paused as she took a long gulp of air.

It was the last peace, the great peace, the deep breath before the last of the Last Days, the final chance to prepare before the scroll of heaven was unrolled.

The golden age of the Restoration had drawn to a close, and the heavens paused and waited for the long plunge ahead.

Over the previous hundred years, freedom had been taken to most of the nations on earth. Wars had been fought and many evils destroyed, with democracies rising from the ruins of totalitarian regimes. As freedom spread, the economic engines began to power a class of leisure in almost every nation on earth, bringing a degree of wealth and comfort unparalleled in the history of the world. And with the rise of freedom, the truth also spread, covering the earth with the power of God until pockets of true believers could be found throughout the world.

But democracies, with all their beauties, are also the most fragile of governments known to man. They are delicate and weak and dependent on good. And when the people turn to darkness, their democracies are doomed, for a government cannot exceed the moral worth of the people it rules. And while the economic and moral prosperity that follows freedom can provide fertile ground for the truth, history has proven that prosperity will inevitably sprout the weeds of selfishness, pride, and decay.

When the people become physically comfortable, the truth is ignored. And when they become wealthy, the truth is despised.

So it was that, as the world grew rich, the Deceiver spread his evil until wealth, power, and ambition became the only measure of success. Like spoiled children in a nursery always crying for more, screaming and pouting because they didn't get their share, the people became so self-centered and selfish they were incapable of good. In this ground of rot, the hate of God began to take hold. Shrill voices began screeching against that which was good. Women cast off their children as if they were scars. Men abandoned their families, while children reviled their parents and lost themselves in new pleasures so acute they bordered on pain. Gender was lost and the concept of marriage destroyed. Some people worshiped their bodies. Some worshiped their minds. Most worshiped nothing.

And the heavens wept for the children who were born into a world without hope.

And still the hate grew. Public figures rose up, brainless and empty, spewing vile rhetoric against their own nations and the freedoms that had once made them great. Great leaders preached the loathing of anything decent or good. Hypocritical of the failings of virtue, endlessly forgiving of the failures of vice, the world grew ripe, like an apple stored in a damp cellar too long. Though the outward appearance didn't show it, the earth had rotted inside. The peel remained red and supple, if perhaps a bit wrinkled, but on the inside the world was a worm-filled and putrid mass of brown pulp. What appeared to be well and healthy was, underneath the peeling, sick to the core.

The signs of the rot could be seen by anyone who cared to look.

But few people did. Why would they want to smell the decay when they were satisfied with following the preachers of money, lust, and hate?

So a golden age faded like the sun behind a dark cloud. The winds began to blow. The flames would soon rise. The earth had been washed, and now the fire was near.

And some people saw it coming. But only a few.

* * *

The aircraft was a military transport flying over the waters of the Mediterranean Sea. The general was asleep in the dim cabin, and the window shades had been pulled down. His long legs were stretched out, his arms at his side, and he dreamed as he slept, a dream of great beauty that turned suddenly cold.

In his dream it was a warm summer day. The air was clean, almost crisp, and the sun warmed his neck. He stood in the middle of a great field, the grass stretching for miles in every direction around him, lush and so green it almost hurt his eyes. And it was quiet, as quiet as he had ever experienced in his life, so quiet he could hear his own heart beat in his chest. The sun slipped behind a shadow, and he looked up to see a line of beautiful clouds, a billowing cluster of thunderstorms blowing in from the east. A cloud shaped like a nearly perfect anvil, dark blue with white edges illuminated by the low sun, blew out in front of the storm. The backlighting tinted the clouds in deep purples and pinks and cast random shafts of sunlight on the green grass below. It was beautiful, simply stunning. It took his breath away.

He felt so small, so insignificant. The sky was so huge, and he was so small. The grassy field rolled for miles, and the clouds were like monsters billowing over his head.

But the storms quickly turned black, and lightning began to flash from the sky. It turned dark, the wind blew, and he felt a deep, sudden chill as the cold air swept down from the heights of the storm.

Then he heard it: a nearly silent whistle. Something fell from the sky and he looked up to see a white burst of light. The nuclear core grew into a white-hot mushroom with deep orange and black edges where the air had been vaporized. Another explosion, then another, on his right and his left. It seemed like the whole world was exploding in flame, the nuclear detonations filling the entire sky. He saw a blast wave move toward him from the closest mushroom cloud, a black wall of fire and heat that emitted from the fireball. It moved across the green grass like the winds of a tornado, a wall of superheated air that was bloated with smoke and destruction, dirt, sand, and flying debris.

The black wall screamed toward him. And he knew he was dead.

* * *

The general awoke with a start, his underarms sweaty. His back was tense, his head hurt, and his mouth had turned dry.

He looked around, disoriented, and realized he must have called out.

"Are you all right, sir?" his aide asked him as he moved to his side.

General Brighton slowly nodded, then rubbed at his eyes.

"A bad dream, sir?"

The general's face flushed, embarrassed. "I'm sorry," he said.

"No problem, sir. Too much stress, I'll bet."

The general reached for the open bottle he had left in the cup holder in his armrest and sucked in a mouthful of warm water. He felt a trickle of sweat run down his left rib and he stared at his lap, where his hands shook like a leaf.

His aide noticed him shaking. "Are you sure you're okay, sir? Can I get you anything?"

"I'm okay," Brighton answered. He squinted his eyebrows, then looked away. "It was just a very . . . unusual dream."

"And not a good one; I can see that from the sweat on your forehead."

"It seemed so real," the general said as he took another sip of water. His aide watched him a moment, then relaxed in his seat.

"Where are we?" General Brighton asked after a long moment of silence.

"Approaching the Middle East coast. You should be able to see Egypt and Israel by now."

Brighton pushed up the plastic window shade and looked out on the sea. Then he gasped and sat back, his chest tightening around his ribs. He passed a quick hand over his eyes, then looked out the window again.

Looking out to the east, he saw the very same cloud formations he had just dreamed: the same shapes, the same colors, the same perfect blue anvil and straight shafts of light.

He gasped as he stared at the scene, and his aide moved again to his side. The general gestured him away and returned his eyes to the sky.

Brighton shook his head to clear it, but the clouds didn't change. He saw the first flash of lightning and swallowed hard.

He thought a long moment as his aircraft flew east, his heart pumping like a drum in his head.

He didn't understand it.

And he almost didn't want to know.

His Fall

"The hour is not yet, but is nigh at hand, when peace shall be taken from the earth."
—D&C 1:35

chapter one

Prince Abdullah al-Rahman lay nearly drunk on a beach on the southern tip of France. Behind him, La Villa de Ambassador II, one of the finest resorts on the Mediterranean coast, rose over the shoreline. Cyprus trees swayed in rhythm with the wind, and the sand was so even it looked as if it had been raked. The grass above the beach was perfectly manicured, the air was clean, and the water sparkled with a million diamonds from the Mediterranean sun. The sky overhead was a perfect blue. Behind him, on the other side of the wrought-iron security gates that surrounded the Ambassador II, the beautiful resort towns of Monte Carlo and Nice lay equal distances away, one city to the east, the other to the west. Around him, the beach was completely deserted, for Prince Abdullah's bodyguards had already chased away not only his own family members but the tourists who had wandered up from one of the other resorts as well. It was late afternoon as Prince Abdullah sat alone on the sand, staring out on the sea.

The prince and his entourage had leased the entire La Villa de Ambassador II for the week—all 225 rooms, three gourmet restaurants, spa, golf course, and private beach. For the next seven days it all belonged to him and his group of ninety-seven security forces, concubines, wives, and friends. Abdullah and his family had come to France to get away from the desert heat—and to shop, which meant that in addition to the cost of the resort, one of his wives had transferred a couple of million dollars into their petty cash account.

But Abdullah wasn't interested in shopping. He had other things on his mind.

At twenty-five, the prince was young and trim, with a finely sculptured face and almost European features, thanks to his mother, a beautiful Moroccan Muslim with mixed European and Arab blood. He had a fine nose and strong eyes over thick lips; and, unlike most of his Arab brothers, the prince didn't consider facial hair an indication of his manhood, so he kept his face clean shaven.

One of the wealthiest men in the world, Prince Abdullah al-Rahman was the second oldest son to King Fahd bin Saud Faysal, monarch of the House of Saud, and grandson of King Saud Aziz, the first king of modern-day Saudi Arabia. As a royal prince in the kingdom that held the largest oil reserves in the world, he and his family were unbelievably wealthy. There was no whim or desire, no pleasure or need that the prince could ask for and not have given to him. Along with his wealth, the royal prince held the reins to great power, for the world economy revolved around oil, and the politics of oil revolved around the Saudi Arabian peninsula.

Yet despite all his power, despite all his wealth, the prince was not satisfied and always wanted more. It was as if he had an insatiable hunger, an unquenchable thirst. Like a dying man in the desert who was forced to eat sand, no matter how much he ate it did not quench what he craved.

It was never enough. He always wanted more.

And now what he had been given was going to be taken from him! His imbecile father was going to package up the kingdom and give it away. In the name of democracy—a completely foreign concept in their part of the world—his idiot father, King Fahd bin Saud Faysal, was going to destroy everything his ancestors had worked for for almost three hundred years. He was going to give up the kingdom and institute a democratic regime.

All of it gone, destroyed in one generation! Like a wisp of black smoke, his family's wealth would disappear. And his older brother was going to help him.

Unless Prince Abdullah stopped them both.

But how? What to do? He was completely distraught.

He cursed violently as the bitter rage grew inside him, a hot, burning furnace of hate for his father—and lust for what he might lose. If it were not for his father . . . if it were not for his brother, the crown prince . . . if Abdullah had played his cards right, he might have one day been king.

But his father had taken that choice away from him.

He was going to give the kingdom away!

The prince pushed his hand through the sand as he sipped at his beer. He was frustrated and angry, more so than he had ever felt in his life. The day before, as he was preparing to leave for France, Abdullah had fought with his father, a bitter argument that had turned so angry three of the king's bodyguards had been forced to step between the two men. And though the prince had argued and pleaded until he was hoarse, his father hadn't listened, but instead cut him off.

"Leave me, Abdullah!" his father had screamed in a rage. "Leave me *right now,* and never speak of this again. I do not have to justify my decision to you. Now go and forget it. I will not discuss it again."

And so it was that Abdullah found himself on the beach,

fuming, his dark heart growing cold, his mind constantly racing, trying to develop a plan. His father was a fool. No, he was worse than that. He was a selfish, stupid, conceited old man who did not care one whit for his children. He was a slithering fool, a spider in the corner, a poisonous snake in the grass.

The sun moved toward the sea as Abdullah raged, leaving a blood-red horizon above the hazy waterline where the prince sipped his beer and kicked at the warm sand.

Then he looked up and saw him, a withery, old man. Abdullah had not heard him approach, and he stared up in surprise; then, cursing angrily, he pushed himself to his feet. He looked around for his bodyguards, but they were nowhere in sight. The old man stared at him and grinned. "How are you, Prince Abdullah?" he asked in heavily accented English. His voice was weak and raspy, and he smelled of cigar smoke and dry breath.

The prince glared with contempt. "Who are you?" he demanded in a sour tone.

The man smiled weakly, looking old and decrepit. Fine white hair and large teeth were his predominate features, but he moved quickly and with an energy that belied his small frame. His eyes seemed to glow yellow from some inner furnace, and Abdullah wondered quickly how old the man was. He could have been sixty or one hundred; it was hard to say, for his face was blotched with liver spots but his eyes were young and intense. He flashed a fast smile, his white teeth jutting brightly underneath a bony nose.

The old man pointed a slender hand to the east. "Your father is a very dangerous man," he said without introduction.

Abdullah glared but didn't answer. The old man waited, then ran a weathered finger across his lips, wiping away a line of dried spit.

"Speak not evil of my father!" Abdullah finally sneered.

The old man scoffed, looked away, then glanced down the beach. "Abdullah, please, don't play the loyal son with me. There's no need to impress me. I know what's in your heart, and I don't have the time or inclination for role-playing right now. We need to focus on our enemies, those we both need to bring down."

Abdullah shot a quick look back at the resort. Three men stood at the top of the trail leading from the beach to the pool. Large men. Caucasian. Dark glasses. Dark suit coats hid the weapons at their hips. None of the faces were familiar, and he swore to himself. He glanced east, down the beach to a line of low trees and saw another stranger standing in shorts and an oversized shirt. An enormous beach towel was draped over his shoulders, and Abdullah knew that it concealed the man's gun. He glanced left and right, feeling naked and alone as his gut tied in knots and his underarms sweated. For the first time in his life, he was alone.

Where had his men gone? He would have them shot!

He glared at the stranger, then nodded toward the hotel. "Who are they?" he demanded.

The old man hesitated.

Abdullah growled. "Come on, old man, tell me!"

The old man glanced at the bodyguards. "They work for me. That's all you need to know."

"Where are my people?"

"It seems they have left."

Prince Abdullah shook his head in disbelief. Could it be true? He *would* have them shot! The old man watched him, then reached down and adjusted his loose T-shirt, pulling it down over his bony hips. "Don't blame your men," he said softly. "My people are better, that's all."

Abdullah felt the panic rising, the fear growing tight in his throat. His eyes darted up and down the beach, thinking of how he might escape. Another man appeared near the tree line. Abdullah looked in the other direction and saw that a small schooner had appeared on the beach. The two men who worked the small anchor kept an anxious eye on the old man.

Abdullah's mind raced. A kidnapping! A murder! One of his rival cousins! He swore and looked down, then glared at the old man.

The stranger read the look on his face. "No harm, no foul," he said calmly. "You are not in danger. Your men are not far away. So relax and forgive me, but I wanted to speak with you alone."

"Who are you?" Abdullah demanded. "What do you want?"

The old man smiled, then reached into his shirt pocket and pulled out a piece of chewing gum. Unwrapping it quickly, he dropped the blue wrapper on the sand and stuck the gum in his mouth. "I want the same thing as you do," he answered simply.

"How do you know what I want?"

The old man smiled again, his yellowed eyes burning bright. "I know the hearts of most men. I know how they think, and I know how they feel. I know what they desire and what they are willing to do. That's what I know. And that's what I know about you."

Abdullah was quiet as the fear began to subside in his heart. He glanced past the old man. "How *did* you get past my bodyguards?" he asked.

The old man dismissed the question but waved a bony finger in front of Abdullah's chest. "We need the royal family to hold on to power," he said. "Your father, the monarch, must not go through with his plans. And your older brother, Crown Prince Saud, *must not* become the next king. They will share with their people their power, and the last thing we need is another democracy in the Middle East. I'd say the filthy Jews are enough—don't you agree?"

Abdullah certainly agreed, but he still didn't answer, and the old man wet his dry lips again. "Your father will ruin everything unless we stop him," he said.

Abdullah snorted in disgust. "My father is a fool," he answered bitterly.

"No! You are wrong. You might as well say the sun comes up in the west as to call your father a fool. The king is a *visionary!* And the most dangerous kind. But he is no fool, I promise, and until you understand that you will be useless to me."

Abdullah stood silent. He wouldn't quibble over words. Fool. Visionary. It didn't matter.

The old man studied the prince, knowing he had not understood, but he also saw the fire of hatred and that was enough to begin. "Your father isn't the only enemy you have, Prince Abdullah," he continued. "You have more enemies than you know. And I'm not talking about jealous brothers, bitter cousins, or betrayed friends. I'm not talking about any man in the kingdom who could do you harm. I'm talking about the only real enemy you have, the only real force that could take from both of us what we most desire in this life."

Abdullah stared at him. "What are you talking about?" he answered bitterly. He spoke sharply. Abdullah always spoke sharply—being raised as a prince made one prone to be rude.

The old man turned to stare out over the water. "Do you want me to show you?" he asked. "Do you want me to show you how to stop your old man? Do you want me to show you the greater enemy at your door?"

Abdullah glanced around him, but remained silent.

The old man nodded. "Yes, I thought that you might. Now, quickly. Come with me, and I will show you the truth."

* * *

After a short flight, the two men sat in a rented car parked on a side street half a block from the American embassy in Paris. It was dark and warm, and the streets of Paris were busy around them. Cement barricades blocked the street twenty yards in front of their dark Mercedes SUV, and a contingent of metro police stood guard at a security booth near the barricades.

Prince Abdullah shifted nervously in the back seat of the Mercedes-Benz. A driver and another bodyguard sat in the front, but a dark, bulletproof glass separated the front and back seats. The old man sat beside him. Abdullah still did not know his name. The old man glanced at his watch, then began to explain. "The American ambassador is hosting a reception for the Saudi OPEC delegation," he said. "You probably know that; it has been in the news. The public explanation for the reception is to strengthen the American ties to the lead OPEC nation, but the real reason for the meeting goes far beyond that."

The prince shot a look toward his new friend. "What else?" he asked.

The old man shifted, moving himself forward in the seat. "The U.S. Secretary of State will be at the meeting. The U.S. and Saudi Arabia are going to sign a highly classified agreement guaranteeing that the kingdom of Saudi Arabia will not reduce its output of oil for at least the next five years. It will also guarantee that Saudi Arabia will exert its influence to ensure that none of the other OPEC nations will reduce their production either. In exchange, the U.S. military will reassign the First Marine Expeditionary Force to the military base outside Dhahran. See, your father knows the transition to democracy may be difficult at times, and having a U.S. military presence established in the kingdom again will likely reduce the threat of bloodshed and instability. So everyone gets what they want. The United States gets cheap oil and a reestablished military presence in Arabia; the king gets the stabilizing influence of U.S. forces for the next twenty years. That is the essence of the secret deal that will be signed here tonight. And your oldest brother, Crown Prince Saud, was the brains behind the whole thing."

Abdullah nodded gravely. He had already heard rumors, and he wasn't completely surprised.

The two men were silent, and the night grew darker around them. The old man reached to the console between them, pulled out a package of cigarettes, and lit up, the orange glow illuminating his scrawny face. He offered one to Abdullah, who took it and lit up with his own silver lighter. The old man pointed to one of the French policemen who stood near the cement barricades. "You see the young sergeant there?" he asked. "The one in the black hat?"

Abdullah moved forward on his seat and nodded.

"He has twenty pounds of plastic explosives strapped up and down his legs," the old man explained.

Abdullah grunted. He didn't believe it. The old man stared at him, reading the expression on his face. "You have a question?" he asked.

Abdullah grunted again. "Your man does not have any explosives on him," he said.

"Why do you say that?" the old man asked curiously.

Abdullah pointed to two guards with German shepherds standing at the barricade. "Sniff dogs. If your man had explosives, they would be going crazy right now."

"Hmmm, of course you're right. But you see, Prince Abdullah, earlier this evening the dogs were exposed to a fifty parts per million whiff of hydrogen sulfide, a strong enough dose to destroy their olfactory abilities for the next ten days or so. Truth is, you could throw those dogs a stick of dynamite and they would happily retrieve it and drop it at your feet. Those dogs couldn't smell a skunk if it climbed on their faces and rolled on their noses."

The old man took another drag, then continued. "In five minutes, at exactly 9:15 P.M., the young sergeant, our man in the black hat, is going to walk toward the embassy and talk to the canine guards at the door. He will be cleared to enter the embassy to use the restroom, but he will have to use the service entrance on the south side of the building. It will take him a little more than three minutes to get inside. Once inside the building, he will make his way through the kitchen, toward the service elevator. The reception for the OPEC delegation is being held on the second floor, just above the main reception hall. He can get to the main hallway from the service elevator. Once he is underneath the reception area, he will detonate the plastic explosives that are strapped to his legs, and most of the east side of the building will come down in a grand fireball." The old man spoke calmly, as if he were announcing the future demise of rats. "We estimate forty to fifty casualties," he concluded. "Some of them will be Americans, but there will be many Saudis as well."

Abdullah turned toward him, his face stretched in surprise. "You're going to kill them!" he muttered.

"No, Abdullah. *You're* going to kill them! The decision is yours."

Abdullah shifted, his eyes wide with sickness and fear. "But why? What is the purpose? What do you hope to do?"

"Our only purpose, Prince Abdullah, is to test you. We want to know who you are. We want to know what you value and how far you will go. That is the only reason we're here. Now, we have chosen to strike the Americans, but that hardly matters to us at the moment, or at least in this case. Our only purpose in this exercise is to see if you will go along with us and to find out who you really are."

"But," Abdullah stammered, "if you kill the U.S. Secretary of State . . ."

"Relax," the old man answered as he pulled another drag on his smoke. "The SecState isn't scheduled to appear for another hour or so. He's not the target. This is just our little test."

Abdullah gasped. "I don't understand . . ." he sputtered.

"Oh come on, Abdullah, it's not that difficult. Say the word, say one simple word, and the entire operation is called off. One word from you and *poof!* not a thing happens here. You and I say good-bye. You'll never see me again. I drop you off at the private airport where the executive jet is waiting to fly you back to the beach. You forget me. I forget you. This whole thing becomes a strange dream, nothing more. Just say the word and you save the lives of your countrymen and some American civilians as well.

"But if you decide you want to join with us, if you decide you want us to show you how to hold onto power, then don't say anything, and at 9:21 fifty people will die, many of them Saudis, your countrymen, even friends. Many more will be injured, but I can't say how many for sure."

Abdullah remained silent, his heart slamming in shock and fear. "I don't believe it . . ." he stammered.

The old man studied him by the glow of the street lights. "You ever see the result of a suicide bomber?" he asked.

Abdullah shook his head.

"Hard to explain what it looks like. Bloody . . . really bloody . . . a horrible mess. Pieces of bodies: bowels, heads, and ears. I've seen dead hands reaching for something that was no longer there. And the smell, oh the smell, it can give you the creeps. You will never forget!"

The old man looked at his watch, then turned harsh. "You've got to decide," he commanded. "What are you going to do? Join with us, and we help you. I can guarantee you power. Join us and I promise you will be the next king. Or say no and we forget it. We call off the mission and just drive away."

"I need time to think!" Abdullah hissed.

"No, Abdullah, you are young and still virile! I'm the old, feeble man. I'm the one who needs time! You don't need any more."

The prince frowned and cursed violently.

"I know it may seem a little rushed," the old man continued, "but you've got to decide now. This is how we do it. This is how we find out what's in your gut. If we give you time, you *will* think, . . . you will rationalize and consider. You will weigh the pros and cons and come to a decision in your head. And that's not what we want. We want to know what's inside of here!" The old man reached over and tapped the prince on his chest. "We have learned this is the best way to know what's inside a man's heart. Will he kill? Will he flounder? Will he hesitate to act? Or will he move with the commitment we hope that he will? Trust me, Prince Abdullah, this is a very effective test.

"If you really want to join us, you've got to have blood on your hands. If you don't want to get bloody, then we're not interested in talking to you. If you're not willing to go the distance, if you're not willing to make the sacrifices of innocent lives, then you're not ready to work with us and we will tell you good-bye.

"But if you think I can help you, then you have to be willing to take a chance. You have to be willing to get bloody. And that's why we're here. So what's it going to be? You've got to decide, my new friend."

Abdullah was silent as his eyes darted widely in doubt.

The old man glanced at his watch. "Thirty seconds," he said. "Tell me to do it. It's up to you. Say you will do it, or we say good-bye."

"No! Not right now! Give me a little time!"

"No, *Prince* Abdullah," the old man sneered his title now. "You must decide *now.* Join us and we can show you a way to be king, king of the House of Saud, one of the most wealthy and powerful men in the world. Join us, and we stop King Faysal's foolish plan. Join us, and we save you. But understand this: You will be joining a battle that goes far beyond what you see. You will be joining a battle that goes far beyond the simple struggle for power inside the kingdom of Saudi Arabia. We have a much larger battle, a much greater war, a much longer vision, and a much broader plan. And you will have to fight those battles with us if we fight this battle for you. Now that is all I will tell you. What are you going to do?"

Prince Abdullah sat speechless, his mouth hanging wide, his cigarette burning to a long, gray ash in his hand.

The old man's voice rose, growing like a snarl in his chest. "Fifteen seconds," he cried as he stared at his watch. "Commit now to join us! Tell me to kill your countrymen. Prove to me we can trust you."

Abdullah leaned suddenly toward him, his eyes burning with fire. "You swear to me, old man, that I will be king!"

"I swear it," he cried in an almost shrill voice.

"Swear you won't fail me!"

"I swear it, Abdullah! Now swear to me you will join us!" he hissed to the prince.

Abdullah didn't hesitate. "I swear it," he said.

"You will bring down this building?"

"Kill them all!" the prince commanded.

The old man looked at him a long moment, then smiled and relaxed. "So be it, Abdullah. And welcome, my friend."

The old man leaned forward to tap on the glass, and the driver started the Mercedes and turned it around.

* * *

As the black SUV drove away, the French guard in the black hat stood and stared down the street at its red taillights. He knew the prince's answer was yes, and he sighed wearily; the massive dosage of Valium was the only thing that kept him calm. He was a dead man anyway; whether he went in a sudden explosion or was tortured to death, it was all the same. If he tried to hide they would find him; they had already proven that. He had a debt. They wanted payment. It was as simple as that. So he had agreed he would do this so he could go with only the briefest burst of pain. In return, they would take care of his daughter and the debt would be satisfied.

He sighed again sadly, then turned away from the receding taillights of the car.

At exactly 9:15, the guard turned and walked toward the embassy door.

* * *

The SUV was two miles away and driving down Lefainte Boulevard when Abdullah saw the flash of orange light behind him. He didn't hear the explosion or feel its expanding concussion, but the flash and rising fireball were strong enough to light up the night.

chapter two

Two days later, the old man and Prince Abdullah al-Rahman sat together at a small café in the Place du Casino. The golden square of Monte Carlo sparkled around them, a sensory overload of beautiful sights, smells, and sounds. Both men had checked into the Hotel Hermitage the night before and were rested and comfortable in the morning air. They wore summer suits and dark shirts, and they smoked as they talked. Native peace lilies, roses, and daisies created a natural bouquet around them; the air was heavy and warm with the smell of flowers in bloom. It was a lovely spring day, and the flower shops, boutiques, art galleries, and small cafés bustled with tourists, most of them overweight working stiffs from elsewhere on the continent and the United States who had come to bask in the reflected glory of the young and beautiful. A few locals hurried through the crowd on their way to minimum wage jobs that couldn't buy them a closet in the city, let alone a flat or small home. Because it was Monte Carlo, constant wealth was on display, and the prince and the old man mingled comfortably with the ostentatious crowd.

More than a dozen security men subtly worked the

sidewalks and streets, some of them Prince Abdullah's, some of them belonging to the old man. The two sat at a small table on a narrow and crowded sidewalk near a flowing fountain. For almost three hours they sipped French coffee and nibbled tiny pastries, deep in conversation. The old man did most of the talking. Prince Abdullah sat straight, his eyes intense, sometimes incredulous, sometimes unbelieving. But behind his stare, he smirked constantly.

He had made a good decision. The old man had a plan. Just hearing his ideas was worth the small price of the blood on his hands.

"You will be responsible to establish liaison with our Pakistani agent," the old man said in his final instructions. "We have planted the seed for this plan, but it will be your responsibility to nourish it and bring it along. It will take several years of your undivided attention. We will take care of the security, but the rest will be up to you."

"And the objective?" Abdullah asked. The old man had been talking around it for hours, and the prince was growing inpatient.

The old man smiled smugly. They had finally arrived. It was time to complete his knowledge. He leaned across the table and whispered, his breath strangely dry and foul.

The Saudi prince listened, then pushed away from the table, his mouth hanging open, his eyes smoldering. "Impossible!" he sneered. "Do you think you are the first ones to try this? It has been tried many times before. Everyone who has tried it has failed. You will fail too."

The old man snapped angrily back in his chair. "Are you stupid?" he asked, an irritated father scolding his child. "Haven't you been listening?"

Abdullah slowly nodded. "I have heard every word . . ."

"Then how can you doubt us?"

"I don't doubt you, my friend."

"Of course you doubt me. Isn't that what you just said? Have I completely misjudged you? Haven't you heard *anything*?"

"Friend, I only wonder if you've completely thought this thing through. Many of the best men have tried, and *none* of them found success. There are too many countermeasures, too much security. Everyone who has tried it has ultimately failed. And I'm sorry to say this, but it is my objective judgment that you will fail too."

The old man thought a moment. "I don't think so," he said softly.

"But why not?" Abdullah prodded anxiously. He wanted to believe him. He really did.

"Because we are patient," the old man explained. "Because we invest in the *future*. We don't demand results right now. We know it will take time, maybe ten or twelve years; but trust me, Abdullah, we will succeed. By then I will be very old, perhaps even dying, but I will live to see it. I will live to see our success." The old man sipped at his coffee, then took a deep breath and leaned forward again. *"I will live to see the burning glory,"* he smirked sarcastically.

Abdullah shook his head. He couldn't help but smile. "The burning glory," he repeated, almost laughing out loud. "Oh, that is perfect," he snorted. "Burning glory! Yeah, that's good!"

The old man laughed with him, then stiffened suddenly and turned serious again. "Take care of our man in Pakistan," he commanded. "That is your only job. And you must learn to be patient. This will take many years. But the payoff will be worth it; I assure you of that."

* * *

A little more than three weeks later, Prince Abdullah al-Rahman made his way to Karachi, Pakistan. For five days he checked out the city, traveling anonymously, moving through the slums and markets, staying in a classic but not luxurious hotel. He posed as an oil-supply businessman from Riyadh hoping to land a $500,000-dollar deal. He camped out at the *Hotel Karachi,* an old brick and marble structure that dated back to the colonial era, one of the very few centers of international commerce in Pakistan. He brought with him only four bodyguards, and he never talked to them or acknowledged them in any way, though he noticed them around him from time to time as he walked.

It was the first time he had ever been in Karachi, and he found it nearly as despicable as he had been told. It was noisy. It was hot. It was the murder capital of the world. Men and women relieved themselves in the open, right out in the street, squatting over rusted holes drilled into the sidewalks before moving on. The children looked hungry and thin. And everything smelled: the food, his hotel room, the taxis and streets—there was a permanent odor of humans, animal feces, garlic, and sweat in the air. Standing beside his bed, he sniffed at his suit. It too smelled like the street. He would have it burned the second he got back to Saudi Arabia. He looked out on the crowded alley outside his hotel window, noting the abject poverty below. How in the world had *these people* developed the technology to build a nuclear weapon? It was an incredible irony he could not understand.

But they had. And he hadn't. And so he was here.

For five days, he moved around Karachi, feigning low-level business meetings, looking and watching, wondering when it would come. He knew his contact was watching him, testing his patience while making certain he wasn't being trailed. So he waited, passing the time as convincingly as he could. By the third day he was growing impatient. By the fifth day he was furious. Who did this man think he was? Didn't he know who he was dealing with? Didn't he have any sense?

Abdullah had been told to wait until he was contacted; until that time there wasn't a thing he could do. He was completely at their mercy. But the whole arrangement made him furious, and he raged inside like a chained bull.

Then, on the evening of the fifth night, Prince Abdullah was sitting alone in a small bar in the back of the hotel. It was quiet and growing late when a small, mustached gentleman approached his table and nodded to him. "Come with me," he commanded without introduction.

Abdullah glanced around. Two of his security people sat and talked at the bar. He caught one by the eye, and the bodyguard turned away, though Abdullah could see he was still watching him through the smoky mirror behind the bar.

Abdullah didn't move, but his heart suddenly skipped. "Excuse me?" he said.

"My master would like to speak with you," the stranger answered curtly.

"And who is your master?" Abdullah replied, drawing a quick breath.

The stranger lowered his voice. "Dr. Abu Nidal Atta, deputy director, Pakistan special weapons section, principal advisor on national security to the Pakistani president."

Abdullah nodded slowly. This was why he was here.

He nodded quickly to his bodyguards, then stood and followed the man.

The meeting took place in a small room on the fourth floor of the hotel. It was a short discussion, direct and all business, and both men left satisfied.

It would be almost thirteen years before Prince Abdullah

would see the Pakistani scientist again. Though they would work closely together, they agreed they would never meet face to face, always communicating through intermediaries, a very few men they could trust.

At the end of the process, the Pakistani scientist would become one of the richest men in the region, and Prince Abdullah would have his treasure of nuclear warheads.

Elizabeth

"And I will give children to be their princes,
and babes shall rule over them."
—Isaiah 3:4

"For behold, angels are declaring it unto many at this time in our land: and this is for the purpose of preparing the hearts of the children of men to receive his word at the time of his coming in his glory."
—Alma 13:24

chapter three

She was young and beautiful, literally heavenly so, far more beautiful than anything that could exist in the mortal world. She was slender and solemn, and she kept her eyes low, waiting, submissively awaiting what was to come. Yet she had been waiting so long that she was prepared, her readiness supported by the determined square of her shoulders. She was nervous, but also confident, and though her face was uncertain, her eyes almost danced with anticipation and hope.

She had the look of a young woman, innocent and sweet, but she did not appear foolish and certainly not naïve—she had witnessed the bitter, and she knew what that was about, and she surely wasn't blind or unaware of what lay ahead. But she had chosen the better part, and was anxious to begin.

Dressed in a seamless white robe that reached to her ankles and was tied with a small bow at her waist, she brushed her dark hair back, then walked forward slowly until she stood directly in front of him.

Teancum, her trusted friend and sometime-protector, turned to face her, taking her by the hand. "Let me look in your eyes, Elizabeth. Let me see the courage and love that I know is there."

Elizabeth gazed at him, eyes beaming with hope and excitement. Then she smiled, a smile that seemed to light up the stars. It was so perfect and natural, a smile without guile, as if there was a great joy inside her that burst to get out.

"Are you ready?" he asked her after looking into her eyes.

Elizabeth nodded. "I'm ready. At least I think I am."

"You miss your brothers who have gone before you?"

"I do. I want to be with them. I think that they need me, and I need them too."

"And have you had your visit with the Father?"

"I have. It was marvelous beyond words."

Teancum nodded his head slowly; Elizabeth's pending departure forced him into a rare moment of introspection. How could the Father love his children so much that he would send them into the dangerous world? he wondered. How does he prepare them for the dangers that lay ahead? It never was easy, and this one had to have been particularly difficult. Teancum knew something of what lay ahead for her.

Teancum had seen many such farewells, each one different. There was always a mixture of sadness and joy. There were words of final counsel, unique to each child. And there was a special sharing of love and affection.

Elizabeth watched him carefully but didn't say anything.

Finally Teancum took her hand and held it, suddenly feeling tender. "What he really wants for us, Elizabeth, is for us to come back to him."

Her bright eyes burned with determination. "I swear to you, Teancum," she whispered, "I will return!"

He gazed at her sadly. He knew that was the standard response. "Do you realize that you are entering a battle from which *most* don't return? And Satan desires to have you, Elizabeth. You are special to him. He remembers how you fought him here in the premortal world and he now lies in wait, looking for the day when he can fight you again."

Elizabeth stood silent. Finally Teancum turned to her slowly and pointed away. "Elizabeth, do you remember Jerusalem? The pools of Bethesda, the porch and the water where the lame and halt used to wait for the angel to stir the water for them? There was a beggar there. His body was broken and feeble. He was so weak and lame, he was unable to walk, unable even to stand. Do you remember him, Elizabeth? Do you know who I mean?"

"Yes, I remember. He was one of the crippled. And my Brother healed him."

"Do you remember how long he waited?"

"I don't remember specifically, but it was a long time."

"Thirty-eight years, Elizabeth. Almost his entire life. Thirty-eight years he suffered alone, waiting patiently. Yet whenever the angel came, he never could reach the water in time, for he was too weak and feeble to be the first to the pool. Can you imagine his discouragement?! Can you imagine how he felt? Thirty-eight years he suffered, waiting for a miracle. He felt so sick and abandoned, so completely alone, for there was no man to carry him and no one who cared.

"And sometime in your mortal life, you will feel like this man. You will feel sick and abandoned, unable to deal with the challenges of the world. You will want to be healed, but there will be no one there. And when you feel that way, Elizabeth, I want you to remember this man. Remember that Christ healed him when no one would carry him to the pool. When he felt most alone, after patiently waiting so long, the Savior came out of nowhere and made him whole. There will be times you feel you have been abandoned, but that is *never so.* Your Brother will heal you. Our Father will always look after you. And from time to time I may be able to help you as well."

"But Teancum, how can all this be true? With the entire universe to manage, how can we matter so much to the Father? With all the suffering in the world, all the long prayers and urgent cries, will he still have time for me when I pray?"

Teancum took a step toward her and looked straight into her dark eyes. "He controls the heavens," he answered. "He controls the seas and the universe and the armies of men. He controls the course of each nation and the course of *each man and woman*. The sun will rise as he tells it to, and he can make kings of men. And if he can do all this, Elizabeth—and you know that he can—then can he not hear your prayers and give you help when you ask? The galaxies, they are nothing, when compared to his love for you. *He can make you holy,* and he can answer your prayers. And remember this, Elizabeth, for this is important too. It is a plan of happiness he has created, not a plan of misery. He sends us to be happy! And he will provide a way.

"So you must trust him, Elizabeth, and trust in the plan. You must have faith when the answers don't come immediately. On earth, when you hear it, the truth will sound familiar to you. Seek for this spirit, then perhaps the Spirit of God will help you remember the feelings and the covenants you made with him when you were here."

"Dear Teancum," she answered after a pause, "I am scared and I'm nervous, but I think I'm prepared."

Teancum thought of the evil men on the earth, those who conspired already to lay their evil plans, plans that would affect this daughter so deeply. He thought of the old man who was Lucifer's servant and the prince he had recently pulled into his service too. He shuddered; then he took her hand and squeezed it again.

He wanted to warn her, but what more could he say? Things would be as they were, and she would find out soon enough.

chapter four

The young Persian was tall but slender, with brown eyes, a clean face, and short, wavy hair. He was handsome, almost regal, with a fine Roman nose and the high cheekbones and widely spaced eyes of a prince. Indeed, in another time, under different circumstance, he would have been one of the kings, for the royal blood that ran through him was a thousand years old, and the fact that he wasn't was but a twist of timing and fate. Had he been born a few generations before, he would have sat on a throne, nobility along with his cousins and uncles, all of them tracing their roots to the trunk of that great royal family.

But it wasn't so. Instead, Rassa Ali Pahlavi was a Iranian sheepherder and sod farmer, a man who scratched out an existence, living from one season to the next, praying for rains, then praying for sun, praying for a harvest that could carry him through. And it was this same twist of fate that sent him to the harsh Agha Jari Deh Valley along the western coast of Iran instead of to the old royal compound in downtown Tehran.

Here, in his country, the old royal family name meant

nothing at all, nothing but memories of disappointments and the failures of generations long past.

So despite the fact that Persian royal blood ran through him, it bought him no advantage, and he preferred to keep his lineage a secret, unwilling to be reminded of how his grandfathers had failed. His own grandfather, the Great Shah Pahlavi, last in a line of Persian monarchs dating back to Cyrus in 559 B.C., had, through arrogance and corruption, lost the claim to his kingdom and been expelled with his family, leaving behind but a few, all of whom were stripped of any prestige, money, or power. When he thought of the royal family's exile, Rassa pictured the ancient royals of Persia packing up their caravans and slipping into the desert. His family, too, had literally packed up their wealth and slipped into the night; they had transferred enormous sums of money into overseas accounts, loaded their jewels and their paintings, the riches of their kingdom, and sulked away with their caravans of wealth, disappearing into the dark. With the fall of the Shah, his family's power and wealth—and worse, their ambition—had slipped into the desert and completely disappeared. Most of Rassa's family lived in lands far away, fat and discontented but too scared to come home.

Yet Rassa was not like them. He was neither fat nor discontented. And he was certainly unafraid.

Still, it appeared there was no turning back of the clock. The age of Greater Persia had passed. The rule of Pahlavi was gone. The timing of his birth had ensured that he would live his life in the mountains, herding sheep and plowing fields, and never sit on a throne.

It seemed ironic to Rassa that so much was left up to fate. Fate and the Master. Timing and place. They could all be so cruel, the young man had learned.

But still, life was good. Rassa said those words to himself

every day. It wasn't perfect; there was sadness; and no, he was not a prince; but that was all right; it didn't matter anymore. Life was *always* worth living. And worth passing on.

And on this night, at this time, that was his only concern. His young wife. And their child. That was all that mattered to him now.

Rassa Ali Pahlavi, twenty-six and broad-shouldered, walked along the narrow trail that led through the trees, away from his village. Twilight fell quickly, and the shadows under the canopy grew dark as he walked. The jungle of trees along his path formed a perfect canopy over his head, and the air was musky and wet, almost salty from the wind blowing in from his back. Behind him, the briny salt flats ran parallel to the shore of the Arabian Sea, some twenty-one kilometers to the west, and the evening air carried the smell of salt water and decaying brine shrimp. The terrain between his village and the sea was steep and rugged, with narrow valleys and foothills rising from sea level to meet the peaks of the great Zagros Mountains, which acted as a barrier to the mighty storms that rolled in from the Persian Gulf, a wall over which the clouds couldn't climb without dumping their load, leaving the valleys on the west side of the mountains rich and green and fertile and wet.

As Rassa moved off the trail and out from under the trees, the evening light broke through. He climbed a grassy embankment that looked over his village, a neat square of squat, clay houses, wood fences, and tidy courtyards surrounded by brick walls. The barnyards were filled with white and brown goats, dark-skinned children, gnarled plum and fig trees, and tangled grapevines, a hundred years old. To his back, the mountain rose above his village, marked by rich green grass and gray rock, with tiny pockets of snow in the highest crevasses left behind from the winter snows. The terrain sloped up to the mountain from his village in a near perfect half-bowl, rising ever more steeply until it merged with the rocks. An enormous wedge of granite, like a huge piece of rock pie, jutted at the peak of the mountain, almost twelve thousand feet up. Lower, on the southern tip of the bowl, a thick forest lay, with large oaks and tall pines swaying in the night, side by side.

Standing atop the rolling crown of the hill that looked over his village, the young Persian looked back to the west where the sun was now low, a deep orb of red on the distant horizon. He could see the haze and humidity rising off the warm waters of the Persian Gulf. The sun soaked through the wet air, blood red and warm.

Blood red and warm. Yes. That was right. Blood red and warm. Like the birth of his child.

Rassa thought of his wife, a woman he loved more than he loved himself, more than he wished to live. She was young; she was beautiful; she was everything to him. And as he stood there in silence thinking of her young face and anguished cries, as he pictured the consternation in the midwife's dark eyes and the feel of her arms pushing him toward the gate, he felt a shudder run through him, and the sickness rose again.

His child was coming. On this night, it would be born.

Then he fell, his knees buckling, his arms heavy and weak. He put his hands together and bowed until his forehead touched the dirt.

He hunched there, unmoving, as the evening grew quiet and still.

Then he sensed it, a feeling, an emotion, he had not felt before, a peace, unexplained, from somewhere deep in his soul. And from his perch on the mountain looking down on his world, he felt a deep calm spreading over him. Then he heard the voice speaking as if to his very soul.

It was silent and peaceful, and he knew it was God.

"This thing that is about to happen, know that it is my will."

Rassa gasped, his heart pounding, his chest tight as wire.

Then he held his breath and listened to hear the cry of his child.

* * *

Standing behind Elizabeth was the great gate that she had to walk through. It was wide and tall and made of ancient stone, heavy and beaten by the passage of men and time. Beyond the gate, a narrow pathway led down a long, winding trail that was covered with huge trees and tangled with deep brush. The path descended and grew dark and seemed to disappear in a mist. She turned and took a step toward it, and the mist seemed to grow darker and even more thick.

She turned back, facing the women who accompanied her to this entrance to the path, and she felt her heart break with the pain of saying good-bye.

If she could just know, if she could just be assured that she could come back one day. But there was *so* much uncertainty. Nothing was sure. So many had failed. Might she fail too?

"Remember," one of the women said, "this is the same plan our Parents experienced. And even though it will be painful, it will also be filled with joy." Her eyes were moist, her face tender and yet also assured, perfect in the knowledge that this had to be. "This is the only source of true and eternal joy," she added.

"I want to stay with you," Elizabeth whispered, looking from one face to another. "I want to stay with all of you." Then she broke into tears and fell into the arms of the woman closest to her.

"We will miss you," the woman whispered. "We love you. But it is time to go. But return! We will be waiting for you."

Elizabeth pulled away and stared into her eyes. "You are ready," the woman whispered. "Now it is time. You must go."

Elizabeth turned, feeling the pull of the gate and the pathway beyond. It waited, dim but promising, and she felt a quick shiver of both excitement and fear. So many she had loved had already passed through this gate, and she wanted to join them, to be with them. She felt a yearning, a tugging, to start her mission too.

Teancum stood off to one side, quietly waiting.

"I really want to follow Jehovah." Her voice tore in her throat.

"He has shown you the way."

"But I feel weak already."

"Sometimes he felt that way too. But you will find strength inside you. You are stronger, much stronger, than you have ever conceived."

"But there are times I might fail."

"Then he will carry you."

Elizabeth dropped her eyes. "I will try to be good."

Teancum smiled gently, then took her hands and held them in a final good-bye.

Elizabeth pulled away, turning slowly to the Father, saving that farewell for last. He stepped forward and placed his hand on her shoulder, then leaned toward her, embraced her, and gently kissed her brow.

She took a quick breath and held it. She pressed her cheek against his chest and thought of a lifetime of his expressions of love and confidence, a lifetime of his promises that he would always be there for her.

Finally she swallowed, mouthed farewell, and turned for the gate. She took a step toward it, and the veil became whisper thin. She stood there a moment, a look of pain on her face, then turned back suddenly. "I know my mother will suffer to bring me into the world. She suffers even now. I feel it in my soul."

"She will know of your true gratitude for the gift of life that she gives," one of the women said.

"But how? How will she know?"

"She will see it the first time she looks into your eyes. She will see it and know the first time she sees you smile. She will know that you love her long before you can speak, for the Spirit will whisper your feelings to her when she sings to you in the dark. And one day, Elizabeth, you will know too. One day when you are a mother, you will catch a tiny memory of this time, and from somewhere inside you, you will know that your child loves you too.

"Now go. It is time. Time to step into the storm."

She took the Father's hand and squeezed it, then took a deep breath. "I'm ready," she answered as she turned back to the gate.

But before she passed through, something else caught her eye, and she paused and looked through the veil that separated the worlds.

She saw her mortal father there, in the distance, a long way away. She smiled as she watched him, looking into his eyes. He watched her and gasped, as if she read his mind. She nodded to him in answer, then stepped through the gate.

* * *

The night fell. Rassa kept his head low in prayer, and it seemed to him almost as if time stood still. He wasn't asleep, but he saw it as if it were a dream. The vision was bright, but still misty, as if he were watching through a great gulf of distance and time. He saw shimmering stairs, wide and gentle, leading to an enormous stone gate, a pathway winding to his left, and a row of tall, silver trees, glistening as if from a heavy rain. There was a dazzling light, bright like the sun, and he had to cover his eyes. And it all seemed so close. He almost reached out his hand.

A girl stood alone on the stairs. He saw the white dress, the dark hair, the thin arms and soft skin. Her eyes danced, and he saw the anticipation and excitement shining through. He almost gasped, and he shivered. She was so beautiful!

He watched her intently. Did she know he was there? Did she see him too?

She lowered her gaze and took a careful step toward the gate, a gaping hole leading to some unknown world. She paused and trembled, and then Rassa understood. She was excited, but scared, maybe even terrified. Yet she continued moving forward, unwavering, committed, so strong and sure!

And as he watched he felt a great urge to speak; he wanted to call to her. He opened his mouth, but his voice didn't come.

But he knew, somewhere inside him, he knew that *this was his child!*

He didn't understand how he knew it, but he knew it was true.

"This is your child!"

He trembled as he watched her move.

Then she stopped and glanced toward him and slowly lifted her head. She stared through the distance, looking into his eyes, then smiled and nodded to him. *"Yes, it is true!"*

He started and gasped. It was a moment of joy so intense, so powerful, so *pure,* he almost could not breathe.

She nodded to him, then glanced over her shoulder and waved to an unseen presence there. She turned back to him and smiled, then stepped through the stone gate.

* * *

Rassa felt his chest tighten and a rush of blood flow to his head. A shadow fell over him, and the enormous space between them seemed to grow suddenly more vast and powerful, a billion miles, a billion days. The vision faded quickly and soon it was gone.

Rassa found himself kneeling in the darkness, his head touching the ground. The night had settled around him, and the hilltop was dark. The evening wind blew, chill and dry from the mountain, and he felt a cold shiver run up his spine.

He didn't move, his eyes closed, his head touching the soft grass. Finally, he took a deep breath, bringing himself back to this world, then pushed himself to his feet and turned and ran through the night down the hill.

chapter five

Rassa Pahlavi ran through the streets of his village toward his home. The half-moon had climbed and was now a burnt orb in the eastern sky, just barely above the rocky peaks of the mountains. The air was calm, the sky was crystal clear, and the stars were shining brightly, for it was almost midnight. Dogs barked as he passed, and he could hear the sheep bells sounding from the pastures to the east; but the baked brick and stone streets were deserted and dark.

He paused on the cement step outside his front door, then let himself in. He walked through the simple kitchen, past a set of wooden chairs and an old table, a worn vinyl couch and small TV, then stopped at the door to his bedroom and listened. He could hear movement and the sound of water being poured into a steel basin, then laughter, then hushed voices, then the cry of a child. He bowed his head and took a breath, then pushed the door open.

Sashajan was sitting on their bed holding their child in her arms. He moved quickly to her. Her face, though drawn and weary, could not hold back her joy as she leaned to the side, her cheeks touching the top of her daughter's soft hair. The midwife worked around them, cleaning and preparing the sheets for the crib. Rassa glanced to her as she pulled a clean cotton cloth across a small mattress and placed it inside the wicker bed, a homemade crib Rassa had constructed from dry reeds and cattails he had pulled from the banks of the small stream that ran through the center of the village. He caught her eye and mouthed a quick "thank you," then turned back to his wife and child.

Sashajan smiled, her dark eyes beaming brightly. She drew a contented breath and held out her hand. Rassa touched her fingers lightly as he sat on the edge of the bed. The smell of talcum powder and olive oil rose from his new baby's body. The child was sleeping, her lips puckered into a tiny O, her hands clenched into tight fists at her chest, as if she were bracing for some unseen blow. She was wrapped in a soft cotton blanket, her legs tucked tightly against her body. Her head was covered in dark hair, thin as silk, and the midwife had already pinned a tiny pearl in her hair.

As the young parents stared at the baby, neither of them spoke, and Rassa felt a shiver run through him as the peaceful feeling settled again.

Sashajan looked at him, thirteen hundred years of tradition pressing heavily on her mind. "You have a daughter," she said, her voice quiet, even apologetic, knowing it was a wife's duty to produce a fine son.

Rassa stared at the child. "Yes, I already know."

Sashajan began to question, then glanced nervously at the midwife, who had stopped her work and placed her hands on her hips, ready to defend the young mother if Rassa were so foolish as to say the wrong thing. Sashajan turned from the midwife and dropped her dark eyes. "You wanted a son," she said simply.

"No!" Rassa answered. "I want *this* child."

Sashajan looked up quickly, her eyes filled with relief. She squeezed the tips of his fingers. "Thank you," she whispered. There was far more meaning in her expression than most could understand, for it was a seal of their commitment, a commitment that surpassed the boundaries of their culture, the boundaries of their people's traditions or time.

Rassa stared at the infant who slept at Sashajan's breast and thought again of the vision he had witnessed, then he reached down and gently placed his hands under the child, lifting her carefully and pulling her into his arms. The baby remained still as he bent and whispered quietly into her ear. *"I witness that there is no god but Allah, and I witness that Muhammad is the messenger of Allah."* The call to prayer, sacred and holy, words of the prophet himself. It was the desire of all Muslims that these would be the first words a child would hear from her father's mouth, as well as the last words she would utter before death. Rassa repeated the testimony, *"I witness that there is no god but Allah,"* then pulled his head back to look into his child's face.

She slept peacefully, taking shallow breaths. She felt as light as a bird sleeping in the palm of his hand. He placed his little finger inside her palm, and the baby girl instinctively grasped it, her tiny fingers barely able to extend around his finger. Then she opened her eyes and stared at him blankly, her eyes dark and deep, her face calm and unmoving, as if she were intent on keeping her thoughts to herself. Rassa stared at her and wondered how much was inside her head. Did she understand things; did she remember things she could not talk about? Is that why God made his infants unable to communicate? Did a child only watch and learn, or did she already know? Was she learning or forgetting during these first moments on earth?

Sashajan watched Rassa, then moved closer to her child.

The tiny baby turned toward her, and it seemed that she smiled. Her lips turned upward, her eyes brightened, and her face seemed to beam. "Did you see that, Rassa?" Sashajan cried in delight. "She smiled at me. I know she did."

Rassa didn't answer, and Sashajan glanced toward him. "Do you think she knows that I'm her mother?" she asked.

Rassa answered slowly. "I don't know, Sashajan. I really don't know."

Sashajan lifted her finger to touch her new baby's cheek. Rassa watched her a moment, then lifted the child to his face. "I saw you," he whispered, dropping his mouth to her neck, feeling the softness and warmth of her flesh against his lips. "I saw you, my child; but I do not understand. Where did you come from? Where did you live before? I have never been taught that! I do not understand."

Sashajan glanced up, a questioning look in her eyes. "Rassa," she asked him, "what are you talking about?"

Rassa looked at his wife. She looked so young and so small, as if she had shrunk from the experience of delivering their child. She was pale and shaking, and Rassa knew she was weak. He turned back to their child. "We will call her Azadeh Ishbel," he announced. "Freedom is my oath to God." He lifted the tiny girl in his arms, offering her to the heavens. "Azadeh, we will call you. That will be your name."

Sashajan leaned forward and placed her head next to his. "'Freedom is my oath to God.' Yes, Rassa, that is a good name. There is something about her—it seems to fit her perfectly."

Rassa smiled. "She is beautiful. She is Azadeh. Thanks be to God." He lowered his arms and kissed the infant's brow. She unconsciously tightened her lips into another tight O. "Azadeh, I love you," he whispered as he placed the child in her mother's arms. "And though I don't understand where you came from, still I welcome you here."

* * *

Before she left, the midwife pulled Rassa into the next room and lowered her voice.

"It was a difficult birth," she said wearily. "She is young, but not strong. It was very hard for her."

Rassa looked worried. "What do I do?" he asked anxiously.

"Let her rest. Keep her warm. *Don't* let her out of bed. I will come by first thing in the morning to see how she is."

Rassa felt his knees weaken. "She will be fine, though?" he asked anxiously.

"Insha'allah." *If Allah wills it.*

The midwife studied the deep worry lines on Rassa's face, then patted his arm, her hands heavy and strong. "She will be fine," she offered as she gathered her things. "I have seen many worse. Birth and death, death and birth, the cycle of life carries on, and who are we to intervene in the will of God? She is young, and there is no reason to assume she will not mend in the next day or two, but she needs time to rest and recover from all the life she has lost. I can't do that for her, Rassa, and neither can you. But if you let her rest, let her sleep, and keep her safe and warm, she will be fine, I am sure."

Rassa swallowed hard. The midwife swept through the room one final time, then, her work complete, her things gathered, she let herself out the door.

Rassa returned to the bedroom. Sashajan opened her eyes as he walked into the room. "We have a family," he murmured as he sat by her on the bed. "We are a family. God has blessed us. We have cause to rejoice."

Sashajan nodded wearily. "I love you, Rassa," she whispered as he gently stroked her hair.

She fell asleep almost instantly. Rassa sat on the bed and held her hand as the child, wrapped in her soft cotton blanket, slept at her side. Sashajan eventually rolled away from him, and he tucked the covers around her back. For a long moment he stood there and watched them by the light of the moon, a soft, gentle glow that filtered through the window over the bed. The night was so quiet that if he didn't move he could hear Azadeh breathe.

He was a man. He had a daughter and a beautiful wife. And one day he was certain that he would also have a son.

Life was good. It wasn't perfect, but on this night it was very close.

After some time, Rassa moved away from the bed, stripped off his clothes, and pulled on a long night shirt. Moving carefully, he lay down close to the child, anxious to keep her warm against the cool mountain air. As he lay on his back and wearily closed his eyes, he suddenly remembered the silent words again.

"This thing that is about to happen, know that it is my will."

The words seemed to cut, and his heart leaped in his throat. He felt his chest tighten, and his mouth seemed to grow dry. It was a warning, he realized, and for the first time he grew scared.

He lay tense, his eyes open, staring into the dark, wondering again and again what God was trying to say. Eventually sleep overcame him, but he slept restlessly.

He woke early in the morning, at the first light of the sun. Moving carefully, he pushed himself out of bed, then turned to look at wife and daughter again. Azadeh was staring at him, her eyes dark and wide. Sashajan was still asleep, and he bent carefully to kiss her cheek. It was cold, almost clammy, and he carefully studied her face. Her lips were tight and so dry that they almost looked blue. He placed his hand on her forehead and felt the shiver of cold. He almost panicked, his heart racing, as he bent to her side. "Sashajan!" he whispered, trying to wake her.

But the blood clot had already lodged firmly in her brain. She never regained consciousness, and by afternoon, she was dead.

* * *

The next day, after the spiritual rituals and time of wailing were through, Rassa led a procession of mourners up a winding, dirt trail. Behind a small hill, ancient stones had been set into the soil in an intricate pattern, establishing the area as holy ground, with the same rights and benefits as a mosque. The nearby cemetery was small and almost eight hundred years old, though the villagers always seemed to find room for one more. Tucked away in a small dell, the cemetery was a little square of grass completely out of sight from the village. The mountain villagers were practical people, having been taught by a hard life, and they accepted death easily. Because of this, they had intentionally placed the cemetery where it couldn't be seen, for once the mourning was over there was no need to be reminded of those who were no more.

But Rassa wasn't like his people. He didn't accept Sashajan's death. Like his ancestors, the ancient Persians, he was romantic and soft hearted, and he missed his wife so much that his heart ached in his chest, each beat pounding at him like a drum of pain and despair. He hardly saw the sunlight around him, so thick was the blackness inside.

But though he didn't see it, it was a beautiful day, warm and sunny, with a light breeze from the sea. The sycamore trees were in full bloom, and the grass was green and full. By late summer, the cemetery would be covered with dead grass and brown plants, but for now it was beautiful, alive, and dark green.

Rassa led the mourners while desperately holding his child. Dressed in a white gown that flowed from her neck to her feet, she was a sparkle of brightness in a sea of dark turbans, long robes, black scarves, and veils.

Rassa laid Sashajan to rest, somehow believing he would see her again, then dropped a handful of dirt on her pine casket and walked away, following the winding path that led to his home.

That night, he held his newborn baby and rocked her to sleep. She watched him intently, looking up from his arms, and he couldn't help smile as she stared into his eyes. "What are you thinking?" he wondered aloud. "What memories and emotions are you hiding behind that deep stare?"

Azadeh looked away, then yawned deeply, clenching her fists to her side. Though she fell asleep quickly, Rassa continued to hold her tight. The house grew quiet and dark, and the rocking chair creaked on the wooden floor. Rassa kissed her cheek softly, then sang in her ear:

"The world that I give you
Is not always sunny and bright.
But knowing I love you
Will help make it right.

"So when the dark settles,
And the storms fill the night,
Remember I'll be waiting
When it comes,
Morning Light."

* * *

Two weeks after the funeral, Sashajan's sister came to him and offered to take the child. "It is not a man's job to raise her," she tried to explain.

Rassa turned away and looked at Azadeh sleeping contentedly in her crib. She had grown full and healthy in her first few days of life, and the formula Rassa fed her seemed to keep her satisfied. He watched her a moment, then shook his head.

Allah had sent Azadeh to him. She was all he had left. He would keep her and raise her. It was Allah's will.

* * *

The next day came and then passed, then another day after that; a week, then a month, then another month after that. It was summer; it was fall; the snows came, then the spring. A year passed, then another, and the cycle repeated itself.

After a while, Rassa fell into a routine. And though he had opportunities to remarry, he never could find the heart, for the image of Sashajan's face never quite left his dreams. Every year, on the anniversary of her death, Rassa left the child with Sashajan's sister and disappeared for a day of private mourning. No one knew where he went, though a few of his friends tried to guess, and when he returned he always brought wildflowers, which he planted on his wife's grave.

Azadeh grew as time passed, and Rassa continued to love her more than he loved anything, for the emptiness inside him seemed to fill when she was near.

chapter six

The war between good and evil had continued on the new battleground, and over time the spirits of darkness had taken a liking to the new place where they fought.

Since the very beginning, Master Balaam, the great teacher who had fallen in the premortal world, had been free to wander and roam, free to tempt, harass, and cause suffering. Those he couldn't tempt he would try to bring suffering and pain. And like all those who had been cast to earth before the first man was put here, like those who had sacrificed their very salvation for He Who Tells Lies, like those who had been damned to wander, hopeless and furious and alone, Balaam was also hollow and desperate and bitter with wrath. His only pleasure came in raging against that which was good, and he found particular satisfaction in finding and tormenting friends from before, those who had worked for the downfall of his master, which had led to his downfall as well. And Balaam wasn't alone in this search. Many fallen angels spent their time looking for old friends they had known from the premortal world.

They remembered these old loved ones. And they hated them now to the core.

Through the years, Balaam had claimed many souls—a hundred, a thousand, he really didn't know, for once he had destroyed them they were quickly forgotten. But through all the centuries Balaam particularly remembered the brothers that had caused him such pain. He knew that they were being saved for the last days, and once the true gospel was restored to the earth he began to search for them.

And when he finally found them, a cold chill ran through his heart.

Though Luke and Ammon had been born into a strong family, he was still optimistic he could lead them to his master, the father of lies. Good old Samuel, on the other hand, hadn't been as lucky as Ammon and Luke. He was alone—and even better, his father was one of the selfish and lazy who had barely qualified to go to earth.

Balaam's lips curled upward as he thought about Sam. He would be easy; indeed, he was almost now in his grasp. The other brothers, Luke and Ammon, would be more difficult, but if there was one thing Balaam had learned it was to not give up. Think of Judas, he said to himself. Think of David; think of a million other souls. Many of the great ones had fallen. Certainly Luke and Ammon were reachable. He and his fellow angels had been destroying God's children for a very long time now, and they had mastered the art. The fact that the brothers had been saved for the last days only made his task easier. With the world so evil, what chance did they have?

After finding the brothers, Balaam had concentrated on locating their sister, Elizabeth, too, searching the world until he had found her. Now if he could just bring them all to Lucifer, how sweet that would be!

Balaam scowled as he thought of the work he must do.

* * *

During the millennia that had passed since Balaam had been cast down to earth, he had spent his time roaming from one place to another, working to perfect the temptations that could cause men to fail. Through the years, he had seen it all. There was no pain or disappointment, no depravity or torture, no betrayal, hate, or hurt he had not taken part in.

Balaam thought back with pride on what he and his fellow angels had done. He had been there and cheered when Cain had lifted the stone against his brother. He had witnessed Abel's blood flow and learned the power of greed. Soon after, he and his friends had discovered the astonishing power of lust and its incredible potential to destroy the families of God. It was a short step from lust to far greater sins, and within a short time there was no aberration or depravity they had not introduced to the world. In one particularly brilliant display, Balaam had convinced a young mother to sacrifice her own children to some pagan god, a moment he remembered with particular satisfaction. And the people had called it *religion!* Even Lucifer had laughed. Balaam then remembered doubling over in laughter in the days of Noah, when the people refused to repent even when faced with enormous floods. How many children had perished, drowned in the flood of their parents' sins?

Over time, the followers of Satan developed a real love for the blood and horror of war. How many battles had they started—then watched the outcome with glee? Armies were their playthings, the cries of the dying sweet music to their ears, and, in his memory, Balaam could smell the smoke from the fires and the stench of dead flesh. He could hear the cries of broken mothers when their children were tortured or taken as slaves.

Then, on a warm night in April, Satan and his followers

had screamed with rage as the angels sang together, giving praise to their God.

Christ had been born in a stable. Their mortal enemy had arrived.

Later, when the darkness fell over Gethsemane, they had watched in despair as Christ paid the price of all sins, buying the redemption they could no longer have. Time had stopped, and they quivered as he groaned from the weight. His head bowed, the angels waited, and the blood seeped from his pores. How long it had lasted, none of them knew, but when it finally ended they knew the war had been lost.

The moment brought such a fury from their master that he almost went mad. In his unspeakable wrath, he reached out to strike back in the only way he knew how. He whispered his promptings in the ears of the soldiers, inciting blood lust against the Christ. Then he stood back and mocked when Christ was placed upon the cross, the skies growing dark as he danced in glee on the hill.

But after two days of storms, the morning dawned bright and clear. Christ emerged from the tomb, and the sun rose again.

* * *

As Balaam thought back on the time he had been condemned to wander the earth, he looked around, taking in all the changes he had seen in his day. He had seen great civilizations rise and fall and great rivers change their courses. He had seen deserts grow out of marshlands and the seas flood their coast. He had seen many changes. The earth was now growing old. And the day was soon coming when the King would return.

Balaam shook his head in anger, his dark eyes burning bright, then snarled in fury, a hot stench of dead breath. He thought of the young ones he had been looking for, then turned to look for his master. Time was growing short, and they had much to do.

* * *

Balaam found Lucifer in a dark room, casting his temptations over his flock, draping them in a cold and passionless blanket of sin and despair. He approached the Master carefully, bowing almost to the floor. "Master," he whispered in a cowering voice.

"Yes!" Lucifer demanded as Balaam crawled to his side.

"If I could, Master Mayhem," Balaam driveled. "I have something for you."

Lucifer turned toward him, his eyes cold as wet stones. Balaam looked away, unable to look into those dark eyes. "Master," he began, "I have found the three brothers I have been looking for."

"So?" Satan sneered. "What concern are they to me?"

"Master . . . if you will recall, these were some of the most valiant. They fought bravely against you. And now they are here."

Lucifer growled, a hollow and evil sound from his chest. "There are hundreds, even thousands, who have been saved for this day. I hate every one! Why are you wasting my time? Go! Do your work. You know what to do."

Balaam shrank back from the rage in Lucifer's voice. It hurt him; it burned him like a hot knife in his chest. But he had an idea, and if his master would just give him time. . . .

"Master Mayhem!" he pleaded, his head almost touching the ground. "I have also located the girl. Do you remember, Master Mayhem, the vision you saw? It was only a glimpse, but parts of it were true, and this young child, this young girl, she is important to them. She is one of the chosen, one of those who made a covenant with the Father about what she will do on the earth. But if we could destroy her, it would help our work now."

The Master turned toward him. "What are you talking about?"

Balaam almost quivered, the knife cutting deeper inside. The Master stared at him, bent on reading his thoughts. "Yes," he finally answered, "I remember her now. And yes, we must destroy her. Now what do you propose we do?"

Balaam clasped his hands together. "I know someone," he stuttered. "His name is Roth. He is one of your angels. . . ."

Lucifer frowned wickedly. "I know Roth," he said.

"Yes, Master. He is slow. He is lazy. But I think he could help."

chapter seven

The ground above the Agha Jari Deh Valley rose sharply to the west. There, on a rocky spot looking over the neat and well-organized village, an ancient guard tower rose like an arm and fist from the ground. The tower was made of stone cut from the mountain and stood almost sixty feet above the sloping terrain. The base of the tower was some thirty feet square, with granite walls six feet thick. Inside the walls was a large and high-ceilinged room. A single metal door allowed access to the room, and a narrow set of wooden stairs along the back wall led to the top of the tower. In ancient days, the tower had been manned constantly to warn villagers of an impending attack. In those early years, the population of the village was small enough that most of the women and children could be crammed inside the base of the tower, where they would huddle listening to the sounds of the battle outside.

The tower, known as *el Umma,* or the community, had fallen into deep disrepair through the years. The huge metal door was nearly rusted off its hinges, and the steps were so dry and rotten they creaked and groaned mightily under even a little weight. But the tower was one of Rassa's favorite places to think, and through the years he had retreated there many times to ponder and pray.

The day before Azadeh's fifteenth birthday, he got up early one morning and hiked the steep trail that led to *el Umma*. Azadeh was sleeping, and he knew he had an hour or so before she would wake. It was early spring, but the hay was coming near to full, and his day would be busy, for there was much work to do.

Rassa climbed to the top of the tower just as daylight was beginning to break. Inside, *el Umma* smelled of mold and dust and ancient, rotting wood. Every ten or twelve feet the walls were scorched and blackened from where oil-soaked torches had been attached to the walls, suspended by steel latches that were embedded into the mortar and stone. But even without a torch, four-inch slits in the rock walls provided a dim light to illuminate his way up the stairs. He climbed carefully, testing each stair, though he was familiar with most of the weakest boards. The sun was just rising between two of the highest peaks when he emerged at the top of the tower, where a round rampart with a short wall provided a barrier to keep him from stepping into space. Rassa knelt, facing Mecca, and bowed his head for prayers, then sat back and leaned against the tower, with the rising sun to his back.

He kept his eyes open, looking out on the sea. The sky was clear; a cold front had moved through in the night, cleaning the air of haze and humidity. From where Rassa sat, he could see most of the eastern coastline of the Persian Gulf, the dark waters stretching north and south, lapping at the brown sands and dry foothills that made up the Iranian coast. The sea was hazy and gray and sparkled in the rising sun. Looking north, he could clearly make out the oil platforms and pipelines that crossed the shallow waters of the Gulf. Further out, he could see the drilling platforms and pumping stations of Khark and Ganaveh, the heart of one of the richest oil fields in the world. A row of tankers, perhaps four in all, lined up at the Bandar–e Bushehr offshore-pumping station to take on their load. Even from this distance, he could distinguish those that were already loaded with oil, for they sat much lower in the water than those that were waiting to be filled. After filling their bowels with Arabian crude, the tankers would steam south and east, through the Straits of Hormuz and into the Arabian Sea. It would take the monsters several weeks to reach their destinations in Japan, Taiwan, and the southern U.S. gulf ports. Rassa watched with only casual interest, for the oil fields of Iran meant very little to him. He benefited not at all from the incredible wealth that was generated through Iranian oil production, and because he had been watching the oil tankers since he was a child, there was little there he had not seen before.

Yet as he stared to the west, something did catch his eye. Far out at sea, maybe ten or twelve kilometers off the coast, a monstrous ship steamed into view. It started as a gray dot on the southern horizon, but grew quickly, and Rassa watched it carefully. As the ship moved closer, he saw the deck and the enormous steel mast, and he knew it was an American aircraft carrier. The carrier cut through the water, its sharp bow slicing through the three-foot seas, and made good time as it cruised to the north. Minutes later, Rassa saw one, and then two aircraft launch from its deck, pointed-nose fighters that disappeared for just a fraction of a moment below the carrier's deck, then formed up together and turned to the west. F-14 Tomcats, Rassa could tell from the sweep of their wings.

The fighters accelerated together, then pulled their noses steeply into the air and disappeared beyond a high strand of gray clouds. Rassa watched them, curious. To his right, along the mountains, he saw two Iranian jet fighters, old Iraqi MiG 29s Saddam Hussein had sent over the border to Iran during the first hours of the Gulf War and which Rassa's government had never returned. The MiGs screamed in from the north, low and fast, following the contours of the mountains before turning toward the brown sands of the coast. The MiGs always stayed away from the international waters, and they certainly never ventured near the American carrier as they circled over the coast, though one made a feint for a U.S. destroyer before quickly turning away. The MiGs were flying very fast, and they soon disappeared behind him, heading back to their base, their engines screaming as they sucked down their fuel.

Rassa watched with interest. He had seen the game of cat and mouse before: an American carrier group would move up the coast, flanked by their escorts and destroyers while launching their Tomcats on combat air patrols. The Iranian (or, in the old days, Iraqi fighters) would follow the American ships, watching and teasing in their own little show of force. Rassa wasn't a military man, but he suspected if the U.S. fighters ever got serious, if they ever made a turn for the Iranian fighters, his brothers would turn tail and run. It was one thing to tease, but another altogether to get blown out of the air.

As Rassa watched, he realized such scenes had been far more common over the past several months than they had ever been before. And he had witnessed other things, things that worried him and were talked about in town. There seemed to be a constant line of army convoys moving up and down the coastal highway. Some said these army units were there to act as a barrier to the constant flow of Iraqi insurgents and foreign fighters that hid out in the Iranian deserts, where they had established base camps from which they would train and prepare for strikes into the newly democratic regime in Iraq. Others claimed the opposite, saying the Iranian army was providing training to the insurgents, as well as food, money, ammunition, and aid.

Rassa had also recently seen many more American warships than he had ever seen in the past. Normally, the Americans would keep their battle groups much farther to the south, rarely venturing much farther north than the northern coast of Bahrain, but lately the American ships regularly docked at the Iraqi ports near Umm Qasr, as well as the ports at Kuwait.

And there seemed to be many more western oil tankers in the Gulf. He glanced again to the offshore loading docks at Bandar–e Bushehr. On any given week, he might see one or two tankers load up at the port, but over the past year or so, and especially over the past several months, the number of American tankers had doubled, even tripled, and Rassa wondered why.

As he watched, the American aircraft carrier turned forty degrees to the west and was soon out of sight, though an escort trailed behind, staying between the carrier and the coast. There were no longer any fighters in the air, and Rassa shifted against the tower to look on his village below.

Agha Jari Deh was an ancient town, with maybe a little more than four thousand people, a number that hadn't changed much over the past several hundred years. From where he sat, on top of the tower that was uphill from Agha Jari Deh, Rassa watched his town come to life. He saw a pair of *mutawwa'in,* the religious police, walking the streets dressed in their black turbans and white robes, ready to enforce the morning call to prayers. In the center of the village, a new civic center was being built, a modern brick-and-glass building going up alongside ancient mud huts stiffened with palm leaves and logs. The village market, or *suq,* was exactly as it had been for almost five hundred years. The money changers were out, already clinking their coins to advertise their business as the merchants set out their wares—flour, copper, peaches, fine rugs, ancient spices (which had been the catalyst of too many wars), coffee, tea, sugar, holy water from Mecca, pistachios, goat's meat, and thin cuts of lamb—everything needed for daily life could be bought in the market. The streets were busy with pedestrians and bikers, but there were also many more automobiles than there used to be, including Mercedes and Land Rovers brought in from Europe. Islam had never preached it was a sin to grow rich, and many of the villagers had grown relatively wealthy from working in the offshore oil fields or trading with the foreigners and city dwellers who came to the market every day.

From where Rassa sat, he could see the fault line that ran almost straight through the middle of the town. Every hundred years or so, his village suffered a powerful earthquake, but afterwards, whatever houses or shops that had been shaken down were quickly rebuilt. His people were not easily rattled, and what they lacked in resources, they made up in tenacity and patience and reduced expectations.

The sun was rising higher now, and it was quickly growing warm. Rassa felt drowsy and peaceful, and he considered a moment, thinking of his home.

Rassa was a simple man, but he was not unlearned, having been educated in one of the finest private schools in the region (one of the few benefits of being the grandson of the Shah), and he knew this place where he stood was truly unique in the world. He surveyed his village, a village that had its roots going back almost 2,500 years, back to the days when men were just learning to plow, when they realized an ox could do more work than a boy, back to the age of the old kingdom in Egypt, the first great civilization that was to rise in the Mideast. He knew that countless warlords and emperors had likely stood in this place. From the first nomadic tribesmen to the Persian kings, from the Roman senators to the Muslim caliphs, from the Russian czars to the British generals—many of the world's greatest leaders had fought for this ground. From the beginning of time, they had considered Persia a brilliant gem, a pearl of desire, a land worth fighting for.

How many men had died, how many wars had been fought, how many empires had risen and settled over Persia, this fertile piece of land that he called home?

Persia. The White Pearl. Treasure of Ancient Days.

The world had been changed here.

Might Persia change history again?

Rassa Ali Pahlavi had a feeling, somewhere deep in his soul, that it was to be. This feeling, this thing he had felt since he was a child, had been one of the reasons he had chosen to stay. In the years following the fall of his grandfather the Shah, most of the royal family (and they had numbered in hundreds) had accepted luxurious exile in various nations outside of the Persian Gulf. There they had retired with their millions, their servants and aides and butlers and wine. But in leaving, they had forgone any influence on their nation, as well as any hope of a respectful return. But Rassa's father, now dead, had chosen to stay, and Rassa had followed his lead; even if anonymous, even if poverty stricken, he wanted to remain in this land, for he believed a time would come when he would see better days, when the glory of Persia would rise once again. And he wanted to be there when the great day arrived.

As Rassa stood in the rising sun, he sensed both good and darkness, the passing of time, the passing of history, of dreams and disappointments, of birth and death, the emotion passing over him like a wave of warm air. Bending, he ran his fingers through the two hundred years of dust and dirt that had settled on the stone bulwark at the top of the tower. It was black, like the soil below it, and he let it sift through his fingers, then lifted his hand and smelled the richness there. He turned in a slow circle, looking from the forest to the mountain, then back to the valley below. Where else could man stand and look down upon more than two thousand years of civilizations, the tracings of wars, long forgotten, but which had shaped the history of the world?

He considered ancient Persia as he stood in the morning sun.

* * *

The history of Iran was one of rise and fall, of defeat and renewal, of brutal oppression followed by tenacious rebuilding. It was a story of both progress and depravity, of faith and disbelief.

It began along the seashore, where the air was cooler in the summer and wet with rain, where the fruit trees grew naturally and the black soil—rich trailings of retreating glaciers—was so thick it extended down to bedrock. The Iranians were a mixture of many nations and races: the Achaemenids and Aryans, as well as Arabs, Turks, and Mongols, but they could also trace their roots to the first race of people who inhabited western Asia, a region extending from the present republic of Turkestan to the Mediterranean. In Iran, the Old Asians, tall people with strong arms and elegantly long necks, first settled along the coast some 2,500 years before, then spread over the western parts of the plateau running to the Zagros Mountains. For centuries, minor battles were fought between the various peoples that were struggling to establish their young cultures there, but eventually the Elamites took over the whole of the Tigris Valley, from Assure to the Persian Gulf. These people then became the first to experience the rising power of Babylon. By the time King Nebuchadnezzar had finished his conquest, little was left of their infant civilization.

Meanwhile, on the other side of the Zagros Mountains, the Aryans, who would become ancestors of people in present-day India, Iran, and western Europe, were moving down from the north, mixing with the native Old Asians while planting the foundation of several great civilizations to come.

As time passed, the Persian kingdom grew up on the upper plateaus, not far from where Rassa now stood. On the other side of the Zagros range, the Babylonian empire continued to thrive, growing in majesty and power until, about the time of Jeremiah in the Bible, six hundred years before the birth of the great prophet Jesus, Cyrus the Great rose up and united the kingdoms into one.

Thus began the reign of the great Persian kings. The first great king, Cyrus, was courageous and generally tolerant of others' religions and beliefs. Upon conquering Babylonia, he retained the king as the governor and eventually freed the Jewish slaves, allowing them to return to their homeland and the ancient temple of Solomon which they so dearly loved. Even the Jews held the great king in esteem, putting the name of King Cyrus on a pedestal of respect and gratitude.

Cyrus was followed by other kings, first his son and then others, all of whom built great highways, postal systems, waterways, and grand cities. These kings set up a system of governing the conquered lands through local governors (a system that was later copied by the Romans), and created the most recognized and accepted coinage in the world. The kings also developed a corps of brilliant engineers, who built the first canal linking the Nile to the Red Sea.

For nearly three hundred years, the Persians grew in influence and power, until they peaked in expansion when King Xerxes attempted to subvert the Greeks. An odd man, probably mad, who worshiped the moon and preferred to sleep on the ground with his dogs, Xerxes did manage to drive his army to Athens, but then he was quickly driven back and his army was nearly destroyed in the retreat. Beaten and demoralized, King Xerxes spent the remainder of his days drinking, shopping for new wives, and lopping off the heads of his army commanders. Soon after, the age of the great kings drew to a close. In 324 B.C., a Macedonian named Alexander defeated King Darius III, leaving the Macedonian kings in control of most of the civilized world.

Meanwhile, a new empire began to rise in the west. The Romans were edgy and ambitious neighbors, and though the two nations lived side by side for a time, their trust of each other was always paper thin. Still, Persia realized the strategic potential of an alliance with Rome, and sought to exploit her location as the bridge between east and west. Just before the birth of the prophet Jesus, Iran established trade relationships with both China and Rome and quickly grew rich from taxing the trade that moved along the Silken Road.

These riches brought great power. Power and riches brought envy. And envy, as it always did, brought conflict and war.

For the next eight hundred years, the Persians warred continually with their neighbors, bitter and bloody wars which, though never quite enough to bring the Persian Empire down, were enough to keep it from growth and prosperity.

So it was that the Persians were easy prey to the Muslim invaders who arrived with their Arabian horses, curved swords, and black robes. The Arabs were eerily determined, almost suicidally so, for to them death brought only the promise of a greater reward. They had one god, called Allah, and he was worth fighting for; so when the battle was pitch and the outcome unassured, the Arabs would cry from their horses, "Allah-o-Akbar!" *Great is the One and Only God.* It was their great call to arms, and it gave them strength.

With the arrival of the Muslim armies, the Persian Empire, decadent and weak, quickly collapsed. Like a sand castle washed away before the crashing waves of the storm, the Persian kings were swept from power by the disciplined Muslim troops.

But what was the power that really destroyed them?

Nothing but the power of God.

The Muslims had a core belief to fight for, a fire inside them that drove them to fight, the belief that, come pain or death, they were fighting the battles of God, that he could not be defeated and they were destined to succeed.

So it was that, along with conquest, the Muslims brought a new religion, a commanding set of beliefs that resonated with such power it could not be ignored. The religion of Islam was gratefully accepted by the Persians, even though it came at the tip of a sword, because, at a time when most Persians were bound by a harsh and unchanging caste system, the followers of Muhammad claimed equality for all, regardless of race or social status.

For the next hundred years the Persians penetrated most of the Muslim world, contributing greatly to Muslim art, literature, science, and culture. They also became great warriors, eventually establishing a state of Persian Islam.

In A.D. 1220, however, the history of Iran took a bloody and bitter turn for the worse.

It came in the form of a dark man on horseback, an enormous man, bloodthirsty and evil and bent on conquering the world. Genghis Khan was a Mongol prince, leader of a bitter and fearsome people, a people born of hardship and suffering, a people who drank human blood as easily as others drank water. The armies of Genghis Khan were hardened, violent, and as loyal as any army ever assembled. Toughened nomads turned warriors, they were bent on conquering the world.

A dark man, huge and evil, with greased-back dark hair and yellow slits for eyes, Khan approached the lands of Persia on a gray horse. Ruling his soldiers with an iron fist while rewarding his officers with the many spoils of war, Genghis was a tactical genius who swept through Persia like a hot blade through ice, destroying entire populations before him. He massacred whole towns, beheading men, women, and children and stacking their heads in gory piles that reached fifty feet high, their dead eyes staring out, their dry tongues protruding from gaping mouths. Those few he didn't massacre he kept as slaves. Rape, torture, and suffering were his preferred methods of dealing with his subjects, and his armies massacred the Persians with no more mercy than if they were killing sick rats. Eventually, Khan ruled the largest empire in the world, from Korea to Hungary, and under his rule the land of Persia became a long and mournful cry of devastation and fear.

But again, God showed his mercy, and Genghis Khan died. His empire was soon divided, and once again small and independent states sprouted along the Persian coast.

Then disaster struck again when Teymoor Lang, a devout Sunni Muslim, entered Iran, bent on destroying the Shiite heretics. Though a learned and cultured scholar of the Qur'an, Teymoor Lang appeared incapable of showing mercy to the followers of the prophet's son-in-law, Ali.

After the fall of Teymoor Lang, the times of sorrow passed, and with the dawn of the seventeenth century, Iran entered the golden age, a time when Rassa's ancestor, Shah Abbas, united the various kingdoms under one glorious rule. The Iranian civilization soon reached unprecedented heights of social and military power and was once again recognized as one of the world's superpowers. Peter the Great traveled with his armies through Rassa's village, selecting a beautiful Iranian princess to take with him back to Russia. Napoleon fought side by side with the Shahs to help oust the British armies. And though the Russians were a constant threat (being jealous of Iran's rich oil fields and warm water ports), the royal family held onto their power, sometimes reigning as monarchs, sometimes reigning through proxies, but always managing to retain their unrelenting control on their country. In the early part of the twentieth century, the Pahlavi dynasty was established, flourishing until the Islamic revolution in 1979 finally drove the royal family from power.

* * *

So it was that Rassa found himself on that morning, looking down from a crumbling tower that watched over his village, not a king, not a prince, but a young farmer looking on a land that would never be his.

As he stood alone that day, considering the cycles of life, he thought of the birth and death of nations, the birth and death of peoples, the birth and death of his ancestors who had lived there before.

The cycle always repeated. It was repeated with nations, and it had already been repeated in his life. There were two people he loved. One he had laid in a grave; one he laid in a little bed every night. There was birth, there was rising, and then there was death. Rassa shrugged. Who was he to understand the cycle of life? Who was he to question what it was all for? He could ponder, he could ask, but he could not comprehend.

Might he know it one day? Insha'allah. *If God wills.*

chapter eight

Rassa glanced at his watch and was just standing to leave when he heard heavy footsteps echoing up from the base of the tower. He listened, relaxed, as the footsteps drew near. Omar Pasni Zehedan emerged at the top of the stairs.

"Rassa," he offered simply as he moved to Rassa's side. From where Rassa had been sitting, it would have been impossible for Omar to have seen him from the ground; the low wall around the embattlement would have hidden him from view. But it wasn't uncommon for the two to meet there, and neither of them was surprised to see the other man.

Omar sat next to Rassa on the embattlement and leaned against the cold stone. Rassa was quiet as he settled in.

"You see the aircraft carrier?" Omar asked after a while.

Rassa nodded and hunched his shoulders toward the sea in reply.

"There were also a couple of our fighters up north."

Again, Rassa nodded.

Omar Pasni Zehedan pulled out a crumpled pack of unfiltered cigarettes and stuck one between his fat lips. He was a huge man, with legs like a tree trunk and a thick, hairy neck. His hands were round as grapefruits and he had a steel vice for a grip. Father of fifteen children, husband of six wives (the Qur'an allowed for only four wives, but he didn't count the two who had failed to produce offspring for him), Omar was wealthy and cynical and wise. As a young man, he had grown rich through adventures and daring, but he was far more conservative now, for he had much to lose. For going on twenty years, Omar had been the dehestan leader, equivalent to a county mayor in the West, and he wielded his influence with the deftness of an Olympic gymnast while holding onto his power with the same iron-fisted grip that he used to seal his secret deals. Over the years, the man had grown rich through illicit trade: selling black-market supplies to the army, smuggling dollars and euros (without which little business ever got done), bribing the port tariff managers to export rare Persian rugs, running dope, alcohol, and guns—there was little Omar hadn't bought, sold, or traded at one time or another. He even owned a silkworm farm, using the silk to buy passports and visas from Tehran, which he then sold to business leaders who wanted to travel abroad. He had many friends, and his enemies weren't a few, but all in all he was as well connected and well financed as anyone Rassa knew.

The dehestan leader's relationship with Rassa's family went back many years. Omar and Rassa's father had fought side by side in the Iran-Iraq war, cringing in sandy trenches while chemical warheads flew overhead and, upon Rassa's father's death, Omar had taken Rassa under his protective wing. Over the years, they had become loyal friends.

Omar spit a tiny piece of tobacco off the tip of his tongue. Rassa watched him shift his weight from one hip to the other, knowing the cold stone hurt his arthritis. Omar cursed and stretched his legs. "I drove up to Bandar–e Mah Shahr yesterday," he then said. "It normally takes me two hours. Took almost four. I was stopped at three roadblocks. There used to only be one. I passed an army convoy that must have been three miles long. I made note of the unit, their commander proudly, and stupidly, had his unit flag waving from his staff car." He spit once again. "They were the Twelfth Special Security Forces," he announced, as if he were breaking important news.

Rassa stared blankly. It meant little to him.

Omar was silent as he lit up his smoke. "The Twelfth is normally posted to the central headquarters in Tehran," he continued. "So I did a little reading." Omar was well traveled, but far more important, he had a computer ***hooked up to a phone line!*** Access to the Internet meant access to the entire world's library of information sources and newspapers, including those in Tehran, and the insights he gleaned were often remarkable. Many nights Rassa had gone to Omar's house and, until the wee hours of morning, read things he would not have believed just a few years before.

"They are posting the Twelfth to protect the oil fields to our south," Omar concluded.

Rassa glanced toward him and shrugged, "Protect them from what?"

"The circumstances beg that question, it would seem. I don't see enemy navies lined up, ready to invade our shores, I don't see an enemy ready to knock down our doors. It seems the mullahs and bureaucrats are growing both suspicious and bold. They don't see an enemy; they only see people like us. But it appears they intend to protect their theocracy, even with Muslim blood."

"You knew they would, Omar. How many times have we said the same thing?"

The older man growled and shifted his weight to his other

oversized hip. He adjusted his turban and glared to the south, then reached under his robe and pulled out a sharp, curved knife from a tight leather sheaf he had strapped to his leg. Extracting a large peach from his pocket, he cut it in half and extended a piece toward Rassa, using the end of his knife. Rassa took it and thanked him as he took a small bite.

"Too much is going on," Omar answered. "Too many rumors. Too many whispers of war. Too many army units on highways, and too many threats from the mullahs who hide in Tehran. But the enemy isn't that Great Satan, the United States, like we used to think. The enemy comes from within. And there is a darkness, a mist, spreading like smoke in the air. I don't like it, Rassa. It is calm now; I know that—but I feel it is the calm before the crashing storm."

Omar glanced at his friend. Rassa nodded weakly. Yes, he agreed.

The world was changing, even here in Iran. There was too much information, too much travel, too much talk for the ultraconservative imams and mullahs to keep their people in the dark. Rassa had heard all their arguments, all of their bile and fear—having been raised in the swamp of their loathing, how could he have not heard it before? But the truth was, he didn't buy it. He knew it wasn't true. The ayatollahs were lying. The men who ran Iran, the mullahs, the local district leaders, the policemen, teachers, and bureaucrats, all of them hated the United States; it was a part of their jobs, one of the qualifications they were screened for before they even applied. But not everyone shared in their hatred, and there was a growing sentiment, especially among the educated and the young, that the people of Iran had a decision to make: enter the twenty-first century or step back five hundred years. Build on the hope of the future or the hate of the past. Take a step toward freedom or back to the Dark Ages again.

Omar glanced to Rassa, expecting to see him rousing with anger. The two had conspired many times, and Omar knew how Rassa felt about the government of Iran. But Rassa's face remained passive as he stared at the calm morning sea.

* * *

Omar crushed his smoke and turned his eyes to the rising sun.

Should he tell him, he wondered? Should he tell his friend? Should he try to explain his dream or keep it to himself? The truth was, he wanted to forget it, to drive it from his mind. But he had had dreams before, and he had always been right. Yet even now, in the daylight, he shuddered as he thought. It had been so violent, so graphic. He wished he could forget.

It was such a horrible dream, he had wakened in sweat.

Now should he warn Rassa? Or would it just worry him?

He glanced uneasily at his young friend. "It has been tough, losing Sashajan," he said in his gravelly voice.

Rassa only nodded. It was only three days short of fifteen years since he had placed her in the grave.

"The little one, Azadeh, how is she now?" Omar asked quietly. He shot a quick look toward Rassa, then turned away. It was considered inappropriate, even rude, to ask of one's daughters or wife, and only the closest friends could make such an inquiry.

Rassa didn't see the flash of concern in Omar's eyes. "She is growing," he answered, a look of pride on his face.

Omar pushed himself up to his feet, anxious to get off the cold stone. "You know, Rassa, I have nine daughters," he said. "Some of them are goat ugly. I don't mean to be unkind, but I am an honest man, and I know what I see. There aren't enough blind men in the valley for my daughters to marry. But thankfully *some* of my daughters look like their mothers and not me. Some of them are beautiful, Rassa, I am proud to say. But I tell you now, there is something in Azadeh. She has a beauty that goes far beyond the eye."

Rassa smiled proudly. "Thank you, Omar," he said.

"No, I'm not just being pleasant, Rassa. She is a vision, an angel who fell from the sky. Sometimes angels fall among us. Where angels fall, why they fall, Allah does not reveal. But Azadeh is an angel and she has fallen here."

Rassa nodded slowly. "Our children are great gifts. We all have angels in our homes."

"Yes, Rassa, that is true. But this generation, these children, I don't know . . . there is something about them, something I don't understand. They are better than we were. They are better than we are now. And we are all the time speaking of how our children need us, but I have come to believe that before this time is over it will be just the opposite. We will be needing them." Omar glanced down at the village and rubbed his hand over his face. He felt himself tremble, and he was embarrassed for himself. He was a hard man, a businessman, a man of great wealth and means. But this dream, this cold warning—it had cut him to the core. And he loved this child Azadeh as much as he loved his own. He turned to the younger man. "You need take care," he instructed as he stared at his friend. "I'm worried for her, Rassa . . ." His voice trailed off.

Rassa rose to his feet, his eyes hurt and intense. "What are you talking about, Omar?" he demanded.

Omar started to answer, but the words didn't come. He remained silent for a moment, his mouth open, then turned away and shrugged, wishing he hadn't said anything. What would he tell him? How could he ever make it clear? *Your child is in danger, Rassa, for I had a dream!* He would sound like a fool if he tried to explain.

"I just worry for her, Rassa," he finally said. "She is young; she is special; and you are left here to care for her yourself. She needs a mother, like we all do, and you need a wife. I worry for you both. That's all I meant to say."

* * *

Rassa watched his friend's face, knowing there had to be more, but Omar waved his hand and moved toward the steep steps. "It is nothing, Rassa. Nothing. Really. I just worry for you. Now I must go. It is getting late and we both have work to do."

Omar stopped short of the stairs, then turned and lowered his voice. "There is a meeting tonight. Are you coming?" he asked.

Instinctively, Rassa looked around cautiously, then shook his head. "I can't," he said. "Tomorrow is Azadeh's birthday."

Omar grunted, "Yes, yes, of course. Give her my love. Tell her happy birthday for me."

chapter nine

Her father was silent during that evening's meal. Azadeh cleared the table and finished the dishes, then sat down beside him as he smoked by the fire. It was cold out. A biting wind blew down off the mountain to claw at the thatched and clay shingles that lined their low roof, and Azadeh could feel the cold draft as she passed by the window.

She sat by her father and stared at the fire. He turned to her, looked away, then turned to her again.

"Let's go for a walk," he offered in a low voice.

Azadeh looked at him, her eyes dark and alive. It wasn't like her father to offer such a thing. More, it was cold and blowing, a hard storm was coming, and the weather on the mountain could be violent and unpredictable. Still, he stood and pulled his coat on. "Come with me," he said. "We'll go to the market and walk around for a while."

Azadeh's heart flipped. The market? At night? She had already completed their shopping. They had milk and eggs, cooking oil and honey. They did not have to go shopping for another couple of days. In her mind she pictured the market, its shops crowded with people, merchants displaying their wares to the wealthy that had come up from the valley to shop. She thought of the multicolored lanterns that would be hanging to light the dark night.

A walk to the market? At night? When they didn't need supplies? It could only mean one thing. He had not forgotten her birthday. He was going to buy her a present!

Azadeh quickly pulled on her hijab, slipping the thin scarf over her hair and neck, then draped a dark shawl over her shoulders and flipped the scarf over her long hair, pulling it forward to protect her eyes, and followed her father out the front door. He waited for her, and she ran to catch up with him as he turned toward the town square. He reached for her hand, and she slipped it into his as she glanced down the dark streets toward the lights in the distance, which seemed to burn with an intensity she had not seen before. Her heart leapt with excitement as they walked toward the square.

Of course he had remembered! He would never forget. But the fact that he always remembered her birthday didn't mean there was always a celebration. Her culture never ran short on reasons to celebrate—birthdays, weddings, Mondays, anniversaries, leap year, government holidays, untold religious celebrations—it seemed they celebrated anything. Still there had been precious few presents or parties in Azadeh's life. "No money," her father would explain in a pained voice. It hurt him, and she knew that—but the truth was there was rarely so much as an extra rial to spare. Rassa was nearly penniless, an anonymous and struggling farmer who had to scratch out a living just like everyone else. And it had been a bad year. The cotton had nearly burned in the fields from lack of spring rains, and then a series of cloudbursts and flash floods had washed away some of the best cows in their herd.

Still, as they walked toward the market, Azadeh stepped

quickly and with hope. Could it be her father had somehow managed to scrape a few rials together? Might there be some extra money, some unknown fountain she knew not of?

Tomorrow was her birthday, but not just any birthday—she was turning fifteen. She would be considered a woman. Just a few hours more, and her childhood would be left behind. It was a time of great celebration, a time to acknowledge her transition into adulthood, a time to celebrate the passing of the young ways and the coming of the joys and responsibilities associated with being an adult. Her entire life lay before her, hopeful and promising.

She shivered from excitement as she held her father's hand.

If Azadeh had been forced to be perfectly truthful, she would have admitted there were times in the past when she felt her birthday had become more a day of mourning the death of her mother than a day to celebrate her birth. Sometimes Azadeh wondered if her father realized that she felt lonely too. And though she wanted a present terribly, what she really needed was some kind of sign that her father loved her as much as he had loved his wife. She needed a symbol of his affection, some indication that he realized that she missed her mother as well.

She lowered her head against the wind. When she looked up again they were almost there.

She knew what she wanted. She had eyed them in the market some three months before. And they were not simply clothing or some playthings; she was almost a woman and far beyond being satisfied by childish toys. She pictured them in her mind, shining and bright, imagining how they would feel if she ever held them in her hand.

Would he have enough money? Almost certainly not.

But they *were* walking to the market. And it *had* been his idea. Who knew what he was thinking? Perhaps a miracle was in store.

The market was not crowded; the cold had chased most of the people away. But the wind had died down now, and though it was cool, it was no longer cold. The lights burned, and the lanterns cast multicolored shadows in every direction. Rassa moved toward a small booth that had handmade dresses hanging in display. They were extravagant and beautiful, a clash of lace and bright colors, but Azadeh hardly looked at them. These dresses were for little girls, the little Cinderella she could no longer be. Her father watched her reaction, then asked the price, hunched his shoulders and moved to the next stall. They worked their way around the market. Dresses. Handbags. Shoes. Denim pants from the West. A silver flute. He checked the prices carefully, occasionally lifting some less expensive item as if to suggest it to her before placing it carefully back on the shelf. Azadeh tried to show interest, but her heart seemed to faint. They were moving in the wrong direction! The birthday present she wanted was on the other side of the market, five rows to the south, almost a full block away.

Rassa lifted a set of small earrings, holding them next to Azadeh's cheeks. "These are beautiful," he said hopefully.

Azadeh smiled and agreed. "They are beautiful, Father."

"How much?" he asked the merchant.

"Forty-five thousand rials," the merchant answered. Fifteen American dollars. Rassa's eyes dropped in a look of despair, and Azadeh watched him, her heart breaking. She heard the sound of the coins clinking in his pocket, and she knew he did not have enough money. What might he be holding? A few thousand rials? Not enough for the earrings. Not enough for anything.

She would not get a present. It broke her heart—but not because of the present itself. She didn't care about a birthday gift, at least not anymore. She cared only for her father and how he must feel. What a failure he must feel like! How disappointed and embarrassed! She watched him carefully, seeing the pain in his eyes, and for the first time she saw a look of complete despair. Everything he had, he had given to her. But it was not enough. He looked away in shame.

She leaned tenderly toward him. "It doesn't matter, Father," she whispered. "I love you. That's all that matters. I know we don't have much money, but that is okay. Come on, let's go home. It will be okay."

Rassa looked at her sadly. "I'm sorry," he said. "It has been a bad year. The cotton. The cows. We'll do better this year. And then I will get you . . ." He gestured toward the shops and the brightly lit kiosks with their playful displays. "I'm sorry, Azadeh," he repeated as he lowered his head.

She took his hand and pulled him toward their home. "It's okay, father. I really do understand."

They walked in silence, making their way up the dusty roadway that led to their home. At the top of the hill they stopped and turned back, looking down on their village. The wind had swept the skies clear, and the moon was bright and orange, a huge ball rising over the mountains. The lights from the village shone in the clear air, and a huge bowl of stars shined over their heads. The Milky Way was full and fat, a bright band of stars—it seemed a trillion in all. They looked at each other, and Azadeh forced a quick smile.

"She is up there," she whispered.

"Who?" Rassa asked.

"My mother."

Rassa slowly nodded his head. "I hope so," he said.

"I know you miss her, Father."

They looked at the sky a moment longer, then turned again for their home.

They were just reaching the light of their front porch when Rassa turned and said, "You wanted something special, didn't you."

Azadeh shook her head. Her father watched her, then pressed. "I could see it in your eyes. I could see it in your actions. Did I even come close to guessing what you wanted? I don't think I did."

Azadeh was silent, hoping she would not have to tell him what she had been hoping for. "It was nothing, Father," she answered coyly.

"This is a special birthday. More so than most. I know you had your eye on something. You have asked to go to the market too many times over the past month or so. I have tried to figure out what you hoped for, but I have no idea. Fathers are not so good at these sorts of things; I think you see that by now. This is where you need a mother. She would know what to get you when I couldn't figure it out."

Azadeh was silent.

"What was it?" her father prodded.

She kicked her sandaled feet through the dirt, then leaned and whispered in an embarrassed voice. He nodded slowly, a look of great sadness clouding his eyes. It would have been far too expensive. "I'm sorry," he apologized for the last time.

"I still love you, Father," Azadeh teased in reply.

* * *

The two walked to the front door in silence. It was dark and late, and Azadeh got ready for bed while her father sat in his chair and read by the light of a small lamp.

After she was asleep, he sat alone for a time, then pushed himself up from his chair and walked to his bedroom and stood by his bed. Leaning down, he pulled out a small chest from under the headboard, then extracted a hidden key from a wooden drawer by his bed. He opened the chest and extracted two American silver dollars, the only savings he had, the only wealth he had ever accumulated in his entire life. He fingered the coins. They were heavy and firm, and he held them tightly in the palm of his hand, then closed the chest and pushed it back under the bed.

* * *

Azadeh woke early. The sun was just breaking over the mountains, and the dawn was pink and dark purple from the clouds overhead. She heard her father working in the kitchen and smelled his special jelly rolls, her favorite treat. She lay on her pillow and smiled. She did love her father. He was the best father in the world. She knew she was blessed. It really was enough.

She lay there a moment, enjoying the laziness of lying in bed, then threw back the covers and put her feet on the floor.

She saw them on the dresser beside her, and her heart almost stopped. Two pearl-handled brushes and a gorgeous silver mirror. They had been laid on a deep purple cloth, and the silver handles glittered brightly in the morning sun.

She didn't move. She couldn't move. For a long moment she just stared as her heart slammed in her chest. She glanced toward the door, to where her father worked in the kitchen, then back to her dresser where the beautiful brushes and hand mirror lay. She shook her head. Was she dreaming? Then she literally squealed. She reached out for the brushes, then suddenly pulled her hand back. She almost didn't dare touch them. The joy was too great. It was enough just to look at them and know they were there. It was enough to know that she had them. That was enough for a while.

She held her hand to her mouth, then jumped out of bed. She ran into the kitchen, slamming back her bedroom door. Rassa turned in surprise as she burst into the room. Running toward him, she jumped into his arms. Leaning into his neck, she buried her face against his shoulders and cried in his arms.

chapter ten

Lucifer stood in the center of the village square, flanked by his two disciples. Balaam stood close, but the small one, Roth, kept back. Roth was a bent and broken spirit who had lost his lust for the fight and now spent most of his time sulking about the things he had lost, while toying with some of the evil mortals who had already fallen to his side. Indeed, Roth had reached a point where he didn't much care if he destroyed any more souls, for he had become more interested in finding ways to pass the eternities of time, seeking any pastime that would provide a moment's respite from the torturing knowledge that his misery would never end.

The black centuries loomed forever before him. This was it. Forever. This was all he would have. This misery, this darkness—it was all he would know. Endless days. Endless years. His misery would never end.

Lucifer watched Roth out of the corner of his eye. He hated all his followers (was there really anything he didn't hate now?), but he hated Roth even more than most others. He considered him lazy and childish, a man who couldn't be counted on, a man who was more interested in his own diversions than bringing souls to his side. Yet Satan had made a decision not to deal with his slothful servants for now. One day, when it was over, when the final battle was through, he would deal with Roth and the others like him. When that day came, he would punish them for their fickleness and lack of diligent service to him, for if there's one thing Lucifer hated above everything else it was disloyalty. When it came time to punish them, Roth would suffer in ways he couldn't even dream about now.

But the time was not yet. Lucifer had more important work to do. He would have all of eternity to deal with lazy servants like Roth.

Lucifer turned back to Balaam. Like Roth, he too had grown pale and thin, with bony fingers, thin arms and a long, slender neck. His face shimmered with darkness, like the reflection of water on a moonlit night, leaving a pale shadow that almost made him look dead. And there was a tension and anxiety in the movement of his head, as if he was always hungry, always looking for the next meal, starving for the taste of joy, love, or success, but forever feeling famished. His hungry eyes betrayed him. Balaam could not be satisfied.

The Master turned away from his servants to study the small village around him. He remembered it well, for he had been there many times, going back to the days when men were just emerging from their primitive shells. He had repeatedly caused anguish and suffering in this place, and he had some fond memories of this very square.

The market was crowded, for it was Thursday afternoon and everyone was shopping, preparing for their holy day. Young children played in the streets, women walked by in dark scarves, only their eyes or faces exposed. On the corner a group of young men talked while they tossed a small leather sack between them, kicking it expertly with their feet.

Throughout the market men haggled over prices and quantities, their voices rising and falling until the deal was done. Lucifer turned in a slow circle, taking in the ancient market, the mud and brick shops with their small apartments on the second floor, the dirty brick streets and tangled electrical wires that were strung overhead. He noticed the tattered banners that denounced the Great Satan, the old movie posters, and the corner latrines. Everything was an earthy brown: the dirt, the cobblestones, the houses and shops. To his back, the great mountain rose over the village. The peaks were still capped with snow, but the hills that sloped up to the rock were covered in deep green grass. He turned away, preferring to look at the shabby, manmade structures rather than the work of his enemy's hand.

Balaam stood in silence beside him. Roth remained in the background, his lower lip trembling, his eyes wide in fear.

Like all the dark angels, Roth was accustomed to being sad and alone, for the dark angels hated each other as much as they hated themselves; and to be around these, the two masters, seemed to rip at his chest. It was painful to have them near him, like a knife in his heart, and he wished with all his being that they would leave.

He kicked the dust anxiously and silently cursed his two masters' names. Lucifer sensed it and glared at him, then took a quick step toward Balaam. "Where is she?" he demanded in a sour tone.

Balaam pointed toward a gentle hill on the south end of the village. A row of small houses lined the road along the top of the hill. "She lives up there, with her father."

"And her mother?" Lucifer wondered.

"She died shortly after her birth."

Lucifer sneered. "So she doesn't have a mother. Well, isn't that *sad!*" His face broke into a sharp grin, his lips curling upward, exposing his teeth. "That should make your task a bit easier, won't it, Balaam."

Balaam looked away. So far it hadn't, but he didn't reply.

Lucifer took in the dirty village, enjoying the sight of the run-down shacks for homes and dirt trails for streets. He studied the tar-paper rooftops, ancient mud-brick stores, and anti-U.S. propaganda that hung on almost every wall. There was no evidence of freedom in anything he saw, no indication of liberty or self-government. All was dark, brown, and ugly, and he couldn't help but smile.

The only thing that kept him going was his bitter hate—hate of his brothers and hate for their God. What man built, he brought down. What they created, he destroyed. If there was anything beautiful, he defiled it; anything innocent, he despoiled. If man were free, he brought bondage; where there was love, he brought lies. If he could not have happiness, then man would not have it as well. *This* is the thing that drove him to work so hard every day.

Looking around the village, he realized there were few other places where the people had been so robbed of their right to free will. He smiled, satisfied, then thought again of the girl. "She lives on the hill?" he confirmed with a tilt of his head.

"Yes, Master Mayhem," Balaam replied.

"And what do they call her?" he demanded in a deep snarl.

"Her name was Elizabeth in the other world. They call her Azadeh Ishbel down here."

Lucifer looked surprised and then swore, shaking his head in disgust while staring at Balaam with a critical eye. "You don't see it, do you, Master Balaam! You are so stupid you missed the significance of her name!"

Balaam stared ahead blankly as the knot in his gut tightened up.

"Ishbel is the Greek variation of Elizabeth," Lucifer announced with revulsion. "That hardly seems like a coincidence. Was her father inspired? Did he hear whispers from God?"

Balaam shook his head, for he had not seen the connection. And though he considered himself a master of every language, able to tempt and deceive with just the right word or phrase, the ancient meanings of her names had completely escaped him. He looked down, embarrassed and ashamed. He was reminded once again that he was not the king, that Lucifer was his master and would always be so.

He bowed toward the fallen son of the morning. "Master, why her father selected her name, I could not say with any authority. I have only recently found her. I would have to spend some time searching and see what I can find."

Lucifer growled, a familiar animal sound from his throat. "All right then, you do that. Now where is the one I came here to see?"

Balaam turned and nodded toward a slender man who sat on the edge of the street. He was tall and lanky, all arms and legs, with a rough face and long nose and a wild, bushy beard. His hair rolled in greasy locks over his eyes, and he leered from underneath the dark curls. He sat on a low stool beside a small cart of poorly packaged cigarettes. A handwritten sign advertised his wares: *"Cigarettes! Tobacco! Rolling Paper!"* A small metal box sat at his feet, and every few minutes he would open it up and count the money again, as if some unseen hand might have stolen from him. A group of three young boys ran up; one extracted an orange from under his dark shirt. The man took the orange, shook his head in mock disgust, then reached into his own shirt pocket and extracted three smokes. He handed them to the boys, who took them and ran.

Lucifer studied the stranger, thinking back, knowing he

had seen him sometime before, but in this world or the previous he could not tell. Balaam stepped toward the Master, keeping his voice low. "His name is Abd al Rahman Al Than," he said. Abd al Rahman, son of Qasim, tribe of Than.

Lucifer turned toward Balaam. "I don't care who he is! I don't care about his name. Just tell me the things I need to know!"

Balaam nodded eagerly, then jerked his head toward Roth. "He plays with him sometimes. He can get into his mind."

Lucifer turned toward Roth, who kept his eyes low, then nodded toward the mortal again. "I'm not impressed," he said in disgust. "I mean, look at him. He is stupid. And lazy. He's just like you, Roth! This mortal isn't a leader. No one is going to listen to him! What can he offer us? What influence can he possibly have?"

Balaam shot a cold glare at Roth. "Let me handle this!" he seemed to scream at him with his eyes. Roth nodded and stepped back into the shadows again. "The mortal will listen to Roth," Balaam explained as he turned to his master. "The mortal listens for his voice. He even tries to make contact with him."

Lucifer turned his dark eyes on Roth. "He will listen to you?" he demanded.

Roth glanced toward Balaam, then anxiously nodded his head. Lucifer moved toward the trembling devil and drew up to his full height. He stood majestic, even beautiful, his black hair falling to his shoulders, his face dark and alive. Roth fell to his knees at the Great Master's splendor and majesty. Balaam cringed but a little, for he had seen it before, and he knew the Great Master could hide his ugliness for only a short time. His mind shot back to the first time he had seen Satan change. The image of the bloody pig's head was forever burned in his mind.

"So tell me then, Roth," Lucifer mocked with a sneer. "What have you ever convinced this man to do?"

"Master," Roth stammered in reply, "I am but a humble servant. I don't claim to have the powers you do . . ."

"Yes, yes, of course. But what have you done? Quickly now, Roth, and don't waste my time!"

The fallen angel fell back, unable to respond, and Balaam moved forward, standing at Lucifer's side. "May I speak for him?" he begged. Satan sneered at Roth, then turned toward the former teacher in the greatest premortal university. "Master Mayhem," Balaam began, his voice pleading now, "the mortal is not particularly bright; I think we all can see that. But we don't need a leader for what we want him to do. As I said, Master Mayhem, he will listen to Roth. They have a special relationship, one that is truly unique. The mortal is a deviant with a dark place in his heart drawn to any kind of pain or abuse. He loves to inflict it. Animals. Small children. He has done many things. And the society he lives in allows him to take advantage of their silence, for he can instill in them a fear that keeps them quiet, it seems. And while it is true, Master Mayhem, that Roth spends most of his time with his diversions, he can speak to this mortal, he can get in his mind. This mortal knows his voice. And if the mortal will listen and do what he says, then why can't we try it? What do we lose if we give Roth a chance?"

Lucifer narrowed his eyes and took a step toward Balaam. "All right," he sneered, his voice piercing. "I will give him a chance to prove he can be useful to me. I will give you a chance to prove you can do something right. But I will not be patient. If he screws this thing up, I will take care of this myself. So don't let me down, Balaam. I am counting on you!"

Balaam backed up, feeling the cut in his chest. He had his instructions. And he was not going to fail.

chapter eleven

The day after Azadeh's fifteenth birthday, it started to rain as a front of foul weather moved in from the coast, wet and soaking and misty and cold. The ground became saturated and muddy, and a thousand tiny rivers of runoff spilled down from the mountains to join the stream that ran through the center of the village, swelling it to a frothy and muddy torrent of broken branches, silt, and debris. It rained hard all day, and by the time Rassa pulled in for the night, he was soaked to the skin, bone-tired, and shivering with cold. He had spent the day moving his small herd of cattle into a lower pasture to inoculate and brand the heifers, work that had to be done to keep the cattle from getting hoof rot from the mud. By early morning, his rain coat had been soaked through, and he had abandoned all pretense of trying to stay dry.

Azadeh was waiting for him at the kitchen table, and she looked up as he walked into the room, dripping and muddy. She smiled, her face brightening as if a light had come on, her eyes wide and happy, her teeth flashing bright. Rassa stopped and looked at his little girl. How it warmed him, how it brightened him just to see her. Her dark hair fell down to the middle of her back, and she was growing tall and strong, the tallest girl in her class. She had her mother's perfect olive skin, his eyes, and her grandfather's strong cheekbones. Jumping up from the table, Azadeh ran to the stove and turned up the heat. "Poppa, I have some tea ready for you," she said.

Rassa took off his wet coat, shook it out, then hung it by the oil furnace to dry. Sitting on a three-legged stool, he pulled off his leather boots while Azadeh worked over the stove, boiling some water and rice. "I would have had supper for you, Father, but I didn't know what time you would be in," she said happily.

"That's fine, Azadeh," Rassa answered wearily. Shivering, he pulled off his wet shirt and grabbed a rough towel to dry off his hair; then he stood over the heater, feeling its warmth. It was cold, but that wasn't unusual, for the mountains had a mean streak when it came to spring weather. The higher elevation caused wide swings in the temperature, and rain might stay for days, even weeks, before finally pushing over the highest peaks to provide needed moisture to the dry valleys on the other side.

Rassa walked stiff and cold and seemed unusually tired. Azadeh watched him for a moment. Turning away, she pulled off a fist-sized piece of bread dough from atop a warming pan she had placed near the stove. She rolled and flattened it to the size of a dinner plate, then tossed it against the burning-hot side of the stove. The dough stuck and immediately began to cook to a crisp and airy piece of pita bread. Two minutes later, she carefully pulled the toasty bread off the side of the stove, cooked the other side, then cut it open and stuffed it with spiced lamb and goat. She threw another piece of bread on the stove, which they would eat with honey and butter, then selected a Lebanese orange from the copper fruit bin, as well as some raisins and dates, seasoned some rice with salt and butter, cut some cheese, and set the food on the table.

Rassa watched with pride but also sadness as she worked. It hurt him to come into a dark house and find her alone. She was alone far too much. She needed a mother. And little brothers and sisters to care for each other. She needed to spend more time worrying about school and her friends and less time worrying about him and why her mother had died. She was so thoughtful of others, it was almost a fault, the way she jumped up, always willing to serve. And though she seemed content, Rassa knew she wasn't, and it saddened him that she felt such a responsibility to keep her loneliness in. She had fought the melancholy from the time she was a child, though she tried to be happy, always forcing a smile when one did not come naturally.

"Men are that they might be happy," she had once said.

Rassa looked at her and thought, then asked, "Where did you hear that, Azadeh?"

She thought a moment, then shrugged and pressed her lips. "I don't know," she replied.

As Azadeh grew, Rassa came to believe she would rather have needles driven under her nails than show him the sadness she hid inside.

But Rassa knew it was there. He was not completely blind. He had noticed it even when he watched her play with her dolls as a child. Azadeh had always played the role of the mother, never the child or sister or friend. She would comfort her babies, sometimes crying for them, telling them that she loved them while holding them tight. As Rassa watched, he realized she was acting out all the things she hoped her mother would have said to her had she lived. And she mothered not only her babies, but every child within a mile of their house, as well as every stray dog or cat that wandered into the village.

One day a few years before, Rassa had made the mistake of bringing a rabbit home from the market for supper. Azadeh had burst into tears and hidden in her room, refusing to come out until he had agreed they would let the poor creature go. So they had walked hand in hand to the fields behind their house, the rabbit inside a brown sack, and set the bunny free. The memory made Rassa smile, but it was a sad memory just the same. She felt everything so *deeply* that sometimes it caused him concern.

Azadeh spent long hours writing, sometimes poetry, sometimes in her journal, sometimes funny stories, few of which she would let Rassa read. One day, not long before, he had found a letter she had written to her mother and hidden inside her small desk. He read the words only once, but that was enough, for they had been burned in his mind.

Dear Mother,

I miss you. Sometimes I feel so alone. Father tries so hard, and I love him more than my heart can express, but I miss you too, Mother, and I wish you were here. Sometimes I think I feel you might be close to us. And sometimes I wonder, if you could hold me tight and talk to me, what would you say? Would you say that you love me? Would you say you are proud of me? I hope you are, Mother, because I have tried so hard.

Your loving daughter,
Azadeh Ishbel Pahlavi

It tore Rassa's heart to read what Azadeh had written. The words cut him deeply, and he would never forget them. But there was also a great pride in the reading, and he would always cherish her words.

Her mother *would* have been proud of her daughter; he was certain of that. And if somewhere she still existed, then he hoped she could somehow see what a treasure she had given him when she had brought this girl into the world.

* * *

As Azadeh finished preparing the meal, Rassa slipped into his bedroom and changed into dry clothes and warm stockings, then sat at the table and sipped at his tea. Azadeh put the food before him, then sat down beside him. Rassa reached out and took her hand. "Thank you, Azadeh," he said.

She bowed her head politely. "You're welcome, Father."

The two ate slowly, talking little, both of them hungry. Then, full and warm, Rassa stood to help Azadeh with the dishes. He had recently installed a new hot water heater, and they savored the steaming water that poured from the tap, as contrasted with the lukewarm dribble they had lived with before. Rassa washed while Azadeh dried and put the dishes into the painted wooden cupboard.

"You know, Father, my friends would die if they saw this!" Azadeh teased as she set a plastic glass on the lower shelf. "A father doing dishes! What is this world coming to?"

Rassa only smiled, knowing it wasn't as unusual as Azadeh might think. Once inside the home, the workings of the relationship between a man and wife were not what they used to be; there was a blossoming women's rights movement abroad, and Rassa suspected he wasn't the only man doing dishes that night. The law of Islam could be interpreted in many ways, and a sentiment of much more equality was taking hold in his land, if not in public, then in private; and Rassa knew that many of the religious police who strolled through the village with their black sticks and frowns were more henpecked at home than they would have ever admitted. This wasn't Arabia, after all, with its Wahhabi Islam; this was Persia, a much more equal and gentle land.

Azadeh began to prattle as they worked. She would start another school year in a few weeks, and she could talk of little else. "Father, might I one day go down to *El-hiram* to the School of the Masters?" she asked again. "I know you really liked it there. Might I go there too?"

Rassa lifted an eyebrow. "What have I always said?" he answered slowly.

"I must wait. I must be patient. But I too am a Pahlavi, Father, same as you, great-granddaughter of the Shah. I need a good education too! I'm bored in my school, and I want to learn more. I think I know as much as my teachers sometimes!"

Rassa nodded and smiled. It probably was true. *"Insha' allah,"* he said.

Azadeh frowned in frustration. That's what he always said. But she knew not to push it. She was young, but not foolish, and she knew when to hold her tongue.

"Come," Rassa said to her, and he sat on the worn, vinyl couch. "Let's read together, Azadeh, before it is time for bed."

The two read together for an hour, then they repeated the words together as she kissed his cheek:

"Remember, I'll be waiting when it comes,

Morning Light."

Azadeh smiled, touched her heart, then ran off to bed. "Think about the School of the Masters!" she called over her shoulder as she turned the light off in the hall.

* * *

The night fell cold and dark, with a steady drizzle that seemed to soak up the light. The quarter moon, low and yellow, was completely hidden above the thick clouds, and the wind blew in sudden gusts, pushing the drizzle through the trees.

The stranger waited in the darkness beyond the light that emitted from the house. He watched from the shadows as they read and stomped his feet impatiently. He had killed the dog already, so she wouldn't be making any noise, and he smiled as he remembered the wet cut of the knife across the mangy dog's throat. The first kill of the nighttime. Other kills lay ahead.

"That is fine. Take your time," the dark voice whispered in his head. *"I have prepared you for this moment. Now you must do as I say!"*

"I will, Master," the slender man cried. "I promise, Master, just tell me what to do."

The angry voice hissed inside him, dark and evil and cruel. An agreement had been made between them. Now it was time to act.

The small man hunched in the shadows, rainwater dripping off his hair and down his neck, soaking the shirt on his back. His face was thin and hungry, his eyes dark and narrow, and his nose flared with each breath, causing a mist in the air. He waited, then started humming an old song from many centuries before, an oath of the ancients who had once ruled the earth. "I am evil," he whispered in a raspy voice to himself. "I am evil, this I know. And now this evil comes."

His eyes glinted, cold and dark in the freezing rain. He was nearly mad, almost drooling, completely out of his mind.

But the dark spirits that possessed him didn't care about his weakened mind. He would do what they told him, and that's all they cared about.

* * *

The hours passed. The house fell dark and silent. The rain backed off, the clouds broke, and the dull moon shone overhead. Still the man waited, his legs cramped, his feet cold, his hands numb and clammy inside his coat pockets. He fingered the knife as he waited. The entire village was silent. *"It is time,"* the voice said.

The man pushed himself up from the shadows and moved silently toward the house. He approached the back door, staying near the shadows of the trees that lined the backyard. His eyes had adjusted to the night, and he saw without using a light. Stepping over the dead dog, he moved to the back door.

It was unlocked. He knew it would be. No one secured their doors in this town. He cracked the door, then waited, listening in the dark. He pushed another inch and waited, then pushed his head inside.

A fire was burning in the oil heater, and the room was almost steamy-warm. A small light glowed from the other end of the hallway, casting a dim shadow through the room. He sniffed the air and listened. He had to be very careful. He must not fail his master. He must not fall short of his goal.

"Kill it . . . kill it . . . kill it . . ." the chant began again in his head. *"Kill it . . . it will hurt us! We want it to be dead!"*

The man stood without moving, only his head and shoulders inside the house; then he slowly pushed back the door and entered the room. He pulled the knife from its sheath; the nine-inch blade glistened red in the dark. He tried to wipe off the dog's blood, but it was already dry, so he licked the blade to wet it, then wiped it again on his pants. He moved his head left and then right, then took a step toward the hall. Stopping at the door on the back wall of the kitchen, he held his breath. Which was the father's bedroom? This had to be it! Pressing his ear against the door, he listened but didn't hear anything. The light shined from behind him, a small bulb glowing yellow at the end of the hall, and he turned and walked silently toward it. A single twenty-watt bulb burned in the bathroom, and he quietly pushed the button to turn the light off. A thick darkness enveloped the interior of the house, and he waited without moving until his eyes had adjusted again, then moved back to the bedroom at the back of the kitchen. He sucked in a quick breath and held it, then slowly, almost imperceptibly, moved the doorknob. The door creaked as he pushed it open an inch. Inside, he could hear the man breathing, deep and heavy and slow. He pulled the door shut again and moved to the other bedroom at the end of the hall, next to the bathroom where he had turned off the light.

He held the knife ready, then placed his hand on the doorknob, turned it gently, and pushed it back. The room was dimly lit from a night light on the other side of the small bed. He listened, then moved inside the room, holding the knife in both hands.

She was asleep, her face down, her dark hair spread out across the pillow, the covers tucked almost up to her chin.

"Kill it . . . kill it!" the voice started chanting again. *"Do what I tell you. This is what I brought you here for. Do what I tell you, and you will be mine. We will live together forever! Now do what I say!"*

This wasn't the first time the man had listened to the evil voice that growled from time to time in his head, but this is the first time the voice had asked him to do such a . . . *permanent* thing. The man hesitated a moment. Could he really kill her? Could he really plunge the knife?

But the devil inside him had become his best friend. He was his comrade, his companion, the only ally that he had, and he would do as it told him. He no longer felt he had a real choice.

"Look at it!" the voice hissed. *"Look at it sleeping! It is innocent now, but it won't stay that way forever. Believe me, it will fight us, it will haunt us one day. It will grow strong and*

wise, and we must kill it while we can! Take your knife and do it. Kill it before it is too late!"

The man nodded, hesitating, as he looked at the child, seeing a glimpse of the perfection that lay in her soul. He could barely make out her closed eyes in the darkness. Her face was peaceful and calm.

He faltered a moment. She was so beautiful! How could she be so dangerous? She was so young and so childlike. What real threat could she hold?

"KILL IT!" his master screamed. *"Do what I tell you or you will suffer, I swear!"*

The man raised the knife slowly.

"Kill her!" it cried.

The man sniffled, then grimaced. He would do as he was told. He held the knife in a death grip, and it trembled in his quivering hand. He reached up with his other hand to steady it and took another step toward the bed.

Then he saw it and froze, almost hissing in dread. A tiny light, like a star, began to shine over the bed. The light grew from a soft glow to a shimmer; then the angel appeared, surrounded by fire and a radiant power. The light was so bright! How it hurt him! He wanted to flee! The angel was dressed in a white robe with a silver hood pulled over the crown of his head, and a single star, like a diamond, shone from a golden headband. He lit up the room with his power and the flaming sword in his hand.

"Teancum!" the spirit inside the mortal muttered in bitter rage and dark fear.

The angel took a step toward him. "I know you," he said. His voice was like thunder, and it rolled through the night.

The mortal wanted to run, but the spirit held him, not letting him flee as the other spirits rallied inside him, speaking for the first time. "We have nothing to do with you, Teancum," the spirits all cried. "This is not your battle. We have come for the girl."

The angel rose up in power and pointed at them. "You will not touch this child," he commanded. "Her name is Elizabeth, and she is my friend!"

The mortal man cowered, and it was he who spoke to the angel now. "But we must," he whispered slowly, his voice hoarse and dead. "Our masters will hurt us if we don't do as they say . . ."

The angel took a position over Azadeh and raised the sword above his head. There was a soft *swoosh,* like night lightning, as the sword stroked the air. "YOU WILL NOT HARM THIS CHILD!" he commanded again. "Now go back to your master! Go back to your hell!"

The angel grew suddenly taller and more brilliant, shining as white as the sun.

The mortal felt the heat from his power and fell back in pain. The fire seemed to surround him. He was consumed by the flame. The angel shook the silver hood from his head, and his fine hair trailed back, blowing over his shoulders as if from an invisible wind. His blue eyes were so piercing they seemed to cut through his soul. "GO!" he commanded, and even the earth seemed to shake. "In the name of my Master, I command you to leave." The angel stood there, unflinching, as if he were ready to spring.

The spirits recoiled, then cried out and departed, leaving the mortal alone. He felt the dark world fall around him, then the crushing weight of desertion and the emptiness of despair. He was alone now. They had left him. The angel moved to stand over his head.

The mortal stumbled backward like a coward, reaching for the bedroom door. The angel lifted his arm and pointed at him, and he squealed in fear. Scrambling like a rat, he ran through the door.

* * *

Neither Azadeh nor her father ever wakened that night, and though Rassa noticed the back door was open when he got up the next morning, he had no way of knowing what had taken place in his daughter's room.

Four days later, a fisherman found the rotting body of the intruder in the swollen river, twenty miles downstream.

After spending a life in the service of his master, inflicting abuse and pain, the mortal had closed his final deal. He had listened one last time to his master and was now in his grasp.

chapter twelve

Two days after the fisherman dragged the bloated body from the river, another stranger pulled into Rassa's small village, equally mystifying, though certainly not insane. He moved comfortably through the crowded streets, for he had been in the village before; in fact, he had been there several times in just the previous two weeks alone. He was a large man and well kept, though he wore unexceptional clothes. His face was hidden behind dark glasses and a neatly trimmed beard. He drove a Swedish sedan, which he parked on the south end of the open-air market; then he spent a couple of hours walking through the village, taking everything in. He talked to each shopkeeper he visited, asking a few questions and occasionally even writing things down. Then he browsed through the market, testing several possibilities before buying some potatoes and garlic sausage for breakfast, along with a cup of thick tea.

It was Saturday morning, the start of another work week, and the market was crowded and noisy and smelly from the usual crowd. A little after eight, after the first call to prayer, Rassa and Azadeh made their way through the market, collecting the supplies they would need for the next couple of days. Rassa bought two liters of goat's milk and some sugar, then fifty nails and some wire to repair the fence around his yard. Azadeh picked out some fresh fruit and cabbage, then eight small carp, which were wrapped in old newspaper and tied with rough string. She dropped them in her basket, then ran to her father's side.

The stranger watched them intently, always staying a comfortable distance behind and acting with care so he did not draw any attention to himself. As the sun rose, the air grew warm and the marketplace became oppressive. Their shopping completed, the father and his daughter left the market and walked the dusty road toward their home.

The stranger watched them go, then melted into the crowd and walked back to his car. Climbing in, he locked the doors, started the motor, then pulled out a satellite phone and dialed a number in Riyadh.

"Crown Prince Saud," he said after his call was put through. He grunted and waited. "Muhsin Al-Illah," he gave as his name.

Then he waited, his breathing heavy, his hands sweaty and cold.

"Sayid," he said when the prince finally answered the phone. "I have been watching the target. There is nothing new to report."

The Arab waited, then continued. "They appear to be of little means, *Sayid,* though they do have their own home, a small brick and mud house on a hill looking over the village. It is small but well kept. They do the best they can."

The large man fixed the air vent to blow on his face as he listened, then answered again. "Yes, Your Highness, I agree. I have come to the reluctant conclusion that it might possibly work. It seems that no one knows, or at least no one cares any longer, that Rassa Pahlavi is a grandson of the Shah. He lives a quiet life, a simple life. And though I pray it never happens, and I hope you are wrong (blessed be your name, your Royal Highness, for I do not mean to ever disagree!), but from what I have seen I believe your plan would possibly work. *If* we were careful, and *if* we were left with no choice."

* * *

A little more than five hundred miles to the west, Prince Saud, crown prince of the House of Saud, future king of Saudi Arabia, thanked his loyal servant, then slowly hung up the phone. He stared a long moment, considering what he should do.

Were they close? Was it real? Was the danger as near as he feared? Was Prince Abdullah as dangerous as his father said he was?

He knew he was. And there was no time to hesitate.

He huffed with emotion, then picked up his secure phone again and dialed the number to his old friend in the United States.

Young Warriors

"And it shall come to pass in the last days, saith God, I will pour out of my Spirit upon all flesh: and your sons and your daughters shall prophesy, and your young men shall see visions. . . . And I will shew wonders in heaven above, and signs in the earth beneath."

—Acts 2:17, 19

"Even as the Allies celebrated victory, the appalling costs of the war began to emerge. It had killed as many as 75 million people around the world. In Europe, about 38 million people lost their lives, many of them civilians, a majority of them in their teens and early twenties. The destruction defies belief. Numbers alone did not tell the story."

—Prentice Hall World History

chapter thirteen

Major General Neil S. Brighton stood and stared through the large plate glass window of his home office in Chevy Chase, Maryland. The old plantation house, a classic two-story brick Victorian with lots of polished wood and white paint, was large and quiet and smelled of a pine disinfectant. The house was almost 125 years old but exceptionally well maintained. It sat atop one of the highest hills inside the beltway, and from his second story window the general could look south and see most of the downtown D.C. skyline. The Mall and national monuments were a little more than seven miles away. The George Washington Memorial, a pointed pillar of white bathed by enormous floodlights tracking skyward, jutted up to the east of the George Washington bridge. Even from this distance, he could see the glow of the lights that surrounded the Mall where he jogged four miles every afternoon, come rain, sleet, or shine; his secretary *always* kept his schedule clear between four and five P.M. It was the only time he ever had to be by himself, and it was also the most productive hour of his day. And though he couldn't see it from his second-story window, he knew the White House was just a little more than a mile to the north of the Mall. He envisioned the security fences around the White House lawn, the covert bunkers for secret service personnel, and the hidden surface-to-air missiles on the government buildings next door.

The general was very familiar with the White House. He worked there every day.

Brighton took a deep breath and wondered again. *Who am I kidding? I'm just a simple ol' farm boy from Texas. What am I doing* here?

He stood still for a moment, thinking back, then glanced at the old English clock on the fireplace mantel. Almost midnight, and here he was, just finishing supper and still dressed in his air force blues, the formal uniform he wore to the White House everyday. He felt the stiff fabric and the pressure of all the ribbons on his chest. He missed wearing his flight suits—they were much more comfortable—and he certainly missed flying, especially after days like today. His day had started with a private meeting with the chairman of the Joint Chiefs of Staff, after which he had suffered through no less than fourteen appointments, then ended with a reception at the Libyan Embassy, a typically stuffy and formal affair, the kind his wife enjoyed and he absolutely despised.

Then he remembered how beautiful Sara had looked in her black satin dress and suddenly the evening hadn't seemed like such a waste of time. "Sara, oh Sara," he thought to himself, "when I asked you to marry me, did you know I would drag you from one corner of the world to the next? Did you envision the challenges of the life we would choose?"

He wondered, supposing not. It had been a wonderful journey, but not without cost.

The general breathed deep, then turned around and snapped off the small light on his desk. He had to get up in five hours, and it was time for bed.

Before leaving his office, General Brighton checked his wall safe, armed the security system, pulled the tab to synch up the secure telephone to the next code-of-the-day, then turned off the overhead light and walked from the room. His wife had turned on the night light in the hallway so he wouldn't have to stumble to bed, and he started unbuttoning his uniform as he walked down the hall. When was the last time he and Sara had gone to bed at the same time, he wondered. Too long ago. And it made him sad. In the old days they would lie by each other and talk and laugh every night. But he was so busy with his new assignment as military liaison to the National Security Advisor, one of the most demanding jobs in the entire Department of Defense, that he hardly had time to think, let alone lie around talking in bed. Nothing was as demanding as the job he held now—not flying fighters, not commanding a combat wing, not even masterminding the air war in Iraq—nothing compared with the pressures he dealt with every day. Eighty-hour work weeks were the norm, and he was exhausted all the time. He knew his family was suffering, but he didn't know what to do.

His only comfort, his only consolation, was that he had been assured this was what he was supposed to do. This was his calling, what the Lord needed him for.

He remembered the blessing his stake president had given him when he had felt so overwhelmed. *"Your Father in Heaven is aware of your concerns. He will take care of your family during this trying time. And He wants you to know that this is one of the purposes for which you were brought into this world. This is part of the work that He wants you to do. The path lies before you. Step forward with confidence and don't be afraid. He will take care of your family as you concentrate on this task."*

It had felt almost as if the Savior himself had placed his hands on his head. *"And I will lay my hand upon you by the hand of my servant."* Major General Neil S. Brighton repeated that scripture all the time in his mind. And he thought of the blessing almost every day, for it strengthened and comforted him as he struggled to balance the demands on his time, especially during the many weeks when he was away. But because of the blessing, he understood a little better. It was like when he had been a bishop: there were many sacrifices, but this was also something he needed to do, part of his schooling, part of Heavenly Father's great plan.

That didn't mean it was easy.

But it meant it was good.

"Sometime soon," Brighton frequently promised himself. "Sometime soon, things will change. Life will slow down. I promise it will."

As he was reaching for his bedroom doorknob, his secure telephone started ringing, and he stopped in his tracks. "Please go away!" he mumbled to himself. "It's late. I am tired. Let it wait until morning."

But the phone continued ringing, and he turned quickly and walked to his office, hurrying to pick up the STU-III telephone before it woke anyone up.

"Yeah?" he said abruptly as he picked up the phone.

"Major General Brighton," the communications specialist replied.

"Yes," Brighton answered.

"Sir, this is Private First Class Bendino at the CIC communications center. I have a call from Prince Saud, crown prince of Saudi Arabia. We have traced and authenticated the phone number to verify it is coming from Riyadh, but we can't confirm his identity. He wants us to patch him through."

"Crown Prince Saud bin Faysal?"

"Yes, sir. This is who he says."

"Then of course patch him through."

"Sir, do we need to notify the operations desk of the call?"

"No, Private Bendino. I suspect this is a personal matter. I have known the crown prince for a very long time."

"Okay sir. But you realize, of course, that as with all communications with foreign heads of states, these communications will be recorded and monitored."

"Fine, Private, fine, now please patch him through."

The secure satellite line clicked and then buzzed and then fell silent again. "Neil?" he heard the prince's deep baritone.

"Your Highness! How are you? I hope everything is okay."

"Okay? Yes, of course. Everything's fine."

Brighton considered the differences in time, knowing it was early morning in Saudi Arabia. "It's good to hear from you, Prince Saud. It's been a long while."

"Too long, general, too long. Listen, I know it is late there, and I don't have much time, but I heard you were flying over here to meet with some of my air force leaders. I would hope we could get together. Nothing special, just an hour or two to catch up on, how do you Americans say it . . . older times."

"Old times, Prince Saud."

"Old times. Yes, of course. Anyway, could we meet?"

"Anytime. Anyplace."

"Excellent, Neil, excellent. Now listen, I'm going to be in Medina for most of the week, but I'm going to fly back to meet you in Riyadh. I'll have my people give your staff a call and work out a schedule. Will that be all right?"

"Of course, Prince Saud. Whatever you want. But let me ask, is this important? Do I need to do anything to prepare?"

The line was silent a long moment, and Brighton could hear the prince breathe. "Nothing important, Neil," he finally answered. "It is a personal matter. I just want to catch up."

The general sensed the hesitation and was about to press,

but the crown prince spoke again before he could say anything. "Same number at the Pentagon?" Prince Saud asked.

"The switchboard will always get you through."

"Okay, then, my friend. I look forward to seeing you."

The phone clicked and went dead, and the general placed the red receiver back in its cradle. He stared at it a moment, then turned again for the office door.

He read his scriptures as he always did, no matter the time, then knelt by his bedside to say a weary prayer. Then he lay on his pillow. But sleep didn't come, for he kept hearing the nervousness in his friend's voice.

The night was quiet, the darkness still and heavy, the moon having set below the horizon. Then a sudden wind blew, gusting through the dry leaves, howling like a banshee, though the skies remained clear. His bedroom windows rattled with each gust of wind, and he lay in the darkness, staring through the window at the blowing branches a few feet away. They swayed with each gust, sometimes bending out of sight, the fall leaves being ripped from the dry branches of the trees.

Brighton lay awake, agitated; he had been restless all day. He had been restless for a week, and he didn't know why. Something was coming. He could feel it deep in his bones, something *moving*, something *watching*, something that brought evil change. He could feel the frustration, but he didn't know what it was. He glanced at his wife, who was asleep on her side, her blonde hair tossed about her, the streetlight on her face. For a long moment he watched her sleep, her breathing heavy and slow; then she winced and pulled back, as if in her dreams, she felt it too. Neil reached out to touch her, placing his palm on her cheek, and she pressed against his fingers and leaned into his touch. But she didn't wake fully and soon was in a deep sleep again.

Neil lay back and listened to the leaves rustle in the yard.

He felt anxious and tight, a sprinter ready to explode from the blocks. He fought the anxiety, then finally sat up on the side of the bed.

He shook his head to clear it, but the fear only settled deeper in his chest. The blackness seemed to consume him, like nothing he'd ever felt before. He glanced at his wife, then pushed himself out of bed.

He walked down the hall, pausing at the top of the stairs. He placed his hands on the rail, feeling the beautifully carved oak. He listened for a moment to the grandfather clock ticking at the foot of the winding stairs, then took a deep breath, fighting the anxiety within. He stood a long moment, alone, in the dark.

Then he thought of his sons and turned suddenly for their room.

His two sons shared a bedroom at the top of the stairs, and he opened the door just enough to let in a crack of light from the hall. As he pushed the door open, he got a whiff of the smell—sweaty jerseys, leather basketballs, gym bags, a half-eaten bowl of popcorn—the tangy smell of youth that he knew so well.

But his sons were no longer children. They were growing into men.

They stirred under the blankets, but neither of them awoke. The older son, Parley Ammon, the blond, eleven minutes older than his brother, lay asleep on his bed, his hair, like his mother's, in a tousle on his head. His younger brother, Luke Benjamin, dark haired and tan, rolled to his side and turned away from the light.

As he stood in the darkness, in the hallway, in the quiet of his home, having been driven from his bed by a dark power that seemed to move across the land, Neil looked at his children and was reminded again of who they really were. They were greater than he was—he knew that inside—more valiant, more clever, more dedicated to the right. "My brothers," he muttered as he stood in the hall. "What are your missions? What is the reason you're here?"

He lowered his head as a sudden warmth filled his chest. He trembled and stepped back, a look of awe on his face. He shook his head suddenly and brought his hands to his eyes. He stumbled, his legs so weak he almost fell to his knees.

"Pray for them," the Spirit told him as he lowered his head. "Pray for your children. Pray for your sons. Pray they will grow into the men that I intend them to be! Pray for Samuel Porter, for he was once a great leader who has lost his way. He is alone now and lonely, and I need him on my side. He has no one to turn to, so you must pray for him too."

Neil shuddered, then pushed himself away from their bedroom and sat on the stairs. All night he knelt in the darkness and prayed as the Spirit had directed him to.

* * *

Balaam watched him, all the time cursing, with Lucifer at his side. They sneered at the father, mocking his prayers. "You're not worthy. You're not worthy," Lucifer lied in Brighton's ear. "What kind of father are you? You are hardly ever here! Your sons, all their faults, you know they get them from you. You've been a terrible example. And yet you pray for your sons. You are tired. God is busy! Why don't you go to bed?"

On and on it went, lie after lie, distraction upon distraction, sneer upon sneer.

But Neil Brighton fought through it. And the God of heaven heard his prayers.

chapter fourteen

The next morning broke brown and dusty from the wind that had howled through the night, leaving a haze of fine dust laying low in the air and tinting the sunrise with dim pink and gray hues. As the sun rose, the winds shifted to a light breeze from the Chesapeake Bay, which smelled of brine and wet marsh weed, humid and cold. The traffic started early as it always did in D.C., the legions of government minions and private sector bloodsuckers heading into the district to fight their unending battles over money and power. On the surface, everything looked normal: a steady stream of airliners took off from Reagan National Airport, the METRO line ran on time, and the 495 Beltway was bumper-to-bumper, the same as it had been for more than thirty years.

On the surface, nothing had changed.

But there was change in the air, a tension and expectation that had finally risen to the surface after bubbling underneath for a generation.

D.C. was a tense city. It had always been high strung, for many of the people who lived there were by their nature ambitious and on the cutting edge. But over the past several years, it had changed from nervous to neurotic, the Twin Towers and burning Pentagon having completed the transition from uneasy to scared. The truth was, D.C. citizens knew they were the primary target, the most likely city to burn, and they seemed to have grown used to the stress of the bull's-eye on their backs. How many other U.S. cities had so many police barricades? How many had antimissile batteries hidden on the tops of their buildings or secret "sniffer" units that scanned the highways and ports, searching for the telltale radiation that surrounded a nuclear device? How many other U.S. cities had already suffered an anthrax attack, revived their underground shelters, or had their hospitals drill regularly to prepare for a mass-casualty attack?

Such was business as usual in Washington, D.C. But something new was astir now, a dark expectation that had been building for years. The people felt the pressure growing like a dark, rising cloud that was ready to burst, until there was an almost fatalistic acceptance that it was only a matter of time. A week, a year, maybe longer than that. But the disaster was coming. It was just a question of when.

* * *

Early in the morning, after his sleepless night of prayer, General Brighton showered and dressed quietly while Sara slept. As he sat on the chest at the foot of the bed to pull on his shoes, she stirred and held out her hand. He stood and went to her, kissing her on the cheek, then sat next to her.

"The boys are going rock climbing this morning," she said in a sleepy voice.

Brighton nodded. He had heard them getting breakfast down stairs.

"You were up late again?" she asked.

"I had some papers to review."

"You got a late call on the secure telephone?"

"Prince Saud called from Riyadh. He wants to get together when I'm in Saudi next week."

"Prince Saud? How is he? You haven't seen him in a long time."

Brighton paused, thinking of the strain in his old friend's voice. "He seemed a little anxious," he answered. "But I can understand that. He's sitting on a powder keg, and most of the people around him are striking matches and tossing them on the floor."

Sara sat up and brushed her blonde hair from her eyes. Brighton watched her and wondered how she could be so beautiful, even in the morning, even barely awake.

Her blue eyes, pale and shining, narrowed as she thought. "Prince Saud is a good man. I have always said that, and it's not because I'm overly impressed because he's the crown prince."

Brighton nodded, knowing that was true. With an advanced degree in education and having lived in some of the most sophisticated capitals of the world, Sara moved comfortably among the most elite circles. She had met presidents, ambassadors, senators, and kings, but she was hard to impress and unafraid to speak her mind, even to argue, if the opportunity presented itself. He remembered a reception at the White House about four months before when she had had a strained disagreement with the French president's wife over the difference between the nature of boys and girls. Raised a traditional Catholic (meaning she actually believed what the church taught) and educated in Boston, she had been a vocal advocate of homemaking as a legitimate career long before being influenced by her baptism into the LDS Church.

Sara watched her husband. He knew he must look worn

out to her, even more than usual. "Anything going on at work?" she asked sympathetically. "You look a little tired."

Brighton didn't answer. The truth was that there was *always* something going on at work. Always. Forever. It would never change. He felt like a kid holding his thumb in the dike. He had only ten fingers, and there were hundreds of holes, gushing cracks in the dam, all of them spurting powerful streams of dark water. He could move to the worst breaks, but more popped up every day. Pakistan was in shambles. Russia was moving into Chechnya again. Their friends in Europe had abandoned them, then sat back and laughed, hoping the Yankees would be brought to their knees. Argentina had just voted in a socialist government and announced they had developed a nuclear bomb, the first nuclear weapon in the Western Hemisphere outside the United States. The new Argentine government was courting ties to Cuba, the bastion of true communism that sat at their door. And North Korea. North Korea! He hardly had time to even think about that! Iraq was a mess. No, it was much worse than that. After forty years of Saddam and near-civil war, the people had yet to prove themselves capable of self-government. The mullahs in Iran were growing bolder, taking hope from the mess they had helped to make in Iraq. Hamas, Hezbollah, al Qaeda, the Fedayeen—there was more bloodshed and hatred flowing from those groups than any one nation could absorb. The enemies of the United States didn't grow weak—they grew stronger—and there was no way to reason with them, absolutely no common ground. General Brighton sometimes felt they would be more successful in reasoning with a snake than negotiating with these radicals, for a snake, if it were to see an option that would benefit its position, would at least consider the move. But not these people. Brighton had seen it enough to be completely convinced. They cared not about bettering their position, their people, their children. They cared only about one thing and that thing was death. Death to their enemies. The glory of death in the cause. The glorious death of a martyr. Death through the holy war.

To the radical Islamist, the Americans weren't human, they were *jahili*. Barbarians, subhuman. Decadent and soulless, without value to God. They were not only ignorant of truth, but they had rejected their God and so were worthy of death and indignity. And whereas most Westerners found value in any culture or society, believing they all were perfectible to one degree or another, it was not so for the Islamists, who considered Western culture completely devoid of truth or value, populated by savages with which they could not coexist. That was why it became acceptable to drag the burned bodies of American soldiers through the streets, why it was acceptable to hang the corpses of soldiers from a bridge leading into the city, why it was acceptable even to kill their children if they could. They would grow up to be barbarians. They *were not* innocent. Was a young scorpion less deadly than the mother who gave it life? Was there any sense, was there any justification or law that insisted they couldn't kill their enemies until they were strong enough to fight back? No, there was no reason to wait. They would kill even the children, for they would only grow up to impugn the glory of God.

This is how their enemies thought. Brighton had seen their thinking illustrated a thousand times. They were not true Muslims, for Muslims did not believe in such hate. These were not true religious people. They had hijacked a religion to further their cause and were as likely, even more likely, to kill fellow Muslims as anyone else in their contest for power. They were enemies of any person who would stand up for freedom, be that person Christian or Muslim, black, brown, or white.

Brighton knew this wasn't a battle between Christianity

and Islam. It wasn't a contest of religions. At its core, it wasn't even a battle between cultures or nation-states. It was a battle for freedom. It was as simple as that. This was good against evil, black against white.

And it was a battle they were losing. At least that's how he felt.

Of course, he believed in God, but he had read the Threat File. He knew they were in trouble. And that's why he didn't sleep at night.

Give him another day, another small victory, another chance at hope on the battlefield, and he would regain his optimism—he knew that he would. He had been down before, and he had always scratched his way up again. But his faith in America's ability to prevail was growing fragile; there was no doubt about that. The battle had torn him, and he was growing scared.

Brighton thought quickly of an instant message the CIA had intercepted just the day before, an exchange between two Iraqi brothers who had forced their younger sister to participate in an uprising in the Iraqi central town of Ramadi. The message was crude and halting and translated loosely, but the meaning was clear:

Al-Anbari: *All the people in the area have started to move. I put our sister in the crowd and stuck my AK-47 in her hand. I see other mothers push their children into the rioting crowd. I didn't think the people here were so heroic.*

Kamal: *Whatever God wants! Blessed be the Almighty!*

Al-Anbari: *She just tried to come back, but I shut the door. I told her I would kill her if she dishonored our name. It doesn't matter she's only nine.*

Kamal: *Oh God! God is great!*

Al-Anbari: *It is done. She was killed by our brothers, our* *own Iraqi police. But we will avenge her. We still have others we can put in the fight.*

Kamal: *Do what it takes, Al-Anbari. You strengthen my pride.*

Brighton thought of the captured exchange between the two Iraqi brothers and wondered how he should answer his wife. *How were things at work?* Truth was, they were losing. They knew, all of the agents and officers he worked with, they all knew they couldn't stop it. It was coming some day. *Did he sleep well? Was he tired?* The truth was, he hadn't slept since taking this job. And yes, he was tired. He was worn to the bone. He was weary physically, mentally, emotionally; even his spirit was worn thin, like a sheet that had been lain on for too many years. There were too many battles. Too many enemies. He had to protect the country, protect the president. It was his responsibility to advise him on what he had to do. But there weren't any answers, at least not enough. Their enemies were like rats climbing over the wall. They were shooting those rats one by one, shooting as quickly as they could, but there were so many! The rats spilled over the wall. Which meant he was failing. But what more could he do?

Brighton thought back on the night and the feeling that had kept him from his bed, the dark wind and dark spirit that had passed over their home. He wanted to tell Sara; he wanted to tell her everything. But most of it, he couldn't. And what he could tell her would have to wait.

He glanced at Sara sadly, then forced a smile as she asked the question again, "Did you sleep okay?"

And like he did everyday, Brighton pretended everything was all right. "I slept okay," he said as he kissed her hand. "Got to go now. I want to talk to the boys before I leave for work."

"See you tonight then," she said to him. "Are you going to be late?"

"Hopefully not, maybe even early. I'll let you know."

He stood up, kissed her forehead, and left the bedroom.

* * *

Brighton walked down the winding staircase and into the kitchen where he found his sons sitting at the table dressed in baggy shorts and oversized T-shirts. Overflowing bowls of cold cereal sat before them, and he noticed the spilled Whammy Charms on the floor. "Morning guys," he said as he walked to the refrigerator and poured himself a glass of orange juice. He glanced at the bowls of cereal. "You could cook some eggs. Or there's frozen waffles in the freezer."

Ammon looked up as he spooned in another mouthful of sugar and bleached wheat. "That's okay, Dad. We're in kind of a hurry, you know."

"You going down on the river?"

"Yeah. Carderock."

Brighton poured himself a small bowl of rolled oats, added some milk, and placed the bowl in the microwave. "Carderock? Is that at Great Falls in McLean?" he asked as he punched the buttons on the microwave.

"Yeah. It's a good rock. Plenty of handholds, but if you don't climb it just right you can find yourself hanging under some pretty awesome outcroppings."

Brighton knew his sons could climb like flies. He was pretty good himself, but he couldn't even come close to keeping up with them. Sometimes they made him nervous. It was one thing to be aggressive, another to be stupid; and sometimes the line was a fine one, and blurred. "How high is the rock?" he asked.

Ammon shot a quick look to his brother, who paused eating long enough to hunch his shoulders.

"I don't know, Dad," Ammon answered, "maybe fifty feet

or so. It's not the highest climb in the area, but because of the angle and outcroppings, it's one of the hardest."

Brighton pressed his lips as he pictured Luke and Ammon hanging from their fingers, their hands gripping the tiny ledges that extended from the rock, their feet and legs swinging through the emptiness as they pulled themselves up and over the sandstone outcroppings by only their arms.

He opened the window blinds that looked out on their backyard. "You don't have any classes this morning?" he asked.

Luke poured himself another bowl of cereal as he answered. "Ammon's got labs this afternoon. I've got calculus at ten. That's why we're in a hurry. We want to get in a couple of hours climbing before I have to get to class."

Brighton watched his sons slopping in their cereal as he sipped at his juice. He knew something was up. He knew his sons well. "Why are you climbing on a Tuesday? Why not wait until the weekend when you won't be in such a hurry?" he asked.

Again they both paused. Ammon shot a knowing look to his brother, then ducked his head.

Though only older by minutes, Ammon had always been more responsible, and it made his father nervous to see the guilty look in his eyes. It was Ammon's nature to take things a little more slowly, and if he was nervous, then his dad got nervous too. Luke, on other hand, was a full-speed-ahead, let's-give-it-a-go kind of guy. If he left a wreck behind him . . . no, *when* he left a wreck behind him, he would zip around to pick up the pieces, apologize for the trouble, then speed off to the next crash.

When neither son answered his question, Brighton asked it again. "What's up, guys? How come you're climbing today?"

Ammon took another spoonful of cereal. "Nothing special,

Dad," he answered. "A couple of guys we met last week want to come with us. They're a couple of big-shot climbers from California, at least they think they are. They were bragging about all the rocks they had climbed out West. We told them there were some pretty good climbs around here, but they didn't believe us."

Brighton sipped again as he filled in the blanks. Luke liked to talk. Talked a little too much. So he had met some new friends from California where there were lots of natural climbing walls and had talked himself into a situation where he not only had to prove there were good rocks to climb along the Potomac River in northern Virginia, but also that he was the master of them all. Now it was time to make good. And Ammon was going along to keep his brother from killing himself.

How many times had he seen this before? Still, he had to smile. "You're going to class though, right?" he asked as he sat down.

"We'll make it, Dad."

"You know how much tuition at Georgetown cost me?"

"Ah . . . yeah, Dad, it seems like you might have mentioned that before."

"So I'm getting my money's worth, right? You're not *just* messing around? Sometimes you go to class? Sometimes you actually learn something, right?"

Neither son answered. "We're learning lots, Dad," Ammon finally said.

Luke looked up suddenly, "Oh, yeah, that reminds me, Dad—my history professor wants to know if you will come in and speak to our class. He's a flaming idiot, I tell you. Revisionist history, through and through. It was his idea to have you come as a guest lecturer, but I was thinking maybe you could set him straight . . ."

"Have him contact my office. I have to schedule through them."

"It would really help me, Dad, if you could come. I'm afraid I might have ticked him off. Sometimes I argue too much."

Brighton cocked his head toward his son. "Can't imagine that, Luke."

Luke lifted his bowl and drained the milk, leaving a white mustache on his upper lip. Ammon looked at him and laughed and Luke wiped it with the back of his hand. "Dad, you know we're doing okay," he said. "Don't worry about us missing class. Anyway, remember we both have partial scholarships, which cuts our tuition by two-thirds; think how much you'd have to pay if it weren't for that. And we know we have to keep our grades up to keep our scholarships. But you know, really, it doesn't matter that much. We'll leave on our missions after the first semester anyway, and by the time we come back, who knows where you and Mom will be living. Germany? California? Outer Egypt somewhere? But you probably won't be here in D.C., so we probably won't be coming back to Georgetown anyway. We'll probably end up going to a college out West, maybe even to the Holy School . . ."

"Not me!" Ammon shot back. "No way I'm going there. BYU stinks. Go Aggies, I say . . ."

"Okay, whatever, but Dad, we're keeping good grades anyway."

Brighton nodded slowly, a sudden sense of sadness passing through him. It was one of the prices his family paid for the military life he led. No roots, not to speak of—his sons didn't really have a home. Home was where their mom and dad were, and that could be anywhere. His sons were happy and adaptable, and they wouldn't have had it any other way; they could make friends in weeks when others took years. But there was a sense of missing roots; there was no doubt about that. They would have their mission farewells in this ward, a ward they had lived in for almost three years, but it was likely that while they were on their missions their parents would move and so they would report their missions in a new ward, a place they had never been to before.

Then he thought of his stake president's blessing for the first time that day, the words repeating themselves almost automatically in the back of his mind. *"This is one of the purposes for which you were brought into this world. This is part of the work that He wants you to do."*

The general sighed, then finished his OJ and straightened his uniform. "Hey, guys," he said, "if you're going to go climbing, I don't think that sugar crap is going to be good enough. Hang on a minute and I'll make you some eggs." He pulled out a large skillet and placed it on the stove.

"No time, Dad," Luke said to him quickly. "And you've got to get to work too."

"It will take me three minutes. Put some bread in the toaster. You'll be glad you did."

Luke hesitated, then walked to the toaster and dropped in four slices of bread. Brighton pulled out an egg carton and scrambled six eggs, dumped in some bacon bits as the skillet grew warm, then poured the eggs and stirred them while watching his sons.

Ammon sat at the table, reading the sports page while grumbling about his Wizards, who had started 1 and 10 (a full game worse than last year!), while Luke grabbed his calculus textbook and started cramming his way through some problems that, no doubt, should have been done the day before. How Luke managed to keep his grades up, Brighton would never know, for he and Ammon took such different approaches to life. While Brighton believed that preparation was 90 percent of the battle, Luke seemed to think that true inspiration came only under great stress, and self-induced stress was the most inspiring kind.

Although they were twins, his sons were as different as any two brothers could be, and though there was a family resemblance, they hardly looked like brothers, let alone twins. Both were eighteen, their birthdays just a few months away, and freshmen at Georgetown University; but Ammon was tall—a little more than six feet, two inches—with broad shoulders and long legs, while Luke was shorter and stockier, with thick arms and thick legs. Ammon had his mother's blonde hair and fine eyes, while Luke had his father's dark hair and Roman nose. Ammon was smooth as Georgia cream; he could talk himself out of any situation, manipulate any teacher, make any friend. He always knew what to say (even if it wasn't always *exactly* the truth), and a successful career in politics was almost assured. Luke, on the other hand, was extremely straightforward; there was no pretense to him. He didn't sugarcoat any situation; in fact, just the opposite: sometimes he made things seem worse just to liven things up. With Luke, what you saw was what you got, and if someone didn't like that, that was okay with him. Love me or leave me was his attitude, though so far as his father could tell almost everyone ended up loving him—or were intimidated enough to stay out of his way. While Ammon played tailback in football, a position that required speed, brains, and skill, Luke's favorite position was fullback. He was a vicious blocker, a let-me-knock-someone-on-his-butt kind of guy.

Parley Ammon (he hated being called Parley and hadn't answered to the name since he was three) had been named after one of Brighton's great-grandfathers, one of the original settlers of Abilene, Texas, a gunslinger and gambler who had found religion soon after meeting a young Alabama blonde and taking her out to the wild west. After going straight, Grandpa Parley Ammon went on to become one of the most feared lawmen in West Texas, a sheriff who was known for getting his man—whether dead or alive apparently didn't matter a whole lot to him. Luke, on the other hand, was named after the missionary who had baptized his father, a soft-spoken but powerful young man who was led enough by the Spirit to see the goodness in Neil Brighton and who had enough faith to see some hope for the cynical and disbelieving fighter jock whose ambition and ego was larger than either his head or his heart.

Watching his sons, Brighton knew he had probably mixed up their names. Luke was the gunslinger, the fearless lawman with the get 'em or kill 'em attitude. Ammon, on the other hand, was the ambassador, the smooth-talking ladies' man. But he was equally proud of them both and loved them as only a father could love his sons. If they had any faults, and both of them did, he often found the same faults in himself, and knew that was where most of their weaknesses came from. Still, like many of his generation, he stood in awe of his children—they were better than he was in almost every way. And when he considered what he had been like at their age—driving drunk around West Texas, shooting up stop signs, and spending Sundays at the lake with his friends—he wondered how such a tainted man could raise such untainted sons.

Brighton looked down to see the eggs were ready, and he spooned them onto two plates, buttered the toast, and set the plates on the table. Ammon offered a morning prayer, and the two sons dug in, eating as if they hadn't eaten in days, their stomachs apparently forgetting the multiple bowls of cold cereal. Ammon scooped his eggs onto a piece of toast, took a large bite, and turned to his dad. "Sam called last night," he said suddenly.

Brighton perked up instantly. "You're kidding!" he said.

"Yeah. He's in Germany this week."

"He's out of Afghanistan?"

"For a while, anyway. He has two weeks in Europe for R&R."

Brighton stared as he thought. Sam, his other son, his foster son, the lost sheep of his fold, the young man he loved as much as he loved his natural sons, was off on his own now, having joined the army right out of high school. No mission, no college, just a jump into life. But ever since joining the army, his relationship with his adopted father had become strained, and it seemed they heard less and less from him now. "Did he say anything?" Brighton prodded.

"Not really. We didn't talk much. He was in kind of a hurry."

"How is he?" Brighton asked anxiously, trying to keep the strain from his voice.

"Seemed to be happy. I told him you were on your way to Saudi this week. He wanted to know if you were stopping in Germany to refuel. If you are, he wants to hook up."

Brighton thought and smiled. It might actually work. And he would love to see Samuel, even if for only a few hours.

"How's his unit in Afghanistan?" Brighton asked, anxious to hear Sam's report. He kept a very close eye on the status reports from the army units in Afghanistan, but word from the theatre was hard to come by, especially from the Ranger units who were working with the CIA.

Luke smiled. "He sounds really happy. He was glad to get a hot shower and sleep in a bed, but you could tell he was really satisfied. He said he's making a difference. It sounds really cool!"

Brighton eyed his son. "It's not as cool as you think, trust me, Luke. Sleeping in tents. Every meal a cold MRE—soup and spaghetti out of warmed-up plastic bags. It's muddy and cold and extremely hard work. Don't even think of enlisting! You've got to be an officer. So do what I say, Luke: enroll in an ROTC program. And for heaven's sakes, Luke, don't be a grunt. Learn to fly! Don't join the army when you could learn to fly jets. You talk about cool, but what could be cooler than that?"

Luke didn't answer. They had had this conversation before, and Brighton knew how Luke felt. Flying? Yeah, Luke thought it would be okay. But he had seen his dad suffer through too many nonflying duties, and he knew the air force took their best pilots and jerked them out of the cockpit and into staff positions long before they were ready. And besides, there was something else, something greater, a feeling Luke had that real men fought their wars in the blood and mud, not from some sterile cockpit at forty-thousand feet.

Brighton sighed and moved to the hallway and returned with his flight cap and briefcase. "Where in Germany is Sam taking his R&R?" he asked.

Ammon and Luke were gathering their climbing gear. Ammon hesitated, then shook his head. "He didn't say. But he said he could meet you at Ramstein if you lay over there."

Brighton nodded. That might work out. "Did he talk to your mother?" he asked.

"No," Ammon answered. "He called while you were at the embassy reception. And he was in kind of a hurry; he wanted to call his old man. He hasn't seen him in a couple of years and apparently the old bag isn't feeling too well."

Brighton shook his head. "Don't call him that," he said.

Ammon hesitated. "He doesn't deserve any better. After what he did to Samuel, he deserves a lot worse . . ."

"Doesn't matter!" Brighton answered, his voice growing sharp. "It doesn't help Sam when you call his father that."

"You should hear what *he* calls him!" Ammon replied.

Brighton looked stern, and Ammon shut up.

The three men were silent; then Luke headed for the door. "Come on, Ammon," he shouted. "We should have left fifteen minutes ago."

Ammon stopped at the built-in locker in the back hallway of the old Victorian and pulled out a pair of gum-soled climbing shoes.

"See you tonight, Dad," his sons called as they walked out the door.

chapter fifteen

Luke and Ammon stood at the bottom of the rock, staring up, the sun shining behind them and warming their shoulders with its early morning light, while a thousand birds sang around them: sparrows, mockingbirds, and robins calling to each other from the trees that lined the riverbed. The air was crisp and smelled of dead leaves and wet sand. The Potomac River ran low as it always did in the fall and swirled behind them, the water twenty feet from the shoreline where the sand and brush met the rocky cliffs. Above them, a sheer wall of sandstone rose up from the river, the remnant of some geological aberration that had piled the sand and sediment, then crushed it into stone before a million years of running water cut the softer sediment away.

Luke reached out and touched the cold wall. It was wet and slimy from a small spring that wept from the underground aquifer, the water running clear and forming a mossy trail that ran down the stone. He pressed his finger into the moss, then touched his mouth as he looked around the falls.

The Great Falls of the Potomac is one of the most spectacular natural landmarks on the entire east coast. Above the falls, the Potomac narrows from a wide and meandering river to a powerful ribbon of water that cuts through Mather Gorge with incredible force. The river drops nearly eighty feet in a little less than a mile, crashing over a series of twenty-foot waterfalls and cascading rapids before splitting into multiple frothing fingers that run through the rocky channels that make up the lower part of the gorge. For the past ten thousand years, the Potomac has cut through the bedrock, eroding the falls and the riverbank into a moon-like terrain, while leaving rock formations that are sheer and jagged and perfect for climbing.

Luke pressed the mossy trail again, then moved a few feet to his right to where the stone was dry and bare. Ammon glanced at the trail that led from the riverbed up the side of the steep bank. "Where are they?" he muttered as he looked at his watch. The two brothers were alone, their California climbing partners having not yet shown up.

"Probably lost," Luke answered as he waved away to the east. "You know those California boys. Get them off the freeway and they pretty much freeze up. They're probably to Gettysburg by now, or somewhere in West Virginia."

"Think they'll stop when they hit the Mississippi?"

"Only if they run out of gas."

"You know what I think? I don't think they're lost. I think they're just smarter than we are. They're lying in bed and laughing at us for getting up so early."

Luke shook his head and smiled, then swept his hand through the air. "That's okay. This is worth it. Is there anything in the world that is better than this?"

"Ahh . . . let me think. Girls . . . ?"

Luke shook his head again. "I mean other than that."

"Ahh . . . steak. Yeah. Both steak and lobster are better than this."

"Okay. Two things."

"Yeah. And sleep. Sleep is *much* better!"

"Be quiet, okay. This is great. Winter's coming. This might be our last time to climb before we leave on our missions."

"Wait, I'm not finished. . . . TV's better . . . yeah, I think I'd rather watch TV than get up at five in the morning just to climb rocks."

Luke looked dismayed. "Okay, I'm sorry I dragged you out here, all right!"

Ammon smiled and cracked his brother on the back. "Just kidding, bro. You know I'd rather be here with you than anywhere else in the world."

Luke looked at him. "A little early for sarcasm."

"Just trying to get things going, you know, lighten things up a bit." Ammon smiled again and picked up the rope and his climbing harness.

Luke studied the wall, lifting his head to study the top of the cliff almost fifty feet above them. Overhead, a six-foot ledge jutted outward from the wall at a 60-degree angle. He studied the cliff for handholds, then pointed to a trail of tiny cracks leading up to the overhang. "I could climb up to that ledge," he said, pointing to where the rock jutted outward from the sheer wall.

"Yeah. And then what?" Ammon asked.

Luke studied the overhang. "It looks like there might be a few holds . . ." He shifted his weight and leaned back. "There . . ." he pointed with his right arm, extending it high, using it to guide Ammon's eyes toward a tiny crack in the rock. "If I could reach behind me for two feet or so, I could jam my hands in that crack."

"Yeah. Then all you'd have to do is hold on to that ledge with your teeth . . ."

Luke glanced at his brother. "You don't think I can do it, do you!"

"No, Luke, I don't think *anyone* can do it. It's too far. You'll be reaching out a full arm's length above and behind you while hanging on with only one hand. No, let me correct that: you'll be hanging on with only your fingers. I don't care how strong you are—no one could reach that far behind them and get their hand into that crack. Not while hanging on the wall anyway."

"But I could if . . ."

"Even if you do reach the crevasse, Luke, what are you going to do then? It's a vertical fissure, it runs *up and down* the rock, not across. You'd have to jam your fist in there and let go of the wall and pull yourself up by only one hand. No one could do it, not even you."

Luke looked up and nodded. "You're probably right," he said in disappointment.

"Bloody straight, good buddy."

"Probably no one could do it."

"It'll probably *never* be done."

"Certainly no one's ever done it before now."

"Certainly not."

Luke continued staring above him. The outcropping was a little more than forty feet up the wall. Forty feet. Four stories. A long way to fall. He lowered his eyes from the ledge and surveyed the scattered pile of boulders and rocks that had been strewn by the river at the base of the wall. Some were as big as his fist, some the size of small tables. All would hurt equally if he were to fall.

Ammon nudged his brother and pointed twenty feet to their right. "There's our spot," he said. "See that—there's a good crevasse we could jam our feet into. And plenty of handholds. We could climb the first forty feet there, then move to our left, come in above the overhang, and go up from there." He took a step back. "Once we're above that ledge, it's easy climbing."

Luke looked up and saw where his brother was pointing. "Yeah, that's a pretty good plan. But you know, Ammon, I'd really like to try climbing up *here.*"

Ammon grumbled. He knew what his brother was thinking. "Luke," he said, "let's not waste our time. There's no way you're going to get over that ledge. Look at it! It juts out at least six feet. And there's nothing to hold onto. So you're going to make me climb up the back side of the cliff to secure the rope, you'll spend twenty minutes climbing the rock and who knows how long trying to get over that ledge, then you'll have to give up and come down. By then, you'll be too exhausted to try anything else. So we'll waste an hour for nothing. Come on, man, let's just climb over there. You can climb first; then I'll take a shot. We'll both get in a good climb before we have to go."

Luke was studying his path up the rock to the overhang. "If I can get a good grip on the crevasse, I could pull myself to the edge of the overhang. Then I could hold onto the lip, swing my legs up, and pull myself over the top."

"No, Luke, come on. You don't have to do this, okay?"

"I know I don't have to. But I want to try."

"Let's just . . ."

"I know what you're going to say: Let's just climb over there. But you know what I was thinking, Ammon?"

Ammon grunted and didn't answer. Luke pulled on his thin leather gloves.

"I was thinking about Samuel. If he were here, you *know* what he would do? He'd want to see if he could climb over that ledge. And if he didn't make it today, he'd come back tomorrow, and again the next day, and the next day after that.

He'd figure a way to get up and over that ledge! You know he would. He'd try a thousand times if he had to, but he'd figure a way to get over that outcropping up there."

Ammon shook his head. "Sam's a stubborn fool."

"Stubborn? Maybe. I guess. But is stubborn a bad thing? Because when I watch Sam put his mind to something and never give up, it doesn't seem like a bad thing, you know."

Ammon shook his head. "I just want a nice, normal gut-wrenching climb. I want to get a good workout, then get back to school. You, on the other hand, want to prove something to yourself. You want to prove something to Sam, and he's not even here."

"I don't have to prove anything."

"Then let's climb over there!"

But Luke was already moving toward the rock and strapping his climbing harness on. "I'm going to try it here, Ammon. Now will you go up the back side and secure the rope, or do you want me to do it?"

Ammon huffed in frustration, then picked up the rope and started up the trail.

* * *

Balaam and Lucifer, their faces contorted in burning jealousy and hate, stood not far away, watching the brothers.

Balaam glanced to the Master and caught a glimpse of his own ugliness reflected in his master's dark eyes. There was something particularly horrible about someone so full of hate. He was pale and deadly, like a floating corpse, his face so lifeless and dreary he couldn't stand the sight of himself. He was hideous and he knew it, but he no longer cared. Unlike his master, who could still hide his ugliness if someone was willing to believe in his lies, Balaam was dark, cruel, and ugly and pretended to be nothing else.

Lucifer walked in a circle around the young men, listening to them talk while thinking to himself. Balaam watched him carefully, but stood out of his way.

Lucifer was dressed in his normal garb: braided sandals, a red sash, and a flowing gray robe, dark as smoke but with a light shimmer as if there was some unseen power there. His hood fell over his shoulders, his hair flowed down his neck, and his feet were as worn and sullied as any homeless vagabond who wandered the earth.

Balaam studied his great master from out of the corner of his eyes, noting the growing strength of his shoulders and the power of arms. His dark hair seemed to shimmer, and his eyes burned with fire. He stood in great arrogance, almost reeking of power while basking in the glory that his hate had produced. The world was more evil than it had ever been, more brutal, more carnal, and more soaking in sin. And the more the world bathed in evil, the more powerful his master became.

But there was growing good among the shadows, like these young brothers here, and Balaam was troubled. Like tiny points of light that penetrated the darkness, the great spirits had arrived to make their mark on the world. And they too were growing powerful, more pure, and more clear. And that made Balaam wonder. . . . He kicked at the ground with unease.

Lucifer looked at him suddenly, as if he read his mind. "You see them too, Master Balaam?" he asked in a deadly voice.

Balaam nodded slowly.

"You think they grow stronger? And you think I grow weak?"

Balaam swallowed and bowed. "No, Master Mayhem," he pleaded in a trembling voice. "You are the Great Master, the king of this world!"

Lucifer dismissed him with an angry wave of his hand. "That is right, Balaam. I *am* the king of this world. I am its glory and splendor, its magnificent power. And I am still rising! My day will soon come. And as my glory grows, the veil between my angels and this world will come down. A few see me now, but in time *all* will see. I will stand in my dark glory before them, and they shall see me as I am. I will step forward in power and claim this world for my own. And then they shall know, and their mouths shall confess, that it is *my* glory that burns bright in this land!"

Balaam nodded eagerly but said nothing as he lowered his eyes, knowing they would betray him if his dark master saw. Inside, his gut crunched into a tight ball. He wanted to believe—he wanted it desperately—but he felt in his heart that it simply wasn't true. He felt his gloom rising as the day of the Savior approached, the day when Balaam would be stripped of his power and brought to his knees, when the kingdom of his master would be shattered and his minions destroyed.

The Deceiver watched Balaam, noting that he kept his eyes low. "Do you believe, Master Balaam?" he sneered.

"Master Mayhem, I *want* to believe!"

"If you ever had faith in me, Master Balaam, then you'd better have faith in me now. You are tied to my future. I am all that you have. So when you pray to me, Balaam, you had better believe your own words!"

Balaam began to tremble in terrible fear. He had seen the Master angry before, and the last thing he wanted was for him to be angry with *him.* He quivered and shuddered, then dropped to one knee. "I believe, Master Mayhem!" he cried in a loud voice.

The Deceiver grunted in disgust, then turned away again.

Lucifer moved a step toward the brothers and faced them, looking them both in the eyes. He *knew* them. He recognized them, especially the strength of their souls. The powers that resided in them were like a bright light to him. But the memory wasn't certain, and he had to force his mind to look back.

It was *so* long ago. It was another world. So long since the light had been taken from him.

But as the Deceiver looked at Ammon, the memories came flooding back. They were hazy at first, extremely vague and unsure, but as he concentrated they began to take shape.

He had fought a great battle with Ammon in the premortal world. He had given his best effort, exerted all the strength he had, but despite his best efforts Ammon had rejected his plan.

Lucifer's face tightened up, and his stomach turned sour as he thought of the frustration Ammon had caused him in the premortal world.

* * *

They stood in a dark stairway in Lucifer's part of the world. It was black and suffocating and smelled of rot and wet soil. A cold rain pelted the rock structure, and the wail of Lucifer's followers lifted through the air, bitter cursings of the Father for casting them out.

Ammon stood and faced Lucifer in the winding stairwell. He took a step up, but Lucifer blocked his way. "Will you just listen?" Satan pleaded in the softest voice he could muster. "I'm begging you, Ammon, for Luke, for Elizabeth, for the sake of the others!" His voice dripped with charisma. It was a beautiful show. He put on his best face, a sincere look of kindness that was impossible to resist, and Ammon's eyes softened at the comforting smile.

Ammon took a breath and wavered, leaning against the rock wall. Lucifer brushed up beside him, getting right in his face, his black cape swirling like a dark mist at his knees. "There is so much I can give you." His voice was rising now. "So much you could have. Imagine worlds without number, power beyond your wildest dreams. Imagine every fantasy, every whim, every lust or ambition, everything I can give you, anything you desire. Anything you can dream of, any human taste, touch, or feel—all the wealth in the universe, I would share it with you. And all I ask is you believe me and do what I say."

Lucifer put his hand on Ammon's shoulders and felt his body shake at his touch. How many times had he felt that, the delicious quiver of fear! He moved closer to Ammon and put his cold arms around him. He sensed the goodness in Ammon as it recoiled from his touch, but he pulled him closer, not letting him go. "Pledge to me, Ammon," he hissed.

Ammon's knees almost buckled. He was overcome by despair.

Lucifer spread his arms and opened a powerful vision of the pleasures of the world. "Do you want it?" he whispered. "Shall I give it to you!"

Ammon paused. Yes, he wanted it. He wanted it so! He swallowed against the vision, then slowly opened his eyes. "You can give me anything?" Ammon asked him.

"Anything!" Lucifer cried.

"Anything that I ask for?"

"Anything you desire!"

"Can you give me love?" Ammon asked him. "Can you take away my sins? Can you give me salvation? Are you willing to die for me? Can you give me the love of my family and the love of my friends? Can you promise me anything besides what you have shown me here? Can you give me the love of my Father, or my older brother, Jehovah, the Christ?"

Lucifer took a step back, a look of rage on his face. "Worship me!" he demanded, his eyes flaming with hate.

Ammon turned away. "You have nothing to offer," he said.

Lucifer shrieked with such a fury that it pierced his own ears. "Let me show you what I'll give you!" he screamed in a rage.

Another vision opened, and Ammon gasped in heart-wrenching fear. In an instant Lucifer showed him all the horrors of the world, all the hate, pain, and disappointment that lay in store. Ammon cried and fell back, a look of dread in his eyes. Lucifer watched him, then stepped forward, cursing his name as he moved. "I will find you!" he promised. "I will remember this day. I will find you and curse you when you go down to earth. So remember, me, Ammon, because I will remember you!"

* * *

Lucifer's eyes burned with emotion as he thought of the memory. He had always hated the brothers, and now he hated them even more.

And look at them. Look! They were strong and happy. Worst of all, they were on a firm path. They would be leaving on missions. He hated the thought. The things they would do. The men they would become. The people they would touch, and the lives they would change. Generations would be blessed if he didn't stop them.

He fumed, his eyes burning. But *what* could he do?

Lucifer glared at the brothers. "I wish I could kill them," he growled. "If I could, I would. I would torture them, beat them, and cause them great pain. I would make them cry for mercy, then beat them some more. I would make them hate their bodies as much as I hate not having one. I could have been their master! But no, they didn't want me. They wanted to learn and grow for themselves. So that is fine. I will teach them. I will teach them of misery and despair!"

Balaam only watched his master. He had heard it before.

Lucifer fumed a long moment, pacing from side to side.

Then he suddenly stopped and smiled, exposing his teeth. He stared at Luke for a moment.

The brothers each had a weakness. And he remembered now what they were. He glared toward Luke, looking at the back of his head. He was the more prideful. So that's where he would begin. "I may not be able to hurt him," he hissed. "But there are a few things I can do. And if we can convince them to be careless, if we can distract them, then that might be enough."

Balaam slowly nodded. Careless. Yes careless. It was a tool that had been used against the young many times before.

The Deceiver muttered angrily as he walked toward Luke. "He is young. He is foolish. There might be a way . . ."

Balaam watched Ammon pick up his rope and begin to walk up the trail. "Stay with him," Lucifer commanded. "Try to distract him. Do anything you can. Make him act foolish. Shout distractions in his head!"

Balaam bowed and followed Ammon as he walked up the trail.

Lucifer watched them go, then moved toward Luke, positioning himself near his head. Leaning toward the mortal, he whispered thoughts of pride into his ear. *"You're the best. This is easy. No reason to be careful here."*

chapter sixteen

It took Ammon ten minutes to climb the trail that led up the backside of the riverbank to the top of the rock. As he walked, he became angry, thinking of Luke. He was always so prideful, so conceited, always proving himself! It was never enough just to have fun. Everything had to be a grand competition, and he had to be best.

Balaam walked beside him, shouting and sneering, planting angry thoughts in his mind. *"Why is Luke always like this? He's just wasting your time trying to climb this impossible rock!"*

Ammon moved up the trail, using his hands to pick his way up the steep path that led around the backside of the cliff. The trail was littered with broken rocks, and he slipped back a time or two, grabbing the brush at the sides to keep from falling back.

"What a waste of a morning," he mumbled, "standing at the bottom of the cliff, holding the safety rope so Luke can prove what a great climber he is.

"I really should be studying," he thought, for he had a test the next day. But no, he was going to spend the morning watching Luke climb an impossible rock. What a waste of time! He should have stayed in bed.

The longer he climbed, the madder he got, and the madder he got, the more distracted he was. Balaam continued working beside him, whispering scornful thoughts in his ear. Irrational. Emotional. Thoughts of envy and rage. *"Luke is better than you are. You know that, and he knows that too. He's just rubbing it in, just trying to prove it again. That's the only reason he's doing this—to make you feel like a loser. He just wants to bug you, to put you down a notch or two. Such a crock, the way he does that. Why can't he just give it a break? With him, it's always* me! *Always* me! *Everyone look at* me! *Aren't you growing sick of it? Will he ever change?"*

Balaam kept it up, a constant barrage of vile thoughts in Ammon's head. And the more Ammon heard it, the angrier he became. Balaam knew the thoughts were illogical and selfish, but Lucifer's temptations rarely made any sense. Yet still people listened. Driven by emotion, the human heart sometimes doesn't think.

Ammon climbed, his head down, the emotion building inside.

Yeah, he loved Luke, sure, and they got along great most the time, but once in a while he could be a real jerk . . .

He suddenly realized he was at the top of the hill. Looking around he saw that because the wall had not been climbed before, there was no anchor he could use to secure the safety rope to. For a moment he thought of tying it to a nearby tree; but instead he took an anchor and small hammer from his backpack and secured his own bolt, driving it deeply into a crack at the top of the cliff. He pulled on the anchor to check it, jerking it back and forth.

The rock around the bolt began to chip away, and he leaned over to check it.

Balaam leaned toward him, intent on his work, his eyes dark and fierce. *"Don't worry about it,"* he hissed, knowing this was his chance. *"How many times have you done this? A thousand times? More? Has a bolt ever broken? No! Not even once. So why are you worried? What are you so careful for?"*

Ammon jerked on the bolt. It seemed to hold. He clipped a carabineer through the anchor and screwed the safety clasp to ensure it couldn't open. Then, standing, he turned and glanced over the top of the rock. It was a long way to fall, and he felt a little dizzy. Truth was, he had never been keen on heights.

From where he stood, he couldn't see Luke, who was hidden from view underneath the ledge. "Luke," he called out, swinging the rope in his hand.

Luke stepped away from the wall to where Ammon could see him. "Heads up," Ammon called as he tossed down the rope. Luke caught it, being careful not to let it touch the ground where the sand or dirt would weaken it and make it less safe.

Ammon ran his end of the rope through the carabineer, then secured it to his climbing harness using a figure-8 knot. He pulled on his gloves, then looked over the edge of the cliff.

"Ready!" he called down to Luke.

Luke snaked the rope through his own harness, then tightened the slack. "Go for it," he called back.

Before backing over the cliff, Ammon looked a final time at the bolt he had driven into the crack.

"It's fine," Balaam whispered. *"You're such a worrier. Come on—go for it!"*

Ammon didn't move.

"Luke's waiting!" Balaam sneered. *"He's looking at you, wondering what you're doing. He's not a pansy. He wouldn't worry. He wouldn't freak out like this . . ."*

Ammon knelt down and brushed the sand and dirt away from the bolt. The sandstone was weak and crumbling from a thousand years of rain and wind, but the bolt seemed to be firmly driven into the rock. Standing, he pulled against the rope, giving a final jerk.

"It's okay!" Balaam whispered quickly, keeping a steady chatter in his ear. *"Go on. Have some fun. The bolt will be fine. What are the chances anything will go wrong?"*

Ammon nodded, agreeing with the whispered thoughts in his head.

And because he was young, and because he was naïve, and because he was angry, and distracted with thoughts about school, and because he hadn't been hurt by inexperience before, Ammon trusted the whispers and didn't check the bolt carefully.

He stood at the edge of the cliff. "On belay!" he cried.

"Belay on!" Luke called back as he braced for the pull of Ammon's weight.

Ammon turned his back and walked off the top of the cliff. It was a sheer drop below him, and he easily bounced his way down, rappelling to the ledge ten feet below the top of the rock. Hitting the overhang, he moved to the tip of the ledge, then pushed forcefully out and away from the wall while feeding out ten feet of rope. The rope tightened, then swung him like a pendulum into the wall, and he spread his bent knees to absorb the shock.

Above him, the bolt slipped, moving against the cracked stone, but Ammon didn't feel it as he swung into the side of the cliff. He pushed again. His weight jerked the rope and the bolt slipped again, pivoting thirty degrees. A small crack, too small to have been seen, spread in the rock, but still the bolt held.

* * *

Ammon stopped his descent directly under the ledge. Hanging there, he looked over his head, his body off balance, his torso hanging back.

The outcropping had more handholds than he had been able to see from the ground. And the ledge wasn't quite as steep as it had appeared. The crevasse they had looked at might provide a pretty good grip *if* Luke could reach it, which was a very big *if,* for it was a good two or three feet away from the face of the cliff. Ammon examined the overhang for thirty seconds or so then let off more rope, bouncing from the rock as he made his way down. The last of the descent was almost a free fall through space, for the overhang kept him away from the wall and he had to balance himself carefully as he descended to the ground.

Luke was waiting, an anxious look on his face. "What do you think?" he asked quickly.

Ammon stared up at the overhang as he loosened the straps on his harness. "I'm not sure about the bolt," he said absently, ignoring the intent of his brother's question. He jerked on the rope and suspended his weight on it by dropping to his knees as he pulled. The rope held firm, and Luke waved at the air.

"Come on, Ammon, the bolt is secure. In all the times we've done this has a bolt ever broken away?"

Ammon stared up, keeping his weight on the rope. "I don't know," he muttered. "It just didn't feel right. Sandstone is notoriously weak, you know, and though I found a good crevasse, part of it broke away when I drove the bolt in."

Luke hesitated. "Come on, Ammon. It's fine. You just don't want . . ."

"No, Luke, really. I just want to be sure."

"Come on!" Luke persisted. "Nothing's going to happen.

How many times have we done this? Nothing has ever gone wrong before. You're turning into Mom, always fussing about something."

Ammon ignored him as he jerked again, suspending all of his weight. The rope seemed to hold firm, and Luke huffed impatiently.

"All right," Ammon finally said. "It seems to be okay."

"Yeah, it's fine," Luke answered. "Now what about the overhang?"

Ammon looked up. "It's going to be even harder than it looks," he answered, lifting his arm and pointing as he talked. "There, you see that?" He motioned toward the leading edge of the overhang. "That crevasse you're counting on to provide a handhold, it looks to be only a few inches wide, just enough to get your hand in and get a good grip. But it's a lot wider than that, Luke, I'd say five inches or so, and it slopes downward much more than it looks like from here. You're not going to be able to use it for a handhold like you thought."

Luke studied the small fissure and said, "But it's got a pretty good lip there that I could hold onto."

Ammon nodded. "You could try. That's all I can say. But listen, Luke, why can't we just move down the rock fifteen feet or so?" Ammon pointed to his right. "It's got better handholds, it's even, and we wouldn't have to mess around with that overhang, which is just going to make you fall."

"So what if I fall? That's what the safety rope is for."

Ammon flipped the climbing rope in his hand, 150 feet of interwoven nylon and cotton. Designed to stretch under pressure, it was a good rope, and expensive, and had saved both of their lives literally dozens of times. He pulled on the rope as he stared at the wall. "One more thing," he continued, still hoping to talk Luke out of trying the climb, "because the rope has to extend over the edge, it will hang away from the wall.

That's going to make it harder for me to keep a proper tension on it. No big deal—I can handle that—but if you lose your grip and fall, the ledge will leave you dangling five or six feet away from the wall. Which means you'll have to trust me to lower you to the ground."

"I don't know, Ammon. It won't be any harder than you rappelling down."

Ammon hesitated. "I just think it's a waste of time to try to climb over that ledge," he concluded. "You can't do it, Luke. No offense, buddy, but no one can pull themselves over the top of that ledge. So I'll sit here for an hour and watch you try, then you'll be exhausted and come down, and that will be it."

"But you'll hang with me, right? You'll give me a chance?"

Ammon watched his brother. "You're not going to pull a Sam on me, are you? Because both of us know what Sam would do. He'd hang on the wall and keep trying to pull himself over that ledge until he either starved to death or we pulled him down. He wouldn't give up as long as he had any strength. He would literally fall from exhaustion before he would quit. Now, you're not going to do that, are you? Because I really have to get to my lab this afternoon. If I'm going to be here all day holding the safety rope for you, then tell me now so I can go and buy me some lunch and a couple of sodas before you get on the wall."

Luke smiled. "I'll give it a reasonable try," he said. "If it doesn't work out, I'll admit defeat and rappel down the wall, and we'll try somewhere else."

"I'm serious, Luke. I'm not going to stay here all day," Ammon warned. "I'll tie the rope to a tree and leave you if you drag this thing on."

"Got it," Luke answered.

Ammon nodded, checked his harness, then flipped the

rope, moving it a couple of feet to his right in order to position it to the place where Luke wanted to climb.

* * *

As Ammon released his weight and flipped the rope, the bolt he had driven into the rock reseated itself and cocked again to the side. Microscopic fractures formed through the rock, spreading away from the bolt like a tiny spiderweb, weakening the stone where the bolt had been set.

* * *

Luke moved to the base of the fifty-foot sandstone wall. Ammon stood behind him, the safety rope secured to his harness. The rope ran over the top of the wall, through the carabineer he had secured in the crack on the top, then back down the wall to Luke, who had tied the other end to his climbing harness. Luke glanced behind him. "Belay on?" he asked.

Ammon flipped the rope to make certain it curled on the small carpet he had laid out behind him, then pulled out the last of the slack. "On belay," he answered.

Luke moved to the wall. "Climbing," he said.

"Climb on," Ammon replied.

Luke stretched his hands over the rock, feeling for the tiny crevasses and finger holds that a nonclimber would have never seen. His gum-soled shoes were like fly paper, giving him an extraordinary sense of security against the rock. He stretched, reaching over his head, and pulled himself up, using his feet and legs to support his weight as much as he could to help save his upper body strength for the ledge overhead. As he climbed, he was extraordinarily aware of his body and used every part: his knees, his elbows, his fingers and palms; he even forced his chest muscles against the rock in order to evenly distribute his weight. He easily climbed the first fifteen feet, using tiny protrusions as handholds and forcing his feet into thin cracks. Halfway up the rock, the wall became suddenly smooth, and he had to hang on a tiny ledge while he searched for the next handhold. Stretching over his head, he felt for a crack that he could hold on to.

Ammon watched from the ground, all the time looking up. He kept the rope tight enough to immediately break Luke's fall, but not so tight as to interfere with him or let it get in his way. He watched his brother search in vain for a handhold, then called up, "Luke, there's a place to put your foot a couple of feet to your right."

Luke turned his head. He stretched out his leg and tried a place or two, but couldn't find anything that would support his weight.

"Higher up," Ammon shouted. "Get your right foot on that tiny ledge right beside you."

Luke stopped and stared down at his brother. "Oh, you must mean this ledge here by my ear!" he shouted sarcastically.

"Come on! It's not *that* high. You can do it, buddy, if you get your knees high enough . . ."

"I'm not a contortionist, Ammon. How many people could lift their feet to their chest!"

"You're exaggerating, Luke. Now come on, you can do it!"

Luke stared at the tiny ledge by his waist, hesitating. He lifted his leg a time or two, measuring the height, but his other foot almost slipped. He stared down at Ammon. "Would you like to come and demonstrate?" he called back.

Ammon started to answer, but Luke ignored him. After several more minutes of searching, he descended the rock a couple of feet, moved two arm lengths to his right, then started climbing again. There was a better route there, with handholds enough for him to sink his fingers onto. Fifteen minutes later he had climbed to the ledge.

"How you feeling?" Ammon asked as Luke studied the overhang directly over his head.

Luke took a free hand and wiped quickly at his brow. "A little tired," he called back. "That wore me out, getting stuck halfway up. And it took a lot longer to get here than I thought it would."

Ammon glanced at his watch. Luke had been on the rock for almost thirty minutes. He knew Luke had to be exhausted. A less experienced climber would have fallen a dozen times by now. A beginner wouldn't have made it ten feet up the wall. But Luke was just beginning. The most difficult part of the climb was directly over his head.

Luke craned his neck back as he held to the rock with his fingers, his feet turned sideways to fit on a one-inch crack in the rock. The rock jutted outward at a sixty-degree angle, extending above and behind him for five feet or so. His hands trembled, and his calves were beginning to cramp from the constant strain of holding his weight on his toes. He had to move quickly or he wouldn't have any strength left to pull himself over the ledge.

He searched in frustration, sweat pouring down his cheeks and under his arms.

* * *

Lucifer stood in the air beside him. *"You can do it!"* he whispered into the exhausted man's ear. *"Ammon doesn't think you're strong enough, but you know that you are! Samuel could do it. Is he that much stronger than you?"*

Luke passed a weary hand over his eyes as he thought.

"Sam has always been stronger," Lucifer hissed bitterly.

"He's better at everything! But you know you can do this. Now prove that you can."

The young mortal looked down. His brother stared up. He clenched the fingers on his left hand against the tiny cracks in the wall, then leaned backward so far he thought he would fall. He clung there, suspended, barely hanging on the cliff. He moved his hand across the overhang, feeling for the crack they had identified from the ground, searching for anything he could sink his fingers into. His shoulders ached, his arms trembled, and his neck muscles cramped.

"Luke," Ammon warned. "Be careful up there."

"I'm okay," he shouted.

Luke moved a few inches away from the wall and the safety rope went slack. "You got me?" Luke called as he glanced down.

"I got you!" Ammon answered as he braced himself, planting his feet and leaning back, anticipating Luke's fall.

Luke gathered his strength and reached back again. He stood on his toes, and his leg muscles cramped. He stretched out his fingers and lifted one leg, but *he . . . couldn't . . . quite . . . reach . . . it!* He huffed in exhaustion, then shifted his weight to his left foot and lifted up on his toes, clawing over his head and behind him. He could see the crack, but it was two inches too far.

* * *

"Jump!" the Deceiver told him. *"Let go of the wall. You can do it, Luke! You won't get hurt if you fall!"*

* * *

Luke stretched out again, almost at the end of his strength. He extended his fingers. *Just . . . a . . . few . . . inches . . . to . . .*

go! He shook his head and looked down, relieving the cramps in his neck, then gathered his strength and repositioned himself on a tiny ledge on the cliff.

"You got me, right?" he called down to Ammon.

Ammon looked a little worried. "Come on, Luke," he answered. "Let's call it quits."

Luke shook his head. Not when he was so close!

He looked back and stretched a final time for the handhold he had been reaching for. It was simply too far. It was jump or climb down.

He made his decision and swallowed hard.

He braced himself against the wall as he gathered his strength, then leapt for the rock while twisting in midair, extending both hands, stretching them over his head.

He grasped the crack with his right hand, but only with the tips of his fingers. There he hung, suspended, his feet swinging wildly through the air. He grasped with his other hand, forcing it against the crack in the wall, scratching and pawing for something to grab.

Ammon braced himself, waiting to absorb the weight of his fall.

Luke almost screamed from the pressure on his arm. The adrenaline shot through him, and he clawed like an animal with his free hand. As he pawed at the rock, tiny pieces of sandstone and dust tumbled into his eyes. Hanging by one hand, he scratched with the other, then felt a tiny crack in the rock. Stretching, he grabbed it with all the strength he had left.

He caught his breath as he hung there, four stories above the ground, then moved his right hand for a better handhold. He pulled himself upward and moved his left hand. Inch by inch, hand by hand, he moved upward toward the tip of the ledge. Another foot . . . another handhold, he moved across the overhang.

His arms ached. It was agony. He could hardly breathe. His fingers trembled with exhaustion, and his shoulders knotted in pain.

He didn't think he could make it. He couldn't hold on anymore. It took everything he had just to hang on to the rock. He was growing light-headed; his entire body was shaking, and his arms cramped in pain.

Just a few inches more. But he did not have the strength.

He wasn't going to make it. It was time to let go. He had tried; he had failed. Now his body was done.

He huffed in disappointment, then reached for the safety rope, snatching it desperately while hanging by one arm.

The rope fell through his fingers, slipping over the overhang and onto the rocky ground. The carabineer was still attached to the climbing bolt, and both clinked when they landed on the rocks below.

* * *

Ammon saw the rope fall and almost threw up on himself. The bolt had broken free from the crevasse. It couldn't be true! His mind flashed in white lightning and he rushed to the wall. He legs turned to jelly, and his gut crunched in a sick knot of dark fear.

He glanced up at his brother, who hung from the edge by his arms. *"Oh God!"* he frantically whispered. *"Please, don't let him fall!"*

He dived on the rope in a panic, as if it could help him now. He laced it through his fingers, finding the bolt. The carabineer was still attached, and he grimaced in pain, then stared at it blankly, an unbelieving look on his face. He turned for the trail and started to run, then pulled up and stopped. He did not have enough time. Luke could not hang on long enough for him to get to the top of the rock and secure the rope again.

He looked up in horror.

He did not want his brother to die!

Then the bitter truth hit him like a baseball bat in his chest. He exhaled in pain, almost doubling over with guilt. He clenched his teeth and looked up, his eyes wide in gut-wrenching fear.

He *thought* the bolt was safe. But he hadn't been sure.

His brother might die. And it was his fault!

He looked up, his mouth gaping, his throat too tight to scream. "I will catch you, Luke!" he tried calling, but his voice only croaked.

* * *

Luke knew he was dead. He simply couldn't hang on. He had drained all his energy, every ounce of his strength. His fingers were slipping, and his arms cramped in pain. He tried desperately to hang on, but there was nothing more he could do.

He felt his grip slipping, and he closed his eyes for the fall.

Time came to a stop, the world freezing in place. He heard his heart beat and felt each pull of breath in his chest. He thought clearly and precisely as his mind raced ahead.

He looked directly below him where Ammon was waiting in terror, his face sick and grim. It looked as if he was trying to call to him, but his voice didn't come. His brother reached up as if waiting to catch him when he fell. The rope lay curled at his feet, glistening white in the sun.

Luke looked up to the overhang. He was *so* close. Just another few inches. But he simply did not have the strength. His fingers slipped again, and he held on by their very tips.

He listened to his heart beat. *Thump!* It slammed in his chest. Then he started praying. "Please, I do not want to die."

"Then fight!" the Spirit said to him. *"This is your choice!"*

Luke almost looked around. Was someone else there? The voice was so clear, it was as if someone spoke in his ear. He blinked his eyes in confusion, at the same time feeling sudden strength in his arms.

"This is not your time," the Spirit whispered. *"You have more work to do. Now are you going to fight so I can help you, or are you going to let go?"*

Luke didn't hesitate. He tightened his grasp on the rock.

"Look to your right! There is a firm handhold there."

Luke turned his head and saw a small protrusion in the rock he had not noticed before. How could he have missed it? Was it *really* there before? He reached out and grabbed it. It fit like a glove in his hand, and he curled his fingers around it, a perfect handhold. He felt a sudden rush of power and reached with his other hand. Another crack in the rock provided another handhold, and he moved slowly upward on the ledge. He reached the edge of the overhang, where he hung for a moment, still suspended, then started swinging his legs while pulling himself up with his arms. He got one knee up and clawed at the overhang with his feet while pulling up with his arms. His other foot brushed the rock, and he felt another rush of power. He pulled one final time, and his feet caught the top of the ledge. With strength beyond his own, he heaved himself over the top, then collapsed in a heap of quivering flesh.

He couldn't move his fingers. He couldn't move his arms. He was so numb and exhausted he barely had the strength to breathe. His head dropped to the side and he saw the bloody scratches on his arm. His stomach turned to water, bitter and tart, and he rolled to his side and threw up a gush of clear fluid from the deepest part of his gut. Then he lay back, exhausted, barely able to think.

Then below him he heard his brother's desperate sobs.

* * *

Ammon had fallen to his knees, then rolled to his side. He pulled his arms to his chest and held himself tight, while great tears of horror and relief rolled down his cheeks to his neck.

He had almost killed his brother. The whole thing was his fault. He shuddered again as his face went pale. A cold sweat drenched his face, his lips almost turning blue.

It was over. *God had saved him.* He had reached down from heaven and pulled Luke up and over the ledge. Ammon had watched it. There was no doubt in his mind. Someone had saved Luke, someone from above.

He stared at the rope that lay curled at his knees, then picked up the carabineer and felt sick again.

He sobbed with emotion, overcome with guilt and relief.

He had almost killed his brother. How could he have gone on if his brother had fallen? ***He had almost killed his brother!*** What was he going to do? Would he ever get over this moment? Would the dread ever pass?

He felt sick and alone. He thought he would throw up. And he knew in his heart he would never be the same man again.

* * *

A long moment passed. How long, Ammon didn't know; it felt like only a few seconds, but it could have been much longer, before he finally pushed himself to his feet, picked up the rope, and ran up the trail to the top of the rock. Looking over the ledge, he saw Luke waiting there, leaning against the cliff, his arms hanging weakly at his sides. Ammon looked down at his brother for several heartbeats before Luke noticed he was there.

Ammon couldn't speak. His mind was a haze. "Hey, that was kind of exciting," Luke said with a smile.

Ammon shook his head. "I'm so sorry . . . so sorry . . ."

"What? What are you talking about?"

"The rope. The bolt! It was my fault."

Luke shook his head and waved a dismissive hand. "Come on, Ammon, don't go soft on me. There wasn't a thing you could do; it's just one of those things. Anyone who climbs knows that it happens. There was no way you could know."

"I knew the bolt wasn't sure. The rock was starting to crack. I should have stopped you . . ."

Luke pushed himself up, leaning into the rock. "That's a crock and you know it! There was no way you could know. Now don't go girly on me, Ammon. Besides, I'm okay. And now I can say I made it over the ledge. Without a safety rope even. Let's see Samuel beat that!"

Luke smiled, but his voice trailed off and both of the young men were quiet.

"I heard something," Luke finally said in a reverent tone.

Ammon's eyes narrowed. "I saw something," he replied.

"I felt such a power."

"It was as if a hand lifted you up."

They both fell still for a very long time. Then they looked at each other, and Luke lowered his eyes. "Can you throw me a rope? I want to get off this ledge."

Ammon secured the rope to the tree and lowered it to his brother. Luke secured it to his harness, and Ammon pulled him the last ten feet to the top of the rock.

The two young men drove in silence the entire way home.

"Should we tell Dad?" Ammon asked as they pulled into the drive.

Luke shook his head. "I don't think so," he said. "Maybe someday, but let's not mention it now."

Neither one of them even considered telling their mom. There were just certain things it was better for moms not to know.

chapter seventeen

Sara Brighton watched her husband pack for the trip to Saudi Arabia as she sat on the edge of their bed, her legs crossed with her feet under her knees, her flannel nightgown pulled tightly around her knees and tucked under her feet.

Like all military officers, Brighton had spent much of his career on the road, and it took him only minutes to pack for the trip. One suit bag and one carry-on—the general had it down to an art. His travel bag was like his schedule, tight and precise. And he always traveled light: no fluffy bathrobes, extra clothes, or personal pillows. The only nonessential items he would carry would be a small set of military scriptures (well-worn but with print so small it was getting difficult for him to read) and whatever history book he was reading at the time. For the major items he kept a prepacked military suitcase in the back of his closet, which contained a fully packed toiletry bag, dark socks, air force shirts, two dress uniforms, dark leather dress shoes, a long overcoat, and athletic gear.

After joining the NSC staff, Brighton was surprised to discover how often he had to travel with only a few moments' notice. (He had to laugh at seeing the look on his neighbor's face the first time a military chopper set down in their cul-de-sac to whisk him away. In a town that lived and died by perks, even the Armani-suited attorney had trouble matching *that* power play.) Because of the short-notice requirements, Sara had learned to launder his clothes and repack his bag immediately upon his return, for neither of them knew when he would have to head out again.

As Brighton stuffed military papers into his briefcase, Sara watched in silence, twisting a strand of light hair in her fingers. She frowned, then adjusted her nightgown, pulling it over her knees.

"How long will you be gone?" she asked intently.

"Couple days," Brighton answered.

Three days in Saudi Arabia. A quick hit and go. Overseas trips like this were no more unusual for him than a trip to the mall.

"Saudi Arabia is a long way to go for just a few days," Sara said.

Brighton pressed his lips and nodded, but didn't say anything.

"You say you have some meetings with the Saudi military commanders?"

"Yeah. We've had a little problem in some of our joint operations we need to iron out."

"Joint operations? As in command and control or operational missions?" After years of being married not only to her husband but also to his job, Sara had the basic concepts of military operations and their lingo down.

Brighton nodded, then dropped to his knees and looked under his bed. Pulling out *A Short History of the World,* he shoved it into his briefcase. "There are some operational options we're looking at," he explained.

Sara considered. Operational missions with the Joint Saudi Forces. She knew what that meant. If one read the daily papers, especially the *Washington Times,* one could add two and two and come up with a pretty good estimation of the top-secret information that was given to the president in his presidential daily brief. For weeks now, even months, the *Times* had been saying that the Royal Saudi king, King Faysal, was preparing to move against many of the terror camps that had sprung up along the Iranian border across the Persian Gulf, many of which were, ironically, originally funded by the Wahhabi fundamentalists that ran his own kingdom. Many of these terror camps had been used as the operations centers from which they attacked targets within the kingdom, and the king had decided he had no choice but to act. A house divided will not stand, and the terror the Islamist radicals were wreaking within his own kingdom had to come to an end.

Sara formulated in her mind some of the issues her husband would discuss with the Saudi commanders. Would the United States provide military or intelligence assistance? How would that play with the terrorists in Iraq? How would it play if they didn't act? If the United States partnered with the already weakened Saudi king, might that more likely lead to his downfall, something that was a tremendous concern in the West? How would the Iranians react if they suspected the United States had aided the Saudi attacks on Iranian soil? Worse, how would they react if they perceived the Americans as too weak or hesitant to take action in a case that so clearly had national security considerations at stake?

Sara bounced the possibilities back and forth, grateful for the thousandth time that she didn't have her husband's job. It was a lose-lose proposition. Indeed, most of the issues he dealt with had little positive potential but were a bottomless pit when it came to the downside.

Which explained why he was so tired and on edge all the time.

She counted the months until the next election. A little more than a year. If the president wasn't reelected, something that seemed likely now, the new administration would reorganize the NSA staff and bring in their own team. Her husband would be reassigned. They would have to move on.

She approached the possibility with very strong and yet mixed emotions. Personally, nothing would make her happier. It would be such a *huge* relief. It would be like casting off irons; her family would be so much better off without the stress of Neil's job. But the president was such a good man, such an honest man, such a loyal and honorable leader, and the thought that the nation . . . her nation . . . might turn its back on him caused her such heartbreak she nearly cried at the thought. He had been so attacked, so smeared, so besmirched. From the day he had entered office it had been nothing but three years of brutal insults and personal assaults.

"HE HAS BETRAYED OUR NATION!"

"POWER IS ALL HE CARES ABOUT!"

The screaming opposition was more brutal and mean-spirited than anything she had ever seen in her life.

But Sara knew the landscape; after years of life in the military she knew her way around, and she wasn't fooled by the things that she read in the press.

Still, it was heartbreaking to watch. It actually cut her inside. Satan had stirred up so much opposition, so much mindless and visceral hate. He stirred the wicked to hate anything that was good, even those who had sacrificed so that they might be free. *"Dumb Jock Killed in Afghanistan,"* one of the opposition newspaper headlines had read in reporting the death of a well-known athlete who had volunteered for the war. Sara had printed the headline from the Internet and pasted it in her journal. As a sign of the times, nothing seemed to say more.

Hate and opposition. It was everywhere she looked. No reason. No logic. No well-considered arguments. Hate and opposition. It came from all sides. She considered the hostility she saw in many national leaders, then thought of the principles Mosiah and Alma had taught:

"The foundation of the destruction of this people is beginning to be laid by the unrighteousness of your leaders."

"Do your business by the voice of the people. And if the time comes that the people choose iniquity, then is the time that the judgments of God will come upon you; yea, this is the time when he will visit you with great destruction."

She knew it was true. She saw it every day. If the people willingly and knowingly chose corrupt and evil leaders, then they would pay.

But so would the innocent. They could not be spared, for they were in the same boat. If one group was punished, everyone paid the price.

Sara considered in silence, completely lost in her thoughts, until the sound of the clock ticking brought her back to the room. She looked at her husband, who was staring at her.

"Did you say something?" she asked him.

"Do you know where my security badge is?" he asked for the second time.

"You left it on the counter downstairs. I tucked it in the zippered pocket in your briefcase."

"Thanks," he answered quickly as he checked to make sure it was there.

Sara fluffed the two pillows and leaned back against the headboard. "So you're coordinating some operational issues with the Saudis?" she asked again.

Brighton nodded quickly but didn't offer more, and she

didn't press. He always told her what he could, which wasn't much anymore, and she had grown used to his silence about the things he was involved with at work.

She shivered lightly and pulled her arms close to her body. A cold front had moved through, and a fall chill filled the air. The house was quiet around them. Luke and Ammon had gotten up early again and were already gone.

"I think something happened while the boys were rock climbing yesterday," Sara said as she watched her husband pack.

Brighton paused. "What do you mean?" he asked as he counted his socks.

"I don't know," she answered. "Luke's arms were all scratched to pieces. I asked him about it and he just seemed . . . I don't know, a little overly anxious to explain. Then both of them were way too quiet. I have no doubt in my mind they weren't telling me something."

Brighton watched, interested. "No missing limbs?" he asked.

"Not that I could see."

"No contusions. No concussions or brain matter exposed?"

Sara winced and grimaced. "No. And yuck! Do you have to be so graphic? These are our sons we're talking about, and I worry about them. They do crazy things. There's way too much testosterone roaming around here!"

"I know," Brighton smiled. "I can't figure it out."

She looked at his smile. As if he had no idea where they got it.

"It was a strange day altogether," she continued.

"How's that?" Brighton asked.

Sara hesitated. "Well, first there was this thing with Luke and Ammon. But then, you know the Burkoughs at the end of the block?"

Brighton hesitated. He didn't know his neighbors well. "He works for State?" he asked.

"No. Other side of the street. Young black family. He's an associate in one of the law firms on D Street."

"Okay. I know who you mean."

"Great family. I like her a lot. She works for the Red Cross."

"Yeah . . ." Brighton answered absently. The comings and goings of his neighborhood would never be of much interest to him.

"They have two daughters," Sara continued. "The oldest girl, I think she's seven, she put her hand in a nest of black widow spiders yesterday. It gives me the willies just thinking of it. She was bitten at least six times, I was told. She's in the hospital. They think she will make it, but she is a *very* sick little girl."

Brighton's eyes narrowed. "You're kidding!" he stammered.

Sara only nodded.

"A nest of black widows! I've never heard of such a thing. They are predatory insects—they don't nest together; they eat each other, I thought."

Sara shivered and looked around their room as if she expected to see spiders crawling up the walls. "I don't know, Neil, I don't know. But she isn't the only one who was bitten. A couple of kids at the school have been bitten too. They say it's the warm winters we've been having. Warm winters, no snow or freezing temperatures to kill the spiders like the normal winters would. I was listening to the radio. They said there's an infestation of black widows that reaches throughout the South." She shivered again. "I want to get our house sprayed," she said.

"Do it," Neil said. "Call the exterminators first thing this morning."

"I already did. They are swamped. Can't be here for three weeks."

"Three weeks!" Neil replied in surprise. "You're kidding."

"No, honey. I wish I was." She looked around the room again and pulled the blanket up. "Yuck again. A ball of black widow spiders! I tell you, I'm not going down to the basement until the exterminators come."

"Have you seen any spiders?"

"No. But I haven't been looking until the past couple of days."

Brighton thought. "Okay," he said. "Stay out of the basement. And keep your eyes peeled anytime you're outside or in the garage. This is an old house; there are too many dark places for them to hide. And be careful in the garden. Check your shoes and gloves. I'll spray the house and yard first thing when I get back. That will get us through until the exterminators come."

Sara nodded. "Okay. I'll be careful. But the first time I see a ball of black spiders rolling toward me, you'll find me somewhere in Maine where the winters are co-o-old."

Brighton smiled and reached down to kiss her cheek. "It's a really nasty thought, isn't it? It would give anyone the creeps."

He checked his watch. His flight, a C-21 military executive jet, was scheduled to take off from Andrews Air Force Base a little after 7:00 A.M. He had a pile of work he would complete as they crossed the Atlantic Ocean; then they would stop and refuel in Germany before heading to Arabia, where he would arrive early the next morning. "Got to go, babe," he said as he stood from the bed.

"All right, General Brighton. Have a good trip, SIR!" she teased as she pretended to salute.

Brighton looked through the open doorway to the twin's room down the hall. "Where are the boys?" he asked.

"I don't know, something at school. Intramural football practice, I think. But they both told me to give you a good-bye kiss for them."

"Cool. I like it when you kiss me. No offense intended to the guys."

Sara smiled and stood up, put her arms around his neck and kissed his forehead wetly. "That's for Luke," she said, then kissed his right cheek. "And this one's for Ammon."

Brighton grinned in pleasure. Puckering his lips, he closed his eyes. "And from you?" he asked expectantly.

Sara looked at his closed eyes, then took his hand and shook it. "That's from me," she said.

He smiled and pushed her back, making her fall on the bed. "I don't think so," he laughed as he tickled her bare feet.

She giggled, then sat up and kissed him good-bye. Before she let him go, she looked at him for a long time, holding his face with her hands as she stared into his eyes. She looked at him like this every time he went away and had done so since his first combat deployment during the Persian Gulf war.

"Couple of days, right?" she asked him.

"Five days. Three in Saudi, a couple of days en route," he replied.

"I always miss you."

"You know I miss you too."

She took a step back and let her arms fall to her side. "You're going to see Crown Prince Saud bin Faysal?" she asked.

"Yes, we're going to get together after my other meetings."

"Where are you meeting?"

"At one of his palaces in Riyadh."

Sara looked worried. She knew something was up. The crown prince didn't call in the middle of the night just to set up a time to get together for a chat. She studied her husband. "He's a good man," she said. "But I think he's in trouble."

"The entire kingdom's in trouble. Everyone's in trouble. It's the times we live in."

"Yes, I understand that. But he is particularly vulnerable. And he is a good friend."

Brighton nodded quietly.

"Now listen, you be sure to thank him for that . . ." Sara hesitated. "What *do* we call that thing he gave us, anyway?"

"Geez, I don't know. What do you call a $300,000 decoration that hangs on the wall?"

"Whatever it is, you thank him, Neil Brighton! Don't forget. Even if we didn't get to keep it, you still have to thank him. You have a tendency to forget these kind of things, but you've got to remember, okay?"

Brighton flipped his Palm open. "Got it written here," he said.

Sara chewed on her lip. "Tell Prince Saud I send my regards. Tell him I love him. Tell him to be strong."

Brighton only nodded, then reached for his black bag. Lifting the strap over his shoulder, he turned to face her again. "Sam's in Germany, you know. His unit has two weeks' recuperation time."

"Yes. I'm so relieved to have him out of Afghanistan for a while!" she answered, then looked at Neil hopefully. "Maybe you could see him while you're over there," she said.

Brighton shook his head. "Don't think so," he answered. "Very tight schedule."

"He's staying not far from Ramstein." Her voice was hopeful, almost pleading.

Brighton put his bags down and looked at her. "I'm only

in Germany for a few minutes. I won't even get off the airplane except to stretch my legs."

"But it's your flight. You're the boss. They will do what you want to."

"Yes, Sara, I understand that, and believe me, I tried, but I have meetings scheduled every minute I'm gone. We haven't given ourselves any dead time; it's over and back, sleeping on the aircraft, eating sandwiches for lunch. I wish I could see him, but I just won't have any time. Next trip, I promise. I will schedule a few days."

"But he won't be in Germany next time. He's only there two weeks. He'll be back in Afghanistan, or Pakistan, or one of those other '-istans.' This is your only chance to see him. Don't you even have a few hours?"

Brighton hesitated, then shrugged. "I'll try again," he said weakly.

But Sara knew that he wouldn't have time. Her husband's schedule was completely outside of his control; every day, every moment was controlled by his staff.

She walked to him and put her hands around his neck again. "Will you please try? If you have even a moment, will you please try to see him? He needs you. He needs us. Will you please try to see him if you can?"

Brighton took her hands. "I promise," he said.

Sara dropped her eyes to the floor. "I really miss him," she muttered. "I wish I understood. I really just wish I understood what he was thinking."

"He's happy. He's doing his duty. God, Duty, and Honor. We can be proud."

"We are proud! But that's not the point. Why has he withdrawn from us? Why has he made it so hard?"

Brighton shook his head.

He had asked the same questions at least a thousand times himself.

The two stood in silence a moment. "Got to go," he finally said, not anxious to talk about Sam anymore. Turning, he walked toward the door.

"Hey, Neil," Sara called to him, and he slowly turned around. "Can I remind you of something, babe?" He nodded his head. "What is the purpose of life?" she asked him.

He paused as he thought. "To return back to God."

"That's right, babe, that's right. That's what this is all about—to return back to God and take our family with us. That's all you can do, Neil, but it is enough. You might not be able to save the world, though sometimes you think you can. There are things you can do, and lessons you must learn, but you might not be able to stop what is coming, not like you might hope anyway. You might not save our country; they have to save themselves. Sometimes you forget that. And you carry more of a burden than I think you should.

"So just remember your purpose. Find your way back to God. Anything else is just gravy. Try not to sweat things too much. It isn't healthy, general, and you're getting too old."

Brighton stared at her, then smiled and walked out the door.

chapter eighteen

Two hours later Major General Neil Brighton was sitting comfortably aboard a military C-21. The aircraft was quiet. Two men sat behind him, members of his staff, each of them immersed in their work. The narrow aircraft was configured for VIPs, so the men reclined comfortably on the large leather chairs, except for Colonel "Dagger" Hansen, his closest friend and personal aide, who had stretched out on the floor. While Dagger was being held prisoner during the first Gulf War, an Iraqi soldier had broken a vertebra in his back, which had never quite healed, and his back, as always, was now causing him pain. A single bodyguard (senior military officers never traveled overseas without a security detail anymore) was asleep in the back of the cabin. Brighton lifted his head from another top-secret report that demanded his signature and turned in his seat to watch the hazy ocean below him as the aircraft flew east, following the same route, more or less, between Europe and the Americas that had been traveled for more than six hundred years: up the coast to Nova Scotia, then across the northern Atlantic, before dropping down to pass over the United Kingdom and the English Channel.

As he stared out his window, he was thinking of Sam and how he had come into their lives almost eight years before.

* * *

Brighton and his family were living in southern Virginia, where he was an F-15 squadron commander at the First Fighter Wing.

The phone call came late one afternoon. "Brother Brighton," the bishop's voice boomed through the phone. Their bishop was a large and direct man, a man who pulled none of his punches, and he had a powerful voice that matched his huge hands and big heart.

"Bishop, if this is about those tithing checks that keep bouncing . . ." Brighton teased as he answered the phone.

"Nope. Not this time, buddy."

"I did my home teaching for the year."

"Yeah, well, ah . . . actually, Brother Brighton, we try to home teach every month."

"Every month! Wow, you're kidding. Why wasn't I told?"

The bishop laughed. As if Neil Brighton wasn't one of the rocks of his ward!

Brighton waited, but the bishop was quiet. Finally Brighton asked, "What can I do for you?"

"Got a little problem, Neil, and I need your help."

"What's up?" Brighton asked, already preparing himself.

"Got a boy I was hoping we could send over to spend a few days with you."

Brighton had no idea what the bishop was talking about. "You've got a what?" he asked in surprise.

"The Hendersons have a foster child living with them. Good kid. A great kid, but he's had a real lousy start. Abusive home. Alcoholic father. Mother hardly ever around. He's been with the Hendersons for a couple of days and, I don't know, . . . it just seems they haven't hit it off like everyone hoped they would."

Brighton's chest tightened. "What has he done? Threatened them. Tried to burn down their home?"

The bishop chuckled, his laugh as powerful as his voice. "Nope, nothing like that; I promise. Like I said, he's not a bad kid, never been in trouble in his life. He's okay at the Hendersons, but it just doesn't *feel* right, if you know what I mean. As I've been working with them, I've had a clear impression. Now you might think that I'm crazy, but I've come to the conclusion there's been a terrible mistake. This kid should be in your home. I think that's what the Lord intended all along; he just had to take a detour to get there. Now what do you say?"

Brighton shook his head. "Look, Bishop. This isn't a stray puppy you're asking me to take in. We've never even considered . . ." He was stammering now. "We're not foster parents. We're not prepared."

"Life is full of surprises. And are we ever really prepared?"

"But, Bishop," Brighton floundered.

The bishop was quiet. Brighton shifted uncomfortably from one foot to the other. Inside, his gut tightened and his heart skipped a beat. But something the bishop said seemed to roll through his head.

"There's been a terrible mistake. This kid should be in your home."

The sound of the bishop's quiet breathing filled the silence on the phone. "Brother Brighton," he said, his voice softening, "do me a favor. I've got to find this kid a place to stay. Will you consider it? Just for a few days? That's all I'm asking. Just a few days, okay?"

Brighton heard the bishop talking, but his voice seemed a long way away. The words rolled in his mind again, and he felt a shiver of light: *"There's been a terrible mistake. This kid should be in your home."*

Another long moment of silence. "How old is he?" Brighton then asked.

"Thirteen. A couple of years older than your boys."

"He's a good kid?"

"He really is, Neil. The problem isn't him; it was the cards he was dealt. He's never been in trouble. He has a good heart. I've got a good feeling about him."

Brighton cleared his throat and shifted his weight again. "I'd have to talk to Sara."

"Of course. Of course. And it's just for a few days. Meanwhile, we'll keep working with LDS Social Services to find him a permanent home."

"Okay," Brighton answered. "Let me talk to Sara; then I'll call you back."

"Great, Neil, thanks. If we could, we'd like to bring him over tonight."

"Tonight," Brighton answered. "That's kind of quick, don't you think."

"The Lord works in mysterious ways, doesn't he, Neil. Now go talk to Sara; and then give me a call. I'll talk to you later. . . ."

"Hey, wait," Brighton stopped him. "What is his name?"

"Samuel Porter Casey. But he goes by Sam."

* * *

The little boy stood in the doorway, clearly as hostile as he was terrified. He was thirteen, but small framed, and he could have passed for ten. He was grim and firm-faced, with the demeanor of a boxer, someone who had fought his way through life. Sara knelt down beside him. "Hi, Sam," she said.

"Where do you want me to stay?" he answered curtly, while grasping a small suitcase in his left hand.

Sara stole a quick glimpse at her husband. "We've got a room upstairs for you," she answered.

"Should I leave my bag here or take it upstairs with me?"

Sara hesitated, understanding his subtle point. "Don't you want to unpack?" she asked him.

"Won't be here that long."

"You could still unpack your things and make yourself comfortable."

"It's hard to be comfortable in someone's else's home."

Sara straightened herself and reached for his hand. Sam didn't take it and kept his eyes on the floor.

Brighton studied him from the foot of the stairs. He saw the bruised cheekbones and the cigarette burns on the back of his hands. Inside, he boiled. Who could do this to him? He knelt down beside Sam and took the suitcase from him. "Come on, Sam. I'll show you around. We've got a swimming pool in the backyard. Do you like to swim?"

The young boy's eyes widened in fear and he pulled back instantly, pressing against the wall. "I can't swim," he said. "Please don't make me get in the pool!"

Neil shook his head quickly. "We won't! We won't! If you don't like swimming, that's okay. You don't have to do anything you don't want to do."

The young boy continued to cower, his face tight with fear. Sara bent down beside him and took both of his hands. "Listen to me, Sam. We're glad that you're here. It's a pleasure to have you. We have two sons upstairs. They are eager to meet you. We want you to feel at home."

He looked at her defiantly. "My dad beats me at home. Are you going to beat me too?"

Sara saw through the manipulation and didn't react. She already understood him better than anyone else in the world. "No, Sam," she said softly, "we're not going to beat you, and you know that. That's not the way this thing works. That's not the way we do things around here."

She took his hand and held it; he pulled back again, but she held to him firmly as she led him up the stairs.

* * *

Later that night, Sara and Neil stood by the kitchen sink and talked in quiet voices. "He's a cute kid," Neil said as he sipped a cup of hot chocolate.

Sara merely nodded as she stared out the window, seeing her reflection in the darkness outside. "What did the bishop say when he called you?" she asked, her voice and eyes far away, absorbed in her thoughts.

Neil grunted. "Not much. Said he needed our help for a day or two. Said the Hendersons were having problems. It doesn't feel right to them, I think that was how he described it."

Sara listened intently. "Isn't that strange. The Hendersons are great people. Hardly flaky. Certainly not naïve. They are so dedicated to the children they bring into their home. And Sam didn't give them problems. What do you think it means?"

Brighton hunched his shoulders. Truth was, he hadn't had time to think about it. Truth was, he didn't think it meant anything, at least not yet.

But Sara saw it differently; that was clear from her face. "He's supposed to be here," she whispered, more to herself than to him. "I feel it. There is something going on. This is a pivotal event. It will change all of our lives, and I'm not prepared. But I'm as certain of this as I have been of anything in my life. Samuel was *sent* here. We have to try to keep him. I know that in my soul."

Neil stared at her a long moment. "Are you certain?" he whispered.

Sara nodded, her eyes clear, her face intent with conviction. "I know it," she told him. "And you will know it too. Until then, you must trust me. We *have* to make this work."

Brighton stared at his mug, slowly shaking his head. "I know we do," he told her. "And the bishop knows it too."

* * *

It didn't come easy. A kid, even a basically good kid like Sam, couldn't have been raised the way he was and not carry a boatload of baggage with him as he grew up. There were long hours in counseling, long hours at school, long hours in the bedroom listening to Sam cry in his sleep, along with thousands of dollars in court costs and untold other bills. There was heartbreak and frustration and occasional hate-filled accusations from out of left field. The progress came slowly, but it certainly came, with milestones of progress achieved along the way. No more crying at night. No more tantrums of anger. Better health, better grades, more friends at school. More affection, more laughter, more smiles.

In time there were two turning points in Sam's life.

The first came when he had been with the Brightons for only eight months. He was still small and vulnerable and utterly confused about who he was or what he really wanted in life. He knew he didn't want his mother to leave him or his father to burn him with his cigarettes anymore, but little else was clear in his adolescent mind. He knew that he liked his foster family, but they were so . . . *good*, sometimes he felt like he would never add up or fit in.

It all came to a head one day after school. Church, homework, helping with the chores, showing respect to his foster parents, saving his money, and not playing football on Sunday afternoons—it all was too much. Sam decided he had had enough. One day he left, screaming to Sara, "I hate you!" as he slammed his way out of the house. He took off without packing, without taking anything but the shirt on his back and whatever money he had in his pockets.

Neil and Sara knew what it would be like for him to live on the street. They knew the dangers. They knew the sins. They searched for two days, along with the police, but he seemed to have melted into the underground of throwaway kids that hung out on dirty beaches and rundown boardwalks that lined Norfolk and Hampton.

Sam was gone for three days; then he showed up, unexpected, knocking at their front door. Sara stood there, her face pale, her cheeks stained from tears. Ammon and Luke stood behind her, holding their breath.

"I'm sorry," Sam told her as he stared at his feet. "I want to stay here. *Will you please let me come home?"*

Sara reached out to hold him, and he took a slow step toward her. Luke and Ammon rushed forward and slapped him on the back. "Hey, Sam," Ammon said as Sam turned toward him, "leave us again and I'll kill you. I will hunt you down and drag you kicking and screaming back home. Brothers don't leave each other. And we are brothers now."

Sam smiled, his lip trembling, then wiped his hand across his red eyes.

This *was* his family. He really was home.

* * *

The second pivotal event occurred when Sam was sixteen years old.

He had been living with the Brightons for most of three years. Because his runaway mother had refused to consent to termination of her parental rights (she would lose food-stamp money and state subsistence if she formally let him go), and though his old man didn't care a whole lot one way or the other, the juvenile courts had directed that Sam spend one weekend a month with his parents. His dad, a former high school football star who still hung out at the ball games on Friday nights and a sometime charter fisherman who rented his cruiser for fifty bucks an hour (forty if the client was willing to furnish the beer), lived in a ramshackle clapboard house near the fishing docks in a small town called Poquoson at the mouth of the Chesapeake Bay. Sam's mom, a good-looking blonde who was just thirty-three, lived wherever she wanted from one month to the next, wherever the party was, wherever a new friend could be found.

One court-appointed weekend Sam was at the old house. It was a hot fall afternoon with a strong wind from the south blowing blustery and dry. He and his dad were in the backyard patching the fiberglass hull of the boat while his dad pounded down beers. Phyllis (as Sam had taken to calling his mom) hadn't been around for nearly four months. Last Sam had heard, she was out in Las Vegas dealing cards at some low-rent casino on the outskirts of town; at least, that's what she claimed she was doing. But Sam had his doubts, for the pock marks in her arms suggested a habit that was much more expensive than minimum wage and drunken tips could sustain.

His old man, Jody, cursed as he applied the liquid fiberglass sealant, then stuffed a burning cigarette into his mouth. He rubbed at his left arm, tracing a four-inch scar, the reminder of a vicious knife fight in some unknown bar.

"You had a birthday last week, didn't you?" the old man asked Sam.

Sam looked at him, surprised. It wasn't like Jody to remember such a thing.

"That makes you what . . . fifteen?" the old man asked.

"Sixteen actually."

"Hmm . . ." Jody thought, then took a step toward him and grabbed the bare bicep on his arm. "Not much there," he miffed at Sam's supple arm.

Sam looked at his bicep and frowned. His dad stood before him and spread his feet wide. He was a tall man, still solid, with thick arms and thick legs. And he was quick with his hands; Sam had seen it before—he could pick a fly out of the air or slap his mother so fast she never saw anything coming. As Sam watched his father, a sinking feeling welled up in his chest.

Jody stared at him blankly. "Can you take care of yourself?" he demanded in a sour voice.

Sam looked away before he answered, then quickly recognized his mistake. He turned back to his father and stared him in the eye, trying to hide any fear. "I do okay," he answered defiantly.

His dad snorted with doubt.

"I can't teach you a whole lot, boy, but I can teach you how to fight. And there's only one way to learn. Just like with swimming, you've got to jump into the pool. And not on the kiddie side—you need to jump in over your head. So I'm going to help you, Sammy. And one day you'll thank me for this."

Sam looked at his father, his eyes wide. The older man took a short step toward him, a shadow passing over his face. He was six inches taller and weighed at least a hundred pounds more. "You're going to need to know how to do this," he explained as he lifted his fist. "Now come on and get me!

There's only one way to learn. It's time to jump in, Sammy, and I ain't the kiddie pool."

Sam stumbled backward. "No, Dad!" he cried.

The old man moved forward. "You coward!" he sneered.

* * *

Jody beat his son so severely that he knocked him unconscious. Stepping over the crumpled body, he dragged him under a tree, then turned back to the boat and started slapping on paint.

Sam came to later that evening. He lay there a long time, trying to clear his head, then forced himself to his feet, washed his head from the hose, and stumbled into the house.

His dad eyed him warily, then slapped him on the back. "You'll learn," he said lightly. "You've got to keep your hands up to cover your face. And you've got to bulk up; you've got the muscle tone of a fly. I'm not asking that you be a jock like I was, heaven knows there's no hope of that, but I won't raise a kid who can't take care of himself. And I bloody sure won't have a son who is afraid of a fight."

A little more than a month later, his dad wanted to bare-hand box him again. "No!" Samuel whimpered. "I don't want to fight you anymore, Jody."

"Come on, boy. Be a man. You got to learn. At least you know I won't kill you, but the next man might. Come on, boy, and fight me. This is for your own good. I'm not raising a woman. I'm raising a man!"

"You're *not* raising me!" Samuel cried as he backed away from his dad.

Jody stopped. "Bloody straight I'm raising you, you snotty little puke," he shouted. "I am your old man! And don't you ever forget it! I don't care what the law says! I don't care if those white-shirted goons from the state came and took you from me. *I am* your father! *I* brought you into this world. I gave up everything just to have you, without anything in return. Now you can spend all the time you want with that goody-two-shoes family where you're living now, but you're still my son and you will learn to fight. This is a tough world—don't I know it—and a man's got to know how to deal with it. I owe you this, Sammy, so let's just get it done."

His father took a step toward him and lifted his fists.

"You don't owe me nothing," Sam said as he pushed his old man away.

"Do what I tell you. Get your hands up. Keep them high, near your face. Yeah, that's what I'm talking about! Now watch for the sucker punch!"

The fight was bloody and furious, a half-boxing, half-wrestling match with dust and blood and spit on the ground. Sam went home beat up and cut, though not as bad as before.

"Oh, Sammy, what happened!" Sara asked him, holding her hand to her mouth.

"Fell on the boat," Samuel lied as he held a rag to his split lip. Neither Sara nor Neil believed him, but he wouldn't say any more. They considered calling the authorities, but they knew Sam would never forgive them if they did, for he followed a code of silence when it came to his dad. And they also knew that Family Services wouldn't do anything if Sam refused to testify—he was now old enough that Family Services would be focusing instead on the many younger and more vulnerable children in their charge. So even though they were furious, they couldn't do anything.

That night as Sam lay on his bed, his entire body aching, his temples throbbing in pain, he made a decision. His old man wanted him to learn how to fight. Then that's what he would do.

The next day he spent every dime he had on a set of

free-weights and started pumping iron at least five times a week. He also started working out with the wrestling coach and running five miles every day.

Six weeks later, after his usual six-pack of beer, his old man took notice. "See there, boy, I helped you already," he said as he thumped Sam on the chest. "Feel that," he sneered. "The kid is building a six-pack of his own. Well, let's see what he's got now." Jody peeled off his T-shirt, flexed his biceps, then dropped the shirt on the ground.

Sam held his ground, his eyes firm and unafraid. "I don't want to fight you anymore, Jody. You made your point. I've learned this lesson from you."

His dad didn't back off. "Who knows if you've learned anything? You ain't proved nothing yet!"

"Stand back, Jody. We don't have to do this, okay?"

His old man took another step forward and spit on the ground.

The fight only lasted eight seconds. Three hits: a right to the midsection, just above the kidneys, a left to the jaw that broke a back tooth, then a right to the eyebrow that sent his old man's brain rattling in his skull like jelly. *Pow, pow, pow,* it was over and his old man went down like a sack of worn bricks. He lay there, his eyes open, his jaw moving up and down like a fish sucking water. Sam went to the hose and turned it on to soak his old man.

"You satisfied, Jody?" he asked as his old man shook his wet head.

His old man nodded, his eyes unfocused, his breathing coming in grunts.

"Have I passed your stupid little test, then?"

The old man grunted again.

Sam leaned down to face him, looking into his bleary eyes. "Then let me tell you something, Jody. You touch me again, and I'll kill you! You understand that? I don't want to fight you. I don't want to fight anymore. But you come after me again, and you won't wake up in this world. And the same goes for Momma. You touch her again, and I'll find you. So grow up, old man."

Sam threw the hose down and walked away. He left his dad sputtering and never looked back again.

That night he locked himself in his room, refusing to speak to anyone. He ignored Sara's gentle knocks on the door as he cried in his pillow.

He knew it was time to start over. Really start over. Forget the old man and old lady. It was time to move on.

He had a chance at another life, a chance to do something more. He had a chance to be *normal.* A chance to make something of his life, a chance to do something besides what his parents did: drink beer and watch football and look for a party or the next sleazy lover who could pay a few bills.

From that day forward he quit thinking of his biological parents as his mom and dad. Sara and Neil were his parents, the only true parents he would ever have; they deserved the honor of being called Mom and Dad. He loved them with a depth of emotion that could be born only in despair, a depth of loyalty that came from a man who had been thrown a lifesaver in a sea of loneliness and fear. And he knew that they loved him. Why? He didn't know. He didn't have any idea. It was a great mystery, something he would never understand, but they really did love him; they weren't just saying the words. And they had saved him from a life of constant bitterness and self-inflicted wounds.

And it was almost a year before he saw Jody or Phyllis again.

* * *

Samuel continued to work out every day. He grew strong and fast. And he also grew smart. His senior year of high school, he went from a struggling C and B student to make almost straight As. He also tried out for football and became a star running back.

"I'm too much like my real dad," he once said to Sara as they sat at the kitchen counter after one of his football games.

She looked at him for a long time. "Who *is* your real dad?" she asked.

Sam looked away guiltily. "I'm sorry," he said. "What I meant was my biological father. I saw him tonight at the game. He used to play football too. I'm too much like him."

Sara kept her eyes on him. "That's not what I meant, Sam. Who is your *real* dad?"

Sam stared a long moment. "Is He really my father?" he wondered. His voice was pained and wounded. "Is there really a God?" He stared at his tight hands.

Sara's eyes softened. "I know there is, Sammy," she answered. "I know that He loves you. And I know that He's proud. You were given a bad deal, Sammy; there's no way around that. There isn't any more I can say. There's no better way to explain. But I really think that what matters is not the hand we've been dealt, but what we do with our cards. We have to play the best game, play the best way we know how. And that's what you've done, Sammy. And I know your real father is proud."

Sam looked at her and smiled.

But Sara could see.

He still didn't get it. He had grown so much, he had come so far. But he still didn't get it. He didn't see the big picture, at least not yet.

* * *

After his senior year in high school, Sam and Jody seemed to patch things up a bit. He started hanging out at the old home on the weekends every once in awhile, though he rarely spoke with Neil and Sara about the visits. He was embarrassed for Jody and Phyllis. They shamed him. They had beaten him. They had treated their dog better than they had treated him. But somehow he had forgiven them—at least that's how it appeared—and he even seemed anxious to have some kind of relationship with them.

The spring before Samuel graduated from high school, his mom came back from Vegas and took a few baby steps to clean up her life. She and Jody got back together, and though they still enjoyed an occasional rip-roaring fight that would scare half the fish in Chesapeake Bay, they settled down in the old house on the bay and took to the slow life. They expanded their business, taking it seriously for the first time. She drove the boat. Jody ran tackle and cleaned the client's fish. Both of them attended Sam's high school graduation. They even gave him a present—a hundred dollars cash and a pair of black-leather Italian dress shoes. Sam held them up, the soft leather shining in the afternoon sun, then looked at Jody. "You're going somewhere," his old man explained. "You're going to be successful. You're going to be someone someday. So you need to dress right. And a good look starts with the right shoes."

Sam smiled at him. It was one of the happiest moments of his life.

chapter nineteen

General Brighton smiled as he remembered the early days and progress of his adopted son, thinking of the words that Sara had said that first night in the kitchen as they talked in low voices by the sink. *"He's supposed to be here."* He remembered her words perfectly. And of course she was right. He had known as well as she did that it was supposed to be.

As the aircraft flew east, he stared absently out the aircraft window, still lost in his thoughts.

Sam stayed with the Brightons for six weeks after graduating from high school. It was a trying time, a period of discontent and frustration, and he spent much of his time wandering around the house, reading in his bedroom or puttering in the garden. Although he had always loved working the dirt, feeling the earth and making things grow, even this seemed to cause him frustration, and he frequently commented on how he was planting new seeds that he would never see grow to maturity. Neil and Sara didn't push him, knowing Sam was anything but lazy—he just needed some time to sort out a plan. They recognized his uncertainty and left him alone, confident he would eventually figure it out.

Sara walked into his bedroom one afternoon to see him standing in front of his mirror wearing one of Neil's Sunday suits, the patent leather shoes Jody had given him shining under the loose cuff of the pants. He filled out the suit nicely, although the legs were too long. He turned from side to side, looking at himself in the mirror as Sara watched him with pride. "Wow, you look great," she said as he pulled on the tie. "There is something about a suit," she continued. "Yeah. Wow. You really look good."

He looked a second longer, then shook his head. "I don't think so, Mom. It feels too tight."

Sara walked to him and tugged on the shoulders. "Oh no, it looks great," she said. "It fits you just right."

He looked at her and smiled. "That's not what I meant," he answered. "But thanks anyway." He disappeared into his closet, took the suit off, hung it up, then pulled on some old clothes and disappeared to the garden.

* * *

Though Sam had joined the Church when he was fifteen, Neil suspected he may have done it more out of respect for him and Sara than out of any real conviction within. And when it came time to consider a mission, the real struggle began.

"Can I talk to you, Dad?" Sam asked him one night.

Neil put down his work and moved away from his desk.

"I'm in trouble," Sam said, his face pale and tense.

"What's going on, Sam?" his father asked, his mind starting to race.

"I'm in trouble," Sam repeated as he took a deep breath. He held the air, then released it and seemed to deflate. "Let me ask you something," he said in a tired voice. "When it comes to life . . . to religion. . . . How do you know what is true? I mean how do you *really* know? What is it that makes you believe?"

Brighton thought a long moment. "I don't know, Sam. There's just something about it. It all fits together. It all makes too much sense. But I guess in the final analysis, I know what is true because of how it makes me *feel.* By their fruits ye shall know them, and I know this fruit now. It is good, it is real, and it brings happiness."

Sam looked away, disappointed. He needed much more.

The two men were silent until Sam finally said, "I just can't do it, Dad."

"Do what?" Brighton asked, though he already knew.

"You and mom were asking me about a mission . . ."

Brighton felt his heart quicken, but he didn't respond. Sam shot a quick look to his father, hoping to measure his reaction, but his father kept his face passive and he didn't reply.

"I wish I could," Sam continued, his voice pleading and tight. He stared at his father, looking him straight in the eye. He wasn't being flippant. This was something he had considered for a very long time. And he wasn't being rebellious. He was just saying how he felt. "If there was any way . . ." he continued, "any way at all I could go on a mission, you know I would. But I just don't know the same things you do. And I can't go out there and fake it; you know I can't. That's not the way I operate. That's just not who I am.

"But I love you, Dad. You know I do. I respect you and admire all the things you believe. And in my head, I agree. I look at the evidence, and I think you have to be right. It is the only thing that makes sense. If there is a god out there, then *surely* this is his church. But I don't know that he's out there. I want to believe, but there's nothing in here." Sam touched his chest. "And until it is here, I can't go out and tell others that I know it is true. Do you understand what I'm saying? Dad, can you accept how I feel?"

Neil pressed his lips together and stared at the floor. His mouth went dry as he swallowed. He didn't know what to say.

"I'm sorry, Dad," Sam concluded. "I really am. I know how much this will disappoint you."

"What is it, Sam? What is it that you no longer believe?"

"Any of it. None of it. Is there a god? Is there a plan? Can we live together as a family? What about my real mom and dad? I don't know, but sometimes I wonder if this life isn't all there is. I just don't feel anything inside me that leads me to believe anymore. All the times I thought I felt the Spirit, I think it was just because I wanted it so badly, I wanted to please you and Mom, so I convinced myself it was real. I have prayed, but got nothing. There just isn't anything there."

"No, Sam," his father answered, his voice more firm now. "That isn't true and you know it. You know it inside. You have received answers many times in your life. You have felt the Spirit—I know you have—but that is not what you are looking for now. You aren't looking for answers; you are looking for reasons not to believe. You think you are asking God. But you're not asking, you're telling. You're demanding to know. You're looking up and saying, 'You *must* answer me, and you *must* answer me now! What you have told me before wasn't good enough and I demand to have more!'

"You're putting yourself above God, Sam. You want to be in charge, rather than submit to his will. But he is the God of the universe. He doesn't answer to you."

Neil paused. They were harsh words and he knew it, but they also were true. Sam looked away, his eyes lost. "He didn't answer me . . ." he muttered, his voice trailing off.

"He *will* answer you, Samuel, but he will test you first. He is testing you now, because he wants to know. Are you willing to trust him? Are you willing to remember the times he has told you before? Are you willing to take that lonely step into the dark, not knowing, not even believing, but still trusting somehow?"

Brighton fell silent, and Sam kept his face low. His father moved forward, sitting on the edge of his chair. "I can see it so clearly, Sam. I can see it as clearly as I see the sun or the moon. Lucifer is standing beside you, shaking his fist in your face. He is lying to you, Sam. 'Stop!' he's saying. 'Turn away! It can't be true. If there is a god, and he loves you, then why didn't he answer your prayers?' That's what he is saying. I can almost hear his words. He wants you so badly, and he knows he's *so* close. He knows who you are, Sam. He knows the good you are capable of accomplishing in this world. He tried to destroy you in the premortal world, and when you turned away he promised to come after you. Now he's here. And he wants you, just like he did before.

"And now you must choose. There isn't more I can say. We are reaching for you, Sam, and we will always love you, but know this, my son, once you have gone off this cliff, your life will never be the same again."

The room grew quiet and still, the mantel clock the only sound they could hear. Sam stared at his hands, then feet, then the floor. "I don't know, Dad," he answered. "I just don't know anymore."

"Then trust me, Sam," Brighton pled. "If you don't know yourself, then trust me for a while. *I know this is true.* There is no doubt in my mind. I have been through the fire. I had to be converted too."

Sam hesitated, and for an instant his father saw a child there: a thirteen-year-old boy, small, beaten by life, and unsure. He saw all the misery and anguish of the past years. But he couldn't change that. It was up to Sam now.

"I'm sorry," Sam muttered, his heart breaking inside. His lower lip quivered as he strained to control his emotions. "But I can't do it, Dad. Perhaps I'm a bad seed. Maybe I don't have it in me. Look at my old man and old lady, and I think we'd agree there's not a lot to be optimistic about. I want to be like you, but I'm just like my old man."

Neil felt his chest crunch. He remained speechless, his throat tight, his mouth dry as sand. The clock kept on ticking, though it seemed a long way away. He stared at Sam. Sam stared at him. "What are you going to do then?" he asked.

Sam locked his jaw. He had made his decision the night before. "My old man taught me to fight," he answered. "That's something I'm pretty good at. I guess that's what I'll do."

* * *

Six weeks later Sam left for army basic training. Twelve weeks after that, he graduated number one in his class. He was indeed a fighter, very good at his job. Upon graduation he was accepted to Rangers' training and once again finished at the top of his class. He was then assigned to the 101st Airborne and eventually sent to Afghanistan to fight the remnants of the Taliban and Al Qaeda.

Two years after joining the army, Sam received a hand-delivered invitation from his unit commander. He opened it anxiously. He had been waiting for months.

The invitation was short and direct. The Deltas were looking for a very few men. Did he want to apply?

Sam stared at the invitation, his eyes unbelieving. A shot of adrenaline ran through him, and he almost jumped in the air.

The Deltas were the *crème de la crème,* the absolute best—the most disciplined and highly trained soldiers anywhere in the world. The Deltas were so secret the army refused to even acknowledge they existed. Their specialty was Special Operations, or Special Ops—covert missions that were so controversial and dangerous that many of the team members had long hair and wore civilian clothes as they roamed around with CIA agents to the hellish spots of the world.

Fifty men would be admitted to Delta training. Three, maybe five would make it through.

Sam was one of the proud ones. His graduation from Delta proved to be one of the happiest days of his life.

Neil attended the low-key graduation, smiling proudly from his VIP seat. Sara wasn't allowed to attend, but it didn't matter, she would only have cried anyway.

And so it was that Sam had spent the better part of the last year crawling through the ghettos of Baghdad and creeping through the spider web of caves that lined the eastern Afghanistan border. His unit had only one mission: to hunt down and kill the enemies of the United States.

* * *

The C-21 jumped, and General Brighton was startled back to the present. He looked at his watch. Almost two hours had passed. He had been completely lost in thought, thinking about his oldest son.

The small aircraft cut through a thin layer of clouds, and the shining ocean below him suddenly came into view. The general stared out the window, watching the sun cast a long shadow over the calm sea, a sparkling trail of light that stretched east for a hundred miles or more. He sat forward in his seat and pulled a bottle of water from his armrest, then sat back again.

As he stared at the ocean, his mind drifted again. In quiet moments such as these, when there were no crises around him and he had a few minutes to think, his thoughts always drifted to Sam and what had happened to him.

Sam had been in the army for almost three years. For the first two of those years he had kept in regular contact with his family; he came home when he could and called frequently. But soon after joining the Deltas, something happened, and everything seemed to change. His trips home became much less frequent, and he didn't call as much anymore. And when he was home, it was strained. He was no longer comfortable.

Sam was not the same person. How many times had Neil and Sara lay in bed and wondered. They were losing their son, and they didn't know why. They had pleaded; they threatened; they tried everything they could think of, but nothing seemed to get through to him. He was cutting them off, drifting away to live a life by himself.

It didn't make sense. Not after all they had gone through together. There was simply no reason for him to drift away like he was. Something had changed him. What was going on?

Then, just six months ago, Brighton had read an eyes-only review from Sam's unit in Afghanistan, a top-secret inquiry into something that had gone terribly wrong. Brighton started asking some questions. Now he thought he understood.

War could be a vicious and terrible monster that often left a trail of victims in its bloody path. Some were guilty, some were innocent, and some were somewhere in between. Sam had been caught up in a terrible battle, maybe even made a mistake, and some of his soldiers had died when he had been in charge. But it was not his fault. After months of investigating, his father knew that was true.

Sam felt differently. And though Brighton had tried to talk to him about the incident he had refused to discuss it. "Let it go, Dad," he had hissed when Brighton had asked. "I can't talk about it. You know that. Just let it go!"

"Sam, it's not your fault!" Brighton had answered. "I've read the report . . ."

"You weren't there, Dad. You have no idea what happened. You have no idea at all what was or wasn't my fault."

It broke Sara's heart to see such a drastic change come over her son. And though Neil had never told her about the top-secret report, she had a pretty good idea. She had been around soldiers long enough to figure it out.

* * *

Brighton sipped at his water, then pulled out his Palm and checked his schedule once more. Evening arrival in Germany. Forty minutes to eat and refuel. Take off again. Three days in Saudi Arabia meeting with their senior air force staff and the crown prince. Another quick stop in Germany. Another quick sandwich while they refueled.

There was just no time to see Samuel. It wouldn't happen this trip.

He was deeply disappointed, for he knew that Sara was right. His son needed him. They needed to talk. And the irony didn't escape him. After months of being separated by almost ten thousand miles, here they were, in Germany at the same time, within a few miles of each other, and no time to get together. It was a bitter pill.

He sighed in frustration. For the hundredth time in a month he wished that he had more time.

chapter twenty

The C-21 touched down in Germany in the semi-darkness and taxied to the front of base operations, the blue and white airport lights glowing softly around it. A fresh flight crew was waiting, but the jet had to be refueled and serviced, so the general got off to stretch his long legs. At six feet, three inches, Brighton was on the upper limit of how tall a pilot could be—any taller, and the cockpit console would cut off his legs at the knees if he ever had to eject—and he was anxious to walk around and get some exercise while they were on the ground. His aides disappeared into the base operations building, and he walked around the jet while the maintenance troops did their work.

Ten minutes later, the crew chief jogged toward him. "Sir," he said, "we've got a little problem with your jet."

"What's up?" Brighton asked.

"I completed the through-flight inspection. Found a leak in the fuel pump on the number two engine. It's not bad, but beyond tolerances and we're going to have to change it, I'm afraid."

"How long will it take?" Brighton asked as he glanced at

his watch, realizing he had no idea what the local time was. It was dark, must be night, but that's about all he knew. At 43,000 feet and two hundred miles away to the west, the sun had gone down about thirty minutes before, but that didn't help him know what time it was there.

"I'm afraid it's going to take us a while, General Brighton," the maintenance sergeant apologized. "I'm sorry, sir, but we don't have another fuel pump in supply. We've been going through them like underwear—seems we change one every day. We got a bad batch of pumps in the last supply load, I guess, and we're going to have to cannibalize one off of our other jets."

"Okay. That's fine. Just tell me how long."

"Couple of hours, sir."

The general shook his head. "Two full hours!"

"Sorry, sir. But it beats the alternative."

"And what is the alternative?"

"Catching fire and exploding at forty thousand feet."

Brighton smiled. That it did. "All right," he said.

"I've already advised the pilots, sir. They say it's your call. Do you want us to fix it now so you can get underway or spend the night here and get a good start in the morning?"

"I've got appointments tomorrow in Saudi Arabia," Brighton answered as he did some quick math in his head. Two hours difference in time . . . five-hour flight . . . 07:30 brief with the military liaison from the CIA team . . . no way they could stay. They had to leave as soon as the fix was complete. "I need to leave ASAP, sergeant. Fix the jet quick as you can and get me out of here, okay?"

"Roger, sir. We will. I'll advise the pilots."

"Tell them to put a delay on your flight plan but keep it in the system so we are ready to go."

The sergeant saluted, then turned around and started moving toward base operations.

"Hey," Brighton called, "what's the local time, chief?"

The sergeant glanced at his watch. "Eight-fifteen, sir."

Brighton thought a moment. "Can you get me a car?" he asked.

"Can do, sir. I'll call the motor pool and have them send something over immediately."

The general raised a hand, indicating for him to stand by, then pulled out a cell phone. The sergeant stood a short distance away as Brighton placed a call to his communications staff in D.C. It took them less than a minute to track down his son and patch his call through.

"Sam!" Brighton said happily when his son answered the phone.

"Dad!" Samuel answered in surprise. "What's going on?"

"Have you eaten yet?" Brighton asked him.

"Ahh . . . no, not yet. What have you got in mind? You going to FedEx me some food?"

"How about I buy you dinner instead?"

"Dinner! No kidding! Where are you, Dad?"

"Here at the base ops at Ramstein. Got a problem with my jet. Will be delayed a couple of hours. Could we meet somewhere?"

"You're here in Germany?"

"Yes I am."

"Great! You name the place and I'll meet you!"

"Ever heard of Miss Lela's?"

"Are you kidding? Who hasn't heard of Miss Lela's?"

"How long will it take you to get there?"

"Give me a half hour."

"Okay, I can be there in ten minutes. I'll order us something and be looking for you."

"Great, Dad. I'm real excited to see you."

Brighton said good-bye and clicked off his phone, then turned toward the sergeant. "Okay," he said. "Get me that car. Tell them to hurry; I don't have much time. And when you go into ops, find my guys and tell them I'm going downtown for an hour or so."

The sergeant hesitated. "Do you want me to get them so they can escort you, sir?"

Brighton grunted. The higher the rank he achieved, the more he had to be baby-sat. "That's okay, sergeant," he answered. "I'm going to meet my son."

"Do you know your way around, sir? I'd be happy to get you a driver."

"No need, sergeant. I was assigned here for three years back in my flying days. I reckon I can still get around."

"Things have changed, General Brighton."

"I'll be fine, I'm sure."

"Really, sir, things are different than they used to be. It might not be a good idea for a two-star to be out and about on his own. Let me get your security man . . ."

Brighton shook his head. "I know he hates bratwurst. And I want to spend some time with my son."

The sergeant couldn't help but smile. "Bratwurst, eh? Are you talking Miss Lela's?"

"Oh yeah," Brighton smiled. "Famous all over the world. You know a good brat when you taste it—I can see that on your face."

"Miss Lela's has the best stinking bratwurst in all of Germany. It's almost worth flying over from the States just to eat there. And her potato bread and kraut . . . !"

Brighton gave a thumbs up. "Roger that. Now can you get me that car?"

The sergeant spoke into his radio. It took only a second to

get an answer for the general. "It's on the way, sir. But, sir, I've got to ask you, have you been to Miss Lela's in a while?"

"I don't know . . . it's a couple of years I guess."

"Then you might ought to be careful, General Brighton. Miss Lela's has changed. She has a pretty rough crowd. And most of them don't like us Yankees. So keep your head low; that's all I'm trying to say, sir."

"Got it," Brighton answered. "Now get me my car and get my airplane fixed. If you do a good job, I'll bring some potato bread and sausage back for you."

* * *

Brighton stood outside the famous Lela's bar and café, a small brick-and-mortar joint at the back of an alley off of Schandelberg Strausse. All through the Cold War, when there were more ex-pat Americans in Germany than anywhere else in the world, when the U.S. army was massed and ready to drive back the Russian hordes by defending the Foulda Gap with the sacrifice of their lives, before the Americans had started withdrawing their troops, a process that accelerated rapidly at the end of the first Gulf War, Miss Lela's had been one of the greatest cafés in all of central Germany. On any given night it was crammed to the walls, smoky and warm from the open pit grills, and bustling with U.S. soldiers and young German beauties looking for American husbands. Seven nights a week swinging jazz or Orleans blues could be heard wailing up from the basement bar, played by an old American blues band that had somehow ended up in Germany and now played for tips and free beer. General Brighton remembered going to Lela's frequently when he was a young fighter pilot attached to the F-15 wing at Ramstein. The food was wonderful and came heaped on huge plates, and for seven bucks

American, one could eat until he was ready to puke, struggle to the bathroom, and then come back for more.

But though General Brighton loved Miss Lela's for the food, there was another, more important reason he was so fond of the place—this was where he had first been introduced to the Church.

* * *

It was 1987 and the young Neil Brighton was on a serious roll. He had just pinned captain's bars on his shoulders and had been assigned to one of the rockingest fighter squadrons in all of Europe. The tension between East and West was at its climax, and President Reagan had just completed his trip to Berlin, where he had stood at the Brandenburg Gate and taunted the Russian leaders to "tear down this wall." Brighton and his fellow flyers enjoyed sky-high morale, and for the first time in his life he had a little time, a little money, and a great world to explore, a world his buddies back in West Texas would never know. Even better (a *whole* lot better), after two years of waiting for his remote assignment in Korea to end, he and Sara had just gotten married. They spent the Christmas holidays touring Europe, staying in cheap bed-and-breakfast joints, and riding the EuroRail to every out-of-the-way village they could get to in two weeks. Anyone who watched the young couple could see that they were madly in love—a serious, hurting kind of love, a lay-awake-and-talk-until-morning kind of love, an everyone-in-the-office-is-jealous-of-us kind of love.

Life was good. No, life was grand.

Then one day in January, Brighton and his flight commander had stopped by Miss Lela's for a long lunch, a stream of bad weather having cancelled their sorties for the day. They were just getting settled at their table when another member of their squadron walked into the café, followed by two young American kids.

The other pilot was a young lieutenant, and Brighton would later learn he was a member of the LDS Church. The lieutenant had found the missionaries riding their bikes through the rain and brought them to Miss Lela's to dry them off and get them something to eat. Brighton watched them a few minutes, then walked over to talk to his squadron mate, not having any idea who the two young Americans were. Abilene, Texas, didn't have many LDS missionaries wandering the streets, and the ranches and cotton farms on the prairie saw them even less, so the white shirts and ties weren't something he had seen before.

"What's up?" he asked as he approached his friend, curiously checking out the American kids.

"I'm Elder Bennion," the first missionary said as he stood up and extended his hand. "This is Elder Rasmussen. We're missionaries for the . . ."

Brighton cut him off. Missionaries, huh. That was all he needed to hear. Having not spent so much as an hour in church for going on almost ten years, he didn't want to be preached to and had no need for religion. Was there a god up there in the vast universe somewhere? He really didn't know. Had absolutely no clue. But he figured that no one else had the answers either, so he wasn't alone. And if he were serious about religion, he would start with a preacher, someone with a white collar and divinity Ph.D., certainly not these dripping wet kids from the States.

Brighton nodded quickly and offered a weak "Good to meet you," then turned away from the missionaries to talk to his flying mate. But the young elder didn't sit down. "You from the South?" he asked cheerfully to Brighton's back.

Brighton turned toward him again. "Southwest, actually. Texas. Go Cowboys."

"Oh, yeah. Texas is cool!"

"Ever been there?" Brighton asked.

"Nope. But it's still cool."

Brighton smiled, but didn't know how to respond. "Ahh . . . yes, it is," he offered weakly.

"How long you been in Germany?" the missionary asked.

"Couple of months. And you?"

"Almost two years."

"You like it?"

"Absolutely. Love it. Best two years of my life."

Brighton studied him a moment, then glanced down at the missionary's buddy, who had remained in his seat. He stared up with a puppy-like smile, overly anxious to please. The two looked like the Bobbsey twins: same goofy haircuts, faded white shirts, almost identical red ties, brown shoes, and polyester pants. "So are you guys really preachers?" Brighton couldn't help but ask.

"Not really. Like I said, we're missionaries."

"You go around preaching the word?"

"Well, yes. But not like you think. We go around talking to people . . ."

"How come you're not in Africa or India somewhere? Most of the Germans I know are already Christians."

"That's a great question, Captain Brighton, but it would take us a while to explain."

Brighton saw the trap. "That's okay, guys," he answered. "I wish you luck, though." He again turned away from the elders and back to his friend. "Aren't you and Crusty flying up to the range tonight?" he started to ask.

"Captain Brighton, are you married?" the missionary interrupted from behind him once more.

Brighton turned toward him. "Got married just a few weeks ago," he answered with obvious pride.

"Cool! Congratulations. Now do you want to know how you can live with your wife forever, even after you die?"

Brighton hesitated. "What do you mean?"

"I mean the way it is now, when you die, *BAM!* it's over. That's it. Think of your wedding vows. Till death do you part. But there's a better deal out there, if you want to know what it is."

The young Captain Brighton looked at the missionary with his mouth slightly open. He paused, thinking, and was about to dismiss him again when he felt such an overwhelming feeling, it was almost a voice. *"Listen! This will be your only chance!"* the voice seemed to whisper in his mind.

He was so taken aback he didn't know what to say. He stared at the missionary a long moment, and then cocked his head. "What are you talking about?" he wondered.

The missionary started talking, and Brighton ended up sitting down.

Four months later, after many long nights of study and prayer, after shocking his family with a phone call back to the States and being cursed by his father for leaving the faith (a faith that his father shared with his mouth but not his heart or his soul, and certainly not his wallet), Neil and his young wife Sara were baptized into the Church of Jesus Christ.

And since that spring day in Germany, their lives had never been the same.

* * *

General Brighton stared at the old brick building, hearing the noisy crowd and the music pounding through the small windows and old wooden door.

It all seemed so long ago. A different life. A different world. So much had changed since that rainy day long before.

He took a step forward and opened the door.

Entering Miss Lela's, Brighton summed up the crowd. The sergeant was right—it was a rough-looking group—and he was surprised not to be able to pick out any other Americans there. He listened to the voices, but heard no English being spoken as he made his way through the crowd and sat down at a tiny round table near the back of the café. He felt suddenly uncomfortable in his uniform, his dark pants and blue shirt with pilot wings on his chest. The café was smoky and warm, just like it had been in the past, but the music wasn't familiar. Instead of the blues, a loud and screaming band from the Netherlands cried from the back wall. What they lacked in talent they more than made up in volume, and Brighton almost wanted to cover his ears.

He ordered three house specials—two to eat in and one to take back to the crew chief—then sat back and waited for Sam.

Five minutes later, his adopted son walked through the door.

* * *

Samuel had put on weight, twenty pounds, all of it muscle in his shoulders and arms. His hair had grown thick and sun-bleached, and it hung in long bangs in his eyes and over his ears. And he was tan, almost dark, from the vicious Afghanistan sun. Brighton noted his goatee, which was so tightly trimmed it was barely a shadow of stubble. Dressed in dark jeans, a tan T-shirt, and thick leather hiking boots, he looked more like a European than an American standing there. And he certainly didn't look army. Brighton was a little surprised. He knew the Deltas often worked undercover, but as a traditional soldier he felt a little unsettled. He expected a GI Joe in a tight haircut and USA T-shirt. What he saw was a Hell's Angel who had just slipped off his Harley.

So these were the new warriors. Well, that was okay with him.

He stared a moment, proudly, then stood and waved to his son.

Sam picked him out and moved through the crowd toward his table. Brighton stood to embrace him, and they slapped each other on the back half a dozen times before they sat down. "Sam, it's good to see you!" Brighton said in delight.

"No kidding! This is great. How are you, Dad?"

"A little nervous, actually."

"Why's that?" Sam cocked his head.

"I was only scheduled for a forty-minute refueling stop at Ramstein," Brighton answered. "I didn't think I'd have time to get together with you, but your mother was so determined that I see you, I'm thinking she snuck onto base and sabotaged my aircraft before I took off. Now I'm wondering what else she might have done. Is my airplane safe anymore?"

Both of them laughed. "You know there's another possible explanation," Sam offered quickly as he leaned back in his chair. "She might have been praying. That's a more likely cause. I've never known anyone who has a more direct line to God. If she wanted you to break down at Ramstein, well, sorry, Dad, but you were condemned to have trouble here the moment she bowed her head."

"Yeah," Brighton laughed. "You got something there."

The two men stared at each other, one a proud father, the other a hesitant son. "You look good," Brighton offered, "but I've got to tell you, your appearance isn't what I have come to expect from a soldier."

Sam pushed his hair back. "Dad, you don't have to have

short hair to kill people. Welcome to the Deltas. This is how it is now."

Brighton pointed to the long hair and rough clothes. "They wouldn't let our air force boys get away with that," he answered.

"Your boys jet around like Space Rangers. They don't play down in the mud with the men."

"I guess not," Brighton smiled.

"And remember, Dad, we have to work with the locals. It helps us to blend in, which is a good thing."

Brighton nodded. He knew that. "Things in Afghanistan okay?" he asked.

"Doing good, doing good."

His father leaned toward him intently. "Really?" he asked.

"Well, Dad, I'm not really sure what you want me to say. It's a hole. Hot. Dusty. Too many idiots who hate the United States. Too many donkeys and not enough rain. The whole country smells like an outhouse on a hot summer day. Chiggers and sand fleas. What more do you want to know?"

Brighton shook his head. "I'm sorry," he said.

"Sorry! Are you kidding? I wouldn't have it any other way! I can't wait to get back there. We're really smacking heads. It's a miserable and lousy mission, and I love every second I'm there. We're killing more of our enemy than any other unit in the world. We're destroying a lot of those hoods who are bent on destroying the United States. That's what I'm fighting. So I'm not complaining. I'm just doing my job."

Brighton cracked a thin smile; there was a little bravado, he knew, in Sam's words. "You should have listened to me. You could have gone to the academy and learned to fly jets," he said.

"And miss getting shot at? Why would I ever do that?"

Brighton shrugged his shoulders. "What was I thinking?" he answered sarcastically.

"And remember, Dad," Sam continued, his emotion on the rise, "these guys don't just want to destroy us in some vague or ambiguous way. They want to kill us. To hurt us. To cause us any kind of pain. Give them a dull knife, and they'd happily cut off your head, all the time laughing while they hacked away. Give them a nuke and they'd take out D.C. in a heartbeat, smiling and laughing while counting a million people dead. And if anyone doesn't believe that then I think they're a fool. If they'd seen what I've seen, then they wouldn't have any doubt."

Brighton watched his son closely. "Hey, Sammy, you're preaching to the choir here."

Sam only nodded. Even in the darkness, his blue eyes burned bright. Brighton lifted his water and tilted it toward him. "I'm proud of you, Sam."

Sam lifted his Perrier. "Thank you, General," he said.

* * *

The five Germans watched them intently while sipping their ale. They were all in their thirties and had missed most of the U.S. glory days. More, they considered Miss Lela's a local joint, off limits to the riffraff from the States, and they thought that had been made abundantly clear by the old BUSH IS HITLER poster hanging near the front door. And if that didn't do it, the upside-down British flag over the bar seemed to make their feelings clear.

What was it about these guys? Were they entirely stupid? Or just trying to get under their skin?

Besides being angry at the world, the five men were also unemployed and drunk. And as they watched the tall U.S. officer and the local kid (some kind of traitor—probably selling secrets about the antiwar movement), they whispered and cursed at the strangers. Hissing among themselves, they quickly decided they hated Americans as much as they hated anything—and over the years they had come to hate a lot: their government, their ex-bosses, their lousy flats, and their wives.

"Look at him!" the largest German sneered. "Big shot American cowboy, just like Bush used to be. On his way to kill Iraqis. That's all they do is kill!"

His buddies shook their heads. The old boy was right. Stinking Americans. All cocky and proud.

"You remember Wolf?" one of them asked. The other men stared. "You know, Wolfgang Struttger, runs the printing service downtown. He married an American, some woman who got a divorce from her soldier when she got over here. Then she dumped ol' Wolf and took off with most of his cash. Cleaned him out completely, then made off with his son. He's never seen the kid, not even once since she left. She's back in the United States now, but he doesn't know where."

The other buddies swore. "Filthy, arrogant witch!"

They stared at each other and sipped miserably at their beer.

"He shouldn't be here," the largest man finally sneered to his friends. "This is *our* place. Our country. None of ***them*** should be here. They bring only death and destruction. They only care about war! They only fight when there's oil they want to get their hands on. They only fight when it suits them. And have you ever noticed, comrades, they always fight *against us.* Look at all the wars of the past hundred years. Did the United States ever help us? No! Never once. They claim they're our ally, but isn't it funny how we always find ourselves looking down the barrel of their guns?"

His buddies all mumbled, boiling even hotter with rage.

"Jew-loving *Amris!*" the leader hissed. "Arab-hating scum.

Closed-minded bigots and self-righteous crusaders is all they are. How many nations have they exploited and crushed through the years?"

The other men mumbled, content to hate from afar. But the big one, the fat one—he had had too many beers. "I'm going to get him!" he said, pushing himself to his feet. "I hate these stinking Americans, and it's time I let them know."

* * *

General Brighton and Sam were working hungrily through a heaping plate of sausage and sauerkraut when Brighton saw the men approach out of the corner of his eye. Four of them followed their leader, who was a large man, tall as he, but at least fifty pounds heavier. He had a dark beard and short hair, and he wore common work clothes. They all looked to be in their thirties, and for a second Brighton thought they were coming to talk to him about flying—back in the old days, it wasn't uncommon for the locals to want to talk about the air force or what it was like to live in the United States—but then he saw the angry looks on their faces and realized these men were not in a talking mood. These men wanted trouble. And they were coming for him.

"Heads up," he whispered to Sam as the five men approached.

Sam had already seen them, and he nodded imperceptibly. "I've been watching them," he answered.

Brighton put his glass down.

"This isn't going to look good," Sam whispered. "A general and his son cracking a bunch of local guys' heads."

Brighton shrugged his shoulders. "We're the ones who might take the cracking. We're outnumbered pretty bad."

"No prob, Dad," Sammy answered as he slowly pushed back his chair. "Just remember, strike to do damage. You've got to get them out of the fight. If the only thing you do is hurt them, then all you've done is tick them off."

Brighton glanced around quickly, wishing he had brought his bodyguard, not because he was scared, but it would have made it much easier to get out of the café without trouble. Though he had popped a head or two in his early days, and had been a pretty good boxer in college, he still swallowed tensely. General officers weren't supposed to get into fistfights with the locals, it was . . . *unbecoming* to their rank. And if the German press got wind of the trouble, they would have a field day. He could almost see the headlines. *"White House Military Officer Brawls in Local Bar."* His boss would freak out. And Sara would faint!

He cursed himself silently. How had he gotten into this mess? He shot a quick look to Sam. "You okay?" he asked.

Sam only nodded.

"If this gets ugly, stay together."

"I've got your six."

"Don't challenge them. Keep your head down, and maybe they'll leave us alone."

The five men drew near. Sam cut a hunk of greasy sausage with his fork and lifted it to his mouth. Keeping his head down was the last thing on his mind. A soldier *always* watched his enemy as they approached.

Brighton heard a deep growl from over his shoulder. *"Er sieht so hungrig aus. Er kommt sicherlich von dem töten vielen Irakishen Kindern zurück,"* the huge German mocked.

He struggled to translate, pulling the German words from way back in his mind. "Look at him, so hungry. He surely comes from the killing of many Iraqi children," the German had said.

The five men laughed as General Brighton looked up and smiled weakly, feigning ignorance.

The German shot a dark look at Sam as if to say "get out of here, boy," then turned back to Brighton, summing him up. "Big shot," he sneered in German to his friends. "Fancy stars on his shoulders, but not smart enough to learn German. Another ugly American soldier, that's all we have here."

Brighton turned away. All he wanted was a quiet dinner. He didn't have time for this. He felt his back tighten and his chest muscles grow taut, but he kept his head down and his eyes on his plate.

Sam looked up and smiled. "Hey guys," he said in English, "we're just having a quick bite to eat. We don't want any problems. Give us a few minutes, and we'll be out of here.

The thug nodded to his buddies, then reached out and tugged on Sam's hair. "You need a haircut," he sneered, leaning across the table to him. "I've got a knife in my pocket. Do you want me to cut it for you?"

Brighton leaned across the table, putting his arm between the fat man and Sam. Sam angrily shook the German off, pushing his hand away. Brighton stared at the strangers and nodded his head. Five against two. Hardly a fair fight. And they probably had weapons, which made it much more dangerous and far more difficult.

The German leaned across the table and stuck his fat fingers in Brighton's food. "Looks good," he snickered. "Don't mind if I do." He swirled his fingers through the meat juice then licked them and wiped his hand on Brighton's shirt.

His buddies laughed loudly, prodding him on. The German turned to Sam. "Why don't you leave?" he said. "This isn't about you. This is between this U.S. soldier and me and my buddies here."

Sam pushed himself away from the table and stood. "You got problems with Americans," he snorted in anger.

"Sit down," Brighton told him, then turned quickly to the

man. "We don't want any trouble . . ." he said softly, being careful not to give any excuse for offense.

Their leader bent toward him. "You're in Germany," he sneered, spit spraying on Brighton's face. "We don't speak English or wear cowboy boots here!"

"We were just leaving . . ."

The German stood in his way. "I said speak to me in *German,* or I'll cut out your lying tongue and shove it down your throat to your heart!"

"Get him!" his buddies taunted. "Take him out, Friedrich. You can do it!" they cried.

General Brighton breathed deeply as his eyes shot to Sam.

"You don't want to do this," he told the fat man.

"Yeah, pig, I do."

Brighton sighed again, and the German sneered. "No stomach for a fight, boy? You just want to kill babies. Is that all you do?"

The German shoved the American's shoulders, and Brighton caught a glimpse of the knife sheath underneath his oversized shirt. He shot a quick look to the others, wondering if they too were armed. The German poked a fat finger in his ear. "I'm talking to you, Pigdog," he shouted. *"Are you not hearing me?"*

"Walk away . . ." Brighton warned him.

"No way, *Amri,* not till I have some fun!" The German grabbed Brighton's shirt and cocked his fist back.

Brighton bolted to his feet, sending the small table crashing to the floor. He grabbed the German's wrist and twisted, almost breaking his hand, then swung him around and jerked his arm upward, and the huge man squealed in pain. His nearest buddy pulled a knife from his pocket and lurched toward Sam. Sam grabbed the metal fork from his plate and slashed it down on his arm. The man cried in agony as the fork penetrated to his bone, just below the shoulder, into the meat of his arm. It stuck from his bicep, and he dropped the knife to the floor. Sam kicked it aside and waited for the next assault. The other men hesitated, then rushed him as one. Sam stepped back and twisted, kicking his right foot high in the air. He smashed his boot into the leading man's throat and he fell back, grasping his shattered Adam's apple, sucking desperately for air. The third man grabbed Sam's hair and jerked his head back while another approached him with a small knife in his hand. Sam grabbed the German's arm and twisted, bringing all of his weight against the elbow while extending his hip and pushing down. There was a soft *crack* and a cry as the man stumbled backward, holding his broken arm.

Three down. Two left standing. It was all even now.

Brighton held the huge German and jammed his arm upward again until he felt the muscles in the man's shoulder begin to tear lose. The fat man screeched in pain, then pulled away violently, using his weight to try to knock Brighton to the side. Brighton moved with the German, using his momentum against him, then smashed his forearm across the man's face and forced his chin to one side until his neck almost snapped. Reaching under the German's shirt, he gripped his collarbone and held it, using it as a handle to force his forearm against the German's face. The fat man shrieked again, almost fainting, then fell suddenly still. Brighton knew it was too painful for the man to move, too painful to scream. He jerked the German's switchblade from his sheath, flipped it open, and tossed it in the air, then caught the handle again. Holding the knife loosely against the man's neck, he felt the German grow limp with fear.

There was only one other German left standing now. He froze, his buddies rolling on the floor around him crying from various sources of pain, then made a weak feint toward Sam before stopping again.

Brighton tugged on the fat one's collarbone and whispered in his ear. "Look what you've done to your buddies. Some of them got hurt. I think you should apologize!"

The huge man huffed in pain. "I'd die first, Pigdog."

"Your choice!" Brighton jerked on his arm and waved the knife in front of his eyes. The German cried in pain. "I'll kill you!" he screamed.

Brighton almost laughed. "Now what is there in this situation that would lead me to believe that!" he asked. "I mean, look at this, Friedrich! Help me understand."

Sam took a step toward his father. "Don't kill him!" he stammered, then quickly winked to his dad. "Don't kill this one, General. Just let him go."

Brighton felt the German's knees buckle, and he jerked his arm up again. He waved the knife around him. "But I haven't killed anyone this week," he shot back to Sam.

"But you're on your way to Iraq. You can kill someone there!"

"Oh, yeah," Brighton answered, and the German went limp again from the pain.

"Help me!" he coughed, but his uninjured buddy didn't move. He had seen quite enough and wanted no more of this mess. Sam took a quick step toward him and he cowered again.

"You think I'm a killer," Brighton hissed. "Should we find out if you're right?"

"Nein, nein!" the German cried, his eyes wide in pain.

"I just came here for a quiet dinner. Now is that too much to ask?"

The German groaned in agony. "Nein, sir, nein. That is not too much trouble. No, sir, not at all!"

Brighton swung his hand sideways, crashing the switchblade into the brick wall. The knife blade broke at the hilt and he dropped the handle on the floor. "Now perhaps we have an understanding," he said in a calm voice. "You don't want trouble. I don't want trouble. It seems we agree."

The German nodded eagerly. "I don't want any trouble, no, sir."

"Then I'll make you a deal. I'm going to let you go. Then you and your buddies are going to get out of here. I think your wives are calling. Is that what I hear?"

"Yes, sir, they're calling. It is time that I go."

Brighton relaxed his grip, and the German almost fell to the floor. He crawled away from the general. Brighton nodded to his waiter, who was standing wide-eyed by the bar. "How much do I owe you?" he asked.

"Nothing, buddy. Just get yourselves out of here."

Brighton stared at him, then nodded. He and Sam walked past the fallen Germans and through the front door.

They stood alone in the alley, and Sam looked back at the café. "That was interesting," he said simply.

Brighton stared back at Miss Lela's and shook his head sadly. "I shouldn't have done that," he whispered.

"Hey, Dad, let's get this thing straight," Sam said as he turned toward him. "We didn't ask for a fight. And that guy would have killed you if we had given him the chance. He was too drunk and too stupid. And they all were carrying knives. You didn't do anything wrong here. Those goons were looking to fight us before I even sat down."

Brighton looked ashamed, then turned quickly to Sam. "Not a word of this to Sara. She would die if she knew this. Not one word, right?"

Sam smiled and patted his shoulder. "No worries, mate."

Brighton watched him, then turned. "Let's get out of here before those goons call their friends."

Sam followed him to his car. "You know, Dad, that was pretty good work back there. If you ever decide you want to join the real army, I know a few people. It's a pretty tight club, but I think I could get you in."

"No, thanks," Brighton answered. "I'm getting too old for this."

"Apparently not," Sammy answered, glancing back at the café. "Not from what I saw back there."

"I just held my own. You did all the hard work."

Sam just shook his head.

"You've got to go now?" he asked his father.

Brighton glanced at his watch and nodded. "I was hoping we'd have more time to talk."

"Next time, I guess."

"Next time," Brighton answered.

The two men stood in silence. "When are you going back to Afghanistan?" Brighton asked as he unlocked his car.

"A couple of days, from what I'm hearing. By the end of the week."

Brighton looked at his son intently. "Be careful," he told him.

"Always, Dad."

The two men stared at each other; then Sammy stepped back and saluted. "General," he said.

Brighton braced himself and returned the salute. "Sergeant," he replied.

chapter twenty-one

A little more than five hours after taking off from Ramstein Air Force Base in Germany, Major General Brighton's C-21 lined up to land at Riyadh's civilian airport.

Sitting in the middle of the Arabian Peninsula, Riyadh is an exceptionally modern and beautiful city, with a stunning architectural mix of glass high-rise buildings and ancient desert mosques. The skyscrapers ascend like something out of a children's drawing book: sweeping arches, enormous space-saucer shaped coliseums, needle-nosed skyscrapers made of steel and glass, and glistening chrome buildings rising like two-forked prongs into the air. Desert browns, whites, and pastels are the dominant colors. Though the city is considered one of the modern wonders of the world, the traditional Arab influence is pervasive and can be seen everywhere in the arched doorways, dome-topped mosques, and caliph-inspired city centers. Enormous highways sweep through the city, the cement having been laid over the trails where Bedouin camels used to trek; though the only camels one would see in the city now would likely be in the back of a truck and on the way to the meat market. The side streets are tree-lined and well lit and swept every day to keep the blowing sands from the desert at bay.

The capital city of the kingdom, with a population of almost 5 million people, Riyadh got its name from an Arab word meaning *place of garden and trees.* Ancient wadis, now dry, run through the center of the city, and the surrounding soil is fertile and rich. Powerful electric motors pump fresh water from the deep underground aquifers to keep the man-made oasis green and desirable.

To the west and south of the city, the terrain rises gradually for four hundred miles until suddenly it juts upward at the rocky Midian Mountains. To the east, the terrain descends through the Summan, where the landscape gradually transforms from barren desert to rangelands to the fertile crescent that borders the Persian Gulf. A constant wind blows from the desert, and the flies seem to swarm when the nights cool down, especially when the date trees are in flower or bearing fruit. To the south lies the *Rub' el Khal*—the Empty Quarter—a land so bleak and brutal few humans have ever trekked across its sands, a land so desolate and miserable even the Saudis were more than happy to give most of it to Yemen and Oman.

Overhead, the sky is almost always a deep gray-blue, a huge open saucer sitting over the land, cloudless and so deep in color it seems as if one is looking at the edge of space. The air is clean and clear, and the lights from the city can be seen for hundreds of miles on a clear desert night. During the spring storms it can rain violently, and the sandstorms can be deadly if one is caught in the open; but 340 days a year the weather is monotonously predictable: hot and dry in December, searing the rest of the year.

* * *

Like the city of Riyadh, the entire kingdom of Saudi Arabia is a bewildering example of contradictions and extremes.

Much of the nation is an entirely inhospitable desert, yet the oases that dot the country are lush and wet and brimming with life. The cities are bright and beautiful and more contemporary than any in the world, but outside the cities the Bedouin nomads live much as they have for almost two thousand years. The royal family jets around the globe, meeting with Hollywood celebrities and foreign heads of state, headlining cultural conferences and human rights events, while the women in some localities are not even allowed to learn how to read. The Saudi infrastructure is modern and up-to-date in every way, but the kingdom still denies basic freedoms of expression and many human rights. The Qur'an teaches love and peace, emphasizing the need for discussion and the give-and-take of discourse, yet the kingdom allows no opposing political parties; indeed, there are no political parties in the kingdom at all—the royal family isn't a party, but a close-knit, manipulative, and fortified group of relatives who guard their family secrets above anything else.

It is as if the government straddles two ice flows that are moving apart, with one foot in the West and one foot in the desert, preaching progress and equality while many times denying both to its citizens. Any expression of antigovernment activity is unthinkable. Women cannot drive or even appear in public without a male family member as escort. Use of corporal punishment is the rule; beheadings, amputations, and lashings regularly take place in city squares. The punishment for various offenses is precisely prescribed in Saudi law—beheading for rape, murder, sodomy, or sorcery, amputations of the feet or hands for robbery, and public lashings for offenses such as public drunkenness. All of the media, including the eight daily newspapers, are owned and controlled by the royal family, and the government maintains the Royal Decree for Printed Material and Publications, a list of topics that are prohibited to be written about or discussed. The Saudi Communications Company controls the backbone network through which access to the Internet must pass, and the list of approved sites is very short indeed. The *mutawwa'in,* members of the state-financed religious police known as the Committee to Promote Virtue and Prevent Vice, are tasked with enforcing the Wahhabi interpretation of religion and scouring the culture for immoral teachings or immodest dress. Every public facility, including Western companies such as McDonalds, Starbucks, and other U.S. firms, enforce a kind of sexual apartheid, with separate entries and facilities for women and men. The men's sections are lavish and comfortable, many exceeding Western standards, while the women and family sections are often run-down and neglected, sometimes not even offering seats.

It is appalling to those who aren't familiar with the culture. It is also, however, the way it has been on the Arabian Peninsula for generations.

But some felt it was now time for drastic change. A few men, a very few, felt it was time to turn the monarchy over to the forces of democratic power.

And His Royal Highness, King Faysal, Monarch of the House of Saud, was one of those men.

King Faysal knew it would take time for the transition to be complete. It wouldn't take place in his lifetime—the upheaval would be too great, and he was too old now to push anymore. But it would more fully take place with his son, who would gradually make the needed changes. By the time his grandson came to power in twenty years, the transition to democracy would be complete.

It would take two generations, and wrench the kingdom

apart, but Faysal was convinced that democracy and the teachings of Islam were not mutually exclusive ideals, and it was time for the kingdom to take the first step. That meant it was time for the monarch to give up much of his family's great power. It was a radical idea. In fact, some called him a heretic and accused him of insanity. But King Faysal had already begun. Over the past twenty years he had reined in the *mutawwa'in,* set up civil courts with professional judges, authorized city councils outside the influence of royal patronage, and, for the first time, named men to senior government positions who were not his nephews or sons. The next step was to free the press. A national assembly would follow, though that was still ten or fifteen years away.

The king had been bold and courageous. Fighting two hundred years of tradition, he had instituted the first steps of reform, and to say there was resistance among the princes was an understatement at best. He knew of their anger, and he wasn't a fool. But after a long life of laying the foundation for change, King Faysal intended to accelerate the transition to democracy by appointing his first son, Crown Prince Saud bin Faysal, to take his place on the throne. Saud bin Faysal had made a covenant with his father to continue the transition to democracy, and while the monarchy would not disappear, it would hand over much of its power.

The king sometimes wondered what his great-grandfather, the first king of the House of Saud, would have thought of his intentions. After much thought and consideration, he had come to the conclusion that his great-grandfather would have been proud.

* * *

The founder of modern-day Saudi Arabia was King Abd al-Aziz bin Abd al-Rahman bin Faysal Al Saud. A nomadic warrior-prince, King Abd al-Aziz captured Riyadh in 1902 by defeating his long-time rivals, the Rashidi clan, in a bloody and violent desert war. Soon after, he gained control of all central Saudi Arabia. His Bedouin army then turned east and west, uniting the tribes under the puritanical Wahhabi Islamic order until the entire Arabian Peninsula was under his command. After American petroleum engineers discovered oil in Saudi Arabia's eastern province in 1932, King Abd al-Aziz began to strengthen the kingdom's relationship with the United States.

King Abd al-Aziz had some twenty wives, producing forty-five sons and sixty-five children in all. Over time, his posterity proved nothing if not fruitful, and in a country of 23 million people there are now more than six thousand members of the royal family.

Approaching old age, King Abd al-Aziz made it clear that the crown would pass from one king to the next by way of the oldest son. Sometimes this happened, sometimes it did not; for the simple fact was that the incredible power and wealth of the oil-driven kingdom was not something that was easily dismissed, and ambition and greed proved to be destructive tools in the lives of many sons. As a result, the transition of power became unpredictable, and Western leaders eventually accepted that it was impossible to predict with any certainty who would be the next king, or who the world would be dealing with from one generation to the next. Over time, the internal struggles over inheritance became a state secret so closely guarded that it made the old Kremlin power struggles look like a third-grade vote for class president.

King Faysal, the current king of the House of Saud, had several wives and many sons. The actual number—who they were and what they did—was little talked about among the Saudi people, but it had already been established that his oldest son, son of his first wife, Queen Isodore, a green-eyed and dark-haired beauty raised in the holy city of Medina, would be the next king. Indeed, the decision had been made many years before, when Crown Prince Saud was still a young child, and every step of the young prince's life had been carefully choreographed in order to prepare him for the day when he would reign as monarch and king. Prince Saud had proven to be a strong but kindly progressive who spent a great deal of time in the West, soaking up the philosophies behind democratic regimes.

Through the years, as the king watched his son grow, he became more and more convinced he had made the right decision. Indeed, he became convinced Crown Prince Saud was nothing short of an emissary from God, a man sent to rule the kingdom during the painful transition into the twenty-first century, the most difficult times the kingdom would ever see. The crown prince had proven capable. He was intelligent and compassionate and strong to the core. Moreover, he had the vision. He agreed with his father. He *knew* what his purpose was.

Did he have the strength and wisdom such a task would require? Did he have the tenacity to place his nation on the road to democracy? The king thought he did. And Crown Prince Saud thought he did too. So he would take over the kingdom when King Faysal passed away.

The only problem, of course, was that there were other sons.

And they were far from convinced that Crown Prince Saud should be king.

* * *

On the outskirts of the great city, at the end of a tree-lined road that abruptly stopped at a cement barricade and steel fence, behind a cement wall with hidden guard towers and razor wire on top, the crown prince of the House of Saud had one of his three dozen homes. One of the richest and most powerful men in the world, future king of Saudi Arabia, Prince Saud was a large man with dark eyes and broad shoulders and short, curly hair. He was forty-seven, but looked younger, though there were days he felt very old. Educated in the West, including a BA from the Kennedy School of Government at Harvard, the crown prince was decisive and sharp-tongued with his subordinates, but warm and easily manipulated by his family and friends.

The prince sat quietly at the end of an enormous mahogany table. To his side sat the American general. They were the only two men in a room so large it could have accommodated a group of a hundred or more. Brilliant tapestries, some five hundred years old, hung on the walls, the floor was imported Italian tile, and the door frames were rare and unnamed woods shipped from the Indian forest. The ceiling moldings were gold plated, and crushed glass had been mixed with the pastel paints on the walls, giving the room a brilliant radiance from the desert sun that reflected through the twenty-foot windows.

The general stared a brief moment, taking in the beauty of the room. The prince didn't notice. He had a lot on his mind. He needed a smoke, and he fidgeted nervously as he tapped on his pack of American cigarettes, but he didn't light up out of deference to his friend.

Moving his chair across the tile, the prince leaned his arms on the table. "Coffee?" he offered.

The general shook his head. How many times had they been through this before?

"I've got some beautiful teas I've brought in from Oman. The leaf is so thick, it will, how do you say . . . knock your feet off."

The general smiled. "I think you mean knock your socks

off, Prince Saud. And no tea, but thank you." He smiled again, knowing the prince was teasing him now.

"How about a Coke then, General Brighton?"

"Yes. That'd be great."

"Diet? Caffeine free?"

"Regular Coke is fine."

"Oh, you sinning fool!" the prince scolded, trying to hide the smile on his face. "Get you away from Sara and you *really* cut loose! Next thing you know, you'll visit my kingdom and take home another wife!"

"I doubt it, Prince Saud," the general replied. "You know Sara. I don't need to say any more."

"Yes, yes, General Brighton," the prince finally smiled. "I do know your wife. If all men were so lucky! And frankly, good friend, I don't understand how she fell for you. You are like a sweaty Bedouin camel herder who somehow married a princess. Despite all your failings, God has smiled on you."

Neil Brighton only nodded. He knew it was true. "And how is Princess Tala?" he asked.

Saud nodded happily. "Beautiful as ever! And did you know we were expecting another son?"

Brighton smiled happily. "Congratulations!" he said.

Prince Saud clapped his hands. "Thank you," he replied. He touched a hidden button under his desk, and an Indian lad hurried into the room holding a silver tray over his head. He poured a soft drink for the American and tea for his master, then laid out a silver tray of sugar cookies and pastries and hurried from the room.

The crown prince studied his friend and smiled with satisfaction. "How long has it been, Neil?" he asked.

"I don't know, Crown Prince Saud," Brighton replied, unable to call the prince by his first name. He thought a moment. "Sometime just before we liberated Iraq," he then said.

The prince grimaced slightly at the use of the word *liberated*. Well, maybe. Depending on who one was talking to. He sipped at his tea. "You are too busy now, Neil," he said over his china cup. "We never have time to talk! I used to see you regularly until you earned your first star."

"Life has picked up a little; there's no doubt about that."

"And you have grown so quiet, my good friend. Tight-lipped and secretive. Are you never going to tell me about what you do now?"

"Your Highness, you already know. I work for the NSA. Long days, piles of paper work, endless meetings, buckets and buckets of mindless reports, huge egos and office politics more bloody than war. There, that's my job. Not much exciting to tell you—I assure you of that."

The crown prince huffed in sarcastic reply. "I think that's not true, my good friend, General Brighton. Fifty years ago, maybe, but not now, not in these times, not with the battles raging against rising tides. You're the military liaison to the White House National Security Advisor. You are the tip of the sword! *Everything* runs through the NSA. Every proposal, every war plan or decision is vetted through you. It is a *very* important position. High visibility. Very fast track. You personally brief the president almost every week. I'd say, my good friend, you are on your way to the top. Chairmen of the Joint Chiefs. Doesn't that have a good ring?"

The general didn't answer, but picked up his glass.

"I think you are involved in quite important decisions that you can't talk about," the prince gently prodded.

Which was exactly why I brought you here, he quickly thought to himself. *If you will just listen! If you will read between the lines. If you will think and remember what I tell you today!*

The prince tapped his pack of cigarettes as he thought to himself. "How are your sons?" he then asked. "Twin sons! Allah, peace and mercy be His Name, has blessed you. How old are they now? They must almost be men!"

"They will be nineteen this winter," Brighton answered. "And Sam—you remember him, our adopted son—he is in the army. I am proud of all of my sons."

The prince smiled happily. "I'm sure that you are. I am happy for you and Sara. You are good parents, I think, even in your old age."

Brighton laughed. "Remember, Your Highness, I am only two years younger than you. And you don't seem to be slowing down in your parenting despite *your* old age. Didn't you just tell me Princess Tala was about to have another son?"

"Yes, yes . . . well, it is one of the responsibilities of a king to assure a crop of future princes for the kingdom. I'm just doing my job. As the crown prince of the House of Saud, the royal line runs through my veins, so I have an obligation to produce future kings. And though I have eight daughters, yes, I have only three sons, which is hardly enough. All of my younger brothers have many more sons than I do."

The crown prince stared at the general, an intense look on his face. *Listen to me, Neil! See the look in my eyes! I can't say it out loud, so remember my words. I have only three sons. My brothers have many more. My oldest son will be the next king, but only IF they let him live! And I need him to live, Neil, for my plans to succeed. I promised my father, but I will need my son's help, for it will take more than one lifetime to bring democracy to this land.*

* * *

General Brighton watched the prince carefully as an uncomfortable silence developed. The prince was thinking of something. He sensed it and frowned, not knowing what to say.

The prince stared at him a moment, then sipped at his tea. *Is this room also bugged?* Brighton wondered to himself. *Do they listen here as they listen everywhere else?*

Brighton pushed his chair back from the table to cross one leg over the other, then brushed his hand through his blond hair. "You know, Prince Saud, for a short time at least we had the most exquisite decoration hanging over our fireplace at home. A silver and gold emblem of the House of Saud. Two crossed swords and a palm tree. It was simply the most beautiful thing we ever owned."

"You enjoy it!"

"Of course." Brighton shook his head as he thought of the gift from the prince. He had been required to appraise it before turning it over to the government. Three hundred thousand dollars worth of gold, silver, diamonds, and pearls! He shook his head again. "It was too much, my good friend!" he said.

"Are you kidding? To celebrate the coming of age of your sons. It was too little, I assure you, and but the smallest token of my affection for you and your wife. When a man reaches adulthood, it is reason for celebration. I just wanted you and Sara to know I was thinking of you."

The general sipped his soda. "Thank you again, Your Highness. Still, you are too generous. And of course you know, I had to register the gift with the Pentagon Ethics Division. They actually own it now; it is the property of the U.S. government. They let me keep it for a while, but it is not really mine. Conflict of interest. I hope you understand."

"I understand, I understand. I even suspected that might be necessary. When you retire, I will send you another one just like it that will truly be yours."

"Your Highness, perhaps it would be better . . ."

The prince waved a dismissive hand. "Please, Neil, it is a tiny thing to me and I want to do it, okay? Now, instead of worrying about the complications of gifts and ethics, let's pretend for a while, okay? Let's pretend we're fighter pilots again. Let's pretend we don't have the weight of the world on our shoulders. Let's pretend that time hasn't changed us and that the world is more simple and less cruel, like it was before. Let's pretend we are back at fighter pilot school, back when you weren't so impressed that I came from the royal family and I was more impressed with your flying. And please, will you not call me Your Highness, at least for a while? When it's just you and me, and no one else is around, can we go back to the way that it once used to be? Let's go back to our call signs. I'll call you Gameboy and you call me Sultan, okay?"

The general laughed suddenly. He had a vision, a quick memory of their days back in flight school when they were young students learning to fly the F-15, a couple of young and cocky lieutenants screeching like thunderbolts through the skies. They felt like the Greek gods. They had the power of flight. Nothing could destroy them. They were invincible!

Both men smiled as they relived their private memories; then the prince spoke, "General Brighton, over the years, you have always been a good friend. We see each other so rarely, but when we do it always seems like nothing has changed."

The American general nodded. "I was thinking the same thing on my flight over. It's been, what . . . more than twenty years since we first met in Phoenix. Remember that place, Prince Saud? I used to complain about the heat, you complained about the cold, playing golf until midnight with those stupid glow-in-the-dark balls, then staying up to study until 3:00 A.M. We were lieutenants. Life was simple. Those were truly good days."

"Yes, we didn't have so much responsibility; that was for sure. Now here I am, the crown prince, and you, one of the youngest generals in your air force. We both carry heavy burdens. It's not quite like the old days, when the only thing we worried about was crashing into each other or running out of fuel." The prince fell quiet, then added, "You know, though, I pretty much have proven I am a better pilot than you."

The general had to laugh. "Oh no, not this conversation again!"

"No, no, really, General Brighton. Think back to when we first met. As I recall, you made a pretty big deal about how American fighter pilots were the best in the world. I took exception. Now I think it's time to lay down our cards and see what we have."

Brighton looked down and pressed the dark blouse of his air force blues. "You know, Prince Saud, we're never going to settle this until we go head-to-head, until we strap on a jet and call 'fights on' in the air."

"No, no, no . . . that's not true. We have twenty years worth of flying to back up our claims. Now let me see . . . how many enemy fighters have you shot down?"

"Not fair, Saud! I was working on General Schwarzkopf's staff during the Gulf War. No one was more disappointed not to be flying than I was!"

"Yeah, yeah, my sympathies, okay. Now back to my question. I've had two confirmed kills. Really had three, but the gun camera jammed so I couldn't confirm that last kill, and you know the rules—no gun camera footage, no kill. Either way, I'm not selfish; I'll let the other one go. So let's see, that's two, really three, and you have . . . ah, how many enemy jets have you shot down in your career?" The prince's voice trailed off, but his eyes twinkled brightly.

The general shifted in his seat. His face remained calm, but he clasped his hands tight, as the competitor inside him started to rise.

The prince looked for the white knuckles. He knew his friend well. "Okay, okay, let's not talk about that," he said. "You're right, that wouldn't be fair. I mean, it's not your fault you were forced to be Norm's staff boy when the big show came to town. Let's take another measure, ah . . . flying hours. I've got almost three thousand. More fighter time in the Eagle than any other pilot in the entire Royal Saudi Air Force."

"Got you there, Saud," Brighton replied. "I'm pushing almost 3,500 flying hours."

"Really! That is impressive." The prince settled back in his chair. "But you know, of course, I'm not including any of the time I've logged as an F-15 instructor pilot. Can't count sitting in the back seat, watching some lieutenant jerk the control stick around. That's not real flying, keeping some insane student pilot from killing himself. Real pilots fly. Watching flying doesn't count! Now Neil, you're not including your instructor time, are you, because if I were to do that, I'd be up around 3,600 hours." Again, the prince smiled. Touché. Game and match!

The general struggled a moment, then shook his head and laughed. "Okay, you win, Your Highness. But let me add, even if I could beat you, do you think I would be so foolish? Show up the crown prince of Saudi Arabia? Can you imagine the diplomatic crisis such a lapse of judgment would create? I am not so foolish. So I will hold my tongue."

The prince laughed quickly, then stared at his glass. A still silence followed, and the *splat, splat, splat* of lawn sprinklers could be heard from outside.

"Prince Saud," Brighton said, "it's good to be here. And it's always enjoyable to remember old times with you. But I know there's a reason why you invited me here. And though you have tried to hide it, I can see there's something on your mind."

The prince lowered his eyes, then looked again at his friend. His face was suddenly serious, and Brighton could see the deep crow's-feet that lined his dark eyes. The prince pushed up from his seat. "Come, let's walk," he said.

chapter twenty-two

The two men stood and walked through an open glass door that looked out onto a garden which stretched for acres behind the villa. They walked through the garden slowly, following a rock path that led to a gushing waterfall.

"The world is changing, General Brighton," the prince said as they walked. "Indeed, in many ways it is too late—too much has already changed. You now have many enemies throughout the world."

Brighton glanced sideways at the prince. "Our friends are few, but that has always been the case," he answered calmly.

"No, Neil. This is different. From the east to the west, you are nearly alone. Europe hates you now unlike ever before . . ."

"Old Europe, perhaps," the general interrupted. "But the new Europe, the emerging Europe—they are on our side."

The prince shook his head. "Maybe. It doesn't matter. Not now, anyway. And what I said is still true. Most hate you now for your strength and the impact you have. You are a drunken giant, a raging bear, and none of them can stand to see you so powerful. And the impact of your decisions! I don't know if you realize how much influence you have. Your economy sneezes, and a dozen nations catch pneumonia. You develop a foreign initiative, and entire governments fall. You institute a new policy, and by the time it reaches your allies, it is the tip of a whip that snaps at their heads. You are *so* powerful, but also naïve. Like a clumsy giant, you wander across the globe, crushing everything that falls under your feet without even looking down. Is it any surprise so many would like to see you brought to your knees?"

Brighton considered a moment. "Perhaps. But a gentle giant is a better description, I think. And all this talk of the United States seeking world domination—it is completely absurd. It is only the rantings of societies who have failed and need someone to blame. Some people despise us; we know that is true. Old Europe. Many Middle Eastern nations. Dictators and tyrants. We have enemies. But there are still a few others who seem to be in our camp."

"Hmm!" the prince scoffed. "I wouldn't be so sure. There are enemies rising, many foes in the world. And this is important, so you need to listen to me, Neil. There are many kinds of enemies one needs to fear. Those you know and can identify—they are the very best kind. You see them; you can study them; you can counter their moves. But there are other enemies, far more deadly—those who plot in secret places but hide in the light. There are friends, even loved ones . . ." Prince Saud's voice drifted off.

General Brighton watched him briefly, seeing the sadness on his face.

Friends. Even loved ones. Why was he so afraid?

"There are those," Saud continued, "who harbor secret hates and ambitions, those who have taken to the darkness and feel comfortable in it now, those who seek to destroy freedom or anything else that is good."

The general came to a stop and turned to his friend. "What are you saying, Prince Saud?" he asked nervously.

The prince looked around, then stared for a moment at the sky. "I am saying," he concluded, "there is great danger lurking. Great danger to me, and great danger to you." He lowered his face to look into the general's eyes. "My father intends for me to transform the kingdom. You know that—we have discussed it. But there are many who would stop me. I don't know how far they will go."

"You've got to be more specific," Brighton prodded anxiously. "Are you talking of your neighbors? Syria? Iran?"

"No! None of those! Those would be obvious. I'm talking of my family. I'm talking of *your* friends."

"I'm sorry," Brighton answered, "but I don't know who you mean."

The prince shook his head in frustration. "General, I can't be more specific. But is it so hard to understand?"

* * *

The call came through on his satellite phone, a phone that could reach him anywhere in the world.

The younger prince, handsome and thin, flipped the phone open and quickly punched in his security code. "Yes," he said simply when the call was linked through.

"*Sayid,* Crown Prince Saud is meeting with the American general," a deep voice replied.

"Where?" the prince demanded.

"His personal office."

"You are listening, right?"

"Of course, *Sayid.*"

"Has he said anything to the American officer?"

"Nothing of note, *Sayid*. Only small talk is all."

"You don't think . . . he hasn't warned him?"

"No, *Sayid,* God be willing. But they have walked into the garden where we are no longer able to listen."

Prince Abdullah pulled anxiously on his chin. "Where is Princess Tala?" he asked.

"She is preparing to leave the mountain. They will be on their way in just a few minutes now."

"And the children are with her?"

"*Sayid,* they are."

Another moment of silence, one that was longer and more uncomfortable. "Your team is in place?" the younger prince demanded.

"They are ready to move."

"All right, Khilid. You know what to do."

* * *

The two friends stared at each other. "General Brighton, do you believe I support the basic concepts of freedom?" Saud asked. "Do you believe my goal is to move the kingdom toward democracy and closer ties with the West?"

"Yes, Prince Saud, I believe that is true."

"Do you believe I am your friend?"

"I know you are."

"Do you believe I am a friend of the U.S. as well?"

The general paused. This was more difficult. The prince had many allegiances, many voices demanding his ear. Many opposing forces were hanging on him as he balanced on the tight wire, and nothing was simple when it came to the tug and pull of international relationships. After thinking a moment, Brighton replied, "Yes, Prince Saud, I believe you are a friend to the United States."

"Do you believe there are many who would like to see our friendship destroyed, those who would see the kingdom rise up and become an enemy of the United States?"

Brighton turned away as he thought. He needed to be cautious. Even though this was a personal conversation, he still represented his government, and he had to choose his words carefully. But he had always been honest with the prince, and he would be honest now. "There are some in my country who think that has already happened," he answered. "There are some who believe, and with some evidence I might add, that many fundamental Islamist groups carry far too much favor within the kingdom."

The prince considered, then answered, "There is no doubt that is true. But there is a fine balance, a delicate subtlety we must seek every day. Have we made mistakes? Yes, we have. And my father has taken steps to remedy any errors that might have been made. But that's not what I'm speaking of. I'm not talking of radical terrorist groups. I'm talking of others, some within my government, some from opposing nations, who would like nothing more than to see the relationship between our two nations destroyed."

"I understand, Prince Saud. We see those forces at work every day."

"Do you see those forces within your own country? Do you see them within your own government? Can you see them, Neil—because believe me, they're there!"

The general was silent, then sadly nodded his head.

"Then listen to me, Neil. Take this moment, and freeze it in your memory so you'll remember what I say." The prince took a step forward and narrowed his eyes. "I believe we are approaching the crossroads of a great clash between cultures. And I'm not talking about a clash between religions or a clash between nation-states. This isn't Muslim against Christian. It isn't Arab against Jew. And it isn't a clash between democracies and totalitarian regimes. I'm talking about something far deeper and far more deadly, a clash between two fundamentally different sets of beliefs, a clash between groups who defy normal cultures or rules. Our enemies are not contained by borders, and when this is over we will find them everywhere.

"I'm talking about a fundamental conflict between those who believe in basic freedoms and those who would make all men their slaves. I'm talking about ruthless enemies who seek to destroy all free nations and free ways of life. I have seen a glimpse of the future, and you've never had a nightmare that compares with their plans.

"We are rushing forward, heading for what the Qur'an calls the Great War. And this war will be different from any we have ever fought before. It will be a war against an enemy that holds no territory, defends no population, and respects no moral law. Such an enemy cannot be deterred. It can only be destroyed.

"And this enemy seeks your country's destruction above anything else. As long as you stand, then you stand in their way. So they *have* to destroy you. But in order to destroy you, they will come after me first."

Brighton looked away as he thought, his eyes clouding with dread. He had never heard a government leader speak so frankly of his fears. And though he kept his face stoic, inside his gut grew tight in alarm.

* * *

There were three children: two young teen-aged boys and a daughter who had just celebrated her tenth birthday. Princess Tala hurried her children, and they moved smartly into the long sedan, a black BMW with bulletproof windows, steel rails in the side doors, and blast-proof metal plates welded underneath the floor.

As Princess Tala, first wife of Crown Prince Saud, followed her children into the back seat of the limousine, she moved carefully, her hand subconsciously protecting her abdomen. She was just weeks away from delivery of her third son, another prince for the kingdom, another son for the king, and she had developed a habit of resting her hand on her abdomen as she walked. Dropping into the back seat, she adjusted herself, smoothing her white dress and blowing a stray curl of hair from her eyes. Tala was slender and beautiful, with deep green eyes and rich chestnut hair hidden under a silk scarf and thin veil. She sat gracefully, every move elegant, her eyes soft and wide like her ancestral mothers, the ancient Egyptian queens. Her dark skin was perfect, and the sight of her long neck and green eyes revealed enough beauty to command the attention of almost any man.

The crown prince had chosen wisely. Tala was a princess in every sense of the word. Beautiful and intelligent, she was the kind of woman a man would fight for, the kind of woman who could start a war.

Which was both a great blessing and a weakness.

Depending on how long she lived.

The three children sat across from their mother in the long sedan, their backs facing their bodyguard and driver. The princess nodded to the men in the front seat, and the convoy began to move down the circular drive that led from the villa to the front gate that protected the grounds. The small summer palace, a mere forty-five rooms and three pools, fell behind the line of cars, and the princess sighed deeply, then quickly rolled down her window to get a last breath of cool air.

Built on the highest peak on the western side of the mountains, which looked down on the Red Sea, the summer palace was a refuge from the brutal desert below. Here on the mountain, the air was cool and tangy with the smell of juniper and pine. Ancient Joshua trees lined the private drive, their heavy branches hanging over the pavement and breaking the sunlight into shadows that flickered through the windows of the passing cars. The princess glanced back at the retreating villa with sadness. She spent more time in this place than anywhere else in the kingdom, and it was always hard to leave. To her, all of the other palaces, no matter how grand (and they were grand indeed), were no more than hotels where she spent a few nights. But this palace, this mountain retreat—it felt like her home, the one place she was truly comfortable, and she would have stayed there forever if the crown prince would have allowed.

Tala watched her daughter stare through the back window, the stone villa growing smaller. She knew her daughter was also happier here than anywhere else in the world, and in this matter, at least, they agreed. "When will we be back?" the little girl asked her mother as the villa fell behind a line of conifer trees.

Princess Tala shook her head. "Soon," she answered. "But we have other obligations. Our lives cannot be only pleasure. We have other things we must do."

"Can we come back next week?" her daughter asked.

The princess cocked her head and smiled. "El-Tasha, if we came back next week, what would you do about school?"

"I would rather be here on the mountain than go to school. Did you know I saw a mountain goat yesterday? It was beautiful and white, way up on the cliffs. You should have seen it climbing. I thought surely it would fall. Can we come back next week and see if it is still there?"

The oldest son eyed his sister. "She's just looking for an excuse to get out of her studies," he teased. "El-Tasha would rather sit on a rock in the middle of the Euphrates surrounded by eel snakes than go back to school."

The princess laughed, and El-Tasha shook her head. "That's not true!" she answered. "I like school. Sometimes.

Well, okay, I don't like the academy but that's not the reason I want to come back . . . at least it's not the *only* reason."

The oldest son laughed again, and Tala turned to him. He had the dark eyes of his father and was filling out in the chest. Though he was just fourteen years old he looked older. Something about the future responsibility of the kingdom made a boy grow quickly, and the princess could almost see the subtle weight of the kingdom begin to settle on his shoulders. He knew the kingdom would one day be his, and from the time he was a child he had been told to prepare, for the final phase in the transition to democracy would fall on him. And he was doing his best. While all of the royal children were educated by private tutors at the royal academies, not all of the students took their studies as seriously as he. He had proven smart and dedicated, and while probably not as smart as his father, what he lacked in intelligence he more than made up for in intuition and a steel-hard willingness to work.

Princess Tala watched her oldest son with pride. He looked so much like his father, it was almost uncanny. It was like a younger Prince Saud sitting there. She leaned over and patted his knee, then glanced through the bulletproof window at the road ahead.

* * *

A twelve-foot-high brick wall surrounded the mountain retreat; and the only access to the villa, which sat back half a mile from the security wall, was through a heavy steel gate. Thick trees lined the road. The convoy of five vehicles sped along the hardtop toward the gate. The first vehicle in the convoy was a black military van containing heavy weapons and surface-to-air missiles. A black SUV followed the van with the royal family's personal bodyguards. Princess Tala and her family were in the third car, the long BMW sedan, followed by another SUV with her personal staff: her physician, the family pediatrician, a personal assistant, a secretary, a trainer, and a masseuse. The chief of security rode in the last vehicle, a heavy truck crammed with military officers and security police.

After years of training (and some painful experience) the chief had grown accustomed to riding in the back of the convoy, where he could more accurately observe the situation and measure the threats. From that vantage point, he could mark the progress of the convoy as it moved down the road.

The chief shifted uncomfortably in the front seat of the truck. As chief of security, he knew the princess and her family were completely in his charge, and he would willingly give his life if it were ever required to save her. The truth was, if harm were to ever come to the princess, Prince Saud would have him killed anyway, so he might as well die with honor. And though he had always felt pressure, he felt it more and more with each passing day. The radicals in the kingdom had grown more bold and more vicious. Like a dog crazed with hunger, they smelled the sweet tang of blood.

So the security chief moved anxiously to the edge of his seat, as the convoy passed through the main gate and onto the descending mountain road.

* * *

The road leading down the mountain was smooth and well-kept, but it was also cut with deep switchbacks and very steep grades. There were few guardrails or retaining walls, and the security chief knew the road was a dangerous place. From the compound at the top of the mountain the road descended more than six thousand feet, cutting and turning and dropping along sheer canyon walls. The terrain was rocky and steep, and the trees gradually thinned out as the road descended until the landscape merged with the barren desert floor.

The convoy moved quickly, the drivers braking expertly at each curve in the road before accelerating again. The princess watched the road tensely, then pulled out a cell phone and punched her husband's private number. The call was relayed to a central switchboard in Ad Damman, where a sophisticated GPS tracking system kept constant tabs on the location of the crown prince; then her call was automatically transferred to the palace on the outskirts of Riyadh.

Prince Saud's personal assistant answered the phone, his voice low and all business. "Yes, Princess Tala," he said.

"Is Crown Prince Saud available?" the princess asked.

"I'm sorry, ma'am, Prince Saud is in a meeting."

It never occurred to either the princess or Prince Saud's assistant that he might offer to interrupt. One did not interrupt the prince. Not even his wife.

Tala thought a moment. "Is he still with the American general?" she asked.

"Yes, Princess Tala."

"General Brighton, as I recall?"

"I believe that is right."

"Do you know how long he will be?" Tala asked.

The older man huffed. "No, ma'am, I do not." Princess or not, she was still just a woman, and the affairs of the prince were not her concern. "May I tell him you called?" Saud's assistant offered. "I will have him get in contact with you at the first opportunity."

"Yes, please. Thank you, Mishal bin Abd Mohammad. Tell him we are leaving the mountain and will meet him in Riyadh."

"I will tell him," the man answered, and the princess flipped her phone closed.

"Are we going to see Father tonight?" her oldest son asked as Tala looked at him. Princess Tala nodded, and all of her children smiled.

The sedan sped ahead, then slowed for a particularly sharp curve in the road. The princess reached for the handhold over her window, then felt her child kick, a strong thump against her abdomen, sturdy and swift. Placing her hand on her belly, she smiled. "Be still, my young prince," she whispered. "We are almost there."

* * *

The five assassins had concealed themselves in the brush on the uphill side of the road, just before one of the last switchbacks. Behind them, on the other side of a crest in the mountain, their helicopter hovered, keeping out of view. The men were dressed in identical black uniforms, leather boots, and thin gloves. The fingers had been cut out of the gloves to allow them to maneuver their weapons with precision, and their faces were concealed behind black masks.

The team leader listened to the tiny earpiece he had shoved in his ear. "Two minutes!" he hissed to his team as he glanced down the line. The men were expertly concealed, spread out twenty feet to his left and right. The gun-blue barrels of their Soviet-made weapons protruded from the brush.

The team leader listened again, then gave his final instructions. "Call ready," he whispered into the microphone at his neck.

"Two's ready," the second sniper positioned to his right replied.

"Two, you've got the first truck in the convoy," the team leader instructed. "Repeat to me your instructions. You have number one."

"Roger that. Two has the lead truck."

"The first vehicle has the 20-caliber machine guns and missiles. You've got to take it or this whole thing is off. Understand, Two! We're depending on you!"

"Got that, Colonel!" the other sniper replied.

"Three, you take the second vehicle, a black SUV," the team leader continued. "The target is in the third car, a BMW limousine. Repeat that . . . target is in the third vehicle. Leave that car alone!" The lead assassin scoffed to himself as he thought of the lone BMW limousine. It was so obvious! No decoys. No deceptions. Which car contained the princess was almost comically clear. Fool of security! He was worthy of death.

He glanced at the two men to his left. "Four and five, you've got the last two cars in the convoy," he instructed. "It is just like we planned." He looked down the line. "Any questions?" he asked.

His men remained silent, and the team leader crouched lower in his hole, then glanced down the line, checking their positions one final time. He saw the four barrels of the RPG-7 shoulder-launched missiles protruding from the brush and smiled. The RPG-7s, recoilless, shoulder-fired antitank weapons, were simple and functional killing machines. Effective against fixed emplacements or moving targets, they had a range of five hundred meters and could penetrate most conventional armor plate. Proven again and again in combat, RPG-7s had been successfully employed against armored vehicles, bunkers, and American helicopters.

Taking out these lightly armored vehicles would prove easy to do.

The sniper nodded, approving, then turned back to the road.

"All right then, my brothers," he said into his microphone. "This is the endgame. Prove yourselves worthy or die in the cause. That is the only choice you have now, so do not let me down."

Twenty seconds passed, and the convoy came into view.

"Praise be to God," one of the soldiers whispered, and the team leader glared. This wasn't about Allah. This was about power. And the kingdom. And the man they would have as their king!

* * *

The convoy was nearing the bottom of the mountain. There were two more sharp curves below them, then a straight line to the electronically controlled gate that blocked access to the road. The line of cars decelerated for a curve, and the vehicles bunched together as they slowed.

Inside the black limousine, Princess Tala laid her head back and closed her eyes, deep in thought. The little girl was asleep, and the two young men were quiet. The BMW bounced lightly as it hit some gravel in the road, then pulled into the turn.

* * *

"Stand fast!" the lead assassin whispered into his microphone, sensing the anxiety in the air. The vehicles were almost directly below them, not more than eighty feet away. "Two, are you ready?"

"Ready!" the second assassin replied.

"Ready . . . ready . . . NOW!" the team leader cried.

The four RPG-7 rocket-propelled grenade launchers fired in a hiss of white-hot smoke and flame. The four missiles trailed forward, reaching their targets in a fraction of a second, and the four vehicles exploded in bright orange and yellow flames. The lead truck rocked up on its front wheels, crushing its bumper against the asphalt, then nearly rolled onto its back. The black SUV with the doctors simply disappeared, swallowed in a fireball of black smoke and orange flame. The other two vehicles exploded a hundredth of a second later. The heat was so intense it started melting the asphalt, the oil-based road catching fire and spewing black smoke. The second assassin reloaded quickly and fired again and the lead military vehicle was blown in two, secondary explosions bursting from its cargo bay and blasting the air.

The black BMW screeched as the driver slammed on the brakes. The road ahead and behind him was completely blocked by fiery walls of melting steel. The sedan didn't move for a moment, the driver momentarily confused; then he threw the car into reverse, the tires screeching as he backed up, crashing into the wreckage behind. The driver gunned the engine and his tires squealed as he tried to push the burning SUV out of the way.

The assassins had already picked up their other weapons, and the sound of automatic machine-gun fire burst through the air. They blew out the fleeing BMW's tires, shredding them in a hail of bullets; then the windshield was shattered, then the engine, then the driver and bodyguard's upper torsos and heads—everything from the front seat of the vehicle forward to the grill was blown to pieces in a hail of gunfire. The BMW came to rest against the hulk of the burning car behind it. Another explosion rocked the hot air as the gas tank in the last car finally burst into flames. A single soldier stumbled from the second automobile, his clothing on fire. He rolled in the dirt, then fell still, his arms reaching out, as he burned to death. Fire and thick smoke billowed from the burning vehicles, the flames curling around the shattered windows and half-open doors. Another soldier crawled from the largest truck, pulling himself on his belly toward the ditch, and the lead assassin fired, the hail of heavy machine-gun fire nearly cutting him in two.

The assassins jumped from their hiding places and ran

down the hill. Behind them they heard the dull *whop, whop, whop* as their evacuation helicopter crested the saddle in the mountain and swooped toward the rising smoke. The assassins reached the road in a matter of seconds and came to a quick stop. Charred bodies, burning tires, blackened pieces of metal and melted weapons were scattered everywhere. The air was heavy with the stench of burning flesh and fuel.

It was a clean hit. A perfect hit. Not a soldier was living. It was all they could ask for.

The team leader turned to the black BMW, the only vehicle in the convoy that had not been destroyed. The royal family was in there. He started to move.

* * *

Crown Prince Saud shoved his hands into his pockets and rocked on his feet. The waterfall gushed around them, cooling the air with its mist. Then he heard footsteps approach from behind a cluster of palm trees forty yards up the trail, and he looked over to see his personal aide running toward them. "Your Majesty!" the servant cried as he ran.

The prince took a step toward him, and the aide came to a sudden stop and bowed quickly, touching his palms to his knees. "Your Majesty!" he repeated as he lifted his eyes. The crown prince saw the panic, and his heart slammed in his chest. The aide grabbed the prince around the shoulders and began to pull him up the path. Behind him, other palace guards began to race into view. "Your Highness, come quickly!" the aide hissed in his ear.

"What is it?" Saud demanded.

The aide's eyes bulged. "A Firefall! Your family . . ." he cried.

Prince Saud's knees grew weak. He knew the code. *Firefall!* An assault on his family. "What? When?" he demanded.

Two bodyguards appeared out of nowhere and started pressing close to him, protecting him from all sides. Prince Saud reached out to the aide. "What is going on?" he cried.

"Princess Tala hit the panic button!" the aide said to the prince. "That's all that we know. Now, please, come with us, Your Majesty."

* * *

Princess Tala sat upright, her jaw tight in horror, her eyes wide and glaring in gut-wrenching fear. She reached under her seat and hit the panic button again. Her daughter was screaming in terror, a high screeching sound, and the princess reached over and slammed her head toward the floor. Dropping to her knees, she held her daughter's head in her hands. Peering over the seat, the princess tried to look out the front of the car, but the bulletproof window that separated the front and rear seats was so smeared with blood and gore that she couldn't see through it.

"Get down!" she screamed to her sons. The oldest one stared blankly past her, looking through the back window at the carnage behind. She followed his gaze and saw a burning body hanging out of the front windshield. Then she felt the tremor of a smaller explosion behind them. The car rolled backward, then suddenly bumped to a stop as the searing heat and smoke began to seep into the car.

The princess stared at her son, her eyes terrified. He reached for the door handle. "We've got to get out!" he cried.

"No!" Tala screamed as she slammed the locks down on the rear doors. "Whatever is out there, they can't get in! We must stay inside the vehicle. It is the safest place we can be!" She reached for her crying daughter and pulled her into her lap, then thrust her fingers under her seat and hit the satellite-monitored alarm again. She heard the dull *whop* of an approaching helicopter and almost cried in false hope before realizing the chopper could not be her friend. She thumped the front window, desperate to see through the blood, then heard voices and saw shadows approaching through the smoke to the side. She pushed her daughter down and lowered her head.

"Get on the floor!" she commanded her terrified sons.

The children dropped to the floor, and Princess Tala fell over them.

The car rocked back from a single shotgun blast to the door. Tala felt someone pull on the door handle, but it didn't give. Another shotgun blast; her daughter screamed; another blast, another pull. The door fell open, and three men in black uniforms were standing there.

Tala looked at them, her face passive. The terror had drained all rational thought from her brain, leaving her unfeeling and calm. *"Don't you dare touch my children!"* she tried screaming, but nothing came out.

The first man moved toward her, then slowly took off his mask. Tala pulled a quick breath, and her heart nearly burst.

What was *he* doing? No! It couldn't be!

She looked into his dark eyes, and he smiled as he lifted his gun.

"Please, Allah, save the kingdom!" were Princess Tala's last words.

Four shots were fired, each carefully aimed, each one to the head. Then a last shot was fired into the princess's abdomen to ensure the unborn child was dead. It was a statement, not a necessity, for the fetus would have died anyway.

But as a message to the crown prince, it pretty much said everything.

* * *

The garden came alive with security forces and military police. Like ants from an anthill, they seemed to appear everywhere.

General Brighton took a step forward, but the prince pushed him back. He stared at him a moment with dark, glaring eyes. "It has started," he whispered hoarsely as his bodyguards pulled him away.

"What's going on, Prince Saud? What is a Firefall?"

"Stay here!" the prince demanded. "Don't move from this place. I will have someone escort you back to your compound. Go with them and do *exactly* what they say! I must go! I must go!" The prince turned and disappeared down the path.

* * *

Twenty minutes after leaving his palace, Prince Saud's motorcade screamed through the gates of King Khalid International Airport outside of Riyadh. The line of black Mercedes and American SUVs rolled onto the tarmac where his aircraft was parked. A huge 747–400 taxied by, but the motorcade didn't hesitate to race in front of it, forcing the *Air Saudi* airliner to come to a sudden halt. Prince Saud's personal jet was waiting near the taxiway, its four engines running. Mobile stairs had already been positioned next to the aircraft, and the prince took them two at a time. The side door was closed, and the aircraft began to taxi the instant the stairs were pulled away from the jet.

Inside, the crown prince's chief of staff was waiting to give him the news. Saud listened, staring straight ahead, then dismissed his staff. He pushed himself up from his chair and walked to his private office at the back of the jet.

Later that night, Crown Prince Saud was escorted into a large chrome and tile morgue in the royal family's private hospital in Medina. His family was stretched out on steel tables and positioned side by side, each of them lying face-up under white sheets. He walked to them, crying, then demanded to be alone. The physician nodded and bowed and silently left the room.

The crown prince fell to his knees between the four gurneys where his dead family lay. He wept for three hours, crying out to his God, cursing and pleading and begging to die. He made outrageous promises if God would bring them back to him, then fell in exhaustion and slept on the tile floor. Sometime later, the physician carefully entered the room to see the prince kneeling by his wife's body again, holding her hand tightly as he stared at the floor.

"Get out!" the prince hissed, and the doctor withdrew.

The prince remained in the room for almost twenty-four hours. When he emerged he was unshaven, smelly, and as frayed as rotten cloth.

But he had made his decision. And he had figured out a plan.

He knew who had killed them. They were not far away.

Forget all his dreams and the promises he had made to his father.

He would destroy the kingdom if he had to. But he would have his revenge!

* * *

Lucifer, the Great Master, watched Prince Saud suffer from the upper corner of the room. He stood still, his arms limp, his eyes staring down at the scene. He smiled as he watched, almost laughing with glee, the pleasure of the prince's suffering causing a cold glint of joy in his eyes.

chapter twenty-three

It was almost six hours before Major General Neil Brighton's military aircraft was cleared to take off because of the emergency hold put on all air traffic in and out of King Khalid International Airport.

As the evening sun settled, his C-21 executive jet was finally cleared for departure, the first aircraft in a long line of civilian traffic that was cleared to take off. The aircraft quickly climbed to 39,000 feet and leveled off, and Brighton undid his lap belt and settled back in his seat. A young airman dressed in a military skirt and blue sweater served the general a light dinner, then brought him a secure telephone and data cable so he could plug his laptop into the aircraft's satellite communications system.

"Anything else?" the airman asked after helping him plug in the phone.

The general stared at her blankly, then shook his head. "No thanks, Airman Rice."

"You look tired, sir."

"Maybe a little."

"Have you been in Riyadh a long time?"

"Just a few days."

"Still, I'm sure you're anxious to get home."

"Always anxious, Airman Rice."

"We'll be changing crews at Ramstein, sir, but I'll make certain they bring on some hot oatmeal for your breakfast. And fresh grapefruit juice and oranges. Did I forget anything?"

Brighton shook his head and thanked her, then turned to his laptop computer and tried to get some work done. It was a five-hour flight to Ramstein, where they would refuel and change pilots for the long flight back to the States. As the aircraft approached the Mediterranean Sea, the air became heavy with humidity and haze. Looking down, Brighton could see a solid cloud layer forming beneath him, and ahead there were growing lines of thunderstorms, huge angry monsters reaching up to 60,000 feet. The sun was off to his left side and setting quickly toward the horizon, and the shadows from the thunderstorm cells cast purple, gray, and blue hues across the lower layers of white. He studied the thunderstorms and saw the first bolt of lightning flash from one of the storms. He knew the small jet would have to weave its way between the storm cells, and the pilot inside him wanted to climb into the cockpit and push one of the two young captains aside, but he fought the temptation and turned back to his work.

Behind him, his two aides fell asleep, while the security officer stared quietly out his window on the other side of the cabin. Another flash of lightning lit up the interior of the cabin, and the officer grabbed his armrest in a death grip. Brighton felt the aircraft begin to climb to get over the storms, then turn a few degrees to the north.

Pulling his shade, he turned back to his work. The aircraft bounced through the rough skies for forty minutes or so and then settled down as they passed through the last of the storms.

Brighton pulled out another report, forcing himself to read, but though he struggled to concentrate, his mind kept wandering back to what Prince Saud's guard had cried. *"Firefall! Your family . . . "* A cold chill ran down his spine.

Firefall? Firefall? What did the code mean? He thought of the stark terror that had fallen across the crown prince's face, the guards falling in confusion around him, the tension in their voices, their weapons and chattering radios, their determined urgency as they had pulled him away.

He knew it was likely he would never know what had happened this day. The flow of information out of the kingdom was extremely tightly controlled, and personal information regarding the royal family of the House of Saud was almost nonexistent, inside of the kingdom or out. He knew there would be nothing in the press, nothing over the wires, nothing in any intelligence report.

But he knew that something had happened, something dangerous and deadly. He knew it; he felt it somewhere deep in his bones. He thought of the warnings the prince had given, the most frank and disheartening conversations with a world leader he had ever had, then pictured the look on the prince's face once again.

Firefall? Firefall? Another shiver ran down his spine.

Three hours later, the C-21 landed, refueled and changed aircrews at Ramstein then took off again, heading back to D.C.

chapter twenty-four

Late in the afternoon, Prince Abdullah al-Rahman stood at the window of his Dhahran penthouse atop the Royal Saudi Oil Company headquarters and stared out on the ports of the city. The office was an enormous room filled with leather and scarce woods from the far corners of the world. Racks of various game animals hung on the wall, some of them legal, most of them not, many of them exotic and endangered African animals shot by Prince Abdullah on one of his hunts. Abdullah was good with a knife and he was good with a gun, the blood of his warrior ancestors running thick through his veins. He loved to track and was good at it; and he loved to kill. He loved to butcher his meat. There was something about it—the touch and the smell, the warmth of the flesh when it was still freshly killed, gutting the animal and feeling the blood—there was just something about it that was appealing to him. Like his Bedouin ancestors, he hungered to hunt and was always successful, though he never brought the meat home but left it out on the prairie to feed other predators such as himself.

To Abdullah's right, a large plaque hung on the wall, engraved with words from the *Covenant of Hamas:*

Israel will exist and will continue to exist until Islam will obliterate it, just as it obliterated others before it. The Day of Judgment will not come about until Moslems fight Jews and kill them. Then the Jews will hide behind rocks and trees, and the rocks and trees will cry out: "O Moslem, there is a Jew hiding behind me, come and kill him." So-called peaceful solutions and international conferences are in contradiction to the principles of the Islamic Resistance Movement. There is no solution for the Palestinian problem except by Jihad.

The prince loved the words from the covenant. They inspired him by reminding him of his comrade's convictions to bettering the world through the spread of jihad.

As for himself, his battle was anything but a holy war. Indeed, it was very unholy, as he would freely admit.

Abdullah looked through the floor-to-ceiling window. His younger brothers stood behind him, letting him think. The late sun sent long shadows across the city, casting the office in a natural glow. He stared out the window to where the gray and blue waters of the Persian Gulf glimmered in the setting sun. A light evening breeze blew in from the coast. The city was busy, the port alive and bustling with men, equipment, and machines. Enormous oil tankers moved toward the sea docks, where they would take on their loads of rich Saudi crude. After filling their enormous holds, the tankers would turn for various ports in both the West and East, where the Saudi oil would help to quench the insatiable thirst for energy that drove the economic machines of the world. Prince Abdullah watched the nearest tanker move through the calm seas, then glanced down and imagined the reservoirs of oil that lay ten thousand feet below, huge underground pools that stretched a hundred miles in every direction. A quarter of the world's known oil supply lay under the Arabian sands: 400 billion barrels, a hundred trillion dollars worth of underground liquid gold. And the oil guaranteed not only the wealth of the Royal Saudi family, but the wealth of their subjects as well, providing each Saudi citizen with one of the highest standards of living in the world. For generations ahead, their wealth and well-being was assured.

But not if . . . not if . . . The prince cursed quietly to himself.

He shuddered in anger and raised his eyes back to the coast.

Once loaded with oil, the tankers would steam out to sea, passing the huge cargo ships that were on their way to Saudi ports. Abdullah turned to the docks on the east side of the city and watched the multicolored container ships unloading their wares: luxury cars, electronics, food, soda, clothing, frozen meat, furniture, steel, plastics, wood, cables, heavy equipment, office supplies, golf clubs, boats, cotton balls, medicine, cement, and scientific equipment. The list of imports was as long as the docks that paralleled the sea, for his nation imported almost everything needed for survival. The dock work was a precise and well-oiled machine, and he was reminded again that this was where the cycle was complete. Oil for cash. Cold cash for things. Oil revenues in exchange for the beautiful things of the world.

He watched in satisfaction. The kingdom was in order. The sun rose; the sun set; there was peace and prosperity. His subjects were well-fed and happy. It was as it should be.

So why did his idiot father insist on screwing it up?

He turned quickly and stared at his two younger brothers, weak men whose only asset was that they always did what he said, two evil and cold-hearted boobs who hated the thought of losing their power almost as much as he.

He studied their faces: twentyish, handsome, identical dark hair and mustaches, fine teeth, and round shoulders. Yet they were so needy, so dependent, it was almost comical. Neither of his younger brothers had worked a day in their lives, and it disgusted Abdullah that they were so incapable of taking care of themselves. They didn't know how to drive, how to cook, or even make their own beds. They hardly knew how to get dressed without their valets selecting their clothes, and neither could draw his own bath without screaming in frustration when the water flowed too hot or too cold. And they certainly didn't know how to fight—that's what their bodyguards were for—though they seemed to fight and scream at each other at the drop of a hat.

Still, Abdullah had learned his younger brothers weren't entirely stupid. Indeed, they had proven they were capable of learning if they were motivated enough. And the plans of their father had motivated them now.

"Are you here alone?" Abdullah asked the younger of the two brothers.

The youngest prince had recently taken a habit of traveling with a young woman he had met in Greece, dragging her around like a security blanket. It seemed she was always around, lurking in the next room, and Abdullah didn't like it. He had to get rid of her.

His youngest brother glanced at the window and snorted. "Of course I'm alone. I'm not stupid," he replied.

Abdullah stared at him in a cold-hearted smile. Yes, he *was* stupid. And when he started a sentence with "Of course," one couldn't presume that was necessarily what he meant.

Abdullah turned away from the window and sat down at his gold-accented, mahogany desk. His brothers watched him carefully, sitting on the edge of their seats. Abdullah lit a cigarette while they waited, taking a long drag, then leaned back and held the smoke in his lungs.

The older prince smiled almost sadly. Sometimes he wished his brothers could be more like him. But they weren't. And the old man had taught him that they never would be. Motivated by short-term pleasure and money, they couldn't see beyond the next day. So he would use them, then kill them. It was the order of things.

Abdullah stared at his cigarette, letting the smoke drift from his nose. He bit on his lip, feeling a piece of stray tobacco there. "Did you show your face like I told you?" he asked.

"Yes, brother, I did."

"And what was her reaction?"

The younger prince thought, then shot a quick look to his brother. "I'm not certain," he answered. "It all happened pretty quickly."

Abdullah waited, inpatient. "Did she die quietly?" he demanded. "Or did she say anything?"

The brother lit his own cigarette and pulled a nervous drag. "She said something . . . I don't know, something about Allah and the kingdom."

Abdullah listened, then smiled. Yeah, that sounded like Tala, always praising their God. "All right, brothers," he concluded, "you did a good job. That will be all for now." Finished with them, he wanted them out of the room.

The two princes looked at each other, then stood up together. The youngest one turned for the door, then glanced back to Abdullah. "And Crown Prince Saud?" he wondered quickly.

Abdullah waved an impatient hand. "Don't worry about the crown prince. That is not your concern."

The younger prince stared at his brother. "You know our

father, the king, will certainly figure this out. That will not be a good thing. We have to be ready to defend ourselves."

"The king is a coward," Abdullah shot back. "He will not do anything."

"But he still holds great power . . ."

"Which is *exactly* my point! He holds the same power that he wants to rip from our hands. He plans to dismantle our kingdom and turn it over to *them.*" Abdullah shot an angry hand toward the docks. "But does he pay the price of his decision? Of course not. We do! He waits until he grows old, enjoying a life of great ease, then commands his oldest son to take our kingdom apart. But I will not allow it." Abdullah cursed. "I swear that on his grave. It is he who betrays us! He is disloyal to the prophet and disloyal to me. He has been planning our destruction since before we were born!"

The older prince slapped both hands on the table, then pointed a finger at them. "Remember this, my brothers," he hissed one final time. "We are trying to save the kingdom. That is all we do. We are trying to save the kingdom from this selfish man and his son."

The youngest prince lowered his head in subjection as he backed for the door.

Abdullah looked away from his brothers and shuffled some papers on his desk. He pushed a hidden button near his knee and the automatic office door opened. Having been dismissed, his younger brothers nodded to each other and walked from the room.

* * *

Prince Abdullah stared at their backs, then closed the automatic door. Seconds later, a side door to his office swung back.

The old man stepped slowly into the office. He walked painfully, shuffling between the chrome handles of a walker, and it seemed to take him forever to make his way to the couch, where he sat down wearily, then looked at the prince.

Abdullah noted the sick eyes and hollow face. His skin was so thin and waxy, he almost looked dead. Abdullah glanced to the side door that led to a small, private study, knowing the old man's doctor was waiting there, then turned back to look into the red-rimmed eyes again. The old man coughed deeply, hacking the collected phlegm from his chest.

Abdullah waited for him to spit, then reported. "His family is dead," he announced.

"Good, good," the old man answered weakly. "You have made me proud."

Abdullah waited, unconsciously gripping a gold pen in his hand.

"Now we must take care of Crown Prince Saud," the old man struggled to say. "That will be the last step. Then we will be ready to move."

The prince relaxed his grip on the pen. After all of these years, it was what he had been waiting to hear. "I have your permission then?" he asked quickly.

"Yes, yes, of course. Do what you will. But remember, Prince Abdullah, if you don't take care of all the offspring, then you still leave a mess. You've got to cut out all the cancer or it will kill you one day, and the crown prince still has another wife and a son."

The prince quickly answered, "I will take care of them."

The old man hacked again, then breathed deeply in a raspy and crackling breath. The prince knew he was dying; he had a few weeks, maybe less. But they were so close. Everything was in place. In a very few weeks they would have the warheads.

Through sheer force of will, the old man had done what he promised, living to see their success. Abdullah thought back on that spring day in Monte Carlo, some twelve years earlier.

What had they laughed about? The burning glory, he remembered. And here it was, so close. His good friend had been right.

"When will you do it?" the old man asked between gasping breaths.

Prince Abdullah thought a long moment. "Soon," he finally answered. "He's still mourning over the bodies. He's been there for hours. And he knows now, of course; he knows it was me. And he will act, I am sure. A few days, a few hours—he won't wait very long. I mean, we just killed his family—do you think he will wait? But he has a mountain of troubles to sort through before he can do anything. He doesn't know who to trust, and if he can't trust his brothers, who can he turn to? So he will take care of his son first and ensure he is safe. And he will do it alone. He won't trust his last child to anyone else. He knows there are snakes in the nursery, and he will want to kill them himself. Until then, he is vulnerable; so we have a few hours."

The old man rasped, then warned him. "Crown Prince Saud is no fool," he said. "It would be a mistake to underestimate him, so be careful, Abdullah. We've come too far, we've been far too patient, we've worked too hard and sacrificed too much to let it slip through our fingers this late in the game."

The prince pressed his lips. "Yes," he answered simply. "It is a dangerous time, I agree."

"Yes, it is; yes, it is. So take care of Prince Saud before he takes care of us."

Abdullah started to answer when the personal phone at the side of his desk buzzed quietly. He picked up the receiver and listened, then grunted a few instructions and hung up the phone. The old man stared at him, and Prince Abdullah smiled. "Seems Crown Prince Saud is planning a little trip," he said.

"Where to?" the old man questioned, a hint of concern in his raspy voice.

"I don't know," Abdullah answered. "But we are going to find out. He has requested his private helicopter. They are completing the preflight now."

chapter twenty-five

Princess Tala and her children were buried in a secret and private funeral at the royal family's ancient cemetery on the outskirts of Medina. Only Crown Prince Saud, his father, and a few trusted kin stood over the dark graves as the gold-plated coffins were lowered into the dry ground. There was no press release, no public offering, no notification to the world that the princess had been killed, and, incredibly, word of the assassinations hadn't leaked to the international press.

The royal family could be discreet when it had to. And when it came to interfamily homicide there was good reason to be mum. The kingdom had been thrown into chaos, and it was about to get worse. Each of the players was holding desperately to his cards.

* * *

Seven hours after the funeral, the crown prince of the House of Saud was driven to one of his personal helicopters, which always stood alert. The chopper blades were spinning when the prince showed up, and the helicopter took off in the darkness without turning on its navigational lights.

The prince watched through the window of the American-made Sikorski S-92, a four-bladed executive chopper that had more gold and leather than could be found in any executive suite looking down on midtown Manhattan. The highly modified cabin, originally designed to seat seventeen passengers, had been modified into a six-passenger configuration, with opposing leather couches running down each side of the cabin, a fully stocked bar, a small office and lavatory, and two massive reclining chairs just behind the bulkhead wall. The carpet was deep maroon and so thick it felt like you were standing on grass. Highly polished teak and mahogany accented the trim, and the seats were white leather, soft as velvet, and emblazoned with the royal flag.

Crown Prince Saud watched in silence as the warm waters of the Persian Gulf passed underneath his chopper, but the night was so dark it was nearly impossible to get a sense of their speed. The winds had picked up, moving down from the north, and the ocean was white-capped with rippled lines of foam reflecting the light of the yellow moon. The chopper flew east, toward the Iranian border, and with each passing mile the emptiness inside him grew more dark and intense. He leaned against the window that looked out the right side of the chopper and felt the vibration of the rotors spinning over his head. The chopper passed the first of the many offshore oil rigs that dotted Iran's western shore, and he knew they would soon be over land. The crown prince could imagine the view from the cockpit—the miles of white-caps below them, the enormous oil derricks casting shadows under the moon, the deep black sands and rising foothills of Iran's western shores, the moon in the pilots' faces, and the enormous saucer of stars overhead.

He glanced at his watch. A little after one in the morning. They had been in the air for an hour and would soon land.

The crown prince took a breath and turned in his seat. The cabin was silent except for the sound of her cry, a soft and heartbroken tremble that she tried to hold in. The prince stared at his second wife, and she wiped her eyes quickly to hide her tears. He reached out and took her hand and held it to his chest, then placed his other hand very gently on the four-year-old boy who was sleeping beside her. "Do you want our son to live?" he asked simply.

The young princess nodded and squared her shoulders in reply.

"Then be strong," the prince demanded, his voice strained but firm. He pressed her hand against their sleeping child's head. "Be strong for him. Be strong for our family. Be strong for the kingdom. Be strong for me."

The princess wiped her cheeks as she stared at her lap.

The prince saw a vision of the four bodies, a single bullet in their foreheads, their faces peaceful and calm. He glanced at his last son, a four-year-old angel who slept, his head resting on his young mother's lap. His face too was peaceful. His heart broke again.

The family. His honor. Their future. Their king. That was all that mattered. The prince knew that was true.

He studied his young wife, reading the pain in her eyes. She looked as if she were dying, as if she were already dead. She looked so lonely, so abandoned. "Are you certain?" she pleaded. "Is there no other way?"

The prince shook his head. "I have decided. We will discuss it no more."

The young princess sat back, her eyes fearful and wet. Her lower lip trembled. She was *trying* to be brave; she was *trying* to be strong . . . but this was so unexpected and so frightening. She stared straight ahead, her face strained with fear.

"Why can't I go home to my family?" she muttered. "Why can't I stay in Saudi Arabia? I know nothing of Iran."

"Which is why we must do this! Are you so blind you can't see? Your life is in danger. And so is my son. Now quit crying of your suffering. Would you rather be dead? Would you rather I have to bury him like I buried my other sons?"

The princess stroked the sleeping boy's face. "But my husband . . . Iran? Why not the southern province? My people are from that region. I want to live . . ."

"That's right! *You want to live!* So you must do as I say!"

"But it is so far away!"

"Pray it is far enough!"

The princess fell silent, and the prince knew she would not say any more.

Prince Saud leaned his head back and stared blankly at the darkness, a trail of tears rolling down to his chin.

Minutes passed; then the prince leaned toward her again. "You are strong, Ash Salman," he whispered. "There is a determination, a wisdom inside you that is rare in my people. You have already shown more courage than most men I know. I will not leave you alone. I do have a plan. But there is a scourge in the kingdom. We suffer a deadly disease, and it will take me some time to hunt my enemies down. This threat, these assassins—I know who they are, but I don't know how deep it goes or who all is involved. It will take me some time to figure out who I can trust and who I should kill. And until they are dead, I need to know my son is safe. It is we they are after, myself and my son. And if they come to power, if they take the kingdom from us, then the move toward democracy will be aborted before it can be born. So until this danger passes, you *must* hide away."

* * *

The princess took a deep breath, then turned back to her window to watch the darkness outside. The helicopter passed over the Iranian border and climbed to five hundred feet. She saw a dark ribbon wind along the foothills to the south—the Khorramshahr highway that ran to the heart of the oil fields. She tried to remember the map she had studied the night before. The tiny village of Agha Jari Deh was but a little farther inland.

The chopper leveled off, then descended again.

The mountains rose up to meet them.

She was almost there.

* * *

Rassa Ali Pahlavi lay still in his bed, awake but unmoving, the bedroom cool in the spring mountain air. Something had awakened him, something far in the distance, the low sound of beating rotors passing over a hill. He lay there and thought, then pushed himself out of bed and pulled on a thin shirt and dark trousers.

He walked silently out of the bedroom and quietly closed the door. Moving into the kitchen, he set a blackened copper kettle on the stove and turned on the propane, setting the flame on high. He moved carefully, making no noise, knowing the walls that separated the kitchen from Azadeh's bedroom were paper-thin. The water boiled quickly under the oversized flame, and he sprinkled in two measures of black tea, stirred quickly, then poured the tea into a ceramic mug and held it tight, letting it warm his hands. He sipped once. The tea was bitter, and he pressed his lips appreciatively as he sat down at the table.

All around him were reminders of his Muslim religion. A large and beautifully framed embroidery hung on the wall, an angular inscription consisting of three words: *Allah, Muhammad,* and *Ali,* devoted follower of the prophet. The name of Ali in the embroidery identified his household as a member of the Shi'a, or Shi'ites, those Muslims who consider Ali the legal successor to Muhammad. The entire house was liberally decorated with religious symbols and verses from the Qur'an, designed to chase evil away.

Was evil coming? Rassa felt a cold chill. *Something* was coming. He had felt this before.

Staring at his meager surroundings, he felt restless and on edge. He sipped at his hot tea, seeking its warmth. Standing, he walked quietly to Azadeh's bedroom and pushed the door open a crack. She was sleeping soundly, and he sat down again. Picking up a copy of the Holy Book, he repeated the cleansing phrase, *"In the name of Allah, most gracious, Most Merciful,"* then started reading, choosing at random a verse.

"It is righteousness to believe in Allah and the Last Day; and the Angels, and the Book, and the Messengers; to be firm and patient in pain and adversity, and throughout all periods of panic. Such are the people of truth, the God-fearing. . . ."

He read the verse again, then looked up in thought.

"To be firm and patient in pain and adversity . . ."

He thought back to the sound that had startled him out of sleep.

A helicopter. Over the village. On this side of the hill.

Choppers in the village? That was never good news.

Pain and adversity. His village had had its fair share.

* * *

Crown Prince Saud unstrapped his seat belt, moved to the small door that separated the passenger cabin from the cockpit, and pulled it open. He was met by the dim, multicolored lights of the cockpit: four eight-inch computer displays, a terrain-following radar, and rows upon rows of digital gauges and multifunction switches. The two pilots sat side-by-side, both of them Saudi air force colonels, old friends, trusted and worthy, their faces an unearthly green in the reflected cockpit lights. Saud stood in the doorway and studied the ALQ-162 defensive/countermeasures CRT, an automated system that searched out ground threats—ground-to-air radars, shoulder-fired weapons, and other heat-seeking missiles. With the exception of the Operations Normal symbology, the screen was a pale, silver blank. Satisfied, he raised his eyes to look through the cockpit window. The world appeared crooked, for the pilot had rolled the chopper into a steep bank. The horizon tilted across the windscreen at an uncomfortable angle, the moon and stars filling the right window, the coastline and lighted highway filling the left. His head spun a moment, and he adjusted his weight to balance himself, then turned to the copilot, who gestured to the north. "Agha Jari Deh," the pilot said, pointing to a tiny collection of mud and brick houses nestled tightly against the rising mountains.

The prince looked anxiously. Even in the moonlight, he could see that the village was surprisingly small; so small, the chopper would overfly it in a minute or less. There was only one road in or out of the village, and except for those who traveled to its market the village was almost completely unknown.

Saud studied the passing huts and small homes. It was so small. It was perfect. Allah had prepared a way. The prince understood that. Years before, in his perfection, Allah had seen the death that would come. And in his infinite mercy and wisdom he had prepared this way.

* * *

The chopper rolled level and began to slow down. The copilot lifted his hand to the collective and pressed his radio switch to answer a radio call. "Transportation is waiting," he announced to the prince.

Saud nodded and watched as the chopper turned to line up on a grassy field, two or three kilometers south of the village. The circle of grass appeared as a dark bowl against the reflective rocks of the mountains. The village was quiet, less than a dozen lights shining to the north. He picked out the headlights of the waiting vehicles as the chopper descended through 300 feet and slowed below 120 knots. A powerful *whoop* emitted from above his head as the blades slapped the air, taking less of a bite as the aircraft slowed down. The pilot switched on the landing light, and the tips of the spinning blades reflected the powerful lamp. Saud nodded, nudged the pilot on the shoulder, then stepped out of the cockpit and closed the door. Moving to the princess, he sat down at her side. She stared ahead, unmoving, her determination building inside. The prince didn't speak to her as he slipped her lap belt on.

The chopper sat down with a bump on the uneven field, and the pilot brought the twin turbine engines to idle and disengaged the rotors. Saud stood and worked the exit door, which dropped into the darkness, the folding steps exposed as the door slipped into place. He turned back to the princess, who was waking their son, and the three of them stepped out of the aircraft and into the cold mountain air.

* * *

Rassa heard his new dog. The young Afghan hound barked lazily from behind his house, out near the barn, along the narrow trail that led to the mountains. He stood up, moved to the window, and looked out on the courtyard that surrounded his backyard. The moon cast deep shadows that wavered as the clouds passed overhead. The air was calm and cold, and he saw no movement in the dim light. The trees stood tall and still. The geese and ducks had scattered to the small pond beyond the mud wall and, besides his dog, the other animals slept. As he stared at the shadows he heard his dog bark again, her head sticking halfway out of her shelter, only half interested in sounds that Rassa could not yet detect. But twenty seconds later he heard the sound of an automobile engine and the soft crunch of tires against the rock and gravel outside.

A sudden chill ran through him. He thought of the earlier whoop of the chopper blades and the roar of the engines. Out here, in the most remote parts of the country, where the warlords and tribal chiefs still had their way, a chopper could mean only one of two things: warlords from the south, coming up to collect recruits for their bloody turf battles, or the Jihadists from Iraq—the lawless Islamist fanatics who had adapted to the presence of Western forces in Iraq by hiding out in the Iranian deserts, where they planned their battles against the Great Satan and Jews.

Standing in the middle of the kitchen, Rassa felt his heart sink with a feeling of blackness and dread. He had seen many men disappear, pulled away in the night. Some had been suspected collaborators. Some had been hauled off to fight. Few were ever heard of again or returned to their homes.

He listened to the sounds of the car doors shutting, then soft footsteps on the porch. He glanced in a panic at the bedroom door, thinking of his little girl, then considered the old rifle stuffed behind the ancient cedar armoire in the corner of the room, a 30.06 that had been used by his grandfather during the First World War. The rifle was his own deadly secret. Having a weapon in Iran was strictly forbidden, but he made no move toward it. If they were coming for him, be it the warlords or the mullahs, it would be dangerous to fight them, especially with Azadeh in the next room.

So he waited, unmoving, listening to the footsteps outside his door. The wooden door rattled on its hinges, but Rassa didn't dare move.

chapter twenty-six

Rassa finally pulled the door open and stared in the dim light onto his porch. Two middle-aged men stood in the darkness, both of them strong and well dressed in dark suits, white shirts, and maroon ties. Though they wore western suits, traditional turbans were wrapped on their heads. The nearest man almost blocked the doorway with his massive frame, and he moved one hand to his hip, exposing a thin leather holster. The second man stood slightly behind the other and off to the side. Rassa glanced past the first guard to see two dark cars parked on the road, their engines at idle, their headlights off. Without explanation, the bodyguards pushed into his home and swept through the room. Rassa stood speechless until one of them paused at the bedroom and glanced to his boss. "Is Azadeh in there?" he asked Rassa in a deep, husky tone.

Rassa moved toward the bedroom door. "Who are you?" he demanded, his eyes flashing with rage.

"Is she in there?" the bodyguard repeated.

Rassa tightened in panic, and he shook his head. "You do not want her," he hissed, his voice husky with rage. It was the voice of a fighter at the edge of a war. "It is me you have come for! *Leave her alone!*"

He took a quick step toward the guard, while glancing at the holster underneath the dark suit. If they had come for Azadeh, then he would die to prevent it.

The leader ignored Rassa and nodded to the bedroom. "Check it out," he said.

The smaller guard nodded back and slowly pushed the door open. Stepping into the room, he pulled a tiny flashlight from his pocket and flashed it inside. He saw the sleeping girl, her head buried on the side of her pillow, then swept the light quickly around the room, taking in the simple bed, small chest, and white wicker drawer. A small collection of colorful dresses, silken Hajib head scarves, and full Burkas were hanging from a rope tied across the far corner. A silver tray of hairbrushes had been neatly arranged on top of the dresser. On the floor next to the bureau was a pair of sandals and another of leather shoes. He studied the room carefully, then stepped back and closed the door.

As the door closed, Azadeh immediately opened her eyes.

Rassa was waiting, a look of rage in his eyes. He relaxed his glare only slightly when the guard closed the door. "Who are you?" he hissed. "What are you doing here? I have nothing to hide! I have nothing you want!"

The two guards didn't answer as they nodded to each other. The larger man moved to the front door, pushed it open, and raised his right hand. The automobiles turned off their engines. Rassa heard the car doors open, then the sound of soft footsteps. He waited, then moved to the center of the kitchen, placing himself between Azadeh's bedroom and the front door.

A young woman entered the room, her face strained, her dark eyes bewildered and red. She was dressed in a dark burka and leather sandals, and she pulled a deep blue shawl tightly over her shoulders. She moved to a position beside the wall, then pushed her burka back, revealing a long mane of dark hair. Another man followed, dressed in an exquisite dark suit. Rassa saw him and stepped back, sucking in a quick breath of air. The intruder walked into the room with the confidence of a king, his shoulders square, his head high, his eyes constantly moving with suspicion but still clear and sure. Rassa dropped to one knee as the prince moved through the room, the social chasm between them demanding he bow with respect.

The prince moved toward him and extended his hand. Rassa stood, and the prince pulled him to his chest, kissing both of his cheeks in a display of respect.

Rassa dropped his eyes in confusion. What was this man doing here?

* * *

The prince stepped back and took in Rassa, measuring his appearance from his head to his feet. The woman remained near the doorway, waiting, her eyes dull with fright. The prince turned back to Rassa and gripped him by his shoulders. "Rassa Ali Pahlavi," he asked, "do you know who I am?"

Rassa nodded as he answered. "*Sayid,* I know who you are."

"Then who am I, Rassa Ali Pahlavi?"

"You are Crown Prince Saud, oldest son of King Fahd bin Saud Faysal, monarch of the House of Saud, grandson of King Saud Aziz, future Custodian of the Two Holy Mosques, keeper of the Holy Cities of Makkah and Madinah."

Prince Saud nodded, his weary eyes shining bright. Good. That was good. His cousin might have been raised in one of the most remote villages in the mountains, but clearly he was not an illiterate fool. He had read. He remembered. And he was aware. Some of the prince's own citizens would not have recognized him, and only one in a hundred Iranians would have known who he was. He nodded with approval, then motioned toward the young woman. "Do you know her as well?" he demanded.

Rassa kept his head low, clearly afraid of meeting her eyes. "I'm sorry, Your Highness, I do not know who she is."

The prince nodded again. That was good too. She mustn't be recognized if their plan was to work. And he had doubted she would be, not here in the Iranian mountains, so far from their home.

The royal sons were rarely photographed inside their own country, and it was strictly forbidden to photograph their children or wives. Saudi Arabia wasn't England after all, with their maniacal fascination with the royal family. It was *The House of Saud, the Kingdom of Arabia, Keeper of the Holy Cities.* Theirs wasn't a monarchy of fairy tales and magic castles, a kingdom of tabloids and gossip and family secrets revealed. The House of Saud was a kingdom of *power,* the kingdom of *Allah;* and pulp-fiction paparazzi were simply not tolerated in their press. The royal wives and their daughters led luxurious but anonymous lives. It had always been thus, and it would always be; for it would have been demeaning to Allah and his prophet for the women of the royal family to live publicly.

They were extremely rich but essentially unknown behind their security walls. Which meant the princess could stay here *if* she would not be recognized.

Prince Saud nodded to the princess. "You do not know who she is?" he asked again.

"No, my *Sayid*. Should I recognize her?"

Prince Saud watched Rassa closely as he searched for any shadow that he was not telling the truth. Did he truly not know her? Would his eyes give him away?

Rassa's face didn't change. He did not know who the princess was.

The prince breathed a shallow sigh of relief.

It might actually work.

He studied Rassa again. His men had been investigating his cousin for almost a year, and there was little about Rassa that the prince didn't know. And though the final plans had been laid some months before, when the prince first became convinced they might actually come after his family, this was the first time he had seen Rassa, and he wanted to take the measure of him.

Rassa held the prince's stare, never looking away. The prince saw in his eyes what he was thinking: This man might be a prince, but this is *my* home. And no man is my master, at least not in *this* place.

Over the years the prince had learned how to measure a man. He had learned to distinguish between enemies and friends, to measure secret ambitions and hidden desires, to recognize those who loved him and those who wished to bring him harm. Staring into Rassa's eyes, he saw no guile in him. This was a good man, straightforward and honest. For the first time in days, the prince began to relax.

* * *

The crown prince took a step toward Rassa. "We are not strangers," he said. "One of my grandfathers, your grandfathers, they were cousins."

Rassa nodded. The genealogy was not unfamiliar to him. "It was many generations back."

"Yes, that is true. But the bloodlines of royalty are extremely pure. We are far more closely related than you might at first guess."

Rassa thought for a moment, getting past his surprise and

fear. "Our forebears were enemies," he added after reviewing his memory.

The prince smiled. "Yes, they traded a share of their men's lives in battles; there is no doubt about that. But they were not unfriendly, I think. They were sheiks fighting for their kingdoms and to protect their gold, but when the day was over, I suppose they were friends. That was business and that was then, and of course this is now. So you and I, we are family. And the bonds of our ancestors that tie us are far stronger than any blood that has been spilt in the past."

Rassa paused, then answered sadly.

"When the battle is over,
And the evening winds come,
When spear tips glint in the twilight,
And the skirmish is done,
Then I hope I am standing,
And, brother, I hope you are too;
For on the other side of the war ground,
I will be thinking of you."

* * *

The prince stood without moving. The lines were comforting and familiar, but he didn't know why. "Where did you hear that?" he asked Rassa.

The Iranian bowed.

"You wrote that?" the prince pressed.

"Yes, *Sayid*," Rassa answered. "The words just come to me sometimes. I didn't mean to insult."

The prince frowned, his eyes narrowing from the heartsickness inside. Then he repeated, his voice gentle, a mere whisper on his lips.

"Then I hope I am standing,
And, brother, I hope you are too;
For on the other side of the war ground,
I will be thinking of you."

He stole a glimpse at his woman, who stared at him in grief.

Not this time. Not his brothers. They only wished he was dead. He stood in mute silence, then suddenly shook his head.

Rassa stood close by, waiting, as Crown Prince Saud looked at him.

"Rassa Ali Pahlavi," he began, "I have come to you because I need your help. My life is in great danger. My wife is in great danger too. And the only son I have left, the son who will one day be king, is outside sleeping in one of my cars.

"I am bringing him to you for protection. I bring him to you so he will live. I am bringing him to you so he will one day be king. But his life is in great danger, for there are many around us who would not have it be so."

The room became deadly silent. Rassa stared at the prince in disbelief, his mouth growing dry. Prince Saud nodded to his bodyguards, who motioned to each other and walked quietly from the house.

chapter twenty-seven

The men were seated on the wooden floor, their legs tucked underneath them as they leaned against round cotton cushions. A cup of *chai* sat between them, thick as molasses, sweet as raw sugar, and strong enough to give an almost instant rush of energy. The smell permeated the room, warm and syrupy, and a thin wisp of steam rose from their porcelain cups. The young princess sat beside her husband but didn't say anything. She reached out her hand and he squeezed it, but then let go.

The bodyguards took up positions outside the small home. Rassa could hear their footsteps through the thin glass windows as they moved around the house and through the courtyard. As he listened, Rassa realized they were keeping to the shadows, never revealing themselves as they moved from the corner of the small house to the line of trees on the north and west sides.

The prince turned toward Rassa and folded his arms. "I'm going to ask you a question," he said.

Rassa's back stiffened, and he drew a tight breath.

"Do you understand why you are here?" Prince Saud asked in a low voice.

"Why am *I* here?" Rassa answered, a puzzled look on his face.

"Yes. Do you know why you're here?"

Rassa stared at him blankly, confusion narrowing his brow. "I am here, Crown Prince Saud, because . . . well, because this is my home."

The prince shook his head. "No, Rassa Ali Pahlavi, that is not what I meant. Why are you *here?* Why did God give you life? For what purpose were you born?"

"The purpose of life is to surrender my will to Allah," Rassa answered automatically, repeating the first words he had learned, the same words he had repeated every day since he was no more than two.

The prince nodded impatiently. "Yes, Rassa, of course. But think beyond the scripture. I want you to tell me more."

Rassa thought in bewildered silence. "Your Majesty . . ." he whispered, his voice trailing off. He stared at his *chai*, keeping his eyes on the floor.

Saud waited, then put his small cup aside. Rassa thought in bewildered silence, but only became more uncertain. He finally shrugged his shoulders tightly. "Your Majesty . . ." he stumbled, "I do not know what to say." He bowed his head lower, and the prince leaned toward him.

"I have spent most of my life studying the holy teachings of the Qur'an," he said. "I am both by nature and training a deeply religious man. I have responsibilities to the kingdom, but more, I have responsibilities to God. Because of this, I have spent my life studying with the masters, the best-educated Muslim philosophers anywhere in the world. And this is what I have come to believe. The Holy Qur'an teaches that each man has a reason for living. Allah fates certain things. And he has brought me here, Rassa, to speak with you tonight. He has a purpose for you, Rassa, and I know his will."

"Whatever you ask, I will do it," Rassa trembled in reply, before quickly adding *Insha'allah.* If it is God's will.

Saud lowered his voice and shot a quick look at the princess. "My kingdom stands on the edge of a precipice," he whispered in anguish. "We stand and look over a terrible and deadly abyss. And there are those within my country, even those within my own family, who want us to fall. There are those in my councils who crave a final battle with the West. And they are willing to do whatever it takes to make their dreams come true.

"They are dangerous. Extremely dangerous. They are a secret band of brothers, bound by blood oaths and lies. And they are not driven by a dedication to Allah. They are not driven by religion or a vision of a greater Islam. They are driven by power. They are driven by hate. They are evil and deadly men who want to conquer our world.

"And like the shadows that spread when the sun has gone down, they grow more and more dark as the evening comes on. Yet no one takes note of their growing power, for the darkness settles so slowly it is nearly imperceptible. But their influence is spreading. And I'm the only thing that stands in their way."

Rassa stared open-mouthed. It was impossible! This was the most powerful man in Arabia, next to the king himself. One of the most powerful men in the world. He could not understand it. But as he stared at the prince, he experienced a cold look of fear he could not deny.

Prince Saud dropped his eyes and a shadow crossed his face. "Early this evening I buried my family," he explained. "My first wife and our children. A daughter. Two sons. Another son who was not even born yet also died in his mother's womb." He shot another pained look at his wife, then slowly went on. "The only son I have left is outside in the car. I have brought him to you, Rassa, because you are my kin. I have brought my wife and child to you because I need to keep them safe. There is nowhere in the kingdom that they could not be found. But here . . . in these mountains . . . in this tiny village in Iran, they will be safe for a few days, and that's all I need to defeat my enemies. But until I have done that, I need a safe place where my wife and young son can hide, somewhere outside the kingdom, somewhere outside of their reach."

Rassa bowed in submission, then gestured to his simple house. "But *Sayid,*" he questioned, "look at my home. It is unworthy of the princess. It is unworthy of your son."

"My poverty is my pride," the prince quoted the Qur'an in reply.

"But I am a simple man, Your Highness. A simple man, a family man, trying to survive on my own."

"Which is why this will work. They will never suspect. And, Rassa, this isn't a decision I came to rashly. I have thought this through, and I know in my heart this is the right thing to do."

"But *Sayid,*" Rassa argued, "a young *prince.* In my home!"

"Listen to me!" Saud answered quickly, his voice growing strained. "You are Rassa Ali Pahlavi! The royal blood runs through your veins as it has run through your fathers for almost two thousand years. You cannot dismiss that. And they can't take it from you. We share royal blood, Rassa. That is why I came to you."

Rassa was silent, and the prince pointed a finger. "They will be looking for him," he prodded, his voice weakened by fatigue and fear. "They will search through my kingdom; they will turn every rock, every reed, every rill. They will follow my movements, always searching for clues. But they will never suspect that I would dare take him out of the kingdom. And to Persia no less! They would not dream I would do this, and that is why this will work."

Rassa stared ahead in silence. He did not know what to say.

Saud watched him, then stood quickly. His gestures indicated that he was finished explaining and it was time for him to go. He nodded to the princess, and she stood up at his side. Turing to Rassa, Prince Saud made his final point. "The time is soon coming when Islam will rise from the ashes of the Ottoman Empire," he said. "She will rise and reclaim her rightful position of leadership in this world. For more than one thousand years, while the West rutted through the dark ages and wallowed in decay, the people of Islam stood as the military, economic, and spiritual leaders of the world.

"And yet from the day Napoleon marched into Egypt, we have reacted like a stunned bull. One shot and we fell in a quivering heap to our knees.

"But the time is soon coming when we will rise again. There will be a Pan-Arabia! But it will take a new way of thinking; it will take a new world; it will take a new kind of leader to lead us there. A new king is required, someone who can purge Islam of her poison and lift her again as a symbol to the world of wealth and peace.

"I am that man, Rassa. And my son will follow me. So we must keep him safe. Now do you understand?"

Rassa nodded gravely, then pushed himself to his knees. "I will do as you command," he whispered as he bowed at the prince's feet.

The prince put his hands on his shoulders. "You must speak of this to no one," he said. "Do you understand, Rassa, how important that is? You will call the princess a cousin who is visiting from Riyadh. Tell no one I have been here, or we both are dead."

Rassa kept his eyes low as he nodded his head.

"Do you understand that, Rassa? Do you see how important our secrecy is?"

"I understand, *Sayid.*"

The crown prince gripped his shoulder, then looked at his wife. He nodded to the princess. "Go and get him," he said.

The princess left the house quickly and returned with her son. The small boy stood shyly, holding tightly to his mother's hand. He had round eyes and dark hair, and he smiled wearily. His father knelt before him and pulled him to his chest. Looking up, he nodded sternly to Rassa, looking him straight in the eyes. "Keep him safe," he demanded as he let his son go. "It will be only a few days, a few weeks at the most before I come back for him. Keep them safe, and I'll reward you beyond your wildest dreams. But if any danger befalls them, then I will hold you responsible. This is your charge, your great purpose, and you simply cannot fail."

Rassa nodded and bowed. *"Sayid,"* he replied.

"It could be dangerous for you, Rassa."

"*Sayid,* I will serve."

Prince Saud pressed Rassa's shoulder, then turned sadly to the princess and reached for her hand. "I will come back for you, Ash Salman," he whispered, leaning his mouth to her ear. "I will not leave you, not a day, not an hour more than I have to. But for now we must do this. We must do this for our son.

"Now stay here. Be strong! Take care of my child, and I will call for you soon."

The princess nodded, her eyes hard, her face firm and proud. Saud leaned over and kissed her cheek softly, then turned and walked from the room.

After the prince left, the young mother stood silent against the wall, holding the child prince in her arms.

Rassa stared at her blankly, a dumbfounded look on his face. He didn't know what to say. He didn't know what to do. He opened his mouth, then shut it, thinking it better to not sound the fool. The young princess stared at him, then let her eyes drift to the floor. Her young son stirred, looking sleepily around the room.

"Mother, where are we?" he wondered. "Where did Father go?"

The princess knelt down to him. "Abd Illah, your father has gone. We are going to stay here for a few days."

The prince looked around the bare room, then reached up for his mother, pulling into her arms again. "I want to go home," he whispered. "Why are we staying? I want to go with Father. Why did he leave us here?"

The young boy started to cry. The princess was not far from tears herself as she lifted him in her arms.

Then the bedroom door opened, and Azadeh walked into the room. She shot a knowing look at her father, and he realized she had been listening. "Azadeh," he asked her, "how long have you been awake?"

She ignored the question as she walked to the princess and her son. "Princess Ash Salman," she said as she bowed deeply with a graceful sweep of her arms. "My name is Azadeh Ishebel Pahlavi. I am Rassa's daughter. Welcome to our home."

The princess stared at her, her eyes hopeful at seeing the girl. Azadeh took the young prince from her arms and said, "We don't have a lot to offer, but anything we have is yours. It is an honor to have you with us, and we will do all we can to make your stay comfortable."

Rassa took a step toward Azadeh. "How much did you hear?" he whispered quickly.

"Everything," Azadeh answered. "I woke up when they first knocked at our door."

"Then you understand . . . ?"

"I understand the princess has had a very long day. I understand the crown prince is in danger, and so is this child. Now we will make them safe and comfortable. We will treat them as our own."

Azadeh turned to the princess, who looked so young and vulnerable. An instant bond formed between them, and the princess smiled wearily. Azadeh held the young prince and moved toward her bedroom door. "You are tired," she said, as she held him close. "Come. You two have my bed. I will sleep here by the fire. Come. You are tired. We will talk in the morning. It will seem brighter then."

Rassa watched in grateful amazement as Azadeh took care of their guests. She got clean sheets and clean towels and placed a bowl of warm water by their bed. She offered them tea and a biscuit, which both of them declined, then shut the door behind her, leaving them alone in her room.

Rassa stared at her a long moment. "Thank you," he said.

* * *

Rassa waited until the others were finally asleep and the house had grown quiet, then slipped out the door and through the backyard, heading toward the center of town.

He found his friend Omar Pasni Zehedan in the back room of one of the dark warehouses he owned along the old docks on the river. Though it was after three in the morning, he knew Omar would be about his business. His friend often worked at night—some things were best done in the dark, and why should he sleep when there was cash to be made.

Walking through a side entrance of the old wooden warehouse, Rassa paused for a moment to let his eyes adjust to the light and listened to Omar berate one of his lieutenants in the next room. Above him, in a hidden attic, behind a trap door, Rassa knew he would likely find a cache of hand-woven Persian carpets on their way to illegal transport to Europe and the United States. He also knew Omar made more money on one pirated shipment of rugs than Rassa could make in a year. But he didn't envy Omar's money. He would have died from the stress.

Rassa listened to Omar go after his subordinate, took a deep breath, then gently knocked on the door. The voices on the other side of the door turned deadly silent, and he heard the shuffle of furniture and footsteps; then Omar slid the bolt back, his thick beard and huge frame filling the doorway. "Rassa!" he exclaimed. "What are you doing here?"

"I need to talk with you," Rassa answered.

Omar glanced over his shoulder. "Could it wait?" he said.

"No, Omar, please."

* * *

Omar stared at his friend, seeing the concern in his eyes, shot another look over his shoulder, then nodded his head. "All right," he answered as he quickly pushed through the door frame. Pulling the steel door closed, he offered, "Let's take a quick walk."

They walked along the river. The moon was just dropping behind the plains to the west, and the lamps along the docks cast a dull yellow glow. "What do I do?" Rassa questioned after he explained everything.

Omar stared at Rassa, his face firm, his eyes narrow. He shook his head in disbelief. His young friend was in deep water, in way over his head. He was in the middle of the ocean.

Did he know how to swim?

Omar shook his head intently. "You've got a problem," he said. "And the truth is, good friend, you are too naïve and too kind to realize how big it really is."

Rassa looked at him, his eyes wide. "Just tell me what to do," he pleaded.

"You have no choice," Omar answered after some thought. "The crown prince of Arabia will not be trifled with. You must do as he asked you to do; you don't have any choice anymore. You are already committed. But you are also in danger. Are you wise enough to see that? Prince Saud is so desperate, he has played his last option, and that option, unbelievably, has led him to you. But he has powerful enemies, Rassa; he lives in a hard, cruel world. It is harsh. It is mean. It is a dog-eat-dog world, even with family. A world that is difficult for you to understand. There is no good and no bad, only the weak and the strong. It is survival of the fittest, and not a thing else. Now is Prince Saud the strongest? We don't know that yet. But those men who seek to destroy him will seek to destroy you as well. So if I have any advice for you, friend, it would be to stay out of sight. Keep your head on a swivel, and keep your eyes open wide. Don't sleep too soundly, Rassa, not for a few days. The first forty-eight hours will be critical. If they are coming for you, I think they will be here by then."

Rassa looked confused. "But you don't think they would . . ."

"Absolutely they would. You are a friend of the crown prince; you are their enemy now. And if they are after the princess, then you stand in their way. The main question—really the only question—you need to consider is whether they will find her. How determined are they? How far will they go? Can Prince Saud protect her? Did they follow Prince Saud? Do they have spies around?"

Rassa stopped and stared out on the river and slowly shook his head. "I would never do anything that would endanger Azadeh," he said.

"Everyone is in danger, Rassa. It is the times we live in."

Rassa didn't answer, but started walking again.

Omar watched him a moment, noting the slump of his shoulders and the drag of his feet. His friend was in trouble. Omar committed to help. He would keep his eyes out; he would keep his own men in the square; he would watch the roads and highways and see what popped up. And he would warn Rassa if the wrong men came around.

chapter twenty-eight

The Sikorski S-92 flew low and fast over the water as it crossed the Gulf on its way back to Saudi Arabia. The moon was setting in the western sky, and a band of thick sea fog was developing below it. The moonlight cast shadows across the top of the fog, creating an illusion of flying over a landscape from the moon, endless miles of smooth and barren nothingness that stretched into the darkness of space.

Crown Prince Saud sat alone in the luxurious cabin. The lights were turned down, and though his eyes were closed, he was not asleep. His body was almost numb with heartbreak and fatigue, and sleep was far from him, for he was in too much pain. Over the past forty-eight hours he had lost everything he had ever loved: his wife and three children and his son yet unborn, his second wife and his last son, who were hiding now in Iran, his kingdom, his power, everything of any value to him—it was slipping away, a fistful of fine sand. He felt a blackness settle over him, a suffocating blanket of defeat, and he stared at the darkness and sucked in a sudden, deep breath.

The helicopter vibrated around him, a smooth hum that

developed from both the tail rotor and main mast spinning over his head, a comforting vibration that settled into his bones. At the front of the cabin, one of the flat screen TV monitors had been tuned to Arabic All News, but the sound was turned down and the prince paid no attention, though the television screen cast black and silver shadows through the cabin, causing his face to reflect in the oval window by his seat.

As the helicopter flew toward Arabia, the crown prince plotted in silence, his mind determined, almost bent, the rage and grief mixing like a black storm inside. He wasn't thinking clearly and he knew it, but he didn't care anymore. Clarity was for cowards and fools. It was time that he act. Prince Abdullah had killed his family. He knew it was Abdullah; he had known all along. His private intelligence officers had warned him there was a growing danger. Now he had to move quickly to protect what little he had left. His father. The kingdom. It was all in danger. They were not finished with their killing. Abdullah would strike again.

Unless Saud acted quickly to take Abdullah down first.

He balled his fist as he thought, his arms taut, his temples pounding with each beat of his heart. He plotted in the darkness of the cabin and the darkness of his soul.

The enormous chopper flew west, moving toward the low fog, and the night grew thick and full as the moon fell toward the horizon. The Saudi coast began to shine in the distance, a silver shadow in the starlight where the fog broke and the seas hit the shores.

* * *

The American-made F-15 fighter flew in a gentle circle at 23,000 feet. At this altitude, the stars were clear and bright, and the light of the moon glinted off the Eagle's gray wings. The pilot, a senior colonel in the Royal Saudi Air Force, had been in the air for almost an hour and was running low on fuel. In another fifteen minutes he would have to return to the base, which meant his career, and maybe his life, would be over. Prince Abdullah had been very clear. Complete the mission or die. And the colonel wasn't stupid. He knew his life was at stake.

He glanced nervously at his fuel readout, a sick knot in his stomach, then scanned his radar again. He had the APG-63 radar looking down, skimming the ocean below him, searching for his target. Why he had to shoot down the chopper—who it was and why it was flying over the Persian Gulf toward Arabia at three in the morning—he didn't know. Bandits. Terrorists. A rebellious OPEC minister from Oman, an Iranian businessman who had crossed the young prince—he hadn't been told. And it didn't matter. All he knew was his instructions came from Prince Abdullah himself. And one did not disobey the royal family, especially *this* prince. He was ruthless and cunning and, many speculated, on his way to the top. So a smart man like the colonel would attach himself to the winner and ride with him for all he was worth, a calculation that made the situation before him very simple. Shoot down the helicopter and get his first star. Fail and be shot. It was easy to be motivated with his life on the line.

The pilot flew the fighter aggressively, whipping the controls as he desperately searched the night sky. His digital fuel readout clicked again, decreasing to eighteen hundred pounds. The radar found nothing. The sky was empty and dark. The knot in his stomach grew. His readout clicked off another fifty pounds, and he went through the numbers again in his head. Five hundred pounds of fuel to get back to base, a couple of hundred to fly his overhead approach, three hundred for emergency reserve, two hundred to land. He had nine minutes, maybe ten, before he would have to turn back to base.

His palms had already sweated through his gloves, wetting the controls. *"Shoot down the chopper or die trying,"* the prince's brutal instructions sounded again in his head.

The truth was, he didn't mind the thought of dying in combat; he'd give his life happily for the Kingdom of Saud. But he bitterly hated the thought of dying because he had run out of gas or, worse, because the prince shot him when he learned of his failure.

He cursed, slapping his fist on his knee.

Where was the target? What was he going to do? He glanced at his fuel gauge, then cursed once again.

Rolling the fighter up on her wing, he scanned the expanse of dark ocean almost five miles below him, staring through the side of his Plexiglas canopy. He counted no less than six oil tankers moving through the Persian Gulf, each of them trailing a long line of sea foam that shimmered in the moonlight. A couple of enormous cargo transports moved parallel to the tankers, heading in the opposite direction toward the ports at Al Kawayt and Abadan. To the west, a bank of thick sea fog had developed, and he watched as it drifted toward the Saudi coastline a little more than fifty miles away. He flew his aircraft slowly north and then east, keeping it constantly banked up on her side, and the enormous oil derricks along the Iranian coast slipped into view, their dark towers rising over the shimmering waters of the Gulf. He rolled the nimble fighter level, then jerked the stick to the right and pointed the nose toward the Saudi coastline.

His radar swept across the horizon, hitting a couple of targets, civilian airliners moving toward Riyadh and Al Manamah, but it was almost three in the morning and the civilian airline traffic was light. He commanded the look-down, shoot-down radar to search low once again, knowing the chopper would stay near the water—all the chopper pilots he knew had a great fear of heights. His radar reflected a deep green shadow on his face mask as he stared at the screen. Nothing. Empty airspace. No chopper there.

He shook his head in frustration, as the sweat from his armpits soaked his flight suit.

Kill the chopper or die. His instructions were clear.

But he couldn't kill the chopper until he found it.

He glanced at his fuel gauge as it clicked through fifteen hundred pounds, then reached up and adjusted his radar out to eighty miles. The Saudi coastline cluttered the display, and the phase-array system sought to cut through the radar energy that bounced back from the rocky coastline. The computer automatically adjusted the beam to cut through the ground clutter, and the radar display was cleaner on the next sweep.

Then he got it—a quick hit almost sixty miles away. It was low and moving quickly toward the coastline, just above the fog. He commanded his radar to hit the target again. It measured the relationship between the distance and ground speed, then began to click in his ear.

Target. Helicopter. Fifty-six miles off his nose. He yanked the fighter twenty degrees to the right and hit the afterburners for eight seconds to get a quick burst of speed; the Eagle accelerated very quickly, reaching almost mach point nine. Lowering the nose, he armed up his missiles, and the targeting computer instantly began to growl in his ear.

He had a lock on the target. In ten miles he would shoot. Ten miles. Fifteen seconds. From here, it was easy. His mission was almost complete.

* * *

The crown prince had barely drifted to sleep when the Sikorski suddenly reeled on its side; his stomach lurching as the chopper fell toward the ocean. His eyes flew open, his heart slammed, and the adrenaline surged through his body as the helicopter lurched again and nosed over. The airspeed picked up, and he heard the building noise of the airstream slipping over the cabin. Faster and faster. The chopper rolled left and then right, and his stomach turned again. He caught a glimpse through the window and saw the sea shimmer lightly, barely off the left side. They were right on the water, no more than four or five feet in the air. He cried as the aircraft lurched, then started climbing again. A sudden burst of light, bright as the sun and moving off the left side, cast a freak shadow under its incredible light. The ocean lit up like at noonday as the flare burned across the night sky.

The helicopter's defensive countermeasures were kicking out antimissile flares!

The crown prince knew what was happening.

And somewhere inside him, though he didn't acknowledge it yet, a small voice whispered that he was dead.

* * *

Grabbing the side of his chair, Prince Saud stumbled toward the cockpit door, but the chopper lurched again, and he was knocked to the floor. The aircraft rolled on its side to almost ninety degrees, and he slid like a rag doll across the carpeted floor, smashing his head against a small conference table. He felt the warm blood in his right eye, but quickly wiped it away and struggled to his feet again as the helicopter groaned around him, vibrating and shaking like an amusement-park ride. They were exceeding their main rotor speed limit; he could tell by the screeching sound. He reached for the cockpit door and jerked it open just as the chopper rolled again. He fell back and smashed his head on the same table. Cursing, he crawled to the cockpit door and pulled himself to his feet.

Entering the cockpit, he saw the amber caution lights and

heard the warning horns. The two pilots were in a panic, the pilot rolling the aircraft wildly. "Coming right!" he screamed as he rolled the chopper again. The prince's eyes shot to the defensive display, and his heart turned to a cold rock in his chest. He saw the readout of the tracking radar behind him, up at fifteen thousand feet. He heard the warning system growling, warning him of attack.

"Who is it?" he screamed to the copilot on his left side. The Saudi colonel turned to him quickly, his eyes wide with fear. "F-15 Eagle," he cried. "He is lighting us up!"

The night illuminated again as the copilot spit out another bundle of phosphorous flares. The flares ejected from behind the main rotors and lifted into the night, trailing above and behind the chopper in a white-hot trail of heat designed to pull heat-seeking missiles away. The copilot reached to punch the flare button again, but the prince slapped his hand back. "Stop it!" he screamed. "That is not going to help!" He jammed a finger toward the threat display. "He hasn't fired a missile yet. And when he shoots, it will be a radar-guided missile, not a heat-seeker anyway. All you're doing is lighting us up like a flashlight, helping him know where to shoot."

The copilot only nodded, ready to panic again. The pilot flew the chopper like a mad man who had been shot in the eyes, rolling it left and then right, rocking her up on her side. The prince saw the ocean rise up to meet them as the pilot rolled the chopper again. The rotor blades slapped the warm ocean, and the chopper lurched to the side. The pilot panicked and climbed and the chopper shuddered toward the night sky.

The prince braced himself, grabbing the top of the pilot's seats; then he turned his eyes and studied the countermeasures display.

He recognized the radar signature. An APG-63 radar. Yes, it was an F-15, forty miles behind them and closing very fast.

His mind raced as he considered their options. They were over the water. Nowhere to hide. Nowhere to land. He knew the spinning rotors and fat body of the chopper would bounce enormous portions of energy back to the F-15's radar receiver. They had no guns, no weapons, only a few countermeasures. He was a fighter pilot—he had targeted helicopters from an F-15 himself, and he knew how really hopeless it was. A helicopter, over the water, against an F-15 with its missiles and guns.

He swallowed, almost crying. Prince Abdullah had won.

The pilot continued flying like a crazy man, breaking right and then left, climbing and descending, trying to break the radar lock that was tracking them from behind. But the chopper was enormous and no more stealthy than a Mack truck in the air. The missiles couldn't miss it. They had seconds to live.

Saud's brain raced, then slowed down as a sudden calm filled his mind.

He was going to die. He knew that already. Abdullah had tracked him to Iran, which meant he would soon find his son. But he might yet save him, if he could just reach his friend.

He turned to the panicked copilot and jerked his headset from his head. "Tune up the VHF," he screamed above the cry of the helicopter engines and rotors.

The copilot stared at him blankly, his eyes glazed with fear.

"Give me control of the VHF radio!" the prince cried again.

* * *

The Saudi fighter pilot checked his airspeed and altitude. Five-eighty knots. Fourteen thousand feet. The target was forty-one miles in front of him, almost straight off the nose. He watched as it rolled left and then right, a lumbering giant warming up for its death dance. As if any of that mattered! It could turn, it could roll, it could climb or descend—his radar couldn't miss it now that he knew the chopper was there. He lifted his eyes and stared through the darkness, searching the open ocean below, and saw a tiny trail of white light burning across the ocean like a falling star. He squinted, then saw another white trail. What was that, he wondered, then almost laughed to himself. Flares! The idiot pilot was shooting off flares! He smiled under his mask. A real genius, yes. He hadn't even fired his missiles. It was pure panic down there.

Then he started, his mind racing. What kind of chopper carried antimissile flares? he wondered suddenly, an uncomfortable knot in his throat. Not a corporate charter. No civilian machine. Was he shooting a military chopper? What other kind of chopper carried flares . . . ?

He wondered half a second, then pushed the thought from his head. What did it matter? His instructions were clear.

The firing computer continued to growl in his helmet. He was in firing range. He checked the distance and lock-on, then moved his left hand on the throttles, flipped off the safe switch, and fired two AMRAAM missiles into the night air. The missile engines fired together in a trail of white smoke and flame and accelerated before him, then began to track toward the target below.

* * *

The helicopter copilot reached for the radio console and flipped the selector to manual. The crown prince leaned over the center console and changed the frequency to 122.5, the emergency guard frequency. Every U.S. aircraft in the air was required to monitor the frequency. The prince pulled on the headset and jerked the microphone to his lips.

"Mayday, Mayday, Mayday!" he said into the mike. "This

is an emergency call for any U.S. aircraft. Mayday, Mayday! Does anyone read?"

The prince released his broadcast button and listened, but the radio was silent. "Mayday, Mayday!" he repeated. "Any U.S. aircraft, this an emergency!"

The helicopter pilot cried and pointed toward the threat screen. Two missiles had been fired and were tracking them. Twenty miles and closing. The pilot screamed in panic as he rolled the chopper and climbed, then threw the nose toward the ocean again. The copilot reached up and released another five bundles of burning flares. The missiles continued tracking toward the helicopter, accelerating as they descended through the night air. The pilot racked the chopper into a tight left-hand turn, pulling back toward the missiles, trying to throw them off his tail. The copilot saw the missiles turn toward them, then slowly bowed his head.

Prince Saud watched the missiles track toward him on the screen, his mind suddenly peaceful and calm. He knew it was over, but he was prepared. He thought of Tala and his children, hoping he would find them there. He believed they were waiting, and he was ready to go to them now. He was an empty hole, the emotion having been drained from his body sometime before. He had lost the battle. This war was left to someone else now.

Then he thought of his son and the last thing he could do for him, only hoping his message would not be intercepted. He pressed the transmit button and broadcasted again.

"Mayday, Mayday!" he said over the radio. "This is an emergency call to any U.S. aircraft in the region. This is Saudi Crown Prince Saud bin Faysal with an emergency message for Major General Neil Brighton of the national security staff. Neil, my friend, all of my family is dead. I have one son who is living, and you must rescue him. The Agha Jari Deh Valley . . . you will find him there. He is there with my . . ."

The missile hit the chopper in the left engine bay. Prince Saud felt the fire and heat and half a second of burning pain.

* * *

The F-15 pilot saw the explosion lighting up the night sky, a yellow fireball with a billowing white and black core. He saw the smoke rising, and the scattered pieces of the chopper began to rain from the sky, pelting the ocean in a hailstorm of smoking metal and burning debris, the fireball disappearing quickly as the pieces fell from the sky. He smiled, satisfied, and turned his jet back toward his home.

His mission was successful. It looked like he would get his first star.

chapter twenty-nine

The hallways of the Pentagon are a wide, windowless, and wondrous maze of interconnecting spokes and rings that start at the center courtyard and work their way out from there. They are crowded and dull and brightened only by the colorful assortment of uniforms in the halls: air force, army, navy, and marines; dress whites, fatigues, air force blues, and army greens. The Pentagon has its own Metro station (the largest and most crowded in the city) as well as half a dozen cafeterias, its own shopping mall, bank, and mail delivery operation. The services the Pentagon offers are equal to those of any small city—which, of course, is exactly what it is. More general and flag officers work in the Pentagon than in any other single place on earth, and most of them are housed in the executive hallway along the outermost ring on the northwest side of the Pentagon. The building is always crowded, and there is a sense of urgency, a sense of purpose and mission, that simply isn't replicated in any other government building other than the White House and the offices of the CIA. Those who walk the Pentagon halls know they are the sword of the nation, the tip of the spear, and they are willing to die for their country and to keep their people free.

Major General Neil Brighton had a small annex office along the outer ring of the Pentagon, one hallway over from the Chairman of the Joint Chiefs of Staff. It was an understated and private setup, a single room with no reception area, secretary, or staff, a thinking place where he went to get away from the ringing phones and constant meetings and appointments that plagued his White House office. Inside the wood-paneled room, he had a small desk set against the back wall where he could turn in his chair and stare out a large window onto one of the huge parking lots that surrounded the Pentagon. In the distance, the buildings of D.C. rose, punctuated by the Washington Monument's pearly-white spire sticking up in the air. Unlike his White House office, which was decorated with pictures of him with various political figures—two presidents, a vice president, the secretary of defense, half a dozen senators and congressmen, and various foreign leaders—the walls of his Pentagon office were decorated with his real love, which certainly wasn't politics but fighters and fighting men. There were pictures of him as a lieutenant standing in front of his first F-15, pictures of him flying in formation along the DMZ in Korea, pictures of him soaring over the pyramids of Egypt and the Brandenburg Gate of the old Berlin wall. There were pictures of him as a captain and a major, always in olive or desert camouflage flight suits, posing in front of a fighter jet. There were pictures of him with his squadron mates in various locations around the world: deep sea fishing in the blue waters of the Mediterranean Sea, riding camels in Iraq, eating sauerkraut at Lela's, and fighting wars in Kuwait, Bosnia, Serbia, and Iraq. A stranger could trace the general's career by looking at the pictures on the wall, from his flying days as a lieutenant to his first staff job at the Pentagon, from squadron commander at Langley to another staff job with the Joint Chiefs of Staff. It was here that the transition to a political animal became complete—where he started having more pictures of him with ambassadors and presidents than military friends.

It was late in the evening. The general had been back from his trip to Saudi Arabia for less than a day. The sun had set over the District, and the parking lot lights had clicked on. Brighton sat alone in his office and stared out the large window, lost in his thoughts as he pulled on his lip. Then came an urgent knock, and his White House aide pushed back the door. "Sir," the colonel said as he rushed into the room.

Brighton turned wearily. "What you got, Dagger?" he asked.

Colonel "Dagger" Hansen took a step toward his desk and thrust out his hand. He was holding a red, covered binder. "Bad stuff in Saudi," he said.

Brighton stood immediately and reached for the folder. "What is it?" he asked as he tore the classified seal on the envelope.

"Crown Prince Saud bin Faysal," Dagger answered.

Brighton paused and looked up.

"He's dead," the colonel continued. "His chopper was shot down a few hours ago."

Brighton's stomach turned, and he took a quick breath, almost grimacing in pain. "What? Are you certain?" he demanded. "How do you know it was him?"

"We know," the colonel answered. "And that's not all, sir. I'm afraid the news gets much worse. But we've got to go. I'll explain while we walk. The national security staff is assembling in the situation room and the president wants a brief in an hour."

Dagger turned for the door and Brighton followed. The colonel explained what he knew as they jogged down the hall.

* * *

Twenty minutes later, Major General Brighton was sitting at the situation room conference table, surrounded by the national security staff. He sat by himself, his head down, reading the transcript of the radio call:

"Mayday, Mayday . . . this is an emergency call to any U.S. (UNREADABLE) in the region. This is Saudi Crown Prince Saud bin Faysal with an emergency (UNREADABLE) for Major General Neil Brighton of the (UNREADABLE). Neil, my friend, all (UNREADABLE) . . . I only have one son (SIGNIFICANT UNREADABLE) . . . living. You (UNREADABLE) (rescue/rescued/resist??) him. The Agha Jari Deh Valley. (SIGNIFICANT UNREADABLE) . . . with my . . ."

Brighton checked the time of the transcription, then the time the interception took place. He studied the UNREADABLE portions of the transcript, trying to fill in the blanks, then turned to the communications specialist on the NSC staff. "Who picked up the message?" he asked.

"One of our recy birds out of Baghdad," the staff member answered.

"It wasn't broadcast to any particular receiver?"

"No, sir, it was not. It was a call in the blind. A couple dozen other U.S. aircraft reported hearing the broadcast, including half a dozen receivers inside of Saudi Arabia. The reconnaissance aircraft had its tapes rolling and was able to get it on tape, but the chopper was so low it impeded the range of the broadcast, and as you can see there are significant portions that are unreadable."

"It wasn't broadcast using Have Quick radio?" he asked.

"Negative, sir," the young lieutenant replied. "No secure means of encryption were employed. Quite the opposite, the radio call was broadcast on the civilian guard frequency. It was the crown prince's intention to get the message to as many people as he could, hoping it would eventually make its way to you. Clearly, that was his intention. He mentions you by name—that much of the broadcast came through loud and clear."

"But if he was trying to send me a message, why not use his satellite radio?"

"Time, sir, or lack of it. It takes a couple of seconds to synch up to a satellite, and when Prince Saud made this radio call, he was already under attack. It was amazing he had the presence of mind to get this much out. We've gone back and looked at some of the reconnaissance information from one of our Looking Glass IIIs. When this radio message was broadcast, the crown prince's helicopter was deep into evasive maneuvers. Missiles had already been fired. They were six, maybe eight, seconds from impact. The broadcast was terminated when the missiles impacted the target."

Brighton sat back and thought, imagining the chaos in the chopper in the last seconds of the prince's life as they tried to evade the inevitable. He considered the courage and calm the prince had displayed. "And the unreadable portions of the transcript?" he asked sadly, trying not to think of his friend.

"We're still working on that, sir. There were a couple of times when Prince Saud slipped into Arabic, so our translators have been going over the recording, trying to complete the transcription, but as I mentioned, the chopper was low and portions of the transmission didn't come through. It might be this is the best transcription we ever get."

The general laid the transcript on the table and stared at the far wall. The staff worked busily around him, but his mind drifted back.

He thought of his conversation with Saud in the garden. The crown prince had warned him. But did he have any idea he was so close to death? A sudden chill ran though him. How much did the prince really know? He thought of the code word. Was this Firefall?

He turned back to his staff. "Who was with him in his chopper?" he asked.

An intelligence officer stepped forward. "So far as we know, besides the pilots he was alone," he said.

Brighton shook his head.

The crown prince of Arabia. Alone. In his chopper. In the middle of the night. Out over the water. It was more than unusual—it was completely absurd. Turning to the transcript, he read it again. "*I only have one son.*" He stared again into space.

Colonel Dagger Hansen moved to the table and sat down next to Brighton as a small group of staff members gathered around them. The colonel's face was taut, and he wet his lips quickly. He stared at the general, then leaned toward him. "Sir, we've been poking around since we intercepted this message," he said. "Our consulate in Riyadh has been trying to talk with King Faysal, but he is staying low. However, he managed to send us a message. We are still trying to confirm its authenticity, but it appears to be real." Dagger paused and wet his lips again.

"Yes?" Brighton demanded.

The colonel looked around anxiously. "I'm sorry, sir, but we think Crown Prince Saud's family has also been killed."

"Killed!"

"Assassinated. A political hit."

"His family?"

"His sons from Princess Tala, Prince Saud's most senior heirs. And maybe Princess Tala and their daughter as well, all of them killed a little more than forty-eight hours ago."

Brighton's face drained of color, and he blinked his eyes

suddenly. He shook his head in doubt. "I don't believe it," he said.

"I'm sorry, sir. I know you and Crown Prince Saud bin Faysal were good friends. It's a kick in the gut, especially with his family . . ."

"I don't believe it!" Brighton repeated, his voice growing sour. His thoughts came to him slowly, thick tar in his mind. "Why would anyone kill his family? That doesn't make any sense! With the security that's around them, I don't see how they could!" His staff members stared at him, none of them willing to reply.

Dagger tapped a finger on the table, pointing to a line on the transcript. He didn't say anything, but his impatience was clear. "I'm sorry, sir, but it happened," the colonel finally said. "I know he was your friend, but the prince was taken out, along with his family. We know they've been killed. Now what are we going to do?"

Brighton turned toward him, and Dagger tapped the transcript again, the surety of his action enough to bring Brighton's disbelief to a close. "We are seeking confirmation, turning over every stone," the colonel continued, "but from what we are hearing from our friends at the Israeli Mossad, and Ambassador Bandar in Syria, it looks like one of King Faysal's sons is making a move."

The general shook his head, his face draining of color.

A power struggle in the kingdom. It was impossible to overstate the danger this could mean to the United States. The instability in the Persian Gulf would send the price of oil to $100 a barrel, money that would be used to breathe more money and life into al Qaeda. It would destabilize the entire region, including the fragile government in Iraq, while bringing out all the snakes and spiders in Syria, Iran, and Lebanon. It could shut down the Gulf to international shipments of oil while increasing the opportunities for nuclear proliferation in the most dangerous part of the world. It would mean the military forces in Israel would be on hair-trigger alert. It would mean . . . on and on. He felt a sick knot in his throat.

He took a deep breath. All right. It was here. He would deal with it; they would deal with it; they would do what was needed to see this thing through. He rubbed his face, then his hair, then took a deep breath again.

He stared at the transcript and thought clearly for the first time since walking into the situation room. "The prince's son?" he wondered, " . . . the Agha Jari Deh Valley." A light began to flicker inside his head.

"Princess Tala?" he asked. "She was killed, along with all of her children."

"Yes, sir. That is what we have been told."

"But there were no other assassinations?"

"Not that we know of right now."

Prince Saud had a second wife. Another child. One more son who still lived. "You know that Prince Saud had another son?" Brighton asked.

The colonel didn't answer. That was something he didn't know.

"They are taking out his heirs," Brighton said. "They're claiming stake to the kingdom—"

"Sir?" Dagger interrupted, then stopped and let Brighton think.

Brighton shook his head; then it hit like a slap on the head. "Get me a map," he demanded.

A map was laid out before him, and one of the specialists pointed at the crash site in the Gulf.

Alone . . . in his chopper . . . out over the water?

The general stared, thinking again of what the crown prince had said, the warning he had given and the fear in his voice. "Where is Agha Jari Deh?" he asked. Dagger pointed at the map. The general drew a line with his finger between Saud's personal heliport in Riyadh . . . the border . . . across the Gulf to Iran . . . through the mountains to Agha Jari Deh. The line was almost perfectly straight and he swallowed hard. "He hid him!" he said.

Dagger looked at him and wondered.

Brighton pointed again. "He was hiding his last son, his last heir. He took him to Iran." His voice was so certain, no one dared argue with him.

Brighton moved toward an illuminated map on the wall. The small group of advisors followed him, Dagger staying at his side. "Prince Saud knew it was coming," Brighton explained. "He even tried to warn me." He pointed to the small village with his finger. "He was over the Gulf, on his way back from where he had hidden his son in Iran."

Dagger stood in silence beside his boss, then cracked the fragile bones in his neck, as Brighton turned away from the wall map.

"We've got to help him," Brighton demanded as he turned to his aide. "What's the closest special operations unit?" he asked.

Dagger shook his head. "You know how thin we are, sir. All of our special ops units are committed to ongoing operations. I'm not sure who's available . . ."

"Find out," Brighton said. "We've got to get them to Agha Jari Deh before it's too late. We're looking for a young boy . . . four, maybe five. And Princess Ash Salman will be with him as well. Agha Jari Deh looks like a tiny village; if Saud took them there, then someone will know. But we've got to move quickly. If we picked up the radio broadcast, then Prince Saud's enemies inside Arabia certainly picked it up as well. They will be moving. We've got to get there before they do."

Dagger turned to an army liaison who had been standing with the circle of advisors a few feet away from the men. The army colonel stepped forward. "We've got a Delta team R&Ring in Germany," he said. "They were supposed to get another couple of days of rest, but we could load them up and get them in-country if needed. If we can get airlift and transports, they could be in Iran within twelve hours or so."

Dagger turned to Brighton. "Sir?" was all he said.

"Do it," Brighton commanded. "Twelve hours may be too late, but we've got to try. Coordinate with the Chairman, the SecDef, and the CINCS to get the orders in place. We need their support. If they have any questions, tell them to call me. And point out this will be a search and rescue mission only; the unit will avoid a firefight if possible, but we might meet up with hostiles, so we have to be prepared to accept casualties. Then prepare the talking papers so I can brief the president. We will need his authorization before we can move into Iran."

The army colonel nodded and moved toward his console. Dagger went with him, all the time talking in his ear. Brighton watched them go, his mind drifting away.

Sam's unit was in Germany. He knew they were the only Delta unit there.

He had just ordered his son into combat. No man should have to do that.

* * *

Prince Abdullah listened to the young communications specialist intently, boring his dark eyes into him. "You are *certain?*" he demanded, his voice deadly but calm.

"*Sayid*, yes, I am."

"He said the Agha Jari Deh Valley?"

"I am certain, Prince Abdullah, that is what he said."

"That's in Iran?"

"Yes, my *Sayid*."

Prince Abdullah closed his eyes and looked up at the ceiling. "My older brother has been murdered," he said carefully. "I need to know everything. I need to know every detail of the radio call. Now try to remember. Did he say anything else?"

The young soldier didn't move as he thought intensely. "I have told you everything," he finally answered. "Everything that I can recall."

"And there are no survivors?"

"No, my *Sayid*."

"No survivors . . . no survivors . . ." Abdullah's voice choked with pain. He forced a look of grief and deep sadness that pulled the corners of his lips into a tight frown. His eyes teared and his lip trembled—it was a spectacular display, with just the right mix of rage and shock and sadness at his brother's death. Every head bowed in respect for his pain. Always emotional, his Arab brothers recognized Abdullah needed a private moment to grieve.

The young prince wiped his hand across his eyes, then dismissed his staff with a wave of his hand. "Leave me," he whispered. "I need some time alone." His aides left without comment, the last one closing the heavy door to his office.

The room was silent a moment before Abdullah lifted the phone. "He went to Iran," he said immediately when his officer picked up the line. "Agha Jari Deh."

A long moment of silence followed before the officer replied. "Iran?" he muttered slowly.

"Yes. It has to be. And I want to move now."

"Prince Abdullah, I don't know that we can . . ."

"Of course we can. And of course we will. Many powerful Iranian officers are indebted to me. Start with General Sattam bin Mamdayh. He'll know *exactly* what to do."

"Prince Abdullah," the general started to plead, "we have

eliminated Prince Saud. His son is no threat to us now. By the time he is old enough, it will be far too late!"

"You will do as I tell you. I want all of his children killed!"

"But *Sayid,* he is but a child, little more than a baby. He poses no threat to you. Why can't we just let him be?"

"Because he will grow up, you fool! Because he knows who he is! He will remember his father, and he will come after us. And his mother is with him. Do you think she won't act? Are you stupid, my friend, or have you just lost your mind? I want all of them killed. None of Saud's children can live."

"But, my prince, if you will just consider for a moment . . ."

"I want them dead!" Abdullah screamed into the phone. "*Now, are you going to do it, or do I have you replaced?* There are others who will follow my orders, General. You are not irreplaceable. Now you either bring me the son, or I'll mount your head on my wall like the female sheep that you are. Choose now, but choose wisely, for I am not in a good mood. And I don't want to hear any more whining about how he is *just a child!*"

* * *

Iranian General Sattam bin Mamdayh truly did know what to do. As director of the Iranian internal special security forces, he was a good friend of Abdullah's and one of the hundreds of powerful and evil men who owed him or feared him or depended on his money.

Prince Abdullah called the general on a secure satellite phone. Abdullah didn't exchange pleasantries but got right to the point. "I need your help," he instructed. "And I need it now."

"Anything," the general answered. "I will do what I can."

"There is a small village on the west side, not far from the sea. Agha Jari Deh. Are you familiar with it?"

The general thought a moment, searching his memory. Yes, he was familiar. The village was nestled in the crest of the mountains. And there was a young man who lived there, a grandson of the former Shah, the traitor Pahlavi, friend of the Great Satan himself. All of the offspring of Pahlavi living inside Iran were under surveillance by his men, though Rassa Ali Pahlavi had spent a meaningless life of herding and farming so far as he knew.

"Pahlavi!" Abdullah breathed upon hearing the name. "Are you certain?" he demanded, his voice strained and tight.

"Absolutely," the general answered. "I have been there myself. He is a dirt farmer, a peasant; my dog lives better than he. He lives in a shack I wouldn't stable my horses in. He is nothing; I assure you."

Abdullah was silent, his breathing heavy and slow. "Pahlavi," he repeated like it was a bad taste in his mouth. "Pahlavi, my cousin . . ."

"You know him?" the Iranian general wondered in surprise.

Another moment passed in silence, the phone humming softly between the two men.

Abdullah was impressed. Of course! It was perfect. His brother was brilliant. He never would have found him. The young prince would have been safe. He *never* would have looked anywhere outside of Arabia. If his brother hadn't made the mistake of making the desperate radio call . . . if his people hadn't heard it . . . all might have been lost.

The Iranian broke the silence. "You know him, Abdullah?" he repeated.

"I know him," Abdullah answered. "He is a distant cousin, if you traced our lines many years."

The general filled the phone with laughter. "I could kill him," he offered. "I could send him to prison, or I could bring him to you. Tell me what you're after, what you want me to do."

Abdullah answered quickly. "There is a boy. A young lad. He is a . . . problem for me. I want you to eliminate the problem. Can you take care of that?"

The general snickered foolishly, drawing conclusions in his mind. A young lad? Sent away? One of the prince's wild oats. And now the princess didn't want the competition around her legitimate sons. How many times had he seen this? It was the same everywhere. "This will be easy!" he chuckled. "I will see it is done."

"Yes, you will," Abdullah answered. "And you will do it today."

"I'll have one of my personal units up there within a few hours."

"Yes, that is good. Before the sun goes down."

"Sayid," the general snapped, "I will report back to you. But you realize, of course," his voice softened now. "This . . . task you have asked, it is outside the official responsibilities of my office. I do this as a favor, a personal favor to you."

"I understand, Sattam bin Mamdayh." Abdullah knew how the game was played.

"Then perhaps we could talk when I have completed this task."

"Yes, we will talk."

"I will report my success."

"And, General," Abdullah added before he hung up the phone, "I don't need to state the obvious, but we don't want to leave any leftovers behind. We don't want any talkers; we don't want any eyes. We don't want any children spouting wild stories to their friends. It would be better if there were no witnesses to tell of this tale—my cousin, this Pahlavi, his wife, or his kin. If we take care of the child, then you'd better take care of *them*. Otherwise we will have residual problems, if you know what I mean."

The general only snorted. "I know, Prince Abdullah, how to do my job. You let me take care of your problem; then we'll talk again."

chapter thirty

Distant thunder rumbled down from the mountain, and the air was heavy with the fresh smell of rain. Azadeh and her father were working in the kitchen, preparing their evening meal. The young prince was asleep, nestled under the covers in Azadeh's bedroom, and the princess worked beside Azadeh, helping her peel potatoes and drop them into a boiling pot of salt and pork rinds.

Rassa heard his name from the backyard and he stopped, then grabbed Azadeh's hand. Azadeh held still, and the princess watched them, her eyes growing wide. She had been in their home for less than twenty-four hours, and she and Rassa had hardly spoken, but she didn't have to speak to see the fear in his eyes.

Rassa moved to the back window. The sky was dark with heavy clouds. The back courtyard was slippery with mud, and the animals were hunkered down under the small olive trees that lined the back wall. Rassa saw a flash of movement as Omar Pasni Zehedan pushed his enormous frame over the mud fence. He stopped and looked around, then ran toward the door.

Rassa moved to meet him. Azadeh followed her father, but the princess stayed back. Omar, soaked and out of breath, stood at the foot of the stairs, his curly hair wet and hanging in front of his eyes. He was puffing and sweating despite the cold air.

"Rassa," Omar said, his eyes darting around. "There are soldiers in the village. They are looking for you."

Azadeh felt her heart crush as she gasped for breath. She reached for her father, but he pushed her aside. Moving through the doorway, he drew it half closed, but Azadeh stayed close so she could hear what he said. "What soldiers?" Rassa demanded.

"I don't know," Omar shrugged. "I don't recognize the uniforms. Special security forces, I think, but I didn't recognize the unit and I don't know where they're from. But they are asking for you, Rassa, and they are only minutes away."

Azadeh moved to Rassa's side and grasped his hand. The princess had heard, and she backed against the far wall, then turned and ran to the bedroom where her son was asleep.

Rassa pushed the door back, then knelt and faced Azadeh. "Listen to me," he demanded. "We've got to get out of here." He fell suddenly silent. The crunch of heavy truck tires on wet gravel could be heard from the front of their house.

Rassa turned to Omar. "Thank you for the warning," he cried, "but you can't help us now. Go. Get away. Get away while you can!" Without waiting for an answer, Rassa slammed the door in Omar's face.

Azadeh looked up at her father, her eyes wide with fear. Her father pulled her close, and she felt him shudder inside. He took a deep breath. "Stay here," he whispered. Azadeh pulled on his fingers, not letting them go. "Don't leave me," she begged him. Rassa knelt beside her and held her in his arms. "Stay with the princess," he told her. "Get into the back room!"

* * *

The rains had quit just twenty minutes before, and a heavy mist hung from the orchard, dripping and wet, moist fingers that sifted through the trees but never quite reached the ground. The fog moved silently, almost as if it were alive, searching for something among the tall leaves. The surrounding mountains cast shadows through the thick underbrush, bringing on darkness before the sun had fully set. Far in the distance, somewhere east of the river, the roll of thunder echoed back through the trees as the rain squall moved away, pushing up the mountains to the east.

The army trucks sloshed to the center of the road and stopped. After years of oppression, Rassa recognized the sound of the trucks. Soviet-made APC-30s. Heavy. Armor-plated. Twelve troops apiece. He listened and counted. At least three, maybe four trucks came to a stop outside his house. Two full squads. Fifty troops. He sucked a quick breath.

Azadeh moved to the back bedroom and huddled with the princess below the window. The young boy remained sleeping in his mother's arms.

Rassa moved to the front door and glanced through the lace curtains. He saw two trucks come to a stop in front of his house, one farther up the road and one at the base of the hill. The road was deserted, all of his neighbors having rushed into their houses, though he knew they would be watching from behind their curtains too. The soldiers spilled from the trucks, and Rassa studied their uniforms: black combat fatigues, dark berets, flak vests, and high leather boots. He pulled away from the window as the soldiers approached, then shot a terrified look at Azadeh's bedroom, his mind reeling in fear.

* * *

The soldiers weren't truly soldiers, at least most of them weren't, but wild-eyed mercenaries who worked for their commander as his personal army of secret police, an off-the-books unit that reported to the general and nobody else. The conscripts were commanded by brutal officers, glaring and arrogant men.

The senior officer, a young captain, emerged from the second truck, swatting the flies and smoking a thin cigarette. He was a squat man, with a thick neck and well-muscled thighs. His nostrils flared as he breathed, and his glare was intense. His job was simple. Do what the general told him—nothing less, nothing more. And *never* ask questions. Just do what he was told.

The captain stuffed his hands into his front pockets, then took a deep breath. He barked out an order, pointing to Rassa's home. "Empty the house. Bring them all out here!"

His soldiers jumped at his voice. They moved to the door and blew it off its hinges with a burst of machine-gun fire. Moving quickly in teams, they rushed inside. The kitchen was empty. They moved like mad men through the room, opening the small armoire, spilling the dishes from the counter, and knocking the chairs to the floor. Moving to the first bedroom, they kicked in the door. It too was empty. Four men gathered around the last bedroom, their guns at their chest. Their leader gave a quick signal, and one of the soldiers kicked in the door.

They burst though the doorway and looked quickly around the dim room. The bedroom was empty except for a small bed, with some covers that had been thrown on the floor, and a small bureau with some dresses that hung from a rope in the corner. The window was open, and a cool breeze blew the curtains back.

* * *

Omar grabbed the princess and pulled her over the mud and brick wall. She held to her son, grasping him in her arms. The boy cried, and the princess pressed her mouth to his ears, whispering to him silently, "Don't be afraid. Go to sleep!" Rassa followed, then Azadeh, and the five of them were over the wall.

Omar glanced at the stranger and the young child in her arms. "The princess, I presume?"

Rassa nodded quickly, pressing against the back of the wall. Looking around desperately, he began to crouch toward the small barn.

"Come," Omar whispered, nodding toward the trail that led up to the mountains.

Rassa stopped and looked up at the rain-shrouded peaks that rose over the village, studying the rocky trail that disappeared in the cold mist. He heard the shots of gunfire, then a crash as the soldiers shot in the front door to his home. He shot a desperate look toward Omar, nodding to the princess and the son in her arms. "Take them," he whispered. "Go. To the mountains, you know that trail as well as anyone. The mist is heavy; it will hide you. Now go! Get away!"

Omar didn't hesitate. He motioned toward the young stranger. "Come," he hissed, and she moved to his side. Omar reached for her young child and took him in his arms. Crouching, he ran through the small orchard and slipped behind the barn. Rassa listened for a moment, hearing their footsteps fading away as they moved up the rocky trail. Then he turned to Azadeh. "Stay here!" he said.

"Please don't leave me, Father."

"Do as I tell you. Stay here. Out of sight."

Azadeh reached out to touch him, and he held her hand tight. "Father, you can't leave me!"

"It is the princess they are after, the princess and her son. They don't want you or me. I think we will be safe."

"But, Father . . . what are you going to do, if you go back to them?"

There came a loud crash from the house as one of the bedroom doors was kicked open. They heard the banging of footsteps and the soldiers' curses.

Rassa turned back to Azadeh. "I have to do something. I have to give them time to escape."

"But, Father, what about me? What am I to do?"

"Stay here, like I told you. Everything will be okay. They aren't going to hurt me; it is the royal family they want."

Rassa glanced toward the mountains. Omar and the princess had disappeared in the mist. Another crash sounded from their house, this time from Azadeh's bedroom. More cursing, more yelling, and Rassa stood up. He glanced quickly to Azadeh. "I love you," he said. "Stay here. I'll be fine. But stay out of sight."

Rassa jumped the fence to his courtyard, then ran toward the house. Azadeh peeked over the fence, then started to cry. She reached out toward him but didn't call his name.

* * *

One of the guards moved to the window in time to see Rassa running past. "Go!" the soldier screamed. "He's running to the road!"

* * *

Azadeh crouched against the wall, then pushed herself back. She moved to the orchard and hid in the mist. She heard her father's footsteps and the guards calling out, then a warning shot being fired as the guards dragged him down.

* * *

The guards worked quickly. They were brutal but well trained, and they knew what to do. First, they searched Rassa's house, tearing it almost to pieces, knocking holes in the walls and tearing up the floors, looking for a hiding place or a secret trap door. Then they gathered Rassa's neighbors, everyone who lived on the hill, and collected them together, herding them like sheep into a tight circle. The guards stood over them, sneering at their countrymen, ready to shoot the first one who moved. Other guards spread out. It only took minutes to tear up every house on the hill. They found Azadeh hiding in a small shed in the orchard, and they dragged her to the circle of cowering friends.

Azadeh looked down on the village. The streets were deserted. The market was empty, and every shade had been pulled. "Soldiers in the village!" The call had gone out. The village looked like a ghost town. Everyone knew what to do when the soldiers showed up.

Azadeh cried in her heart to her neighbors. "Please, help us!" she said. But she had lived long enough in Iran to know that help was not on the way.

The captain of the guard approached Rassa. "Name?" he demanded.

Rassa swallowed, his Adam's apple bobbing. "Rassa Ali Pahlavi," he said.

The captain nodded, his brown teeth protruding from receding gums. "The woman!" he demanded. "We want to know where she is!"

Rassa stared at him blankly. "I don't know what you mean."

The captain smiled a sick grin. "Someone came here last night," he demanded in a raging tone. "They brought a young woman and a child, that much we know. Now tell us where they are, if you have any hopes to live."

Rassa shook his head weakly. "I don't know, my *Sayid*."

The officer turned to the group of women and children that had been herded into the circle. He studied them carefully. All the women were old, the young and healthy ones having left the village for a better life somewhere else. A few children cowered at the back of the crowd, the older women gathering around them like old mother hens. The princess was not among them. And the child wasn't there.

He walked toward the captives. "All right," he said. "We are looking for a young woman and a boy. It is *very* important we find them. Do any of you know where they are?"

The villagers were silent. The hush was heavy and long.

"If you do not help us find them, we will have no alternative."

Again, only silence. The villagers kept their heads low.

He turned back to Rassa as he considered what to do.

His instructions from the general were simple. Find the woman and child. Make sure they were dead. Not a difficult job.

Who they were, why they had to die—he was not even curious. Following orders was all he had been trained to do. And he had seen what had happened to other officers who had dared question the general's commands. Ugly and painful. They had lived far too long as they bore the consequences of their choices.

So he would not make the mistake of thinking too much.

Find the targets and kill them. A simple job. But there were a couple of ways he could accomplish his task.

He thought awhile, then turned back to Rassa. Though he kept his head low, Rassa stuck out his chest. "Rassa Ali Pahlavi," he said, "you know why we are here?"

Rassa shook his head in terror. "No, sir," he lied.

"We will find them, Rassa. They have to be here somewhere. We will tear down your whole village if you don't tell us what we need to know."

Rassa lifted his eyes. "Sir, I swear . . ."

The captain swung violently, striking him on the side of the head. "Don't lift your eyes to *me,* pig!" he screamed in a rage.

Rassa forced his head to his chest, the skin on his neck folding into tight rings under his chin. The officer stepped to the side, clearing a visual path between the terrified man and the group of huddled women and children. "Rassa," he asked, "do you have family in this crowd?"

Rassa shuddered visibly, his shoulders slumping now. He looked across the clearing toward the huddled group from his village. Azadeh cowered, seeking refuge behind the wall of human flesh, but she still caught his eye, and Rassa turned away. "I have no family, Captain," he lied.

The captain snorted. "We know you do, Rassa Ali Pahlavi. We just don't know who it is. But it doesn't matter. We don't really care. You see, Rassa, there are other ways, other things we could do. Now this is your last chance. Where is the child?"

Rassa lifted his eyes, knowing it hardly mattered what he said. The officer had made his decision, and his fate was now sealed. He knew from experience, from watching others die, that there was nothing he could say now that would change the outcome. Yet he felt almost calm, like a blanket of peace had settled over him. He looked at the captain, staring him in the eyes. "Look around you," Rassa answered. "You can see he's not here. And I doubt you will find him. He is gone. You have failed."

The captain snorted in rage, then turned abruptly and screamed to his sergeants, "Tie this man to the tree!"

Four of the conscripts came forward and pulled the man by his arms, dragging him through the wet mud as he struggled to stand. Lifting him by the neck, they threw him against the nearest tree. The villagers were quiet as Rassa was tied and bound.

There was no trial, no words, not even a condemnation of death, nothing to mark the decision that had already been made. The captain walked to the army truck that had carried him to the village. Reaching behind the front seat, he pulled out a large leather flask. He had come prepared for something new, something different today. The liquid sloshed in the flask as he approached the condemned man. Pulling the soft cork, he doused Rassa with diesel fuel. After soaking his hair, head, shirt, and trousers, he poured the last cup of fuel around on Rassa's bare feet.

A young lieutenant moved forward, his rifle in hand. "What are you going to do, Captain?" he hissed under his breath.

The officer didn't answer. Wasn't it obvious?

The lieutenant lifted his hand. "This was not our instruction," he said.

The captain reached into his trouser pocket. "Step aside, Lieutenant," he sneered, "or you will find yourself also tied to the tree."

The captain pulled out a small box of matches, then heard a faint cry of despair. Turning, he saw a wide-eyed girl. He smiled at her happily, cocking his head to the side. "Your father?" he mouthed to her.

Azadeh stared wide in fear, then nodded her head.

The captain extracted a match from the box and struck it against the metal sheath strapped to his thigh. The wooden match sizzled to life, and he let it burn a moment, staring at the flame, then looked at the girl and dropped the match at her father's feet.

The fuel was slow to catch, for it had mixed with the water and soaked into the mud. Several seconds passed with no indication of fire. Then a thin stream of black smoke began to issue from the ground. A yellow flame began to flicker, quickly catching at Rassa's clothes.

Azadeh screamed, and an old woman cried from the back of the crowd. Rassa took a deep breath and turned his face away from his daughter. The flames caught at his trousers, then the coattails of his shirt. Deep yellow, almost orange, the flames began to lick higher. Every eye, every head, was turned to the fire now. Smoke began to waft through the low trees.

Rassa cried out in anguish, and Azadeh bolted from the crowd, running desperately to her father. A conscript stepped forward, but she pushed through his grasp, tears streaming down her face as she ran to the tree. She tripped on a low stump and fell at her father's feet. "No, Father! No! You promised you would not leave me," she sobbed.

The fire grew higher, and she was forced back from the heat. The flames cracked and burned, reaching ten feet into the sky. She reached again for her father, leaning into the heat. "I want to come with you!" she cried. "Don't leave me, Father. Please, I want to be with you."

Rassa looked down, then closed his eyes for the last time. The officer watched, a satisfied smirk on his face. The fire reached an apex, burning with a bright yellow flame.

Azadeh rolled onto her back, swallowing the sickness inside. The captain looked down, and their eyes met briefly again. She lay there, unmoving, tears brimming in her eyes, then moaned once in anguish and curled into a tight ball. She pulled at her knees, and her eyes slowly closed. Her breath became heavy, as if she were asleep.

The captain turned to his men. "All right," he cried. "There is a young boy in this village. Our instructions are clear. Find every boy in the village who is younger than five. Round them up and shoot them, then let's get out of here."

* * *

Thirty-nine children were murdered in the village that evening. Those who opposed the soldiers saw their homes and property burned. Those who fought them were murdered along with their sons. Those who sought to hide their children were eventually found. The carnage was sickening even to the most bitter heart, and the smell of death and smoking buildings filled the dim, evening air.

The Iranians were working through the last few blocks of the village when they heard the echo of helicopter blades bouncing off the steep mountain walls. They looked up to see American Blackhawks coming over the hills to the south. The Iranian captain stood unmoving, in pure shock and surprise. He wiped the blood from his hands, then shaded his eyes. Some of his men gathered round him as his mouth grew tight with fear. "American soldiers," he cried. "We've got to get out of here!"

The soldiers didn't move. Americans? Here? It simply couldn't be.

The captain screamed again, his voice piercing the air. "Go! They are coming. We've got to get out of here!"

The spell broken, the NCOs turned to their soldiers and shouted instructions to them. "Load up. Leave your gear. Evacuate the area. *Now!*"

The Iranian security forces in their special black uniforms fell into a panic as the American helicopters passed over their heads. Yes! U.S. choppers! It was actually real!

The killers ran to their armored carriers. The engines

started, spitting diesel fumes, and the troops ran up the small ramps into the bowels of the machines. The sound of the choppers beat against the canyon walls as they set up to land. The APCs revved their engines and lurched away, moving toward the narrow and broken road that led from the village to the plains in the west.

chapter thirty-one

Army Special Forces Sergeant Samuel Porter Brighton moved slowly through the village dressed for battle: black fatigues, tan leather boots, leather gloves, full flak gear, strands of ammunition, a first-aid kit, grenades, radios, GPS receivers, emergency rations, binoculars. He wore a Velcro name tag, but no other insignia identified him as being from the United States. The sun had set, and the light was dim, and he looked slowly around him, feeling the contents of his stomach rise to his throat. He had seen combat and death; he had seen destruction and loss; he had seen blood and horror in close-up and gory detail; he had seen men that he loved slip away into death—but he had never in his life seen anything equal to this. He had never imagined a scene straight from hell—the burning buildings, the smoke, the smell of spent rifles and blood. And the carnage concentrated on children! His mind tumbled and reeled.

He held a gloved hand to his nostrils and prayed he would one day forget. He counted the bodies, most of them young boys. Young boys and their mothers. It was a gut-wrenching sight. His heart ached like a muscle that had been twisted in two as he stopped and looked down, hearing a muffled cry at his feet. A young mother, her face covered with a thin veil, her long, black burka covering her body from her neck to her feet, tightly held a child who had been shot in the chest. The boy was no more than three, with tangled hair and fat cheeks. He appeared to be sleeping, but Samuel knew he was dead. His mother rocked back and forth in the grass that lined the road and sang to him softly between her deep sobs. Samuel didn't speak Farsi, though he understood a bit, and the song was familiar, for he had heard it before. She sang slow and in rhythm, so he picked up most of the words.

> *"I have loved you so deeply,*
> *I have held you so tight,*
> *Go to sleep, little baby,*
> *Rest in God,*
> *Close your eyes."*

Sam turned away, gripping the handle of his rifle, the barrel pointed upward, his thumb on the safety. He wanted to help her, to comfort her if he could, but what does one say to someone holding a dead child in her arms? How does one explain something so evil, so utterly useless, so utterly cruel?

All the dead children . . . How could he ever explain?

But he wanted to listen; he wanted to hear her soft cry. He wanted to remember the pain she suffered this night. He wanted to share it and keep it, like a hot flame in his chest.

One day he would find them. He swore that he would. He didn't know when or how, but he would find them one day. Then he would remember this mother and the song she sang.

A soldier didn't fight battles for personal reasons or revenge; it was a job, a duty. Defending freedom was a call. But this scene of carnage, it drove him somehow. And he was going to remember. He was a different man now.

So he listened, his back to her, to the young mother's crying and the gentle swish of her burka against the tall grass. He listened to her sobbing as she held her son tight.

Then he turned and walked toward his commander, who was making his way from a small field on the south side of the village where the choppers had set down. The U.S. captain stopped before him, and the two men stared grimly, measuring the displeasure in each other's eyes. "Report?" the captain asked, his voice businesslike.

Sam shifted his feet. "Nothing more, Captain. Nothing you haven't seen. A bunch of dead babies." He gritted his teeth.

The captain nodded to his right, toward a low hill on the western side of the village. "It started up there," he said. "The locals said there were soldiers . . ."

"I told you," Sam shot back, his voice seething with rage. "I told you I saw old Russian APCs. We could have gone after the soldiers and taken them down in their tracks. But no! That's not our mission, you said. We are here for the child. Well, what is our mission now, Captain? You want us to bury these children? Is that why we're here? We could have taken the soldiers, but what can we do now?"

"Sam," the captain answered calmly. "I'm not the enemy here."

Sam took a step back and sucked in a deep breath. He pressed his lips and looked around, then slowly shook his head. "I'm sorry," he answered. "I was way out of line. I was venting on you, sir, and there is no excuse for that."

The young officer watched him closely. "Apology accepted," he said, but his voice was still firm, a warning to Sam. "And I made the right decision," he continued. "We did the right thing. This *isn't* an op. It's a rescue mission only. We could have gone after the APCs, but they were already pulling away.

What were we going to do, chase them all the way to Tehran? And we *did* do some good here; we interrupted their work. More important, we followed orders. Now, come on, get a grip; we don't have much time. Let's do what we can, then get out of Dodge. We're still in enemy country, let's not forget that."

Sam moved his automatic rifle to his other hand. "Roger, sir," he answered. And though his eyes still burned with rage, it was directed at the carnage around him, not at his boss. He slipped his hand down the butt of his rifle, bringing the short-barreled machine gun to his chest. "And the boy we are looking for? What do we do there?"

The captain worked a wad of gum in his mouth, a stony look on his face. "Any suggestions?" he wondered.

Sam hunched his shoulders. "It's possible he might still be alive."

"Yeah. Possible. Not likely, from the looks of it, but possible perhaps. But who is he, where is he? . . . I doubt we'll ever find out. We don't have the men or the time to sort this thing out."

Sam snorted in disgust. "Freakin' mess," he said.

The captain nodded gloomily, then cocked his head to the hill. "Your squad is almost finished sweeping up there. The interpreters have been talking to the people. Go find out what they've learned. I've got Alpha squad working the other homes near the square. Let's get an estimate on the damage, then get out of here. I'll give you five minutes, then I want your squad in the choppers so we can get in the air."

Sam clenched his jaw, then saluted. "Aye, aye, boss," he said.

"Five minutes," the captain warned him as he walked away. "Not one second more. I want your squad ready when the chopper blades roll."

* * *

Sam jogged to the burned-out homes on the hill. The smoke hung low in the trees, heavy and still, like a deep gray-and-black blanket that had nowhere to go. The air was deadly still, and the thick smoke burned his dry eyes.

His squad had done everything they could to clean up the mess. The medics had treated a few of the wounded, but the Iranian attackers had been thorough. They were efficient with their weapons, and almost all of their targets had been killed instantly. The children proved an easy target, for their bodies were fragile and they didn't fight back.

Sam jogged to his waiting squad, who stood grim-faced and angry, their eyes dull, their pale faces stretched thin. The shock was universal. None of them was prepared to see such a thing.

"Okay," Sam said, turning to his Farsi interpreter. "Anything to report?"

The sergeant tucked an unlit cigarette between his lips. "The stories are pretty consistent," he said. "Four APCs moved into the village sometime late this afternoon, probably not more than an hour, maybe an hour and a half, before we got here. They asked for Rassa Pahlavi . . . that's his house over there." The interpreter nodded to a small cinder block and mud house to his right. "The Iranians were looking for someone, a young woman and a child, and though Pahlavi was a widower, the soldiers seemed to expect they would find them there. Apparently they weren't there, or they might have escaped. When Pahlavi didn't help them, the soldiers freaked out. This is where it ended, with what you see here."

Sam wet his lips, then turned and looked around. All the villagers had retreated into what remained of their homes, as terrified of the U.S. soldiers as they had been of the Iranians before. "Did you notice?" he asked the sergeant, while motioning to the remains of the village below.

The interpreter hesitated. "Yeah," he replied.

"All of their targets were children. All of them boys."

The other soldier was silent. It was painfully obvious.

"Which meant," Sam continued, "that they didn't find who they were after."

The interpreter swallowed. "So they made a sweeping generalization. All the male children must die."

Sam shook his head in disgust. "A rather harsh method to accomplish their mission."

"But effective," the sergeant muttered in a cynical voice. "You've got to give them that. When it comes to the mission, these guys are a dedicated bunch."

Sam wiped his face in frustration, then turned back to his men. "This Pahlavi," he asked. "Any information on him?"

The interpreter nodded toward a smoldering tree. "That's him over there," he answered. "They burned him alive."

Sam took a step to the right to see past his men, his shoulders slumping as he looked at the smoking tree. The lower branches had been scorched, and all the leaves burned to ash. The corpse lay in a heap at the base of the tree. "Anything else?" he demanded as he looked away.

"No, Sam, that's all."

"All right, then, let's go. There's nothing more we can do, and the Honcho wants to get out of here. Move to the chopper. Let's get out of this hell."

"Roger," the soldiers muttered. They all wanted to leave. There was too much death, too much darkness, too much destruction and despair. And it seemed to be for nothing. None of it made any sense. His unit gathered their gear and moved down the hill in a run. Sam watched them go, then stood alone on the top of the hill.

A slight wind picked up, blowing up from the valley and lifting the smoke to the tops of the trees, bending it over the branches like the long, misty fingers of an enormous dark hand. Sam turned his face to the breeze, hoping the wind would remove the stain from his memory and the smell of smoke from his clothes. He closed his eyes and listened, feeling the breeze on his face and the weight of his gear pressing against his shoulders and chest. The tiny radio receiver beeped in his ear as the other squads announced they were ready to go, but he pulled out the earpiece and let it hang at his neck. He needed a moment of silence; he needed a moment of prayer.

He bowed his head slowly. "Father," he began, then paused for a time. He wanted to say something, and he felt that he should, but try as he might, the words didn't come.

He didn't feel like praying. He felt like kicking someone in the head.

He paused, then finally mumbled the only prayer he could say. "Please bless them," he muttered, then lifted his head.

Turning, he started to walk down the muddy road. He had walked only twenty paces when something spoke in his mind. He tried to dismiss it, but the feeling remained. He paused, then looked back at the smoldering tree.

He saw her crawling from the high grass on the other side of the road. She was young, wet, and muddy, with long hair and a tan dress. She moved toward the body at the base of the tree and knelt down beside it, holding her hands over her mouth. He saw her shoulders heaving and heard her muffled cries.

"Go to her," the voice said. *"She is your little sister, and she needs your help."*

Sam stared in frustration. "But what could I do?" he thought desperately to himself.

The voice didn't answer, and Sam didn't move. The sound of the chopper blades began to beat behind him as the pilots spun the rotors up to operating speed. He turned to the landing zone to see that his squad had loaded up in the choppers and were ready to go. He heard his name being called through the tiny radio earpiece that hung at his neck. "Sergeant Brighton," his captain called him. "Brighton, let's go!"

He stared at the choppers, frozen in his tracks, then glanced back at the girl who wept by herself in the mud.

"Go to her," the voice repeated.

The chopper blades spun, ready to lift in the air. His captain moved to the side of the lead chopper and stared up at him, motioning to his radio. He slipped in the earpiece and heard his captain's voice. "Sam, come on, man, we've got to get out of here."

"Please, Sam," the voice pled. *"I can't do this alone!"*

His captain broadcast again. "Let's get out of here, Brighton! Come on, soldier, let's go!"

Sam reached for the transmit button. "Stand by," he said.

"What are you doing up there, Brighton?"

"Stand by!" Sam replied.

He turned away from the choppers and looked at the girl near the tree. She kept her head bowed and her hands at her mouth. Sam took ten steps toward her, and she finally looked up, her eyes wide with fear. She started to back up, pushing herself through the mud, and Sam lifted his hands, holding them away from his body in a gesture of peace. She cowered, her head low, almost bowing to him.

Sam took another step forward, and she slowly raised her head. She looked at him, and his heart seemed to wrench in his chest. She was so young and so childlike and so beautiful. She was small and as vulnerable as a piece of ash in the wind.

Her eyes were brimming with tears, which left a small trail on her cheeks.

Looking at her face, Sam's heart seemed to leap. The feeling was so strong it was like a kick in the chest. He stared, then stepped back. "I know you," he said.

She watched him intently, then cocked her head, not understanding his words. Her face softened, and she quickly wiped a rolling tear from her cheek. Samuel saw the pain and desperation, and he felt his heart wrench again. He felt breathless and hollow, his chest growing tight.

He moved to her slowly, and she backed up in the grass. She kept her eyes low, too terrified to look at his face. Sam stopped a few paces from her, then knelt down at her side.

He shot a quick look over his shoulder. His boss and two soldiers had come up the road and were watching in silence from twenty paces away. They didn't move toward him, letting him talk to the girl.

Sam leaned a few inches toward Azadeh. "I'm sorry," he said. He spoke slowly in English, hoping she would understand.

She forced herself to stop crying and lifted her eyes.

And Sam saw it, a flicker of recognition, as if *she knew him too!*

He thought desperately, searching for the right Farsi word, then gestured to the body. "Your father?" he asked, keeping her locked with his eyes.

She nodded in despair, then turned away from the tree.

"Your mother?" he asked her.

She only stared back.

"Mother?" he repeated.

Azadeh shook her head while saying something in Farsi that he couldn't understand.

"You are . . . alone?"

She looked at him. "Now . . . yes . . . I am."

Sam leaned slowly toward her and reached for her hand. "Look at me," he told her.

Azadeh kept her head low, and Sam lifted her chin to look into her eyes. *"Khorramshahr,"* he asked her. "Do you know where I mean?"

She backed away from him slowly, her face uncertain with fear.

"A refugee camp," Sam said in English, pointing with one hand to the north. *"Khorramshahr,"* he repeated. "I will have someone waiting . . . someone will be looking for you. Go there. We will help you."

Though she nodded slowly, Sam could see she did not understand.

"Khorramshahr!" he repeated. "If you can make your way there . . ."

"Sam!" Brighton heard his platoon leader's voice. The captain moved to his side and placed his hand on his shoulder. "Sam, we have to leave. Come on, man, let's go." He pulled on Sam's shoulder, then put a hand under his arm, lifting him up and pulling him toward the road.

"Khorramshahr!" Sam repeated. "I will have someone waiting, they will be looking for you."

Azadeh moved away from the platoon leader, who was tugging on Sam's arm. Sam reached for her desperately as he was pulled to the road.

"Khorramshahr," he called, but she disappeared in the grass.

* * *

Forty seconds later, the choppers took to the air, flying over the village to keep away from the mountain peaks on the east. Sam sat at the open door in his chopper, his feet hanging over the side. And though they flew directly over the village, the smoke was too thick to see if she was still there.

chapter thirty-two

Azadeh remained hidden in the grass until long after the sounds of the choppers had faded away. By then it was dark and the smoke had cleared from the air, though the sky was still obscured by high clouds. The night turned chill, and her muddy clothes clung to her skin. She started to shiver. She felt bitterly cold. Forcing herself to her feet, she walked in a daze toward her gutted house. Their furniture, their dishes, their books, and their clothes—almost everything they owned had been tossed through the windows and the broken front door. She stared at the scattered belongings, then walked into her home, her teeth chattering from the cold and despair.

She moved to her bedroom, her eyes adjusting to the light, and looked around desperately, feeling a sudden sense of panic. Her room was in tatters, with her mattress and clothes on the floor; but under the broken dresser she saw her brushes and mirror. She picked them up quickly, clutching them to her chest, then fell on the mattress and buried her head in her arms.

She was alone. Completely alone. She had no mother, no

father, no family, no friends. Even the house wasn't hers—a young woman couldn't own property, so the house would be taken and sold, and she would be left on the street.

"Father," she whispered in her crushing despair. "I want to come with you. I want to be with my mother. How will I survive? Can I *please* come with you?"

In that black moment, Azadeh felt all the pains of her world: the aloneness of her breaking heart, the bitter buffetings of Satan as he cackled in her ear, the agony of spirit as she remembered the past: the happy days with her father, the warm home, the warm bread, and the sadness of knowing that it was all gone. She felt a crushing doubt and deep anguish as Satan and angels laughed at her.

Did any of it matter? Was there *any* sense in the world? Was there any good, any love, *any* devotion at all? Her father had spoken of hope; he had used the word *faith*—but none of it mattered, for it all was gone. None of it made any difference. None of it was real.

The only thing that was real was the darkness and the tattered remains of her home. The only thing that mattered was that she was alone.

"Please, Father," she whispered, "please don't leave me here by myself. I did everything you've asked me. I have tried to be good. But now you have left me. So tell me now, Father, what am I supposed to do?"

Then Azadeh rolled to the floor and started to pray, a universal reaction to what she had been through, a human reaction, not Muslim, not Christian, but something even more, something deeper, more permanent than the religions of the world, a reaction from her spirit that hovered within.

"Great Allah," she prayed as she prostrated herself on the floor. But that was as far she went, as far as her teachings could take her. She didn't know what to say or how to ask any more. "Dear Allah . . . dear Allah . . ." she repeated again.

Then her mind started drifting, thinking of her father again, the best example of love she had ever known in her life. But she didn't think of his burning or how he had died. She thought of his living and how she wanted to see him again; she thought of her longing to look in his eyes, to feel his arms around her and see his kind smile. But mostly she thought of the words he would say. He had a way of making her feel better, of making her feel strong, like life was worth living and everything would be okay.

"You were always proud of me, Father," she wept. "You always made me feel better. Can you comfort me now?"

* * *

Rassa Ali Pahlavi knelt beside his daughter as she lay on the floor beside her bed, and stroked her face lightly, feeling the softness of her cheek. And though he looked at her sadly, the hurt in his own eyes had passed, for he was beyond the pains of this earth. The world didn't hurt him; he had completed his mission and passed his great test. "I *am* proud of you, Azadeh," he whispered in her ear. "You are strong, you will make it, and God will be at your side."

He continued to gently stroke her face. "I love you, Azadeh. And we will be waiting and watching and caring for you." He leaned down and lightly kissed her brow.

It was time that he go, at least for a short while. Sashajan was waiting. And there was a great work to do.

* * *

Azadeh felt a soft breeze, and she shivered again. She felt a soft touch on her temple, and she opened her eyes. And though she didn't see him, she knew he was near. Then the Spirit of God whispered to her, "Your father still lives. He loves you. He is proud of you. And I am proud of you too. I promised I would never leave you. And I will comfort you now."

Then she felt a warm blanket falling over her soul. It was soft and so gentle. It wrapped completely around her, from her head to her feet, and kept the piercing arrows of Satan from touching her heart.

She slipped away into a deep sleep, where a deep comfort waited. She slept peacefully through the night, dreaming of a far better world.

epilogue

KARACHI, PAKISTAN

The Palestinian moved through the crowd easily, for he was comfortable there. Though he was not among his own people, the sounds and scents were the same. He felt the constant press of flesh against him, the movement of the crowd, the chatty voices of women and the guttural growls of men, too busy, too grand to respond to their wives. He smelled the tang of old bodies and felt the gritty dirt on his feet. He felt the uneven pavement beneath him and the glare of the sun, white hot and oppressive, wringing great drops of sweat from under his arms and around the small of his back. Everyone sweated in Karachi; they sweated to keep cool, and they sweated to survive. No one was clean in Karachi. That was just the way it was.

The Palestinian moved around a brown and rusted cement hole in the sidewalk, one of the public toilets that was built without the benefit of even a curtain for privacy. He moved through the crowd, working his way toward a small, open-air market half a mile down the street. In the distance he heard gunfire, a series of quick *pops* and *ratta ta taps* in reply, but he paid no attention, for it was almost a full block away, and gunfire in Karachi could be heard every day. In any given twenty-four-hour period, half a dozen citizens lost their lives to petty thieves, gang wars, drug runners, hate, or revenge. The slave trade that flourished on the outskirts of the city was a significant source of the dangerously high murder rate, but also a significant contributor to the local economic machine. Teenage captives from China, India, Pakistan, and Afghanistan were harbored in Karachi before being shipped off to brothels throughout the Pacific Rim. Even as he walked, the Palestinian passed a group of three teenage girls bound together. For thirty *dinre* he could have bought any one of them.

Stopping on the corner, the Palestinian waited for a break in the traffic. He glanced quickly around him, turning his back on the street to look in the direction from which he had come. To his side, a roughly mortared brick wall sported an old movie poster. Tom Cruise smiled at him, his long black hair drooping over one eye. The Palestinian frowned and turned quickly away. A break came in the traffic, and he moved into the street.

Ten minutes later, he sat down at a wooden table at an outdoor café. The owner moved toward him, then recognized his face and instead turned for the kitchen. Seconds later, he emerged with a mug of hot *cheka* tea in hand.

"Amid," the owner said as he placed the mug on the table. "God be blessed, you are safe. It is good to see you again."

The Palestinian, a tall man with dark eyes and enormous ears, nodded to the restaurateur. "How is your fish?"

"Very fresh, *Sayid*," the café owner lied.

The Palestinian grunted and pointed to his plate. The restaurateur nodded and moved through an open door and into his kitchen.

Minutes later, the Palestinian was eating his meal: a charcoaled slab of sea trout, with its head and bones still intact, and a bowl of white rice with hot mustard sauce. The crowd thronged around him, moving up and down the street. An occasional automobile passed by, forcing pedestrians onto the narrow sidewalk and around the small tables of the outdoor café. A group of children played in the street, gleefully chasing each other. A mule pulled a decrepit wagon with one wheel on the sidewalk and the other on the street.

Halfway through the Palestinian's meal, a Pakistani man emerged from the crowd, approached, and sat down without saying a word. In contrast to the Palestinian, who was dressed in a traditional flowing *dakish,* the Pakistani was dressed in black slacks and an open white shirt. Neither of the men was distinguishable in the crowd.

As the Pakistani sat down, Amid looked up and held his fork to his mouth.

The Pakistani lit up a smoke. "Amid Safi Mohammad, how is your meal?" he asked.

Amid Mohammad didn't answer, but pushed in another mouthful of fish. The Pakistani watched him chew, then leaned forward in his chair. Mohammad pulled away as he caught the whiff of cologne. He studied his supplier, then wiped his mouth with the back of his hand. "Brother, I have to disagree with you on this meeting place," he said in a heavy voice. "I don't believe it is wise." The Palestinian paused and glanced to the sky, almost as if he expected to see an American satellite hovering there. His eyes darted down the street. "The rats have eyes, eyes like spiders—they can see everything."

The Pakistani nodded. He appreciated his fellow warrior's fear. But they were in his territory now, and he was not concerned. This was his city, his territory; his tribe controlled everything, and he knew every movement of the American spies. His crew had identified every one who was near, and they kept a close eye. And yes, the Americans got around, but he also had evidence they were not watching today.

He dramatically crushed out his cigarette. "Mohammad, you have to trust me," he answered knowingly, while nodding almost imperceptibly to the roof of a squat cement building on the other side of the street. "The Great Satan has many eyes, but this is my lair. We are safe here, I assure you; my people are near. That is, of course, unless you allowed yourself to be followed . . ." the Pakistani's voice trailed off. The accusation was clear.

"No, no," Amid Safi Mohammad quickly replied. "I was careful. I followed your instructions to the letter."

"All right then." The Pakistani sat back and picked at his teeth. "Now let's get it done."

Amid Mohammad pushed his dirty plate aside. "This will be our last meeting. Our work is almost complete."

"Good. I agree. It has been a dreadfully long year."

"You have done very well, doctor. My people are pleased."

The Pakistani only nodded. If Mohammad only knew! If he had any idea what the Pakistani had gone through! For more than twelve months, he had lived on the edge of a knife, a simple breath away from being discovered. He wanted this over. He wanted it done. It was time to relax, time to enjoy his money. He took a deep breath and forced a thin smile. "The arrangements for the final delivery have been made," he said. "All we have left is to transfer the money."

The Palestinian nodded. "How is your memory?" he asked.

The Pakistani frowned. "Not good, as you know."

"Then get out a pencil and start writing this down."

The Pakistani reached quickly into his back pocket and pulled out a small pen. He grabbed a napkin as the Palestinian started to speak.

"The payment will be deposited into an account drawn on the Soloman Bank of Malaysia. The account number will be forwarded to you by private messenger later tonight. The withdrawal instructions and authentication codes are thus—authenticate zulu, one, four, whiskey seventy-nine . . . that's seventy-nine, not seven nine, then today's date and my birthday."

The Pakistani scribbled furiously.

"The money will remain in the account for only three minutes," the Palestinian continued. "That's three minutes, Dr. Atta, not one second more. If you haven't transferred the money out of the account within the three-minute window, we will take repossession and move it ourselves. And if that happens, it is over. Our business is done. We will have the hardware, and you won't have anything."

The Pakistani looked up from his writing and frowned. "That will not be necessary," he answered defiantly. "I will make the transfer; don't you worry about that."

The Palestinian glanced down the street. "I'm not worried, Doctor Atta, but the instructions from my client are clear."

The Pakistani nodded. Amid went on. "Our people at the bank will be monitoring every transfer. Once the money has been deposited into this first account, you will immediately move the money into another account at the same bank. A second messenger will provide you with the specifics pertaining to this account. Once again, the money will remain there three minutes. Three minutes to make your transfer, or we take possession again. From there, you will move the money into twelve separate accounts drawn on various banks in the Philippines. After that, you are on your own. We wash our hands of the paper trail."

The Pakistani looked up from his paper. "And the messengers?" he asked.

"Same men as before. You will recognize them both."

The Pakistani sat back and pulled out another cigarette. "Fifty million?" he confirmed.

"As we agreed."

"And the final installment?"

"Upon delivery of the last nuclear warhead," The Palestinian wet his cracked lips.

The Pakistani tightened his fingers around the butt of his brown cigarette. Suddenly, without reason, he began to sweat like a pig. He pressed his lips together and folded the paper napkin into a small square. He studied his client. "So that is it?" he concluded.

The Palestinian nodded. "I believe it is."

"We will not meet again."

"There is no reason to."

"So tell me, before we separate, I would dearly like to know. Where did you get your money? One hundred million U.S. dollars—that is not a small sum. Who is your financier? I'm dying to know."

"A poor choice of words, Dr. Atta. Be careful what you ask for, or you might get your wish."

The Pakistani scowled. "I am providing you with five nuclear warheads, not an easy thing to do. I am taking an enormous risk, more than you could ever know. I control many generals, but I do not control every one. I have put my neck in a noose here, and I deserve to know who is financing this operation."

The Palestinian pushed himself away from the table. "Too many questions, Dr. Atta, is not a good thing. The money will be delivered. That is all you need to know. We want the third warhead by Friday. Now our business is done."

The Palestinian dropped a couple of dirty *dinres* on the table and moved for the street.

* * *

Two days later, a rusted container ship, an enormous old freighter loaded with barrels of refined kerosene, lubricants, and refurbished electrical generators, left the port at Karachi bound for the Straits of Hormuz. It took only three days to reach the port of Ad Dammam, the huge Saudi port on the eastern shore of the Persian Gulf.

On the burning pavement of the seaside dock, two enormous but nondescript crates were loaded onto the back of a two-ton army truck. The truck pulled away from the warehouse and turned to drive south. Overhead, two helicopters followed its path.

That night, the third, fourth, and fifth nuclear warheads were placed in an underground storage facility on the Saudi air force base of Al Hufuf.

* * *

Twenty hours after the last warhead was delivered, Dr. Abu Nidal Atta, deputy director, Pakistan Special Weapons Section, principal advisor on national security to the Pakistani president himself, didn't wake up after his customary afternoon nap. When his wife couldn't rouse him, she immediately called for his personal doctor. He arrived within minutes, but it was already too late. The doctor's heart had ruptured. There was not a thing he could do.

An autopsy was requested by the physician, but the president of Pakistan turned down the request. Following local tradition, the body was cremated before sundown that day.

* * *

The Saudi prince in Dhahran smiled when he was informed of the news. He waved his advisor out of his office and immediately picked up the phone. "Get my money back," he commanded. "I want every dime."

* * *

DHAHRAN, SAUDI ARABIA
THREE WEEKS LATER

Prince Abdullah, oldest surviving prince of Saudi Arabia, sat in the center of his office, an opulent and oval-shaped room with gold-plated walls, muraled ceilings, and diamonds imbedded in the molding around the windows and floors. His desk was huge. Three computers and a row of telephones were positioned to his left. A seventy-inch flat screen TV, the satellite dish tuned to CNN, was built into a wooden console to his right. A wall of huge windows, twenty feet high, looked out on the expanse of desert to the east. The sun beat through the windows, forcing the air conditioner to run overtime and the new crown prince to work in his shirt sleeves to stay comfortable.

One of the most aggressive sons of his father, a possible patriarch of his family, a family that was on the rise, Abdullah was a great empire builder, just like the sultans before. Living in a world of power, ambition, and pride, he believed in predestiny, and from the time he was young, he knew he was chosen. It was as simple as that. His father didn't believe him, nor did all of his kin, but he had proven them wrong, proven it again and again.

* * *

There was a soft knock at his office door and, after a respectable pause, the American was escorted into his office. The crown prince stood up from his desk as he approached.

"Drexel, good to see you," the prince extended his hand. The American walked toward him and shook it weakly. "Prince Abdullah," he greeted, his voice raspy and thin.

The crown prince studied his guest. He is growing tired, the Saudi thought as the old man approached. He looks wrung out and defeated. We need to keep a close eye on him.

While appraising his visitor, the prince kept an easy smile on his face. He pointed to an arrangement of seating chairs, and the two men sat down. Black coffee was ready, and the prince poured for his American guest. The cavernous office was quiet.

"You are ready?" Drexel Danbert asked as he sipped at his coffee.

"Yes, my good friend." The prince sat back and relaxed against his leather chair.

The two men stared at each other, each playing his best poker face.

"Before we get started, I've got something to show you," Abdullah said. He opened a packet and threw half a dozen photographs on the table: mothers wailing in front of a smoky wall, children in various poses of death, small boys, even babies, all of them shot in the head or the chest. Drexel picked up the photos, his face unemotional, his pale eyes puffy, his hands shaking and weak. "Ugly work," he offered. It was the only thing he would say.

Abdullah held another collection of photographs in his hand and he tossed them on the table as well: American choppers. U.S. soldiers. Weapons. Hard faces. Smoke and burning houses. The Rangers walked through the village and stood over the dead. Though grainy and tilted, the images were clear.

"This is the story I want you to put out," Abdullah said. "U.S. soldiers are to blame for the assault on Agha Jari Deh. They were looking for al Qaeda. When the villagers didn't cooperate, they punished them. We have witnesses. Testimony. Everything you will need. Al-Jazeera will run with the story when I give them the word. You take it from this side. You know what to do."

The old man studied the photos, then nodded his head. "They'll deny it, of course."

"Of course they will. And eventually they'll prove the U.S. was not involved, but it will be too late; the damage will be done. Remember, good friend, the truth doesn't matter that much anymore. Those who hate the United States will believe it, no matter what evidence is eventually revealed. The *New York Times* will front page the story for five weeks, at least. It will weaken the administration and divert them from their work; there'll be hearings in Congress, special investigations, the whole bit. And remember, Drexel, all we're after is another chip in the wall, another crack in the foundation, and this certainly gives us that."

The old man picked up a photo showing a dead child on the street. A U.S. soldier stood behind him, smoking a cigarette while talking to his comrade and pointing away. The image was clear enough, he could read their name tags. Sanchez and . . . Brighton? Maybe Bingham; he couldn't tell, but either way, it didn't matter; they were about to be famous, their images slapped across every newspaper in the world.

"I'll get some people on it," he said, tossing the photograph on the table. "When will the story break?"

"Later tomorrow afternoon."

"That isn't much time."

"It's a big story, Drexel. It's My Lai again. U.S. military atrocities make very good press, so it will be hard to sit on a story, if you know what I mean." Abdullah's voice was curt and sarcastic, but he smiled as he spoke.

The American sipped at his coffee. A few moments passed

in silence. "On the *other matter*, you know, I've been thinking," he finally said. "Talking around, getting a few opinions, talking in the abstract, of course, but trying to get a feeling for how this will be received. And I have to tell you, Your Majesty, that I believe you are walking on tenuous ground."

"We know we are, Drexel. But you will take care of everything."

The old man was clearly uncomfortable and shook his head hesitatingly. "I don't know, Your Highness. We can do many wonderful things. We've done miracles for you in the past. We are very powerful—our partnerships span the whole of the globe; our friendships are personal; our contacts are cultivated and nurtured through both the good and bad years. But there is, after all, only so much we can do, and this plan is far more than we had ever envisioned. Destroy an entire nation! How would you suggest we manipulate the political consequences of that?"

"We won't destroy them. We will move them. There is an enormous difference, my friend."

"But they will not be moved."

"Then that is their choice. If they stay, they will die, but I cannot choose for them. We can't make them be reasonable, though Allah knows we have tried."

"They will not go away. They have nowhere to go. And even if they did, even if they were given other options, they would choose to die in their homeland. It is that important to them."

"Again I will say it: I cannot choose for them."

The American sat back in frustration. It was criminal and inhuman, and though he had sanctioned human suffering, this was crossing the line. He pressed his lips together, and his heart beat in his chest. "How many people will die?" he asked in a low voice.

The crown prince thought and then said, "That is not your concern. This is a conflict between nations, not a criminal case. You are my lawyer, but I am not a citizen of your country. I represent my own interest; I am a sovereign entity. So don't confuse our relationship or overestimate your input here. You are to advise and represent, but don't interfere or give counsel when it is not asked of you."

The American understood and nodded his head.

"All right, then," the prince continued. He paused and then said, "If it would make you feel better, I will tell you that it probably won't be as bad as you think. The nuclear weapons are tactical in nature and are relatively small. What we are proposing isn't much different from what has been done before."

The lawyer shook his head. "How can you say that?" he cried.

The prince leaned forward and narrowed his eyes. He spoke with indignation, his voice sharp and on edge. "Dresden," he sneered, "one-hundred fifty thousand civilians firebombed. London. Two hundred thousand. Twenty thousand dead in a single attack. Leningrad, three hundred thousand civilians killed in combat, another half million starved. Berlin. Two hundred eighty-nine thousand killed in the last month of the Bolshevik advance alone, and who knows how many in the months before that? Hiroshima. Nagasaki. *Poof!*" The prince brought his fingers together and blew them apart. "A hundred thousand gone. *Poof!* Just like that.

"So get my point, Drexel? This is nothing new. War isn't for the weak. And we've seen this before."

The lawyer frowned and swallowed. The prince's eyes flickered yellow and Drexel startled back. Something stirred inside him. Where had he seen that flicker before? He swallowed again, forcing himself to calm down. "Tell me, how many people will die?" he asked as he lowered his eyes.

The prince hunched his shoulders. "Maybe twenty-five thousand in the initial attack. Perhaps another twenty from the radioactive fallout."

The old man stared at his coffee and tried to steady his hands. "And your target is Jerusalem?"

The crown prince sat back and laughed. "Jerusalem! Are you kidding? Do you think I'm stupid, Drexel? Don't you understand me yet?" The crown prince whistled in disgust. Did this man understand *anything*?

The old man stared in confusion. "But if not Jerusalem . . . ?"

The prince waved an impatient hand. "My target is Gaza," he said.

Drexel stammered and choked. "Gaza! You're kidding! That's a Palestinian city! A hundred thousand refugees live in the Gaza Strip."

"I know they do, Drexel. And those who die will die as martyrs. And Allah will receive them unto his own.

"And remember, that is not all that is going to happen, my friend. Once we have destroyed the Little Satan, the Jews and other cockroaches who have stolen our sacred land, we will turn on their big brother, the Great Satan himself. That is our primary objective, everything else is only a prelude to that. With these weapons, these gifts, we will bring the Great Satan down. We will cut off his tail—that is the first thing we will do—but we will not stop our work until we have stabbed at his heart; and if you have lost sight of that objective, then you have forgotten our cause."

"Where do you start, then, my master?"

"Where it hurts them the most. They are weak, and fat-bodied, and unable to take care of themselves. With these warheads in hand, I can cut off their oil. Not a drop of Saudi crude will move through the Gulf, not a drop of OPEC oil will flow to the States. And our oil is the furnace that drives their machines; they are powerless without it, nothing but a motionless car. They have so little of their own, and what little they have they have chosen to lock away, afraid of getting dirty, afraid of spilling a little oil. Fools! Silly women and stupid children, they are. What were they thinking to do this to *themselves*?

"The U.S. economy, like its soul, is a great paper temple. It looks firm on the outside, but there are no stones in the walls. It is as hollow and fragile as a decomposed log. It's an incredible web, but when one thread is missing, the entire structure falls down. Once we cut off their oil, it will collapse in the wind. It will take only a month before we see panic in the streets.

"And if you don't believe me, Drexel, then consider the past. Think of what happened when we blew a few of their towers down! Think of the economic upheaval. It lasted three years. Now try to estimate what will happen when they lose *most* of their oil. It will be an economic devastation unlike anything since the last world war. No, it will be better, far better—there is nothing to compare. How long will it take before the food stores run short? *Just-in-time* inventory—what idiot came up with that? Most Americans are not able to feed themselves for a day; some of them won't even drink water if it comes from a tap! So we cut off the oil, and the whole thing falls down. No fuel for their semis, no fuel for their ships, no fuel for their factories, hospitals, or trains. The grocery shelves will be empty long before the panic sets in! It will be instant hunger and chaos. What a marvelous thing!"

The American didn't answer. He didn't know what to say. "You're going after the Americans?" he stuttered after a pause.

"The Americans and Israel! They are two evil nations, the greatest pox on the world. I will destroy them together or die in the cause."

about the author

Chris Stewart is a *New York Times* bestselling author and world-record-setting Air Force pilot. His previous military techno-thrillers for the national market have been selected by the Book of the Month Club and published in twelve different countries. He has also been a guest editorialist for the *Detroit News,* commenting on matters of military readiness and national security. Chris is president and CEO of The Shipley Group, a nationally recognized consulting and training company. In addition to the highly acclaimed series *The Great and Terrible,* he is the coauthor of the bestselling book, *Seven Miracles That Saved America.* Chris and his wife, Evie, are the parents of six children and live in Utah.